SADIE WAS A LADY

SADIE WAS
A LADY

Joan Jonker

LONDON NEW YORK SYDNEY TORONTO

Typeset by Avon Dataset Ltd, Bidford-on-Avon, Warks

Printed and bound in Germany
by Graphischer Großbetrieb Pößneck GmbH

To Lady Sheila Butlin who for twenty years has been a loyal supporter of the charity Victims of Violence, and who has been my confidante, my shoulder to cry on when I've been down, and is now one of my dearest friends. To her and all her family I send my love.

A children's ditty learned at my mother's knee:

> I'll tell my ma when I go home
> The boys won't let the girls alone
> They pulled my hair and pinched my comb
> I'll tell my ma when I go home.

Chapter One

Brenda Fielding linked her arm through her workmate's as they turned out of the factory gates. 'Ooh, it's good to get out in the fresh air after swelterin' in that place all day. Me flamin' clothes are stickin' to me.'

'Mine too! If I had tuppence I'd go to the public baths an' wash this smelly sweat off.' As Sadie Wilson turned to her friend, her long curly hair swung about her shoulders. She was an attractive girl, was Sadie, with her mass of blonde hair, vivid blue eyes and a peaches and cream complexion. And at fifteen and a half years of age, her figure was beginning to blossom. 'The sun's been shining all week, but I bet when we're off tomorrow afternoon and Sunday, it'll be teeming down.'

'Let's make the most of it while we can, then.' Brenda was a pretty girl with black hair and melting brown eyes, but her looks were put in the shade by her friend. 'Come down to ours tonight and we'll go for a walk in the park. Yer never know, we might just get a click.'

'I haven't got the money for the tram, Brenda – I'm broke. I think yer forget it costs tuppence there an' back.'

'Well, I'd come to yours, but you won't let me!'

'I won't invite anyone to my home, Brenda, 'cos it's like a flippin' pigsty.'

Brenda tossed her head. 'I wouldn't know, would I, seein' as yer won't even tell me where yer live . . . except it's near the factory.'

'Take my word for it, yer not missing anything. Anyway, I don't want a click. I'm not interested in boys – me dad's put me off them for life.'

'Go on, yer daft thing, yer can't tell me yer never going to have a boyfriend.' Brenda squinted sideways. 'With your looks, yer could have any feller yer wanted.'

'Oh, I'll have boyfriends when I'm good and ready, but it'll only be for what I can get out of them. I'm going to be a gold-digger, Bren, out for all I can get.'

'Oh dear, I hope yer don't start bein' a gold-digger before tomorrow night,' Brenda giggled. 'Yer still comin' to the pictures with us, aren't yer?'

They'd reached the tram stop where Brenda would catch a tram to Walton, where she lived. 'You are comin' to the Broadway with me, I hope?'

'Yeah, it's pay-day tomorrow and I'll get me shillin' pocket money.' Sadie saw a tram trundling towards them. She waited until her friend hopped on board, then waved. 'Ta-ra, Bren, see yer in work in the morning.'

Sadie was thoughtful as she walked the short distance to her home. Brenda was the only friend she had; they'd started work on the same day and had been drawn to each other. She'd visited Brenda's house several times and was always struck by the cleanliness, warmth and good humour of the family. It was in stark contrast to Sadie's own home, and she was too ashamed to allow her friend to see the conditions in which she lived.

The front door was open and Sadie grimaced when she heard the racket coming from the living room of the small two-up two-down terraced house in Pickwick Street, Toxteth. Her sisters, Dot and Ellen, aged fourteen and thirteen, were trading blows with their brothers, Jimmy and Les, aged twelve and nine. And above the noise they were making came the loud wailing of the baby of the family – eighteen-month-old Sally.

'Hey, knock it off!' Sadie stood between the squabbling youngsters. 'Yer'll have the neighbours complaining.'

Red in the face, and glaring at his sisters, Jimmy said, 'Mrs Young's been bangin' on the wall for us to shut up, the miserable old cow.'

Sadie sighed as she looked around with disgust. The table in the middle of the room, its covering a piece of torn, stained oilcloth, was full to overflowing. Swarms of flies were swooping down on the dirty plates still there from breakfast, feasting from an open tin of conny-onny, a jam jar and a topless bottle of tomato sauce, while the blue-bottles concentrated their attention on the baby's bottle and dummy, and scraps of stale bread. The sight was enough to make Sadie feel sick.

'Where's me mam?'

There was a sly smirk on Dot's face. She was fourteen in years but thirty in the head. 'She's in bed with me dad.'

Sadie closed her eyes. 'Has me dad had his tea?'

The smirk was back on her sister's face. 'No, he came straight in and pulled me mam upstairs.'

Anger was building up in Sadie. Fancy coming home to this after working all day! But it wasn't only that, it was the fact that her parents had no shame, no thought for their children who had been deprived of their innocence. They all knew what was going on above their heads because there had been times when her father wouldn't bother going upstairs to satisfy his craving, he'd just close the kitchen door. Sadie

2

had never forgotten the day she'd come home from work and used the back door. There was her father with his trousers around his ankles and her mother with her skirt riding high. And neither of them had been embarrassed. Her dad had just nodded for her to go through to the living room without even a pause in his grunting and groaning.

The memory of that incident fuelled Sadie's anger. She walked to the bottom of the stairs and yelled at the top of her voice: 'There are six children down here waitin' for somethin' to eat. Will you come down and feed them!'

'You'll get it off me mam, our Sadie,' Dot said. 'She'll give yer a belt around the ears.'

'An' I'll give you one if yer don't see to the baby,' Sadie told her. 'You're the eldest at home, yer should help to keep this place tidy. It looks like a muck midden.' She eyed the table, the clutter of clothes and shoes covering the sideboard and floor, then shook her head. 'I'm not doing it, I've been workin' all day.'

Lily Wilson pushed the door open with her foot while patting her hair into place. 'Who the bleedin' hell d'yer think you are, shoutin' like that? The neighbours are nosy enough without you goin' filling their mouths.'

Sadie tried to keep her emotions in check. 'Mam, I've been workin' all day in a hot, stuffy factory. And this,' she waved her hand around the room, 'is what I come home to. Not only that, but there's no sign of any dinner.'

'I haven't been feeling well today, so stop yer moaning.'

Dot stood beside her mother, a falsely innocent look on her face. 'Are yer havin' another baby, Mam?'

The slap across her face was hard and loud. 'Any more lip out of you, yer little faggot, and yer'll get another one. Now get upstairs an' ask yer dad for a tanner. Then run to the chippy an' get a tanner's worth of chips and scallops.'

Dot didn't wait to be told twice, she hot-footed it out of the room holding the side of her face.

Sadie gazed at her mother. Lily Wilson had been a fine-looking girl, but she'd let herself go, too lazy to keep up appearances. She looked far older than her thirty-three years, with her blonde hair uncombed for days on end, teeth that were rotting through lack of cleaning and a sickly complexion due to too little exercise and fresh air. After six children her waist had disappeared and her breasts sagged.

'Yer said yer weren't feeling well today,' Sadie said. 'What was wrong with yer this time?'

'I don't have to explain to you,' Lily flared. 'Now get off yer backside and clear this table.'

Sadie shook her head. 'No, Mam, I've been workin' all day, I'm not coming home to start work again. Not when you've had all day to do it in.'

George Wilson heard what was said as he came through the door. 'Yer'll do as yer mam says or yer'll feel me belt on yer backside.'

Sadie weighed up her father with sadness in her heart. She could remember when she was little how she'd adored him. He'd been such a handsome man then, with a mane of black hair and flashing brown eyes. Now, at thirty-seven, he had a beer belly hanging over his trousers and a bloated face. His heavy drinking was taking its toll. But it wasn't his changed appearance that had killed Sadie's love. At thirty-seven he was still a young man, but for years she'd thought of him as a dirty old man. She would never forget the Friday nights she'd trembled with fear when he would offer to bath her in the zinc bath in front of the fire. He'd always make an excuse to get her mother out of the house – send her to the corner shop for ciggies or the *Echo*. And while she was gone he would pretend to be playful, splashing water over his daughter and laughing into her face. But all the time he was touching her in what she called her private parts. At the age of six she was frightened of him; at the age of ten she hated him.

'No, Dad, I *won't* do as me mam tells me! When I was younger than our Dot and Ellen, I was made to help in the house, so why can't they? In fact, why can't me mam do the work herself? She's got all day to do it in, the kids are all at school except for the baby. I've been workin' all day, like yerself, and I don't see why I should come home to all this. If you feel sorry for me mam, then you start tidying up because I'm not.'

Sadie was staring him out and George was flummoxed. The belt was no threat to her now, he could see that. He could also see something else in her eyes, something he thought she'd long since forgotten. Better tread carefully with her or she'd cause trouble. But he had to exercise his authority so he turned on the other children who'd been watching and listening intently. 'Ellen, Jimmy, get that table cleared and start washing the dishes. Les, you amuse the baby an' stop her from makin' that bleedin' racket.'

'The baby doesn't want amusing,' Sadie said calmly, crossing her shapely legs. 'She wants something to eat – she's starving.'

George turned to his wife. 'Make the baby's feed for God's sake, and shut her up.'

'Are yer goin' to let this cheeky madam get away with it? Sittin' there like Lady Muck, tellin' us what she will do an' what she won't do? What she needs is a smacked backside.'

'Oh, yer can forget that, Mam!' Sadie said with bitterness. 'The days of me dad touchin' my backside are long gone.'

George was beginning to get agitated. If this carried on there'd be a lot of things coming out that were best left forgotten. 'Look, Lily, just see to the baby, for Christ's sake. I'll be glad to get down to the pub for a bit of peace and quiet.'

Sadie gazed down at her scruffy shoes, bought second-hand from the market. They were the only pair she possessed and the soles were coming apart on both of them. Her stockings were full of ladders, and the dress she was wearing had to do her for work and for going out. Yet her father could go to the pub every night, and most nights her mother went with him. They didn't seem to notice the mess the house was in, or that their children didn't have a decent stitch on their backs. And as for getting a good meal – well, they wouldn't know what that was. It was so long since they'd had a proper dinner, her mother had probably forgotten how to cook one.

Sadie sighed. As soon as she was old enough, and earning enough money, she'd be away from here like a shot. There had to be a better life than this.

On Saturday afternoon Sadie handed over her wage-packet and waited expectantly for her mother to open it and take out her pocket money. But Lily pushed her aside, saying curtly, 'Yer'll have to wait until yer dad comes in. I don't know where he's got to – he's usually well in before this. I haven't got a thing in the house for the weekend, so I'll have to use your money until he comes home.'

'Mam, I want me pocket money. I'm meeting me friend at a quarter to six at the Broadway. I can't let her down.'

'Don't start moaning, yer'll get yer money as soon as yer dad gets in. I need all this,' she waved the buff-coloured packet, 'to pay me ways. I've had tick from the corner shop an' if I don't get down there with it I'll have her feller comin' to the house banging the door down. Beside that, I've got to get the rest of me shoppin' in.'

A lump was forming in Sadie's throat. It just wasn't fair! She'd worked all week, she was entitled to the measly shilling. 'What happens if me dad's not in by the time I've got to leave?'

But Lily wasn't listening. She'd ripped the packet open and emptied the seven and sixpence into her hand. 'Dot, take this five bob up to the corner shop, then come back an' I'll have a list ready of what I want from the Maypole and the greengrocers.'

Sadie tried again. 'Mam, are yer sure me dad will be home in time for me to go and meet me friend? I can't leave her standin' outside the Broadway on her own.'

'He'll be in any minute, so stop yer frettin'.'

But it was four o'clock before George put in an appearance, half-drunk and looking very sheepish.

Lily rounded on him. 'Where the bloody hell d'yer think you've been? Hand yer money over quick, before the ruddy shops close.'

When George fell backwards into a chair, the springs creaked in protest. With the stupid grin of a drunken man on his face, and his words slurred, he said, 'I had a flutter on the gee-gees an' I lost.'

Sadie's heart sank. 'How much did yer lose, Dad?'

'All me bleedin' wages.' He hiccupped several times. 'But I'll win it back next week, don't worry.'

Lily stood over him, her hands on her hips. 'What d'yer mean, yer've lost all yer money on the bloody horses? How much have yer lost?'

'Well, yer see, love – hic – this horse was supposed to be a dead cert – hic – an' me an' me mates put our shirts on it.' He made a grab for her. 'Come an' sit on me knee an' give me a kiss.'

'Yer'll get more than a kiss, George Wilson, it's a ruddy big black eye yer'll be gettin'. Now, stop actin' daft and give me a shillin' for our Sadie. I borrowed one off her.'

'I haven't got – hic – a shillin', I've told yer. I haven't got a penny to me name.'

Sadie had the urge to run to him and punch him in his stupid-looking face. Instead she could feel the tears starting and ran from the room. Down the yard she fled, and into the back entry. There she leaned against the wall and closed her eyes. She'd never felt so miserable in her life. And how was she going to explain to Brenda? She couldn't tell her the truth, she'd be too ashamed.

The tears were running unchecked down her cheeks but she didn't care. She just felt like curling up and dying. Her head was so full, she didn't hear the bike being ridden down the cobbled entry.

'What's up, Sadie?'

Sadie opened her eyes and saw the boy from next door through a blur. She shook her head. 'Nothing, I'm all right.'

Harry Young leaned his bike against the wall. 'Come on now, Sadie, yer don't cry for nothing. Yer dad hasn't been hittin' yer, has he?'

Sadie rubbed the heel of her hands across her eyes. Harry was looking at her anxiously. At eighteen, he was a handsome lad with dark curly hair, strong white teeth and dimples in his cheeks. He was always pleasant with her, even though his mother barely acknowledged the whole Wilson family, whose house was an eyesore with a dirty front step and filthy curtains hanging behind windows that were seldom cleaned. It spoilt the appearance of the Youngs' house, which was always spotlessly clean.

'No, me dad hasn't been hittin' me. I wouldn't let him.'

'Well, why the tears? A pretty girl like you shouldn't have anything to cry over.'

The sympathy in his voice was all Sadie needed to make her pour her heart out. 'And me mate will be standing waiting for me . . . I feel terrible.'

'You mean your father has gambled all his wages?' Harry was shaking his head. 'It's a mugs' game, bettin' on the horses.'

'I was going to say me dad *is* a mug, but then I'm a bigger mug than he is! Fancy working all week and not having sixpence to go to the pictures.'

Harry had long ago decided that Sadie didn't belong to the Wilson family. She was the prettiest girl in the neighbourhood, but her clothes were always shabby and she didn't make the most of her looks. Any other parents would have been proud of her natural beauty and helped her make the best of it, because when she smiled, it was as though the sun had suddenly begun to shine. And she was beginning to curve in all the right places. Another year or so and she'd be a stunner.

'I'll give you sixpence, Sadie.'

'Oh no, Harry, I couldn't take yer money off yer. I'll be all right, don't worry about me.'

'Sell me something for sixpence then, and you won't be in my debt.'

Sadie's smile was weak. 'I've got nothing to sell, Harry.'

'You could sell me a kiss. I think it would be well worth the money.'

'A tanner for a kiss? I'm not Jean Harlow, yer know!'

'I still think it would be worth it, and it's my tanner.'

Sadie's mind was working overtime. Harry looked as though he meant it and it would be no heartache to kiss him 'cos he was nice and clean and he had no pimples like some of the lads in work. And his offer meant she wouldn't have to let Brenda down. 'Are yer sure?'

Harry nodded. 'Very sure.'

'Now?'

'I don't think this is the right place, do you?' Harry grinned so she wouldn't take offence at his words. 'After all, a sixpenny kiss is a smacker, not just a peck. What time will yer be coming home from the pictures?'

'We go to first house 'cos Brenda's mam won't let her stay out late. I'll be getting off the tram about half-past eight.'

'I'll be waiting at the tram stop for yer – is that okay?' When she nodded, Harry smiled. 'I'll find a nice shop doorway.' He put his hand in his trouser pocket and Sadie could hear coins jingling before he pulled out a sixpenny piece. 'Enjoy the picture, Sadie.'

Sadie gazed at the small silver coin nestling in her palm then turned those vivid blue eyes on him. 'Are you sure about this, Harry? It doesn't seem right to me. Your mam would go mad if she knew.'

'Unless you tell her, she will never know. Not that I care – I wouldn't care who knows. You're a very pretty girl, Sadie, and if I want to kiss you it's got nothing to do with anyone.'

'It'll be me first kiss.' Sadie lowered her head. 'I won't be very good at it.'

'I'm not exactly Rudolph Valentino meself.' Harry began to chuckle. 'All you have to do is pucker your lips an' I'll pucker mine.'

When Sadie stepped off the tram and saw Harry emerge from the shadow of a shop doorway, she was a bundle of nerves. She'd never be able to kiss like Moira Shearer had in the picture tonight, with her eyes all gooey and a soppy smile on her face. Still, she'd made a bargain and she'd keep to it. 'Have yer been waiting long?'

'Only five minutes,' Harry lied. It must have been at least half an hour, if not more. 'Did yer enjoy the picture?'

'Yeah, it was all right but I'd rather have a comedy. It's me mate that likes romances . . . she cried all the way through it.' Sadie felt conspicuous standing by the tram stop and she looked around. 'Can we go somewhere else? I feel daft standin' here.'

'There's plenty of shop doorways, Sadie, but it's so light everyone would see us.' Harry cupped her elbow. 'It's only five minutes' walk to the park. Shall we go there?'

'If yer like, but I don't want to be too late getting home. Not that anyone would worry. Me mam and dad are probably knockin' the ale back in the pub.' Sadie had to skip to keep up with Harry's long strides. 'Me dad must take me for a sucker. There's no way he'd leave himself without his beer money.'

'He wouldn't do that to yer, surely?'

'Don't kid yerself, Harry, my mam and dad are dead mean with their children. They see to themselves first and if there's anythin' over then the kids might get a look in.' Sadie glanced sideways, thinking how smart he looked. She wished she had some decent clothes to wear, she felt a right frump in the washed-out cotton dress.

They reached the park gates before Sadie pulled him to a halt. 'I feel terrible, takin' a tanner off yer for a kiss. Why don't yer let me pay yer back out of next week's pocket money?'

'I don't want me tanner back, Sadie, I want a kiss. And yer don't have to be frightened – I won't eat yer.'

Sadie allowed herself to be propelled forwards. 'I'm not frightened,

I just think yer want yer bumps feelin', paying for a kiss off me when yer've probably got lots of girlfriends.'

Harry didn't answer as he led her to a deserted spot behind some trees and bushes. He stood in front of her, put a finger under her chin and raised her face. 'Sadie, if yer really don't fancy kissing me, just say so and we'll go home and forget all about it.'

'It's not that, Harry. I'm just frightened I'll make a mess of it and yer'll be disappointed.'

'Sadie, close your eyes and pucker yer lips.' Harry didn't intend to make a meal of the kiss, the kid was only fifteen, after all. But the second their lips met he felt as though he'd been struck by lightning. His arms went around her and he held her tight as the kiss lingered. When he finally broke away it was to gaze into a pair of beautiful vivid blue eyes.

'Was I all right, Harry?'

He coughed, feeling embarrassed at the effect she'd had on him. He'd had plenty of girls, but never before had a kiss set off fireworks in his head. 'Sadie, it was better than a tanner's worth of chips any day.'

Sadie smiled. 'Yer not just pullin' me leg?'

'Scout's honour, it was a real hum-dinger.'

Sadie wrapped her arms across her tummy and hugged herself. 'Me very first kiss. I feel all grown-up now.'

'Did you enjoy it?'

She was silent for a while, then decided she'd go over it again in bed tonight and make up her mind whether she'd enjoyed it or not. But for now she wanted to please Harry. She didn't want him thinking that he'd parted with a tanner for nothing. 'Yeah! Yeah, I did!'

'Then next time yer father does the dirty on yer, come to me. I've always got a spare tanner, especially for a kiss from a pretty girl like you.'

Sadie narrowed her eyes. 'Yer very trusting, Harry. I mean, I could tell yer a lie, just to get a tanner off yer.'

Harry let his head fall back and he roared with laughter. 'Fancy thinkin' of that! Yer sound like a proper little gold-digger.'

'That's what I'm goin' to be when I'm older, a gold-digger.' There was no smile on Sadie's face. 'I'm determined not to end up like me mam, with a gang of kids and a lousy husband.'

Harry took her elbow and led her towards the park gates. 'Yer'll feel different when yer meet someone yer like. Not all men are like yer dad, yer know.'

'Me dad probably wasn't like he is now before he was married. Once they get a ring on yer finger, that's when they change. Well, they've taught me that married life isn't all sweetness and light, so I'll stay clear of it. As I said, I'll be a gold-digger and take everything I can lay me hands on, without givin' anything back.'

Sadie lay on her back staring up at the ceiling. She had to share a bedroom with her two sisters and brothers, while the baby slept in her cot in the front room. There was no privacy; her small camp bed was set against the end of the double bed where the boys and girls slept, top to tail . . . girls at the top, boys at the bottom. Apart from a rickety old wooden chair and the beds, there wasn't another item of furniture in the cramped room. Even if I had any decent clothes, I wouldn't have anywhere to hang them, Sadie thought as she turned on her side and tried to make herself comfortable so she could go over the events of the day in her mind.

She could picture her dad, sitting in the chair, half-drunk, saying he'd lost all his money. She'd really hated him at that moment. And her mam was no better; neither of them cared that she'd worked all week for nothing. They weren't worried that Brenda would be left standing outside the picture house like one of Lewis' dummies. The only ones they cared about were themselves, and they made damn sure they never went short. They'd proved tonight just how selfish they were. When she'd got in about nine o'clock it had been to find Dot minding the children while her parents were up in the pub. They didn't have her pocket money, but they had money enough for their beer. It was no wonder the children were wild and out of control; they'd been left to fend for themselves ever since she started work. Up till then she'd been mother to them and skivvy to her parents. Now the role had been handed over to Dot, who was ill-fitted for it. She was more likely to give the younger ones a clout than a hug.

Sadie plumped the pillow with her fist. Why couldn't her parents be like Brenda's, or Harry's? Brenda was happy and contented because she came from a loving home where there was constant laughter. And the Youngs next door were always laughing – she could hear them through the walls. A long sigh came from deep within Sadie. There was no contentment in this house, no love and no laughter. She felt sorry for her sisters and brothers; it wasn't their fault they were cheeky and ignorant. They'd had to be tough to survive in a home that resembled a pigsty, where their tummies were always rumbling with hunger and the clothes were falling off their backs.

Full of anger, hurt and resentment, Sadie vowed to make a new life for herself as soon as she was old enough. She'd get a little place of her own and she'd keep it spotlessly clean and cheerful. And she'd never get married and have children because the man might turn out to be like her dad. She wouldn't put any defenceless young child through the fear and shame she'd experienced because of him. Not all men were the same, as Harry had rightly said, but she didn't intend taking a chance.

A picture of Harry's face flashed through her mind, bringing back the memory of her first kiss. Had she enjoyed it? She knew Harry had, because she'd opened her eyes when his lips were on hers and she could tell by the look on his face and his low groan of pleasure. Herself, she didn't think it was anything to get excited about, but she'd do it again for the money. In fact, she'd be more than willing to do it every night if she got sixpence each time. She'd be able to buy herself some decent clothes and shoes, and wouldn't have to be ashamed of wearing the same dress day in and day out, or walk around with the soles hanging off her only pair of shoes. And she'd be able to go out on a Sunday instead of being stuck in the house wearing one of her mother's old dresses while she washed hers ready for work the next morning.

Sadie's eyes began to close and she drifted into sleep seeing herself walking down a street with her head held high, wearing a pretty dress and a pair of stylish high-heeled shoes. And a smile came to her face as, in her dream, she stopped halfway up the street in front of a little house where the step was pure white, the windowsill red-raddled and polished, and crisp curtains showed behind the gleaming glass panes. And Sadie saw herself putting the key in the lock and opening the door of a place of her very own.

Chapter Two

On the Sunday morning, in the cold light of day, Sadie bitterly regretted taking the money off Harry. She didn't think she could ever look him in the face again, remembering how she'd cheapened herself. So for the next three weeks she avoided him, ducking down entries whenever she saw him before he caught sight of her. But on this Thursday night, on her way home from work, she'd just turned the corner of the street when he came whizzing around on his bike. He braked sharply, cocked his leg backwards over the saddle and fell into step beside her, wheeling the bike in the gutter.

'Hello, stranger! Have you been avoiding me?'

Sadie's hair bounced as she shook her head. 'No, of course not.' She gazed at him out of the corner of her eye. Even though he was coming home from work too, he looked smart in a crisp white shirt with his hair neatly combed back, and she was conscious of her own appearance. Her washed-out dress was coming apart at the seams and was far too tight on her now her breasts were growing. She really should be wearing a brassière like her friend Brenda, because her nipples could be clearly seen through the flimsy material. 'Why should I want to avoid yer?'

'Search me! But it just seemed funny that we live next door to each other and usually come into contact every day or so, but since a certain night, when a pretty girl got her first kiss, I haven't seen hide nor hair of yer.'

'There's nothing funny about it, it's just coincidence.'

'Was my kiss that bad it put yer off selling me another?'

Sadie could feel herself blushing. 'I should never have sold yer one in the first place. It was a dead mean trick I pulled on yer.'

'You've got it all wrong, Sadie. It was me who pulled the trick – not you. You would never have thought of it in a million years, would yer?'

'No, I suppose not, but it still wasn't right.' They were nearing Harry's house and Sadie slowed down. 'You go on, Harry. If yer mam sees you with me she'll have a duck egg. She doesn't have much time for the Wilson family, and I can't say I blame her. I wouldn't like us for neighbours.'

'I'm not me mam, Sadie, and you are not the whole Wilson family.' Harry lifted the bike onto the pavement. 'I choose me own friends and

I want to be friends with you. So don't forget that. Any time yer in trouble, or if yer ever left without money again, come to me and I'll help yer out.'

Warmed by his words, Sadie smiled. 'Still willing to pay a tanner for a kiss, Harry?'

She has no idea how pretty she is, Harry thought. Her family have pulled her so low she has no self-esteem. 'More than willing.'

'Thanks, Harry.' Sadie gave him another smile and went on her way. A few women were standing at their doors, their arms folded, watching with undisguised interest. She'd bet a pound to a penny that as soon as she was inside her own front door, one of them would be over like a shot to ask Mrs Young if she knew her son was getting very friendly with the Wilson girl. Oh well, while they were pulling her to pieces they were leaving someone else alone.

Sadie always braced herself when she walked into the living room. She knew what to expect, but nevertheless the dirt and the smell never failed to depress her. The children were sat around the table dipping pieces of bread into bowls of watery soup, while her mother was sitting on the couch feeding the baby from a bottle which looked as dirty on the inside as it was on the outside.

'What's for me tea, Mam?'

'The same as we're all having – home-made soup.' Lily Wilson's hair was dishevelled and her face looked as though it hadn't seen soap and water all day. 'See to yerself, I'm busy.'

Sadie groaned as she battled to keep her temper under control. She was hungry after working all day, and to be expected to make do with a bowl of soup that was made of water with an onion and a few vegetables thrown in, was too much to ask. But she wasn't going to argue, not tonight when she wanted to ask her mother for something.

When her father came in, the children all ran out to play, leaving Sadie facing George Wilson across the table. While she was trying to get the unappetising soup down without balking, a plate of bacon and egg was set before the master of the house. Sadie's anger mounted, but still she kept her feelings to herself. She needed Lily in a good mood.

George pushed a piece of bread around the plate to soak up the bacon fat, and then sat back in his chair, undid the top button on his trousers and belched loudly.

Sadie closed her eyes and lowered her head in disgust. It was no wonder the children had no table manners; they'd never been set a good example. 'Shall I put the baby to bed for yer?' she asked her mother.

'No, I'll take her up,' Lily said. 'You wash the dishes.'

'I'll come up with yer.' There was a leer on George's face. 'Give yer a hand to put her to bed.'

Lily grinned knowingly. 'Yeah, come on then.'

Sadie gathered the dirty dishes and carried them through to the tiny kitchen. She filled the kettle for hot water to wash them in, and after lighting the gas she leaned against the sink, deep in thought. She could picture in her mind what was happening upstairs. The baby would have been put down and left to look through the bars of the cot while her mam and dad behaved like animals. What sort of a life was it for a baby? Or for any of the children for that matter? Living in a house where there was never any simple affection, only lust; never any hugs and kisses left over for them. They'd grow up thinking that married life was what they saw happening here.

The kettle started to whistle and Sadie poured the boiling water into the sink. The kitchen was filthy, but it could stay like that for all she cared. It would take her hours to clean it properly, and for what? It would be back to normal in no time because her mother didn't believe in doing housework. The only thing her mother did willingly was what she was doing now.

'Can I have a drink of water, our Sadie?' Jimmy rubbed the back of his hand across his running nose. 'We're havin' a game of ollies.'

Sadie filled a cup; as she handed it to him, she noticed he was barefoot. 'Have you been playin' out without yer shoes on?'

'I haven't got no shoes.' Jimmy thirstily emptied the cup in one go. 'The sole came off an' me mam had no money for me to take it to the cobblers.'

'What are you goin' to do for school tomorrow?'

'I dunno.' Jimmy shrugged his shoulders before running out, leaving Sadie anxious and frustrated. If her mam and dad would only stay away from the pub, they could keep their children decently dressed and fed. But their own pleasures came first – the pub and bed.

'Haven't yer finished them yet?' Lily's face was flushed. 'Yer takin' yer time about it.'

'Mam, can I ask yer something? Yer remember that shilling yer owe me from the other week, when me dad lost all his money? D'yer think yer could let me have sixpence of it this week?'

'We'll see.' Lily made to leave the kitchen but Sadie held onto her arm.

'Mam, I need it to buy a brassière.' She touched her breasts. 'Just look at me, I can't go around like this!'

Lily's smile was more of a sneer. 'What yer worryin' about? Yer'll be very popular with the fellers when they get an eyeful of them.'

15

'Mam, please. Yer do owe it to me.'

'I don't owe yer nothing, me girl, so don't come that with me. It was yer dad what lost the money, so ask him.'

'No, Mam, I don't want to ask me dad. I'd be too embarrassed.'

'Sod off, Sadie, there's nothin' to be embarrassed about. Yer've only got the same as everyone else.' With that, Lily gripped her daughter's arm and dragged her through the door. 'Hey, George, yer daughter wants to ask yer somethin'. Can she have sixpence off the shillin' yer owe her, so she can buy a brassière? She doesn't like her tits bouncing.'

George's grin was that of the dirty old man he was in his daughter's mind. He gazed with relish at her firm, round breasts. Even though his passion had just been satisfied, he could feel himself responding to her youthful body. A trickle of saliva ran down one side of his chin as he left his chair and walked towards her. Sadie tried to pull back but her mother's grip tightened. It was as though she knew what her husband had in mind and was egging him on. But the second his fingers closed on her nipple, Sadie's free hand swung around and she smacked him across the face.

'Don't you dare touch me! If you ever do that again, I'll go to the police and tell them.'

Lily laughed like a madwoman as she grabbed Sadie's other arm from behind. 'Go on, George, have a good feel. She won't go to the police 'cos she'd be put in an institute for wayward girls.'

George's two hands covered Sadie's breasts and he kneaded them while leering into her face. 'Pair of beauties, they are.'

'If yer don't take yer hands off me, I'll scream the house down an' all the neighbours will hear. And I'll tell them what yer were doin' to me from when I was six years of age.'

Lily's grip loosened. 'What d'yer mean?'

Sadie took advantage and pushed her father's hands away. She ran to the door and turned around. 'Ask me dad what I mean, but I doubt he'll tell yer the truth. I'll be home later 'cos I've nowhere else to go, but if he so much as looks sideways at me, I swear I'll not only tell the neighbours, I'll tell the whole of Liverpool.'

Near to tears, Sadie ran through the open front door and fled down the street. Her eyes blurred, she turned into the main road and was running as though she had wings on her heels. She didn't see Harry standing at the tram stop until he stood in front of her and put his hand out to bring her to a halt. 'Hey, what's the big hurry?'

Sadie tried in vain to pull her arm free. 'Leave me alone, Harry, I don't want to talk to yer.'

Harry saw a tram approaching and knew if he didn't catch it he'd be late for his date. But there was something about Sadie that told him she was in trouble, so he let the tram go. 'Come on, what's wrong?'

They began to walk slowly past the shops. 'I've had a row with me mam and dad, that's all.'

'What have they done now?'

Sadie was too ashamed to tell him the truth; she'd never tell anyone. 'I asked for sixpence off the shillin' they owe me and it started a row.' Anger flared, bringing words to her mouth she really didn't want spoken. 'They can spend money in the pub, but they can't give me what they owe me. And they won't fork out for food or clothes for their children. Our poor Jimmy's got no shoes to his feet, but do they care? Do they heck.'

Harry cupped her elbow. 'Have you no money, Sadie?'

'I haven't got a bean to me name, but I don't need any until I get me pocket money on Saturday. It's just that I wanted to buy meself something and I needed that money they owe me.' She waved her arm. 'Just look at the state of me! I feel ashamed not havin' any decent clothes or shoes while me mate, Brenda, always looks so smart. I feel like Orphan Annie when I go out with her.'

'I'll give yer the sixpence yer need, Sadie, and yer can buy whatever it is yer wanted it for.'

Sadie shook her head. 'No, I'm not takin' any more money off yer, it wouldn't be fair. After all, why should you give me money?'

'Because I want another kiss off yer. I've forgotten what the other one tasted like, so yer can remind me.'

'I'll give yer a kiss, Harry, but I'm not charging yer.'

'No, that's no deal.' Harry thought briefly about the girl he was supposed to be meeting. She wouldn't be very happy next time they met at the Grafton, but the relationship wasn't serious anyway. 'If I went into a shop for something I wanted, I'd have to pay for it. I want a kiss off you, so it's only right I pay for it.'

Sadie sighed as she glanced down at herself. Why not take what was being offered? She was desperate for clothes and she'd never get them if it was left to her parents. Out of her shilling a week pocket money, she had to buy a pennyworth of chips every day for her lunch. So with the one night she went out with Brenda, which was the only pleasure she got, all her money was spoken for. 'Okay, Harry. When shall I meet yer?'

'What's wrong with now? We're almost at the park gates.' He didn't give her time to refuse, and as he was leading her forward he was telling himself he was only doing it to help her out. But a little voice in his brain told him that was a load of rubbish.

They went to the same clearing between the trees, but this time Sadie was nervous. And although she had nothing against Harry, she blamed her parents for bringing her down to this. She shouldn't have to sell herself to buy a brassière or a second-hand dress.

Harry lifted her chin. 'Cheer up, Sadie, it's not that bad.'

'It is, Harry! I can't wait to get away from that house. Away from the misery and the dirt, from being skint every week and always looking like a tramp. But most of all I can't wait to get away from a mother and father who are not even kind to their children, let alone love or cherish them.'

When tears threatened, Harry pulled her close. 'In a couple of years yer'll be earning enough money to buy yerself all the things yer want. Then yer won't have to worry about yer family. An' yer can take it from me that this friend of yours, Brenda, no matter what she wears, she could never look as pretty as you.'

Like a child reacting to comfort and kindness, Sadie buried her head in his shoulder. And when she fixed her vivid blue eyes on him, he put his arms around her to give solace and sanctuary. But her slim waist and the thrusting breasts he could feel through the thin material of his summer shirt caused his tummy to do a somersault and his heartbeat to quicken. Back off, the little voice in his brain told him warningly. She's a lot younger and more inexperienced than the girls you usually knock around with. So he moved back, leaving a space between their bodies. 'I'll have me kiss now, Sadie, if yer don't mind.'

The lips that covered hers briefly were as soft as the touch of a butterfly, and Sadie opened her eyes to look at him questioningly. 'Is that it?'

Harry gave a crooked grin. 'I thought yer'd had enough excitement for one night without me givin' yer one of me famous smackers. I'm known all over Liverpool for me smackeroos, yer know. If yer went down to the Grafton now, yer'd see a long queue outside and they wouldn't be waitin' to get into the dance, oh no – they'd all be waiting for me. It's even been known for the police to have to come and restore order.'

Sadie giggled. 'Go on, yer daft ha'porth! Yer'll be telling me next yer pay them all sixpence.'

'Not on yer nellie!' Harry realised it was the very first time he'd heard her laugh. Smile, yes, she always had a smile for him, but never a hearty laugh or giggle. 'I think we'd better be making tracks. I was on me way to meet someone when you came along.'

'Oh, I'm sorry, yer should have left me! Go on now, I'll make me own way home.'

'I'll walk with yer to the top of Northumberland Street.' Harry glanced sideways, wondering how to put into words the thoughts running through his mind. He didn't want to spoil the fragile friendship there was between them, but her parents didn't seem to care about her and she was so vulnerable. There were a lot of unscrupulous fellows around who would take advantage of her. 'Do yer go out with lads, Sadie?'

She shook her head. 'No, I only go out once a week and that's with Brenda, me mate from work.'

'With your looks, I'm surprised they're not around you like flies around a jam jar.'

'Oh, I've been asked out, but I'm not interested. Even if I was, I haven't got any decent clothes to go out on a date.'

'If yer do, then be careful. There are some fellers who are only out for what they can get.'

'I might not know much about life, Harry, but I do know something about men.' Sadie's tone was bitter. 'Me dad taught me the hard way, and I wouldn't trust one of them.'

'Hey! Present company excepted, I hope?'

'Yeah, course it is.' Sadie gave him a push. 'Go and meet yer friend.'

Harry handed her the sixpence he had ready in his hand. 'Saturday night, half-eight, I'll be waiting at the tram stop for yer. An' I want to know what yer've bought yerself.'

Sadie was about to object but she closed her mouth on the words. There were scarecrows better dressed than her, and she was fed up looking a sight. 'See yer Saturday, Harry.'

The children were all in bed when Sadie got home, and there was no sign of her father. Not that she expected to see him; she knew he'd be propping up the bar in the pub on the corner. Her mother was sprawled out on the couch reading the *Echo* and she only raised her head long enough to throw her daughter a dark, menacing look. Sadie sighed, knowing her life was going to be made unbearable from now on. And what for? Just for telling the truth! Perhaps she should have told her mother years ago, but even at such a young age she knew she'd get no sympathy from *that* quarter. Lily Wilson was besotted with her husband and would believe only what she wanted to believe. But as she was forced to spend every night except one in the house, Sadie knew she couldn't stand being ignored. So she broke the silence.

'What's our Jimmy going to do about shoes?'

Lily looked up, her face sullen. 'What's it got to do with you?'

'I was only asking, Mam.'

19

'Yer can ask away, but I don't have to answer yer.' Lily put the paper down at the side of her and leaned forward. 'You just listen to me, yer little faggot, and listen good. If yer ever open yer bleedin' mouth about what yer said tonight, so help me I'll swing for yer. Did yer hear what I said?'

'Oh, I heard yer, Mam, I'm not deaf. It's you that's deaf, because yer want to be. What I said was the truth, and if yer were any sort of a mother at all, yer'd be worried. Because what he did to me he could have done, and still be doing, to our Dot and Ellen. Haven't yer thought it funny that bath night has been changed from Friday to Saturday . . . the one night I go out? Does he offer to be the good father and bath the girls for yer? And does he still send yer to the corner shop on a message to get yer out of the way?'

The telltale look in Lily's eyes told her daughter all she needed to know. Her father was abusing the other two girls like he had her. 'What a fool yer are, Mam, and what a lousy mother. I've had me suspicions for a few years, because of the way our Dot behaves. She's far too advanced for her years, and if you haven't noticed the sly looks that are passed between her and me dad, then yer must be blind as well as deaf.'

Lily moved quicker than she had for years. She was upon Sadie before the girl knew what was happening. But even though the look of hatred on her mother's face frightened her, she stood her ground. 'Go on, Mam – hit me if yer dare.'

'I'd like to break yer bleedin' neck, causing all this trouble.' Lily's hands were clenched into fists ready to strike, but her daughter's defiance held her back. 'Yer've made it all up, yer little faggot, there's not a word of truth in it. And while yer live in this house yer'll do as yer flamin' well told and keep yer mouth shut.'

'I live in this house because I've got to, I've nowhere else to go. But as soon as I'm old enough, yer won't see me heels for dust.' Sadie outstared her mother. 'Until then, while I'm payin' yer most of me wages, I expect to be spoken to in a proper manner – *an*' I expect a dinner on the table now and again.' She sighed and lowered her gaze. 'Fancy having to talk to me own mother like this. But then, yer've never been a proper mother to me or the rest of the kids. In fact, let's face it, yer not even a good housewife. Just look at this place – I've seen cleaner muck middens! The only time you act like a wife is when me dad's behavin' like a dog on heat – and that's every day. Even when the children are looking on, it doesn't stop yer performing yer wifely duty then.'

Lily was almost foaming at the mouth. 'Yer dirty-minded little bitch! Just wait till I tell yer dad what yer said – he'll take his belt to yer.'

'I'm not frightened of him any more, Mam, so please yerself. If he comes near me I'll scream the ruddy house down an' have all the neighbours running in. Yer see, I'm past caring – that's what you and me dad have done to me. Since I was old enough to carry a shovelful of coal in from the back yard, I've been treated like a skivvy. Thanks to you and me dad, I have no self-respect and no pride. And the sad thing is, because I've learned the hard way that I can't trust me own parents, I don't trust anyone else, either.'

Sadie walked into the tiny hall, then turned. 'I haven't enjoyed saying the things I have, but they had to be said. I've kept them bottled up for too long. If you and me dad don't want to treat me proper, then I'll see if I can find lodgings somewhere. It's up to you.'

'But why can't yer come to the pictures with me tomorrow night?' Brenda's eyes were wide with shock. 'We always go on a Saturday!'

'I know, Brenda, and I'm sorry to let yer down. But I can't afford it, not this week. I've got to buy meself somethin' decent to wear, I can't go out in this dress every day for the rest of me life.'

'You're mean, Sadie Wilson. Yer know yer leaving me in the lurch. If you don't go, I can't go!'

'I've said I'm sorry, Bren, I can't do any more. It's all right for you, your mam buys all yer clothes. I've got to see to meself – and yer know how much pocket money I get.'

'Your mam must be the most horrible, mean woman in the whole world.'

Sadie tucked her hand into her friend's arm. They were on their way back to work after spending their half-hour dinner break outside the chip shop, eating chips from a piece of newspaper. 'She'd certainly be in the running, Brenda, and that's a fact. But don't let's fall out, yer the only friend I've got. It's just for this one week, I promise. I won't ever let yer down again.'

'There's nowt I can do about it, is there? I can hardly drag yer by the hair.' Brenda didn't sound a bit happy. 'Anyway, it beats me how yer can buy yerself anythin' with only a shilling. Yer'll only get a pair of stockings for that.'

'I'll have one and six, and I'll get a damn sight more than a pair of stockings.' Sadie looked at her friend through narrowed eyes. 'If I tell yer something, will yer promise to keep it to yerself?'

Now there was a glint of interest in Brenda's eyes as she stiffened a finger and made a cross on her chest. 'Cross my heart and hope to die, if this day I tell a lie.'

'I'll never speak to yer again if yer break yer promise.' Sadie wondered if she was doing the right thing, but she wanted to make amends for letting her friend down. 'I'm goin' to Paddy's market – there's some stalls there that sell good second-hand stuff.' She saw her friend wrinkle her nose in disgust and was sorry she'd spoken. 'Beggars can't be choosers, Brenda, and I'm desperate.'

'Yer'd have to be, to wear someone else's cast-offs.' Brenda shivered even though the sun was shining brightly in a lovely clear blue sky. 'Yer wouldn't catch me doing it.'

'I'm not as lucky as you, Brenda. I don't have a doting mam and dad who buy me anything I want.'

Brenda was immediately contrite. She put an arm across her friend's shoulders and squeezed. 'Don't take no notice of me, Sadie, I'm just upset that I won't be going to the pictures tomorrow night. I'm a miserable bitch, aren't I? Like a spoiled little brat, crying because I can't have me own way. Someone should stick a dummy in me mouth.'

Sadie grinned. 'I'll see if I can get a second-hand one at Paddy's market tomorrow.'

Chapter Three

There was a spring in Sadie's step as she set out to walk to the market on Saturday afternoon. It was a long walk, but she wasn't going to spend any of her precious one and sixpence on tram fare in case she saw something she wanted and was a couple of coppers short. She didn't notice the heads that turned to look at the pretty blonde whose mouth was turned up at the corners in a half-smile. She wasn't expecting miracles, but she had a feeling that today was going to be a lucky day for her.

A twenty-minute brisk walk brought her to the bustling market. It was packed with people seeking bargains, and the air was filled with the shouts of the Mary Ellens selling their flowers and vegetables, and the stall-holders vying with each other to attract customers to their wares. You could buy anything at the market, from clothes pegs to furniture, but today Sadie was only interested in seeking out second-hand clothes stalls.

With her tattered purse gripped in her hand, Sadie elbowed her way through the mass of people. The brilliant sunshine had brought more folk out than usual, many of whom were just passing an hour away browsing. But the atmosphere was cheerful and good-natured, and Sadie's spirits were high as she glanced at the goods on offer on the stalls she passed. It was when she came to a stall where women were pushing each other out of the way to sort through clothes piled high on the makeshift table, that her interest was roused.

'How much is this?' A middle-aged woman with a black knitted shawl covering her shoulders held up a child's crumpled dress. 'It can't be much 'cos the bleedin' thing's nearly worn out.'

'Are yer askin' me, or tellin' me?' The stall-holder, a small wiry woman with bright red hair, had a voice like a fog-horn. 'If yer askin' me, then it's tuppence. If yer tellin' me it's no good, then put the bleedin' thing down an' see if yer can do better anywhere else.' She looked to another potential customer for understanding. 'Honest to God, she'll be askin' me to give her money next, to take the bleedin' thing off me hands!'

'There's no need to be bloody sarcastic,' said the woman, still holding the dress aloft. 'I'll take it, but I still think it's a downright swindle.'

23

'Just give us the tuppence and sod off.' The stall-holder was smiling as she held out her hand for the money. 'See yer next week, Aggie?'

'Yeah, I suppose so, Mary Ann. Our Billy's got no arse in his kecks.' The woman called Aggie looked down at the overflowing basket at her feet. 'I don't suppose yer've got a bag for this dress, Mary Ann?'

'What? Yer get a dress for tuppence, an' yer want a bag to put it in! Where d'yer think yer are, Aggie – George Henry Lee's? It's a wonder yer don't ask me to wash and iron it for yer.'

'I would if I thought yer were soft enough.' Aggie took a deep breath before lifting the heavy basket. 'If I were you, I'd wash and iron it for me. But then, some folk are not as obligin' as others.'

'Sod off, Aggie! If I come across a pair of trousers for your Billy, I'll put them to one side for yer. Can't have him goin' around bare-arsed.'

Sadie grinned as she inched her way forward. How she was going to find anything in that pile she didn't know, but her optimism remained high.

'Can I help yer, girl?' Mary Ann had noticed the pretty blonde girl who was allowing the older women to push her out of the way. If two women spotted something at the same time, and both went for it, they'd think nothing of coming to fisticuffs. 'Anythin' in particular yer lookin' for?'

Sadie tried to get nearer, not wanting to have to shout over all the noise. 'A dress for meself, and a brassière, if yer've got one.'

'What size are yer, girl?'

Sadie looked at her blankly. 'I don't know. Yer see, I've never had a brassière before.'

'Come round to the side an' let's have a look at yer.' Mary Ann waved a few customers back. 'Let the girl get through.'

Feeling all eyes on her, Sadie stood before the stall-holder who weighed her up with an experienced glance. 'Hang on a tick, I've got two here that should do.' She bent down and rummaged in a box by her feet. 'These are both the same size, love, so either of them will fit yer.'

Sadie took them both in her hands. One was white cotton with a lace inset and the other was a pretty pink with a satin bow between the cups. 'Ooh, er, I like them both.' She grinned at the woman. 'Yer spoilin' me for choice.'

'I keep them down there, otherwise, sure as eggs someone will nick the bleedin' things.' Mary Ann was keeping a close eye on her stall, and when she saw a woman with a pair of trousers in her hand, looking around furtively, she whispered, 'They'd steal the bleedin' eye out of yer head and come back for the socket. You make up yer mind while I sort this woman out.'

'How much are they?' Sadie asked the retreating figure.

'Thruppence each – an' that's a good buy 'cos they're in good nick.'

Sadie's brain was working overtime. She liked them both, and really she could do with two so she could wear one while the other was being washed. If she bought them both, she'd be left with a shilling. Would that be enough to buy a half-decent dress?

'Made up yer mind, love?'

'I'd like them both, but I need a dress badly and I've only got one and sixpence. I don't know what to do.'

'Yer'll get a dress for a bob, girl! Have a root through there, yer'll find something.' The stall-holder held out her hand. 'Here, give us those, I'll keep them here for yer.'

But Sadie was too shy, no match for the older women who were desperate for clothes for their children and kept pushing her out of the way. The stall-holder watched with growing impatience. In the end, she bawled, 'Hey, girl! Use yer bleedin' elbows on them or yer'll never get a look-in! If yer too polite, they'll walk all over yer.'

So Sadie got stuck in. She watched the other women delving into the piles and turning them over, so she did the same. It was then she glimpsed a piece of blue and white material. As she pulled it from the bottom of the stack, she prayed it wasn't a child's dress or an overall. And her prayers were answered. It was a summer dress in pale blue, patterned with small white leaves. It looked just about her size and Sadie could feel her excitement rising as she held the dress up. It had short cap sleeves, a sweetheart neck, fitted bodice and a flared skirt.

'I told yer, didn't I, girl?' Mary Ann was almost as pleased as Sadie. 'All yer needed was a bit of patience. It hasn't been worn much, either; it's in good condition.'

Sadie held the dress to her shoulders. 'D'yer think it'll fit me?'

'I'll bet yer a pound to a pinch of snuff that it fits yer like a bleedin' glove.' The stall-holder was thinking that the blue of the dress was exactly the blue of the girl's eyes. 'If it doesn't, yer can bring it back next week an' I'll swap it for yer.'

'How much is it?'

Mary Ann stared hard for a few seconds, thinking she must be going soft in her old age. Then she decided she liked the look of the girl – and what the hell, anyway! You had to be tough, working the markets, otherwise you'd never make a living. But you couldn't go through life without showing some charity. 'Come and stand behind here with me. Bring the dress with yer.'

Looking puzzled, Sadie made her way to stand beside the stall-holder. 'How much is the dress?'

'I'll give yer a little lesson in life, girl, and next time yer come to the market, think on what I'm going to tell yer. I know yer've got a shilling 'cos yer were daft enough to tell me. Rule number one, never do that because many of the people selling on the market would tell yer the dress was a shilling, even though it might not be worth it. Wait for them to tell yer how much it is, then bargain them down.'

'But I've got a shilling,' said a bewildered Sadie, 'and I think the dress is worth it.'

'Oh dear, oh dear, oh dear!' Mary Ann tutted. 'Yer haven't listened to a word I've said, have yer? I know yer've got a bleedin' shilling! How do I know yer've got one? Because yer ruddywell told me! Why I'm bothering I don't know, but I'm trying to get through yer thick head that yer should never tell anyone who's trying to sell yer something, how much money yer've got 'cos they'll take it all off yer. Now, is that clear?'

Sadie nodded. 'I understand what yer saying, and I'll be more careful in future. But yer still haven't told me how much the dress is.'

'Wait until I go an' serve that woman before she has a fit. She's blue in the face shoutin' for attention.' Shaking her head, Mary Ann left her to see to an elderly lady. 'Yes, love?'

Sadie felt someone tug on her arm and turned to see a fat, grey-haired woman holding up a pair of washed-out, blue fleecy-lined bloomers. 'How much is she askin' for these?'

'I don't know.' Sadie hesitated, then looked along the table to where Mary Ann was serving a couple of people at once. 'I'll go and ask for yer.'

'Tell her I'll give her a penny for them, they're not worth any more.'

When Sadie relayed the message, Mary Ann looked to where the fat lady was standing. 'Oh, it's you, Florrie, I might have known. The bloomers were tuppence, but seein' as it's you, we'll split the difference and yer can have them for three ha'pence.'

The deal suited Florrie, but she wasn't going to let the stall-holder know that. 'Yer a hard woman, Mary Ann!'

'Oh, I know, Florrie! I've been to the doctor about it but he said it's incurable an' I'm goin' to have to live with it.' Mary Ann winked at Sadie. 'Give her the bloomers and take the money.'

Business was brisk and Sadie found herself serving more customers. Her nervousness soon vanished and she began to enjoy the experience. You certainly saw life working in a market; it beat slaving in the factory every day. All life passed you by here – people of every size, shape and disposition. The people were poor, they wouldn't be there if they weren't, but what they lacked in money they made up for in humour, and Sadie had a permanent smile on her face.

Trade slowed down and Sadie stood back with the dress over her arm, waiting for Mary Ann. She could have been home by now, had the dress washed and on the line. Then she could have worn it tonight when she went to meet Harry.

'Nice little rush, eh, girl? That should keep my feller in ciggies for the week.'

'I enjoyed it, it was very interesting.' Sadie opened her purse. 'Now, how much do I owe yer?'

'Well, let's see if we can come to some agreement. What are yer most in need of – a blouse or a skirt? Have a look through and see if there's anything yer fancy, an' I'll let yer have it, with the dress, for that bleedin' shilling which is goin' to come between me an' me sleep.'

'I haven't got a blouse or skirt.'

'Oh, don't yer wear skirts? I like them meself, feel more comfortable in them.'

'It's not that I don't like them, I just haven't got any.' Sadie felt at ease with the woman. She'd often wished she had a mother figure to confide in, especially when she'd been growing up and the changes in her body were frightening her. But there'd been no one to turn to. Her parents' families had disowned them years ago, disgusted and ashamed of the conditions they were living in. So Sadie warmed to the stall-holder, the first woman who'd treated her like an adult and showed interest. 'To tell yer the truth, the dress I've got on is the only one I possess.'

'Go 'way!' Mary Ann looked shocked. 'Are yer an orphan, girl?'

'Oh no, I've got a mother and father, and three sisters and two brothers. But I haven't got good parents. All the money me dad and I earn goes in the pub. Me and the other kids don't get a look-in.'

Mary Ann shook her head as though dazed. She believed every word the girl said 'cos yer could see in her eyes that she was telling the truth. 'They don't deserve yer, girl. If yer were mine, I'd be that proud of yer I'd have yer dressed up to the bleedin' nines.'

'Well, I will be dressed up to the nines tomorrow, in me new dress.' Sadie opened her purse. 'How much do I owe yer?'

'Give us a tanner for the two brassières and a tanner for the dress.' When Sadie went to protest, Mary Ann said, 'I'll take the other tanner off yer when yer come next week. By that time I'll have a nice skirt an' blouse for yer.'

'I didn't tell yer about me mam and dad so yer'd be sorry for me. I only told yer because yer've been very kind to me and I'm not used to kindness.'

'D'yer know, me blood's boiling! Your mam and dad want stringin' up by their flamin' feet!' Mary Ann's dander was up. Fancy having a daughter who looked like a film star and dressing her like a tramp. My God, she'd tell them a thing or two if she ever met them. 'Do as I tell yer, girl, give me a shillin' and come back next week. I'll root something nice out for yer.'

Starved of affection for so long, Sadie put her arms around the startled stall-holder and gave her a hug. 'I wish me mam was like you.'

'You don't know me when I'm in a paddy – I can be a real she-devil when I want. Now, give us the shilling and scarper, I've got to make a few more bob here before I go home.' She took the shilling and put it in the big pocket of the apron she wore. 'I hope the dress looks nice on yer.'

'I wish I'd got it yesterday, then I could have washed it to wear tonight. I'm not goin' anywhere special, it's just that the boy I'm meeting has never seen me in anything other than this old rag I've got on.'

'That'll be all right to wear, yer know.' Mary Ann pointed to the dress draped over Sadie's arm. 'It looks clean enough to me, and I can promise yer there'll be no bleedin' fleas on it. Just give it a good shake, hang it on the line for an hour in the fresh air, then run the iron over it. Yer'll have all the lads fallin' over themselves when they see yer all dolled up.'

'They needn't bother themselves, I'm not interested in fellers.'

'I thought yer were seein' one tonight?'

'Yeah, I am, but I'm not going out with him. He's not a boyfriend or anything, just the lad from next door.'

'Enjoy yerself, anyway, girl, an' I'll see yer next week.'

Sadie smiled. 'Thanks for bein' so good to me, I really appreciate it. Not many people would have taken the trouble you have and I'll definitely be back next week,' she grinned, 'with another bleedin' shilling.'

Harry was leaning against the doorway of a shop waiting for the tram that would bring Sadie home from the pictures, when he happened to turn his head and saw her walking towards him. The breath caught in his throat and he whispered to himself, 'My God, she's absolutely gorgeous! A real stunner if ever I saw one.'

Sadie's spirits were very low. She'd run the gauntlet of her mother's snide remarks and they were still ringing in her ears. She hadn't expected to be heaped with praise because she couldn't remember ever receiving a compliment from either of her parents, but surely it wouldn't have hurt Lily to say she liked the dress? Instead she'd killed off Sadie's pleasure and confidence by calling her, among other things, a slut and a tart. She'd still been screaming obscenities when Sadie came out of the door. It was no wonder the neighbours steered well clear of the Wilson family, thinking they were the lowest of the low.

Harry walked towards her. 'Where have you come from?'

'I didn't go to the pictures tonight, so I've just come from home.' The admiration on his face told Sadie he was pleased with her appearance and it gave a little boost to her ego. 'I went to Paddy's market this afternoon to do some shopping, and I couldn't afford the pictures *and* the shopping.'

They fell into step beside each other, walking with unspoken agreement towards the park. 'You look lovely, Sadie.' Harry couldn't take his eyes off her. With her blonde hair bouncing off her shoulders, a dress that fitted her to perfection and a figure that would turn any man's head, she was a real beauty. 'Did yer buy that dress today?'

Sadie nodded. 'Yeah, and a couple of other little things.'

'It doesn't half suit yer. The blue is the same colour as yer eyes.'

'I bet yer'd have said the same thing if I'd bought a pink dress, wouldn't yer?' Sadie's broken pride was slowly being mended. She needed, and craved, a few kind words – just to be told now and again that she looked nice. 'Yer a flatterer, Harry Young.'

They stopped in the clearing. 'I'm only tellin' yer the truth, Sadie. You look lovely.'

'I'm glad yer like the dress, 'cos you bought it!'

Harry laughed. 'Come off it, I haven't had *that* many kisses.'

'Well, the one yer getting tonight is on the house. I don't want no money off yer.'

'If you can get a dress like that with the tanner I gave yer, then I'm definitely paying yer. It's worth it just to feast me eyes on yer.'

Sadie shook her head. She didn't need any money; she had enough to buy her chips every day and that was all she wanted. 'On the house tonight, Harry.'

'I'll tell yer what, we'll have a "buy one, get one free" offer. I'll pay yer the tanner tonight, while I'm still flushed, then have one free on Tuesday or Wednesday night. How does that suit yer?'

'Oh, all right,' Sadie said, thinking if he wanted to throw his money away she might as well take it. She could do with another dress to change into, and a decent pair of shoes. After that she'd start buying some lipstick and some of the scented soap she'd seen in the chemist shop window. If she didn't look out for herself, no one else would.

Harry put his hands on her waist, marvelling at how slim she was. In fact, everything about her was perfect. 'Sadie, how old are yer?'

'I'll be sixteen in a few weeks. Me wages will go up by sixpence a week then, but I'll probably have to hand it over to me mam. She gets me wage-packet so she'll know I've got it.'

'Will yer come to the pictures with me on yer birthday?'

There was a flicker of fear in Sadie's eyes. There'd be ructions if Mrs Young knew her son was going out with one of the Wilson family. She'd play merry hell, and that was the last thing Sadie wanted. 'I don't think so, Harry. I always go out with me friend.'

'You can go out with her another night. Come on, Sadie, let me take yer out as a birthday present.'

'We'll see, it's a few weeks off yet.'

Harry cupped her face with his two hands and gazed into her eyes. 'Don't forget I asked first. And another thing, remember what I told yer about goin' out with fellers. Always be on yer guard and keep them at arms' length.'

'You're a feller,' Sadie said. 'Do I have to be on me guard with you?'

'I respect yer, Sadie, you have no need to fear me.' Harry groaned inwardly, telling himself no red-blooded man could hold this girl in his arms without wanting more than a kiss. But he'd told her she needn't fear him, so even if it gave him sleepless nights, he wasn't about to go back on that promise. Not until she was a bit older, anyway, and knew what she was doing.

The kiss was somewhere between brotherly and passionate. It sent Harry's blood-pressure up but left Sadie wondering what he got out of it. The kiss didn't do a thing for her, she certainly wouldn't pay for one. Still, he seemed to think it was worth it and he'd been so good to her she wanted to please him.

Sadie was nearing the factory gates when she heard her name called. Brenda was standing on the platform of a tram which was shuddering to a halt and she signalled for her friend to wait for her.

'You're all dolled up today.' There was a flicker of envy in Brenda's eyes as she caught up with Sadie. 'Did yer get that dress on Saturday?'

Sadie nodded. 'Paddy's market, but keep that to yerself.'

'And look at the bust on yer – it's twice the size of mine! Yer'll have all the fellers droolin' over yer.'

'They won't see anything when I've got me overall on. Anyway, why should I worry about them? I needed to wear a brassière an' I feel better in one, so to hell with what anyone thinks.'

A young apprentice hurrying past them, called over his shoulder, 'Put a move on, girls, or yer'll be late clocking on an' yer pay will be docked.' Then he stopped in his tracks, turned around and pursed his lips to let out a low whistle. 'Yer lookin' very glamorous today, Sadie.'

'Thank you, Alec, nice of yer to notice.'

Then Alec, seventeen and an apprentice mechanic, remembered he only had about three minutes to clock on, and he hastened away. 'Nice of him to notice?' Brenda eyed her friend with more than a little jealousy as they quickened their pace. 'He'd have to be blind not to notice those two things stickin' out! My mam wouldn't let me out like that, she'd have made me wear a cardi to cover meself up.'

'My mam's still in bed, Brenda, and even if she wasn't she wouldn't care if I walked out as naked as a newborn baby.' Sadie grabbed her card and punched it in the time clock. 'We just made it.'

Sadie and Brenda worked in the packing department of a factory that made sheets, pillowcases, tablecloths and other commodities from the finest linen. It was a tiring job, standing on their feet all day packing goods into large wooden crates. So when the bell sounded to herald the dinner break, Sadie heaved a sigh of relief. 'This concrete floor's murder to stand on.' She kicked off her shoe and rubbed the sole of her foot as Brenda looked on. 'All this, just to get a lousy shilling a week.'

'It might only be a lousy shilling, but you seemed to have done all right out of it. How on earth yer managed to get a dress and a brassière for a bob, I'll never know.'

Sadie was saddened by Brenda's attitude. Her friend was the one person she thought would admire the dress and be pleased for her. Instead, she looked more angry than pleased, and this Sadie couldn't understand. But Brenda was the only friend she had so she didn't want to fall out with her. 'Come on, let's get to the chippy, I'm starving.'

Alec Gleeson was leaning against the factory wall with another apprentice, Bobby Bennett, beside him. They were eating their carry-out while enjoying the sunshine. As soon as the girls appeared, Alec straightened up. 'Sadie, can I see yer for a minute?'

'I haven't got time now, we're on our way to the chippy.'

'Come on, it'll only take one minute.'

Sadie let go of Brenda's arm. 'You walk on an' I'll catch yer up.'

'What does he want?' Brenda wasn't very happy. 'He's never wanted to talk to yer before.'

'I'll let yer know as soon as I find out meself.'

Alec was a tall, well-built lad with a mop of mousy-coloured hair and hazel eyes. His best feature was a set of strong white teeth which he showed as Sadie approached. 'I was wonderin' if yer'd like to come to the flicks with me on Saturday?'

31

Sadie shook her head. 'I always go out with Bren on Saturday. I wouldn't let her down.'

'Ask her if she'd like to make a foursome up with Bobby here. We'd show yez a good time, wouldn't we, Bobby?'

Bobby was a foot shorter than Alec, and slightly built. He had ginger hair, greeny-grey eyes and a face marked with pimples and blackheads. He never had much success with girls, so he jumped at the chance of making up a foursome. 'Yeah,' he said, nodding his head vigorously, 'we'd have a great time.'

'I'll ask her, but I know she won't come. Yer see, her mam doesn't like her bein' out late, so we go to the first house.'

Alec wasn't interested in Brenda, or her mam, but he was interested in Sadie and she hadn't said she had to be in early. Once Brenda left them he'd soon get rid of Bobby. 'We'll go to the first house – it's all the same to us.'

'I'll ask her and let yer know.' Sadie had no intention of asking her friend because she didn't fancy going herself. But as her feet covered the ground a little voice in her head told her that if they went to the pictures with them, then the boys would pay. And the money she'd save would buy her a bottle of that Californian Poppy perfume all the girls in work were raving about.

Brenda was being served when Sadie got to the chip shop and she handed one of the parcels over. They stood on the pavement outside the shop while they made a hole in the newspaper wrapping so they could get to the chips, then started the walk back to the factory.

'What did Alec want?' Brenda asked, blowing on a chip before popping it into her mouth. 'Anythin' exciting?'

'He asked if we'd like to go to the pictures with him on Saturday night.'

'Him take the two of us, yer mean?'

Sadie shook her head. 'In a foursome with Bobby Bennett.'

'Bobby Bennett?' Brenda nearly choked as a piece of chip lodged in her throat. 'Yer've got to be kidding!' Then she narrowed her eyes. 'Ay, yer not soft, are yer? You with the big handsome one an' me with that pimply-faced little twerp! Anyway, me mam wouldn't let me go 'cos she said I'm too young to be goin' out with fellers.'

'D'yer have to tell her? We'll meet them outside the picture house and leave them there when we come out. What harm is there in that? We'd only be sitting in the seats next to each other like we always do, but they'd be paying. And yer'd be home at the same time, so yer mam wouldn't know the difference.'

'I'll go if I can sit next to Alec,' Brenda said, a petulant droop to her mouth. 'But not unless.'

'You can sit by who yer like, I don't care! As long as someone wants to pay for me to go to the flicks, I'm not worried who I sit by.'

'You've changed,' Brenda said. 'Yer never used to be so hard.'

'Oh, I've changed all right, I've had to!' Sadie said heatedly. 'And I'll tell yer why, shall I? We've been friends since the day we started work and although I envied you yer family and yer nice house, I've never been jealous of all the new clothes you get. I've always paid yer compliments and told yer how nice yer look, even though I only had the one scruffy dress to me name. But when I manage to scheme to get a second-hand dress from the market, which I think looks nice on me, what do you do? You put me down, just like me family, as though I'm a nobody and haven't the right to a decent life.' Sadie screwed the newspaper into a ball. 'I've always given you yer own way, like going to the first house pictures because that was what you wanted. But no more, Brenda. I'm goin' to look after number one from now on because nobody else will.'

Brenda was taken aback. Sadie had never spoken to her like that before and the home-truths hit the target. 'The dress does look nice on yer, Sadie – in fact, it looks lovely.'

'A bit late in the day for that, Brenda. A compliment is no good if yer have to beg for it. So keep looking, kid, 'cos I intend to become as hard as nails so no one can hurt me any more. In future, if there's anything I want, I'll get it by hook or by crook.'

Lost for the right words, Brenda said hesitantly, 'If yer still want me to, I'll go to the pictures with yer on Saturday as long as yer don't leave me on me own with Bobby Bennett.'

'You can go straight home when the first house lets out, Brenda, same as me. I want to be home for half-eight.'

Sadie thought of Harry, the one person who always treated her well. She wasn't going to let him down on Saturday. Then a picture of Mary Ann came into her head and she remembered how kind the market woman had been to her. The thought that she would be seeing her again on Saturday was enough to cheer Sadie up. She slipped her hand through Brenda's arm and squeezed. 'Stop sulking, Brenda, it doesn't suit yer.'

Chapter Four

The people around Mary Ann's stall were six deep and she was rushed off her feet. So when she saw Sadie's blonde head at the back of the crush, she gestured wildly. 'Come an' give us a hand, girl, I don't know whether I'm on me bleedin' head or me backside.' She glared at a woman who was thrusting several items of clothing in her face. 'Hey, missus, just wait yer turn, will yer? I've only got one pair of hands, or hadn't yer noticed? I'm not a ruddy octopus!'

'Yer right there, Mary Ann,' called a voice from the rear of the crowd. 'Yer don't never see no octopus with red hair like yours.'

Sadie slipped her purse into the deep pocket of Mary Ann's overall. 'Mind that for us.' She moved to the other end of the long table. 'Can I help yer?'

Over the next hour, Sadie made dozens of trips from one end of the counter to the other, asking Mary Ann for sizes and prices. And she enjoyed every minute of it – the hustle and bustle, the humour of the stall-holders as they enticed people to their stalls and Mary Ann's everlasting flow of jokes. It was really exciting and Sadie felt at home with these people who were rough and ready, down at heel, but still managed a smile and a joke.

'I've never been so glad to see anybody in me life, girl, as I was to see you.' There was no immediate customer needing to be served, so the stall-holder stood by Sadie to get her breath back. When she'd left the house this morning her bright red hair had been piled on top of her head and held in place with a tortoiseshell comb, but half of it had escaped and was now hanging down the sides of her face. 'I bet I look a bleedin' mess,' she groaned, trying to repair the damage. 'I've been on the go since ten this morning.'

'Hey there, Mary Ann!' A woman was holding up a black knitted cardi. 'If I can 'ave this for thruppence, I'll take it.'

'Yer can have it with pleasure,' Mary Ann said, holding out her hand for the money. 'It was tuppence, but I'll let you have it for thruppence.'

'Thanks, Mary Ann, yer a real pal. I don't know . . .' The woman stopped, her brow furrowed in concentration. Then she wagged a finger, 'Here, give us me thruppenny bit back, yer thievin' swine.'

'Uh, oh, Lizzie, we don't give money back on this stall.' As Mary

Ann shook her head, all the curls she'd just combed up came tumbling down. 'Yer asked if yer could have it for thruppence an' I agreed. Now I can't do fairer than that, can I?'

'If yer don't give me me penny change, I'll come over this counter an' take it out of yer face.'

'Lizzie, don't be gettin' so excited,' Mary Ann said. 'Yer know what the doctor said about yer heart.'

'Doctor! What ruddy doctor? I haven't got no doctor!'

'No, and yer've got no ruddy sense of humour, either.' Mary Ann kept her face straight although the crowd were in stitches. It was better than going to the pictures. 'Here's yer bleedin' penny – now take it an' sod off.'

Shaking with laughter, Lizzie pushed her way through the mass of people. 'See yer next week, Mary Ann!'

'Okay, Lizzie! But don't forget what I said about the doctor now! Don't want yer fallin' down dead, do we? Not in front of my stall, anyway. It wouldn't be good for business.'

Sadie had been watching, holding her sides with laughter. And when the stall-holder returned to stand by her, she said, 'Oh, you are funny, Mary Ann.' Then she covered her mouth with her hand. 'I'm sorry, I shouldn't have called yer by yer first name.'

'It's the name I was christened with, girl, so it wouldn't do yer no good to call me any other 'cos I wouldn't know yer were talkin' to me. They'd be cartin' yer away to the loony bin for talkin' to yerself.'

'Yer don't mind me calling yer Mary Ann, then?'

'Not at all, love. Yer can call me anythin' yer like as long as it's not too early in the morning.' The stall-holder patted her arm. 'While there's a bit of a lull, I'll show yer the things I've put away for yer.' She bent down to the box where she kept small items that were easy to pilfer and brought out a paper bag. 'There's a blouse and skirt in there, and a dress that took me fancy. Pick out which yer like the best while I tend to me business.' She strolled over to the counter, muttering under her breath, 'Yer need eyes in yer backside with some of these.'

Sadie pulled a white blouse out first. It was very plain with short sleeves and a round collar, but the material was beautiful; it felt like silk in her fingers. She'd never handled anything so fine before and she tried to imagine what it would feel like against her skin. She sighed as she dipped her hand in again and brought out a skirt in a deep pink cotton. From the waistband it was fitted to the hips then gradually flared out until it fell into folds. Sadie could see herself spinning around and the skirt swirling out. Oh, it was lovely, and it would go so well with the blouse. She could feel the weight of the dress in the paper bag and wondered whether she should look at it or not. She only had one and six, and she really wanted to keep sixpence in case Alec and Bobby didn't turn up. Or if she didn't see Harry and had no dinner money for next week.

But curiosity got the better of her. It wouldn't hurt to have a look at it; she didn't have to buy. Seconds later she was sorry she'd given in to her curiosity because she fell in love with the deep burgundy dress. It had a low-cut round neck, three-quarter sleeves, a fitted bodice and a flared skirt. It was far too fancy for her; she couldn't wear it for work and if she walked out of the filthy house she lived in, dressed in this, she'd be a laughing stock. But one of these days, when she had a place of her own, she'd have a dress like this.

'Made up yer mind?' Mary Ann saw sadness in the eyes that were as blue as the sky on a summer's day. 'What's wrong, girl?'

'I was just thinking that one day, when I'm older, I'll have a dress as nice as this. And I'll be living in me own house, miles away from me family, so there'll be nobody to make fun of me. Nobody to drag me down in the gutter. I'll be able to live and dress like a real lady.'

'Yer a real little lady now, girl, an' don't you let anyone tell yer any different. Stick yer nose in the air, hold yer head up high and say to hell with everyone. And when yer've got a little wardrobe together, enough clothes and things to keep yer happy, then start salting a few coppers away every week towards that place of yer own. It'll take yer a few years 'cos no one will rent a house to a youngster like you, but in those years yer can be saving up to furnish the house. A few coppers every week will soon grow into shillings and then the shillings will turn to pounds. Yer've got a good little head on yer shoulders, girl, and if yer set yer mind to it, yer'll get what yer want.'

'Mary Ann, if you were my mother I wouldn't be thinking of a place of me own because I'd have everything I wanted at home. I don't ask much out of life, just a bit of love, understanding and warmth. It's not asking much, is it?'

'No, it's not, girl – and if I ever meet yer parents I'll break their bleedin' necks for them. But before yer've got me bawlin' me eyes out, and before everything on me stall has been nicked, tell me if yer takin' the skirt and blouse.'

'Yes, they're really nice. I'm sorry about the dress 'cos it is beautiful, but I'd never have the opportunity to wear it and I can't afford it anyway. So how much d'yer want for the skirt and blouse?'

Mary Ann's tummy started to shake and her nose twitched with laughter. 'Have yer still got that bleedin' shilling?'

Sadie laughed with her. 'It's not the same bleedin' shilling, but yer'd never know the difference.'

'Give us it then. I won't charge yer for washing and ironing them.'

'Yer haven't washed them, have yer?'

'I have, 'cos I knew yer'd be wanting to wear them tonight. Now, will yer sod off and let me get back to earning a living?'

'Can I keep the paper bag, please, to carry me things home in?'

The stall-holder rolled her eyes. 'Go on, take it.'

Sadie folded the skirt and blouse and carefully laid them in the bag. From now on, that bag would have to be her wardrobe. 'See yer next week, Mary Ann.'

'I hope so, girl, otherwise me takings will be down.'

Brenda clung to Sadie's arm as they neared the Gainsborough where Alec and Bobby were waiting for them. 'I'll never speak to yer again if yer leave me alone with him.'

'Don't talk daft. How can I leave yer alone with him in a picture house full of people! Be yer age, Brenda.'

Alec made straight for Sadie, who was looking very attractive in her new outfit. His eyes were full of admiration as he took her elbow. 'We thought yer weren't goin' to show up.'

Sadie pulled her arm free. 'Before we go in, me and Brenda don't want to be split up. We want to sit next to each other.'

'Suits me, it's no skin off my nose.' Alec had visions of sitting in the back row with his arms around Sadie and couldn't care less what happened to Brenda. But his hopes were dashed when the usherette told him the back rows were full. The lights dimmed for the start of the first house and after she'd torn their tickets in half, she shone her torch to lead them down the aisle. 'There's four.' She lit up the empty seats then hurried back up the aisle.

Alec took charge. 'Bobby, you go in first. Then you, Brenda.'

Sadie saw Brenda's face as she squeezed past the people in the occupied seats. 'You get in now, Alec,' she said in a low voice. 'You can sit between me and Brenda.'

'But I thought—'

'Never mind what yer thought, just get in.' In the light from the flickering screen, Sadie saw her friend's angry look change to one of pleasure. I knew that would please her, she thought, having a handsome lad sitting next to her. But I'm not coming out in a foursome again 'cos there's no pleasure in it. I should be enjoying myself, not worrying whether Brenda does or not.

After two short comedy films and the newsreel, the lights went up for the interval. 'D'yer want an ice cream, Sadie?' Alec asked.

'No, it's all right. Yer've paid enough out for us.'

'Don't be daft, have an ice cream.'

Sadie leaned forward. 'Are you having an ice, Brenda?'

'If you are.'

'Okay, then, Alec, we'll have one.'

Alec stood up, pushing his seat back. 'Come on, Bobby, you can give us a hand.' He had just about enough to pay for two ices; he certainly wasn't well-off enough to pay for four.

Sadie watched the two lads walk down the aisle to where the usherette was standing with a tray of ice creams. The tray was attached either side to a wide leather strap which hung from the girl's neck, leaving her hands free to serve.

'D'yer want me to change places and sit next to yer, Brenda?'

'No, it's all right.' Brenda tried to sound nonchalant, as though she didn't care one way or the other, when in reality she was floating on cloud nine, sitting next to Alec. Their arms had touched on the wooden armrest between the seats and she'd been thrilled. He was the nicest-looking lad in the factory and all the girls were after him. She'd never been this close to him before but now they'd been out together she could stop and talk to him without needing a reason. She knew he had his eye on Sadie, but it had only been since she'd been getting all dolled up. In future, she'd ask her mam if she could buy her own clothes and she'd choose something more glamorous to compete with her friend.

'Are yer sure?' Sadie asked, although she knew what the answer would be. She'd heard Brenda talking to Alec when the comedy films were on, and although he'd only grunted in reply, it hadn't stopped her friend from chatting away. Good luck to her, Sadie thought. She can have him as far as I'm concerned. 'Just don't come moaning to me on Monday that I broke me promise.'

The lads came back, each carrying two tubs of ice cream. Brenda took hers from Bobby with ill-grace. Never a smile or a thank you. Then she turned to Alec, a silly smirk on her face and her eyelashes fluttering. 'I'm looking forward to the big picture, are you, Alec? Douglas Fairbanks is one of me favourites.'

Oh, dear God, Sadie thought, dipping the tiny wooden spoon into the ice cream. If I ever had to act like that to get a feller I'd take a running jump off the Pier Head. And she's being dead mean to Bobby; she hasn't given the lad a civil word after him paying for her to come in. I know he's no oil painting, but the poor lad can't help how he looks.

When the lights dimmed, Alec half-turned his back on Brenda and reached for Sadie's hand. 'Does yer friend ever stop talking?'

'She's not usually so talkative.' Sadie wasn't sure about the hand-holding. She could see couples in front of them holding hands, some of them even had their arms around each other. Better leave it, she thought, otherwise he'll think I'm childish. I don't want him to know it's my first time out with a boy. 'I think she's got a crush on yer.'

'Too bad,' Alec said, his face close to hers. 'My sights are set on a girl with blonde hair, blue eyes and a figure like a film star.'

He's a charmer, probably used to girls falling for his flattery, Sadie thought. But she wasn't displeased because compliments didn't come her way very often. So she played him along. 'Oh, and why aren't you out with this film star tonight?'

'I am, but she's doing a Cinderella on me. She says she has to run when the clock strikes eight.'

Sadie didn't realise it, but she was having her first lesson in how to flirt. 'Ah, poor Prince Charming. Never mind, your Cinderella will come along again and you might have more luck.'

'D'yer mean that, Sadie?' Alec's voice was eager. 'Will yer come out with me one night, just the two of us?'

'Yeah, okay, but make it on a Friday because I don't want to leave Brenda in the lurch.'

'Next Friday?' Alec would have to borrow the money off his mam until he got paid on Saturday, but it wouldn't be the first time. 'It'll have to be second house because I don't get home from work until six.'

'All right, next Friday. But will yer shut up now and let me watch the picture?'

Alec sat back, contented now he'd got what he wanted. The furthest he'd get tonight was holding her hand, but next Friday, when they were on their own, he'd get a damn sight more.

Harry was waiting when Sadie stepped off the tram and the sight of her filled him with pleasure. He'd always thought her pretty, even when she was dressed in clothes that a rag-and-bone man would be ashamed to sell, but the last week had seen her blossom into a real beauty.

'Did yer enjoy the picture?'

'It was all right, I suppose, but me mate's beginning to get me down. I seem to spend me life just tryin' to please her.' They were walking, hands by their sides, to their usual destination. 'We made a foursome up tonight, with two fellers from work, and Brenda was a real pain. She wanted the feller I had, and because he wasn't having any she got a real cob on. I'll never ever go out in a foursome again.'

The jealousy Harry was feeling made him speak abruptly. 'Yer better off with yer girlfriend, 'cos yer too young to go out with a bloke on yer own. I've warned yer, don't trust them as far as yer can throw them.'

'I can look after meself, Harry, don't you worry about that. No feller will ever get the better of me.'

To fuel Harry's annoyance, another courting couple had taken over their special spot in the park. There they were, their arms holding each other tight as their lips were glued together. And while he blasted them in his temper, he also envied them.

Gripping Sadie's arm he marched her along until they came to another clearing. 'Now,' he said, his hands on her shoulders, 'the bloke you were with tonight – he didn't try to get fresh with yer, did he?'

Sadie stared back. 'He'd have had a hard job tryin' to get fresh with me outside the picture house in broad daylight, wouldn't he?' She pushed her face closer to his. 'What's it got to do with you, anyway?'

'Because I worry about yer, that's why.'

'You're the only one in the world that does, Harry, so I wouldn't bother if I were you.'

'It's no bother, Sadie.' Harry calmed himself down, afraid she'd walk away and leave him. 'Yer a nice girl an' I don't want yer to come to any harm, that's all.'

'I know all about the facts of life, Harry, I was taught them at a very early age.' Sadie sighed. How could she tell him that even the baby, eighteen months old, saw sights that no child should see? And why was she shouting at him anyway? Harry Young was the only person in the street who still had a smile for her when the rest of the neighbours were openly showing their distaste as the Wilson house deteriorated into a hovel. But for all that, he was still a man and had admitted that most men were only out for what they could get. Wasn't her father the best example? And Alec? Oh, she was under no illusions about him. He was handsome all right, but he didn't half know it. He thought he only had to crook his finger and any girl would come running. Well, he was in for a big surprise with her because she wasn't going to be the one doing the running. 'Remember, Harry, I'm one of six children and it's a long time since I believed the fairies left us under a cabbage leaf.'

'I hope yer as wise as yer make out, Sadie, 'cos with your looks there'll always be men after yer.'

'Haven't you got a girlfriend, Harry?'

'Yeah, there's a girl I go out with, but it's really only for dancing. She's a smashing dancer, a dream on the dance floor.' Harry grinned. 'I think she'll be giving me the heave-ho soon, because she's getting fed up with me being late every Saturday. By the time I get there it's nearly the interval.'

Sadie's eyes held his for a few seconds, then she asked, 'Why d'yer waste yer time on me? Surely yer can get as many kisses as yer want from yer girlfriend?'

'Let's just say I like a variety, eh? Yer know what they say about variety being the spice of life.'

'If yer don't put a move on yer'll be losing yer girlfriend and then yer'll have no variety.'

Harry took her hands in his before dropping a light kiss on her lips.

'That was just a taster to get meself warmed up for the big one. And while I'm building meself up for the main event, can I ask if it's two for the price of one again this week? Will yer meet me on Wednesday again?'

'It's your money, Harry, and although I think yer've got a screw loose spending it on me, I'm not goin' to stop yer.' Sadie's mind was on a pair of shoes she badly needed. The old pair were nearly dropping off her feet and spoiling the effect of her new clothes. And it was Harry's sixpences that were getting her the things she wanted. 'I'll meet yer here on Wednesday.'

'Move that paper out of the way.' Florrie Young waited until her son had folded the *News of the World*, then she set his breakfast before him. 'Get that down yer.'

Harry eyed the bacon, egg and black pudding with relish. 'Mmm, that looks good, Mam.'

'I want me head testing, givin' yer a breakfast this late – it's nearly dinner-time. Yer a lazy article, sleeping till eleven on a Sunday. Most people have been to Mass and back by now.'

Her husband, Jack, came through from the kitchen drying his hands. 'Yer Mam's got you and me down for the fires of hell, son. She reckons we'll never see the pearly gates.'

Harry reached for a piece of bread. 'D'yer think Mr Watson from number six will make it to heaven, Mam? He goes to Mass every Sunday morning as regular as clockwork. And just as regularly he beats his wife up every Saturday night after he's had a bellyful of ale. If he makes it to the pearly gates, and I don't, then there ain't no justice. What do you think, Dad?'

Jack picked up the paper and made for his favourite chair. He was a well-made man, tall and muscular. He and his son were very alike in looks and temperament, with their dark curly hair, dimpled cheeks and an easygoing manner. 'I agree with yer, son. That Norman Watson is a real bad 'un. He's a bully and a blackguard. I'm used to bad language on the docks, but some of the things he comes out with make me cringe. I'm surprised the church doesn't fall down on top of him.'

Florrie was clasping and unclasping her hands as she watched her husband bury his head in the paper and her son concentrate on his breakfast. She was a good-looking woman, with a girlish figure, laughing hazel eyes, a good complexion and a happy disposition. The one disappointment in her life was only having the two boys. She would have dearly loved a daughter, but after Paul was born she was told she would never have any more children. Paul, who had gone out to one of his mates, was two years younger than Harry, and in looks he favoured his mother. He also had her sense of humour, and when the two of them got together there was bound to be laughter.

'What are yer thinking about, Mam?' Harry asked. 'Yer miles away.'

Now is the time to get it off me chest, Florrie told herself. But how to find the right words without starting an argument? 'I've been told yer were seen talking to Sadie Wilson, is that right?'

Harry laid his knife and fork down and pushed the empty plate to one side. 'Is that a crime, Mam?'

'It all depends. There's no harm in talking to the girl, but I wouldn't like yer to be seeing her.'

'That's a funny thing to say, isn't it, Mam? Yer don't mind me talking to her but yer don't want me to see her! What should I do, take a blindfold out with me in case I bump into her?'

'You know what I mean, so there's no need to be funny. All I'm asking is, are yer seein' the girl?'

'Mam! She lives next door, I could hardly miss her! Unless you need yer eyes testing, you see her as well.'

The newspaper rustled and Jack's gruff voice came from behind it. 'I hope you two don't come to blows. I refuse to referee a fight on me day off.'

Florrie wagged her head. 'It's him, he's trying to be funny.'

'I thought you were the one being funny, Mam, not me. I mean, what does it matter if I see the girl and speak to her? She lives next door, for heaven's sake! And she's a nice kid – yer can't blame her for the rest of the family.'

'She's one of them and that's enough for me. Any decent feller wouldn't touch her with a bargepole. I'd be ashamed to hold me head up in the street if one of mine got involved with scum like them. So you keep well away from her, d'yer hear?'

Harry leaned his elbows on the table and rested his chin on his clenched fists. 'Did yer say you'd been to church this morning, Mam? If yer have then yer've been under false pretences because there's nothing Christian in what yer saying. I thought yer were supposed to help those not as well off as yerself, not condemn them.'

43

'No one could help the Wilsons, they're past redemption.' Florrie was getting her temper up. 'There is no need for them to live in filth like they do. He works full-time and there's the girl's wages goin' in. Many a folk get far less but manage to live a decent life because they don't go out pubbing it every night.'

'I agree with yer, Mam, on that score. But Sadie . . . the one you call the girl . . . is only fifteen years of age – what can she do about it? D'yer think she likes living the way she does?'

'Yer can talk till yer blue in the face, Harry, but yer won't change me views on the Wilsons. They're a bad lot and there's no gettin' away from it. If I see her trying to get pally with you. I'll have something to say to her, believe me.'

Jack shot forward in his chair. 'No, love, you mustn't take off on the girl, that wouldn't be fair. As Harry said, she's only a kid and it can't be much of a life for her with the mother and father she's got. After all, she didn't ask to be born into this world.'

Florrie bit on her lip. She wasn't expecting so much opposition. 'Harry, just answer me one question. Are yer goin' out with her?'

'No, Mam, I'm not going out with her. But I will see her and I'll speak to her whenever I feel like it. She's a human being and I'll treat her as one. So go back and tell that to the nosy parker who started all this off. Tell her I said it's a pity she's got nothing better to do.' He pushed his chair back. 'Give us a couple of pages of the paper, Dad, and I'll lie on me bed and read it.'

Chapter Five

'Are yer wearin' that dress to go out in tonight?' Brenda asked, a dozen pairs of sheets in her outstretched arms ready to be laid with care in the packing crate. 'Alec saw yer in it when we went out for our chips, so if I were you I'd put something else on.'

'Brenda, I don't need you to tell me what I should do.' Sadie was trying hard to be patient, but her friend had talked about nothing else all week and it was grating on her nerves. 'If it makes yer feel any better, I'll be getting changed.'

'It doesn't make me feel any better.' Brenda's lips were pursed as she packed the sheets. 'I don't know why we couldn't have gone out in a foursome, like we did last week.'

'Some hope you've got after the way yer treated Bobby. I felt really ashamed of yer. The poor lad probably left himself skint all week after forkin' out for yer, and yer never spoke one word to him! He won't be wanting to take you out again in a hurry.'

'He would if you asked him.'

'Not on your life! I wouldn't put the poor lad through that again, not for all the tea in China.' Sadie decided now was the time to get it all off her chest. 'Anyway, this first-house lark is ridiculous. Young people our age are just goin' out at eight o'clock, all set to enjoy themselves. As their night begins, we're toddling home like two young kids. No bloke is goin' to put up with that.'

'I can't help it if me mam's strict with me. She says only cats and loose women are out late at night.'

'And I can't help it if yer mam doesn't trust yer. All I know is that in two weeks we'll be sixteen, old enough to look after ourselves. So it's no more first-house pictures for me after the next two Saturdays.' Sadie ran a hand over the top sheets in the crate before pulling the lid down. 'I'd like to learn to dance, or go over on the ferry to New Brighton and see the fairground . . . anything but be stuck in the routine of goin' to the pictures every Saturday.'

'My mam wouldn't let me do anything like that.' When Sadie didn't show any signs of sympathy, like she usually did, Brenda went on, 'Anyway, clever clogs, where's the money coming from for all this? Yer'll not do it on a shilling a week.'

'Oh, no? Well, just you watch me.' Sadie looked around for the floorwalker and when she caught his eye she held up her hand, a signal that she needed the full crate replacing with an empty one. Then she turned to Brenda. 'I'll start gettin' dates and they can pay for me.'

'Yer'll get yerself into trouble, Sadie Wilson, if yer start going out with every Tom, Dick and Harry.'

'Is that you talking, or yer mam, Brenda?' Sadie smiled as the floorwalker approached. He was a nice bloke, was Benny, always had a smile and a cheery word for everyone. He was over six feet tall, pale-faced and as bald as a billiard ball. The empty wooden crate he was carrying looked too heavy for his painfully thin body to bear, and Sadie rushed forward to give him a hand. 'Yer should get one of the young lads to do this, Benny, otherwise yer'll be doin' yerself a mischief.'

'It's all right, lass, I'm no Tarzan but I'm stronger than I look.' He positioned the crate in front of Sadie before casting an eye on Brenda's work. 'Give us a shout when yer ready.'

Brenda nodded, then waited until he was out of earshot before turning on Sadie. 'You have no right to talk about my mam like that.'

'Like what? I've got nothing against yer mam, she's never done me any harm. In fact, I've always envied you your family and nice home. But I do think she's doing you more harm than good by wrapping yer in cotton wool. There's a big world out there; some of the people in it are good, some are bad. By the time your mam thinks yer old enough to be let out on yer own . . . probably by the time yer twenty . . . yer'll have had no experience of people, especially boys, and it's you that'll get yerself into trouble, not me.'

Brenda thought on this for a while. Sadie was the only friend she had; none of the girls in the street where she lived bothered with her because they knew how strict her mam was and they weren't prepared to put up with it. 'Will you come to our house an' ask me mam if I can go to the second house at the pictures? She might say yes if you ask.'

'No.' Sadie shook her head. 'Yer've got to learn to stand on yer own two feet, Brenda. I haven't had the cushy life you've had – I've had to stand up for meself for as long as I can remember. I've got to scheme to get the things you take for granted, so there's no way I'm going to take on your troubles as well. Fight yer own battles, kid, and learn to grow up in the process.'

'I'll have a word with me mam tonight. But we're still going to the first house tomorrow night, aren't we?'

Sadie closed her eyes in exasperation. 'Yes, and the Saturday after. But the following week you can forget it. We're sixteen within a few days of each other, old enough to do what we want.' She pointed to the crate in front of Brenda. 'Unless yer want to lose yer job, get cracking and fill that crate.'

'Okay, don't be gettin' yer knickers in a twist.' But Brenda's hands were slow while her mind was busy. If she fell out with her friend then she'd lose contact with Alec and that didn't bear thinking about. She was determined to make him notice her, and every night in bed she would dream of how she'd stun him with the new clothes she'd get even if she had to defy her mother. 'You're lucky going out with Alec. He's so nice, and very handsome.'

Sadie didn't answer because she could see no point. Brenda would have to find out the hard way that being handsome didn't automatically mean the person was nice inside. If she couldn't see that blokes like Alec were wolves in sheep's clothing, then it was God help her.

Sadie was filled with despair when she walked up the street that night to find Jimmy and Les sitting on the front step looking like urchins – with filthy torn shirts and trousers, no shoes on their feet, faces as black as coal and hair matted.

'Is me dad in?' Sadie asked, her mind screaming at the injustice. No child deserved to look like they did, not when they had a father who was working and earning money.

'Yeah,' Jimmy said, scratching his head vigorously with both hands. 'He got in about five minutes ago.'

I'll bet he stepped over them and didn't even take any notice, Sadie raged inwardly. He wouldn't feel any shame, not like I'm feeling now. And certainly no pity for the children, who were ostracised by the rest of the kids in the street.

'Have yer had yer tea?' Sadie lingered to give her temper time to subside. If she went in and gave vent to her anger there'd be a slanging match which she couldn't hope to win, not with her mother and father both ranged against her. It would end up with her crying, frustrated at not being able to get through to them the harm they were inflicting on their children. And she didn't want to turn up for her date with red-rimmed eyes.

'We only 'ad two rounds of toast an' I'm starvin'.' Young Les squinted up at her. 'Me mam said she's got no money.'

Sadie sighed as she slipped a foot between them to reach the top step. She'd help them if she could, but how could she when she couldn't even help herself? Perhaps it would be better if she was nice to her mam, buttered her up like their Dot did. If she got her in a good mood she might be able to appeal to her motherly instinct. That's if she has any, Sadie thought, I've never seen any sign of it. Still, complaining and shouting hadn't got her anywhere, so she'd try a change of tactic.

Sadie pinned a smile on her face as she walked through the living-room door, and she kept it there even though the sight and the smell made her feel sick. 'Hi, Mam. Hi, Dad!'

George's greeting was a grunt, Lily's a brief nod. But Sadie wasn't going to be put off. After all, when did anybody ever get a welcome in this house? She passed the table where Dot and Ellen were sitting, watching wide-eyed as their father tucked into two fried eggs on toast, and made for the couch where the baby was sitting. 'Hi-yer, Sally.' After chucking the baby under the chin, Sadie turned quickly away from the sight of the angry red sores on the child's legs, caused by constantly wearing a wet nappy.

'What's for tea, Mam?'

'An egg on toast.' Lily's tone was hostile. 'An' yer can think yerself bleedin' lucky 'cos the kids only had toast. It's hard-up day an' I haven't got a penny to me name.'

'That's all right, Mam, an egg on toast will do me fine.' Sadie made for the kitchen before her thoughts turned into words. Surely it was a mother's place to get a meal ready for her children? Especially when one of them had been working all day. And as for not having a penny to her name, it was a pound to a pinch of snuff that her dad would be in the pub tonight, as usual.

Sadie carried the plate through and sat next to Ellen. 'I'm going to the second-house pictures tonight, Mam, so shall I take a key or will yer still be up?' She didn't need to ask because her dad never rolled home before half-ten, but she'd stick to being nice and see if it got her anywhere.

Lily's eyes narrowed. 'Where yer gettin' the money from to go to the pictures?'

'I'm going with one of the lads from work and he's paying.'

'Oh aye, hard clock? At fifteen yer shouldn't be goin' out with boys. I don't want yer comin' home here with a bun in the oven.'

Sadie closed her eyes at the crude words used in front of her two sisters. 'I'm sixteen the week after next, Mam, I'm not a child.'

Lily caught the message in George's eye and was silent for a while. Her husband had told her he thought Sadie would live up to her words and go and get lodgings if she was pushed too far. And they'd miss her wages coming in, especially as they'd go up when she was sixteen. 'All right then, but in future, ask.' A sly grin crossed her face. 'If he takes yer down a jigger, just make sure his hand is the only thing that goes up yer skirt.'

George's head fell back and as he roared with laughter crumbs spurted from his half-full mouth. 'That was a good one, love, very funny. I'll have to remember that to tell me mates.'

Sadie stared at her plate. What was the use? They would never change, not in a million years. She finished her meal and carried her plate out to the kitchen. 'Can I get washed at the sink before our Dot starts on the dishes?'

'Yer'll have to make do with water 'cos we've got no soap.'

Sadie popped her head back in the living room. 'No soap!'

'You heard what I said, yer haven't got cloth ears. An' before yer start complaining, Miss High and Mighty, yer not the only one in the house. We've all got to do without.'

Sadie walked back to the sink. She couldn't help the bad thoughts that were running through her head. Her mam wouldn't miss soap because she only got a good wash every Preston Guild. And her dad was no better – sometimes you could smell him a mile off. How his cronies in the pub could stand next to him she didn't know. That's if he had as many mates as he said he had, and this she doubted.

Sadie ran the water over her hands and rubbed them together to get as much dirt off them as she could, then she filled her cupped hands with water and swilled her face. There was a towel hanging from a nail on the back of the kitchen door and she reached for it, only to draw her hands back when she saw the state of it. It was used as a flannel to wipe the children's faces and runny noses, and served as a tea towel to dry dishes and as a dish cloth to mop up any spillages, including grease.

'Won't we be havin' our bath, Dad, seein' as we've no soap?' Dot sounded petulant. 'We could still sit in the water an' some of the dirt would come off.'

George glanced nervously towards the kitchen door. 'Shut yer trap about the bleedin' bath, yez can have one tomorrow.'

Sadie was rooted to the spot in horror. Surely her mother wasn't so bad, or so stupid as to let him wash a fourteen-year-old-girl? But Sadie couldn't feel pity for her sister because she was old enough to know it was wrong and to stop it. Instead she seemed to be egging her father on, always sitting close to him and whispering in his ear. She was as hard as nails for her age and Sadie thought that what her father had started he might not find so easy to finish. In his desire to satisfy his perverted craving for sex, it hadn't even entered his head that Dot wasn't just putting up with his advances because she was afraid not to; that she actually liked it and was a more than willing participant. And she was crafty enough to know she would always have a hold over her father. He had created a monster who, in a year or two, would be calling the tune: a girl of fourteen with blackmail on her mind.

49

'I'm glad we've got no soap,' Ellen said. 'I hate bath night.'

Sadie's heart went out to her younger sister. She knew how she felt because at her age, Sadie was just getting out of her father's clutches.

'You look good enough to eat, Sadie.' Alec grinned down at her. She had to be the best-looking girl he'd ever been out with. Funny thing was, he hadn't realised quite what a beauty she was until he'd seen her figure in that blue dress. She looked good tonight, too, in her blouse and skirt. 'Come on, let's get in before all the best specks are taken.'

He held her elbow as they mounted the two steps into the picture house and when he asked the girl in the ticket kiosk for 'Two in the back stalls, please', she knew he'd make for the back row. But she didn't care. His compliments and the admiration in his eyes were like a salve, soothing away the anger, hurt, humiliation and utter despair. She needed someone to tell her she looked nice, needed to bask in the warmth of someone's smile and feel the touch of another human being, if she wasn't to go through life feeling completely worthless.

During the Charlie Chase short comedy, Alec held Sadie's hand. He appeared to be quite content, sitting back in his seat and roaring with laughter at the antics of the funny man. It wasn't until after the interval and the lights dimmed, that he lifted the armrest between the seats, slid his arm across her shoulders and pulled her closer. 'Are yer comfortable, Sadie?'

'Yeah, I'm fine, thanks.' This wasn't said just to please him, she really did feel comfortable and secure with his arm holding her close. The tension was leaving her body and she wished life could always be like this. There were two thoughts niggling at the back of her mind but she tried not to dwell on them. One was that she hoped Alec wouldn't get fresh and spoil it for her, and the other was that at the end of the night she had to return to the hovel that was not her home, but her prison.

Alec was bored with the film, there was no excitement in it. Claudette Colbert and Ronald Colman were not among his favourite film stars. He preferred sirens like Joan Bennett or Jean Harlow, and he-men like Randolph Scott and James Cagney. So he spent more time looking at Sadie than he did at the screen. She was nicer-looking than Claudette Colbert any day of the week and had a better figure. He knew who he'd pick if he had to choose between them.

When the film ended and the lights went up, Sadie said, 'You can have yer arm back now.' She noticed the grin on his face. 'What's so funny?'

'I'll tell yer when we get outside.' Alec pushed his way through the mass of people making for the exit, pulling Sadie behind him. 'I'll be glad to be out in the fresh air.'

They stood on the pavement while Sadie asked, 'What was the joke?'

'I was telling meself I'd rather have a date with you than Claudette Colbert, then I thought chance would be a fine thing! Anyway, she lives in Hollywood, too far away to be walking her home from the pictures.'

Sadie answered with a smile on her face. 'You were right about chance being a fine thing, Alec, 'cos yer not walkin' me home, either!'

Alec's face dropped. 'Why not?'

'Well, for one thing, I told me mam I was going out with a girlfriend, and for another, we live miles apart. I live in Toxteth and you're the other side of the city in Seaforth. We're halfway between both places, and it would be crazy for you to take me all the way home and then have that long journey back.' She saw the disappointment on his face and hated herself for telling a lie. But if he saw the state of her home he'd never want to see her again. 'Why not walk me part of the way then catch a tram back?'

'Yeah, okay.' He put his arm around her waist as they started walking. 'It would be daft 'cos I'm up at six in the morning for work. Saturday is the best night for a date, then we can have a lie-in the next morning.'

'I'm goin' out with Brenda, I told yer. But it's only for this week and next week. After that, if she can't get round her mam to let her stay out later, she's on her own.'

'I don't know why you put up with her; she's so childish she'd get on me flippin' nerves.'

'Oh, she's not so bad.' Sadie didn't want to be disloyal to the girl who'd been her friend since the day they started work together. She'd been glad of Brenda as she had no other friend, so she wasn't going to pull her to pieces. 'It's just that her mam's so strict, she's frightened of the wind blowing on her.'

They strolled along the main road for about twenty minutes, then Sadie called a halt. 'I turn off here, so your best bet is to jump on a tram. You can get one from the stop over the road that'll take yer right to Seaforth.'

'Yer not packing me off without a good-night kiss, are yer? Come on, Sadie, don't be so mean.'

'Oh, all right.' Sadie looked towards a shop doorway. She couldn't really refuse, not after he'd taken her to the pictures. 'Let's go in there where we can't be seen.'

Sadie was expecting a gentle kiss, like the ones Harry gave her. But Alec wasn't Harry, and the speed with which he moved took her breath away. They just stepped into the shadow of the doorway and before she knew what was happening, she was being held tight in his arms and his lips were crushing hers. She felt his tongue trying to prise her lips apart and her first reaction was to pull away and ask what he was trying to do, but a little voice warned her against it. She was new to the game of dating, and for all she knew, all the boys kissed like this. After all, she only had Harry to compare Alec with, and the boy next door was more like a brother. But she didn't relish the thought of someone else's tongue in her mouth so she kept her lips clamped tight.

Alec's hands moved upwards, under Sadie's shoulderblades, and as they did so his thumbs touched the sides of her breasts. It was just an accident, she told herself as her body stiffened; he didn't do it deliberately. But when he kept repeating the movement she knew it was no accident, he was trying it on. Well, she wasn't standing for that! She put her hands on his chest and pushed with all her might. 'What d'yer think yer playing at, Alec?'

'Oh Sadie, I could eat yer.' He could tell she'd never been kissed properly before, she was as green as grass. But he didn't want to frighten her off by moving too quickly, so he wisely kept a distance between them. There'd be plenty of other times and he'd get a great deal of pleasure out of teaching her the ropes. All girls were shy at first, but they came round in the end. He'd never met a girl yet that he didn't get his own way with. 'The figure you've got, no man could keep his hands off yer.'

Sadie was asking herself what was wrong with her that she appeared to attract people who only seemed interested in getting what they wanted out of her. She wasn't a bad person, she'd never done anyone any harm – so why couldn't they like her just for herself? Her parents had always used her for their own ends and Brenda had used her for two years because Sadie was the only one who would fit in with her mother's strict rules. And she could tell by the way Alec was eyeing her up and down now that he wasn't seeing her as a nice girl, but as someone who had a good figure that he couldn't wait to get his hands on. He would use her if he got the chance, so why not turn the tables and make use of *him*?

She looked at him with her vivid blue eyes, a coy smile on her pretty face. 'No man will get his hands on me unless I want them to, Alec, and that won't be until I'm good and ready.'

Alec thought she was playing hard to get and he went along with her. 'I hope I'm around when yer ready, Sadie, 'cos I like yer a lot.'

'Yer not so bad yerself.' While Sadie was learning fast, her heart was hardening. From now on she'd do things to suit herself, no one else.

'Will yer come out with me again next week, Sadie?'

'D'yer ever go dancing, Alec? I've never been to a dance and it would make a change from the pictures.'

'I'll take yer to one if that's what yer want, but I've got to warn yer I'm not a very good dancer.'

'Well, I can't dance at all, so that makes two of us. We could practise on each other.' Sadie's spirits were lifting. She'd got her way over going dancing, and she'd make damn sure she got her own way over everything else. 'Anyway, it's late and I'll be gettin' into trouble. So I'll see yer in work tomorrow, okay?'

Alec was reluctant to part, even though he knew his mother would have a job getting him up for work in the morning. 'We're definitely on for next week, though?'

Sadie nodded. 'Yeah, as long as we can go dancing. But if yer really don't want to go, Alec, just let me know and I'll go with someone else.'

The little minx! She's not as green as she looks, Alec thought. But he didn't doubt for one moment that she'd have no trouble finding someone more than willing to take her where she wanted to go. So he found himself in the unusual position of giving into a girl. 'I've said I'll take yer and I will. We'll make arrangements through the week, eh?'

She gave him her sweetest smile. 'Yeah, okay. And thanks for tonight, Alec, I've enjoyed meself.'

As she walked on alone, Sadie had plenty on her mind. She'd learned tonight that if she played her cards right, she could exert power over a man, and that made her feel good. If her looks and figure were going to get her what she wanted, then she'd use them. From now on she would kowtow to no one.

George opened the door to Sadie and she could smell his beery breath before she stepped into the tiny hall. She made to pass him to go straight up to bed, but he grabbed her arm. His leering face just inches from hers, he asked, 'Well, did yer get a hand up yer skirt?'

Sadie looked at him with undisguised disgust. 'If I did, it certainly wasn't yours.'

Chapter Six

Mary Ann saw Sadie's blonde head and waved. 'Come an' give us a hand, girl, I'm rushed off me feet.' She turned back to the woman holding a jumper up. 'What are yer bellyaching about now, Nellie?'

'There's a hole in this bleedin' jumper – look.'

'Nellie, there's bleedin' holes in all the jumpers! If there wasn't, how would yer get yer head an' arms in?'

Nellie looked at the woman standing next to her. 'She's that ruddy sharp she'll be cuttin' herself one of these days.' Then she pushed the jumper over the counter, stuck her finger through the two-inch hole and wagged it in Mary Ann's face. 'I'd look funny with me head or me arms stickin' out of the waistband, wouldn't I?'

Mary Ann cocked her head as though giving the possibility some thought. 'I don't know, Nellie, I think it would be an improvement.'

'Any more cracks like that, Mary Ann, an' I'll be over this ruddy counter to make some improvements in your face.' Nellie began to get cocky; just for once she was going to get the better of the stall-holder. 'Come to weigh it up, any change in your face would be an improvement, even a broken nose.'

But it was not to be, for Mary Ann had an answer for any eventuality. She pulled a face as she shook her head and the thirty people crowded round her stall held their breath because Mary Ann had never been bested before. 'No, Nellie, my feller broke me nose once 'cos I burnt his flamin' dinner and it didn't improve me face at all.' She cupped her chin in a hand. 'Let's see, I was going to say yer could knock a few of me teeth out if it would make yer feel better, but as they're not mine it wouldn't do yer no good. Yer see, I borrowed these off the woman next door while me own are bein' repaired. Silly sod that I am, I bit into an apple and broke me denture in two.'

Nellie knew when she was beat. 'I dunno, yer'd have to be up early in the mornin' to get one over on you. Proper bloody clever clogs, that's what yer are.'

'Well, let's see whether I'm clever enough to sell yer that jumper for thruppence or not, shall we?'

'Thruppence!' Nellie gasped and her false teeth left their moorings.

'Well, the flamin' cheek of you! It's not worth that – look at the ruddy big hole in it! Go on, have a look!'

Mary Ann winked at Sadie who was now standing beside her, before continuing the exchange. 'I won't charge yer for the hole, Nellie.'

'Charge me for the flamin' hole? Well, have yer ever heard anythin' like that in yer life! Next thing, she'll be chargin' us for breathin' the air by her stall.' Nellie's teeth clicked back into place. 'How yer've got the bare-faced cheek to stand there an' ask for thruppence for a jumper with a hole in it as big as me fist, I'll never know.'

'It only needs darning, Nellie. Surely yer capable of that?'

'Oh, I'm capable all right, but I've got no money to be forkin' out for wool. If I had any money, d'yer think I'd be standin' here arguing over a ruddy jumper? No, I'd be on the tram down to TJs.'

'Hell's bleedin' bells, Nellie, it would cost yer more in tram fare than it would be to buy that ruddy jumper.' Mary Ann's eyes swept around the crowd. Many of them were holding goods they wished to purchase but they were in no hurry, not when they were enjoying themselves. They never missed a Saturday coming to Mary Ann's stall, she was noted for her humour and quick wit. And you always got a fair deal off her; she never tried to diddle anyone. But the stall-holder thought they'd had enough entertainment for one day. 'I'll tell yer what, then,' she said to Nellie, 'just to show yer me heart's in the right place, I'll knock a penny off for the wool.'

This was what the woman was hoping for, and a satisfied grin crossed her face. 'Oh, go 'ed, then, seein' as how yer twisted me arm.'

There was a spontaneous round of applause from the crowd which Mary Ann acknowledged with a bow. Then she held out her hand. 'Tuppence, please, Nellie.' She pocketed the two coins before beckoning the woman to move closer so she could whisper. But Mary Ann's whisper was loud enough for all to hear. 'D'yer know when yer go for the wool? Well, get a pennyworth of elastic, 'cos when yer were comin' towards us, I noticed yer knickers were hanging down. The elastic must have snapped.'

Nellie looked horrified. Had she walked all the way down Scottie Road with her knickers hanging down? Oh, she'd never live with the shame of it! Then she heard the laughter around her and the penny dropped. 'Yer a real case, Mary Ann, an' I could kick meself for fallin' for that!'

'For goodness sake don't kick yerself, Nellie, or yer knickers *will* fall down.' Mary Ann shared the woman's smile, then said, 'Bugger off home to your feller, Nellie, an' let me earn some money. While you've been arguing over a measly tuppence it's cost me a bleedin' fortune in lost customers.'

For the next half-hour Sadie worked hard to help clear the backlog of customers. And she enjoyed every minute of it, feeling more at home here than she'd ever felt anywhere. Never before in her life had she laughed so heartily, and as she grew in confidence so her sense of humour came to the fore and she was beginning to give back as good as she got.

'How much are these, girl?' An elderly woman with pure white hair, her face a mass of wrinkles and wearing a black knitted shawl across her shoulders, was holding out a garment which she'd rolled into a ball. 'Ask Mary Ann for us.'

'What is it?' Sadie unrolled the ball to find it was an old pair of men's combinations with an opening flap at the back. She tried hard to keep the laughter back but it rang out loud and clear, causing heads to turn. Feeling mischievous, she held the combinations against herself and asked, 'Do they suit me?'

Mary Ann had turned from the customer she was serving and joined in the laughter. 'Ay, girl, yer wouldn't half get a click if yer went out wearing them.'

Even the old woman was laughing. 'I'll tell yer what, girl, if they looked as good on my feller as they do on you, I'd marry him again temorrer. The trouble is, he's as thin as a ruddy drainpipe an' if he wasn't wearing clothes, yer wouldn't be able to see him! He's got legs on him like knots in cotton and he daren't walk over a grid in case he falls down it. In fact, he's that thin he hasn't even got a shadow.'

Five minutes later the woman walked away with the combinations tucked under her arm and her purse lighter by fourpence. She turned to wave to Sadie. 'Wait till I get home an' tell my feller. He'll laugh his bleedin' head off.'

'Tell him to mind he doesn't catch cold from that flap in the back.' Sadie called after her. 'One strong gust of wind an' he could be blown sky-high.'

Mary Ann came to stand beside her. 'Yer've taken to this job like a duck to water, haven't yer, girl? I'll have to watch I don't get me nose pushed out.'

'I love it, Mary Ann. I feel as free as a bird when I'm here – all me troubles are forgotten.' Sadie tucked her arm into the stall-holder's. 'Wasn't that old lady a little love? I felt like giving her a big hug and a kiss.'

'Yeah, she's a character, is old Sarah. She's been around for donkey's years, as long as I can remember, so she must be knockin' on eighty if she's a day.' Mary Ann removed Sadie's arm and bent down to her special box. 'I picked a dress out for yer.'

'No!' Sadie put a hand out to stop her. 'I can't buy anythin' off yer today. I've got to have a pair of shoes – these I've got on are fallin' to pieces.' She lowered her eyes, shame flooding her body. 'And me two brothers are goin' around barefoot.'

Mary Ann was aghast. 'They shouldn't be your worry, girl. It's yer mam's place to see to them.'

'I know it should be, Mary Ann, but if she doesn't do it then someone else has to see to them. They look like ragamuffins all the time, clothes fallin' off them and filthy dirty, but I can't let them run around with no shoes on. All the kids must be laughing at them.' There was fire in Sadie's voice as memories came flooding back. 'I know what it's like to be laughed at. I had me bellyful of that all the time I was at school.'

Mary Ann opened her mouth then closed it again quickly. It was no good pouring oil on troubled waters. The girl was distressed enough without her adding her tuppennyworth. So when she spoke, her voice was gentle. 'That stall over there sells shoes, and he's a decent bloke, he'll do yer a good deal. But yer'll have to haggle with him over the price, same as the people do with me.'

'I'm having an argument with meself inside,' Sadie told her. 'I'm desperate for shoes, and like yer said, the boys are not my worry. But I'd feel dead selfish if I saw to meself and left them running around barefoot.'

'How much have yer got, girl?'

'One and sixpence.' Once again Sadie hung her head in shame. 'I know it's not enough for three pairs of shoes, but I thought if I could get meself seen to, and one of the boys, I could fix the other one up next week.' She raised her eyes. 'I've got a date to go to a dance on Friday and I couldn't get on a dance floor in these, I'd be a laughing stock. If it weren't for that, I'd leave meself until next Saturday.'

'Look, let me go an' haggle for yer, eh? You can mind the stall for me 'cos yer know by now roughly what to charge.' Mary Ann grinned. 'With a hole tuppence, without, thruppence.'

'No, I couldn't let yer do that, Mary Ann. Yer've done enough for me.'

'I wouldn't be doing it for you, girl, I'd be doin' it for meself! It's a long time since I was on the other side of the counter and I want to see if I've lost me touch in wangling a bargain.' Mary Ann untied the canvas apron she wore around her waist to keep the money in. 'Put this on, in case yer need change. And if yer'll give me the shoe sizes, and the eighteen pence, I'll go and see what I can do.'

'The boys take a size four and seven, and I'm in a five. But skip mine – I'll tell the boy I want to go to the pictures instead of a dance.'

Mary Ann lowered her gaze to Sadie's feet. 'Listen to me, love, if ever anybody needed shoes, it's you. Those canoes on yer feet don't bear inspection.'

Sadie giggled at the description. 'Go on, I've got customers waitin' to be served.'

'Huh! Hark at you! Yer'll be takin' over from me next.' Mary Ann waved to a customer as she made her way to a stall opposite. 'My assistant will look after yer, Lizzie.'

There were a few people rummaging through the shoes on Tony Henshaw's stall and when his eyes lit on Mary Ann they flew open in surprise. 'Well, well! It's not very often I have the pleasure of serving you, Mary Ann. Down on yer uppers, are yer?'

'I'll laugh at that when I'm havin' me tea tonight.' Mary Ann walked to the back of the stall where Tony was standing. 'I'm not down on me uppers, but see that girl servin' on my stall? Well, she is.'

'I've seen her there for the last few weeks,' Tony said. 'She's quite a looker, isn't she?'

'Keep yer eyes in yer head, Tony, she's not sixteen yet. She's a crackin' kid, but she doesn't have a very good home life . . . lazy mother and drunken father. The first time she came to me she just had the one dress to her name an' I felt sorry for her. Took to her right away, I did. Anyway, I'll tell yer the full story about Sadie some other time. Right now I need your help.'

'Yer'll not get three pair of shoes for eighteen pence, Mary Ann,' Tony said after being given the details. 'And don't try and soft soap me 'cos I've got a wife and six children to clothe and feed.'

'Ooh, it's six children now, is it? Yer a busy lad, aren't yer?'

'I can't sleep, yer see, Mary Ann, an' I can't stay awake all night doin' nothing, now can I? And the wife just happens to be handy so it helps me pass the time away.'

'Why don't yer learn to play patience? Or, better still, tell yer wife to take a rolling pin to bed with her. There's nothing knocks a man out quicker than a bash on the 'ead with a good old-fashioned rolling pin.'

'Yer a hard woman, Mary Ann. If I was married to you I'd probably have nothing to do in bed but go to sleep.'

Mary Ann eyed him up and down, a cheeky twinkle in her eye. 'I dunno, Tony, I do have me moments of reckless abandonment when my feller thinks it's his birthday and Christmas all rolled into one.'

Tony chuckled. 'Am I gettin' the come-on, Mary Ann?'

She chuckled back. 'Yer'd run a mile if I tried it on, wouldn't yer, Tony?'

'You ain't kiddin', Mary Ann – yer wouldn't see me heels for dust.

Yer see, it's not me what can't sleep, it's the missus.'

Mary Ann clapped her hands. 'Come on, Tony, hop to it! I want two pair of boys' shoes sizes four and seven, and a pair of ladies' high heels size five.'

'All for eighteen pence? Not askin' for much, are yer?'

'Okay, I'll put a tanner to it, so that's two bob. Now see what yer can do for us.'

Sadie couldn't believe her eyes when Mary Ann came back holding three pairs of shoes in her arms. 'Yer didn't get all them for one and six?'

'No, it came to two bob. But before yer say anything, just listen to me. I put a dress away for yer as a little thank you for helping me out on the stall. But I'll keep the dress until next week and yer can give me sixpence for it. That way I've got me money back and you've got a dress and shoes. Not a bad bargain, eh, girl?'

'You don't have to give me nothing to help yer out 'cos I enjoy it so much I should be paying you!' But the offer was tempting. Sadie would have a decent pair of shoes and she wouldn't have to feel guilty about the boys. 'I'll make it up to yer, Mary Ann, I promise. I'll come and help yer out every Saturday afternoon for a few hours.'

'Don't be makin' rash promises before yer've had a look at the shoes. Yer might end up throwin' them at me.'

The two pairs of boys' shoes were well worn, down at heel and the toe caps scuffed. But there was still some wear in them and anything was better than running around barefoot. They'd probably look quite respectable if they were given a good brushing with black polish, but Sadie knew they'd fall to pieces without ever having a cloth run over them.

'I got these for you, but if yer don't like them, Tony said yer can take them back and choose another pair.' Mary Ann waited with bated breath for Sadie's reaction. Tony had been reluctant to part with the shoes for the money offered and it had taken all the stall-holder's powers of persuasion to talk him around.

Sadie was stunned into silence. She'd never had a dressy pair of shoes, they'd all been flat-heeled, heavy and ugly. But the pair Mary Ann was holding up for her inspection had high heels, they were in black, shiny patent leather and had a narrow strap across the ankle which fastened into a silver buckle at the side. Never in her wildest dreams had she imagined herself wearing anything as glamorous.

'Well? Has the cat got yer tongue?'

Sadie couldn't speak so she showed her gratitude by flinging her arms around Mary Ann and sobbing into her shoulder. 'God was looking after me the day He sent me to your stall, Mary Ann. Nobody has ever been as good to me as you've been.'

Mary Ann patted the girl's shoulder as though she was a baby. 'There now, sweetheart, there's no need to cry.' She was feeling emotional herself and was having a job keeping her voice steady. 'If yer don't behave yerself I'll take the bleedin' shoes back.'

Sadie sniffed up. 'Oh no, yer won't! They're the most beautiful shoes in the whole world.'

'Yer haven't even tried them on yet! Come on, girl, get a move on. I've got a couple of customers to serve.'

Tony Henshaw watched the scene from his stall opposite. And when he saw Sadie's obvious pleasure and gratitude he suddenly felt good inside. He could have got a bit more for the high-heeled shoes but now he was glad he'd let Mary Ann talk him round. And when he saw Sadie tottering in her first pair of high heels, grabbing the table for support, his laugh was as loud as hers, Mary Ann's and the customers. He felt quite bucked up and cheerful, thinking life wasn't so bad after all.

'I'll never walk in them,' Sadie said. 'I'll fall flat on me face.'

'In ten minutes, girl, yer'll think yer've been wearing them all yer life. I remember my first pair of high heels, they crippled me for a while till I got used to them.' Mary Ann grinned, pushing one of her bright red curls back into the comb. 'I'd have worn them whether they crippled me or not 'cos I wanted to be in the fashion. There were no flies on me in those days, girl, I can tell yer.'

Sadie took her hand from the table and ventured a few steps. 'Ooh, er, I feel as though I'm on top of a ladder.' Another few steps and she felt more confident. 'I'll do it even if it kills me.'

'See if yer can make it over to Tony's stall to thank him. He did yer a favour, girl, an' yer never know, yer might need his help again.' Mary Ann watched Sadie walk across to the stall opposite with her arms sticking out to balance herself. Then she turned to the customer who'd been waiting patiently. 'If I had legs like hers, Florrie, I'd wear me clothes up to me backside.'

Florrie grinned to reveal her pink, toothless gums. 'Wear them up to yer waist, Mary Ann,' she raised an arm as though to protect herself before adding, 'then no one will notice the gob on yer.'

Sadie was jubilant as she walked home, until she neared the street where she lived. How was she going to explain that she'd bought three pairs of shoes on her shilling pocket money? She daren't tell them she'd been getting sixpence a week off Harry because they'd jump to conclusions and call her a slut. And she was going out with Brenda tonight. She'd had to hide that sixpence under her pillow in case she was tempted to spend it. She wished she wasn't going out with her workmate, then she'd have been able to pay Mary Ann and she'd have been straight. She wasn't going with Brenda next week, even though it meant breaking a promise. There were so many things that she wanted, the money could be better spent than going to the pictures. And it wasn't luxuries she was after, it was for things that people like Brenda took for granted. Like a comb that had more than six teeth in it, or soap to get washed.

As she turned the corner of the street, Sadie made up her mind to tell a lie. It was only a little white lie, so God would forgive her. And it wouldn't be necessary if her parents clothed their children properly.

The shoes were wrapped in newspaper and Sadie hugged the parcel to her chest when she saw her brothers sitting on the front step. 'Come on in, kids, I've got something for yer.'

The boys scrambled to their feet. 'What is it, our Sadie?'

'Wait and see.' Sadie entered the living room and tried to stop her spirits from sinking. What an absolute mess! And there was no need for it because Dot was sitting at the table with Ellen playing a game of Ludo, and her mother was sprawled on the couch with the baby by her side. All they had to do was get off their backsides and get stuck in.

'Mam, I've been to the market an' I got the boys a pair of shoes each. They're not much cop 'cos I only had a shilling, but they're better than nothing. I got a pair for meself as well.'

Lily Wilson roused herself. 'All that for a shillin'? What d'yer bleedin' take me for – a ruddy fool? What tricks have yer been up to, yer little faggot?'

Sadie managed to control her temper and feign surprise. 'What d'yer mean, Mam? I haven't been up to no tricks.'

The boys were pulling on her skirt. 'Let's see them, our Sadie. Can we put them on now to play out in?'

When Sadie looked at their excited faces she knew all the trouble she'd gone to, and the lie she'd told, were well worth it. But the look of dislike on her mother's face gave her the nerve to bluff it out. 'Yer'd better ask me Mam. If she doesn't want yer to have them I can take them back to the man and get me money back.'

'Ah, ray, Mam!' Jimmy glared defiantly at his mother. 'You promised yer'd get us shoes weeks ago, but yer didn't, did yer? So I want the ones our Sadie's got for us 'cos I'm not goin' to school again in me bare feet an' have everyone laughin' and pokin' fun at me.'

Sadie raised her eyebrows. 'Well, Mam? I don't mind takin' them back, I could do with the money. Those shoes were bought with me next week's dinner money.'

'No! Yer not takin' them back, our Sadie!' Les was nearly in tears. 'Mam, tell 'er we can have them. I've got all sores under me feet an' they don't half hurt.'

Lily sank back on the couch. 'Oh, let them have them. I don't care where yer got the bleedin' money from.'

Sadie unwrapped the parcel and took out the boys' shoes, leaving her own in the paper. She just wasn't in the mood for the sarcastic remarks she knew would come her way if her mother saw the black patent leather high heels. They would come when they saw her dressed to go out, but by then her temper might not be so high.

She looked down to where the boys were sitting on the floor sorting the shoes out and the delight on their faces was a joy to behold. But the mother who should have been happy for them, showed no interest at all. She glared at Sadie with a sullen look on her face, making the girl's temper soar even higher and causing her to blurt out, 'I'm glad to see yer looking so happy about yer sons having shoes on their feet, Mam. And it was nice of yer to thank me for spendin' me money on them.' She turned to the door, then spun around. 'There's not many mothers in this world like you, Mam, thank God.'

'But you promised!'

They had come out of the first-house pictures and were standing on the pavement in front of the cinema. 'I know I promised, but I'm breaking me promise, Brenda, because I want to.' Sadie looked at the sulky expression on her friend's face and thought what a spoiled brat she was. She wanted everything her way and couldn't understand when she didn't get it. She reminded Sadie of a young child, crying because she couldn't have the lollipop she could see in the shop window. But she wasn't a child; she would be sixteen in ten days' time – old enough to behave like an adult.

'But I'll be on me own, I've no one else to go with.' Brenda's bottom lip trembled. 'Just this once, Sadie?'

'No.' Sadie hardened her heart. Never again would she let anyone make use of her. 'I want to spend what bit of money I've got on buying meself some things I badly need. And I'm going out with Alec next week, anyway. He's taking me to a dance, and when I've learned how to dance properly I'll be going to places like the Grafton or Rialto.' She averted her eyes so she wouldn't see her friend's woebegone face. She wasn't going to give in like she usually did, not this time. 'The pictures are all right now and again, but not every week like we've been doing for the last two years. There's got to be more to life than that.'

'So we won't be friends no more?'

'Of course we'll still be friends! I see yer every day in work, don't I? And yer can always come dancing with me, if yer want to.'

'Me mam won't let me!' Brenda wailed. 'I know she won't.'

'I can't help that, Brenda. All I know is that your mam can spoil your life, but I'm not going to let her spoil mine.' Sadie let out a deep sigh. 'Anyway, I'm going. I'll see yer in work on Monday morning.'

'You're looking very smart in yer high heels,' Harry said as they walked through the park gates. 'They suit yer.'

'Harry, they're killing me. I'm not used to walking on me toes and I've got cramp.' Sadie turned to grin at him. 'I shouldn't have put them on to go to the pictures, so it's me own fault for wanting to swank.'

There was nobody in their clearing; in fact, the park seemed unusually empty of grown-ups out for a walk, or older children playing. 'Let's have a good look at yer.' Harry stood in front of her and feasted his eyes on her beauty. The blonde hair that framed her face was long and curly, her black eyebrows were perfectly arched and the long lashes fanning her cheeks were dark against her flawless complexion. Her nose was slightly turned up at the end and her lips were made for kissing. Her slim figure was perfect, and her legs long and shapely. 'You are one very lovely girl, Sadie.'

Sadie blushed. Alec's compliments went over her head because she knew he'd say the same thing to every girl he went out with, but it was different with Harry because she knew he wasn't just flirting, he really meant what he said. But she didn't know how to answer him so she resorted to humour. 'I'm a girl who's got her heels dug in the grass, Harry. I'm two inches smaller than when we came in.'

Harry laughed as he reached for her hands. 'You'll soon learn not to shy away from compliments, Sadie, because there'll be plenty coming your way. But I'll not embarrass yer, so tell me what your day's been like.'

'Work this morning, the market this afternoon and the flicks tonight. I didn't enjoy work, the market was brilliant and Brenda spoiled the picture for me by acting like a child when I said our Saturday night dates were over. I thought she was goin' to cry on me flippin' shoulder.'

Harry lifted one of her hands and pressed it to his lips. 'What did yer do at the market that made it brilliant?'

Sadie felt at ease with Harry, knowing in her heart he wasn't with her because he wanted something from her. So she told him about some of the customers at the market and the laughs they'd had. Then she explained about the boys having no shoes, and how Mary Ann had helped her get three pairs for two shillings. 'Our Jimmy and Les were over the moon, but me mam's attitude made me mad. I mean, it's up to her to clothe the kids, but she's always saying she's got no money. And yet when I spend all me pocket money to put shoes on their feet, she doesn't even look at the shoes, never mind saying a thank you to me.'

Harry listened, while at the back of his mind was the question – why does she have to be one of the Wilsons? If she was any other neighbour's daughter he wouldn't have to meet her on the quiet. He could call on her without the wrath of his mother coming down on his head. He knew now that his feelings for Sadie were not those of a friend; he was falling head over heels for her. And she was such a sweet girl. It wasn't fair that she was paying for the sins of her parents. He sighed, thinking things would have to run their course. He loved his mother dearly and didn't want to upset her, but the time might come when he would have to. That's if Sadie felt the same way about him. She was still very young so there was time for the matter to resolve itself.

'Anyway,' Sadie was saying, 'I'm goin' me own way from now on. I've got a date next week to go to a dance, so that's a start.'

Harry felt his heart miss a beat. 'Who've yer got a date with?'

'A bloke in work. He's one of these smarmy fellers, thinks because he's nice-looking all the girls should throw themselves at him. But I've got him taped. He won't get very far with me.'

'Well, if yer think that about him, why date him?'

'Because he can take me to a dance, that's why! I can't afford to buy me own clothes and pay to go anywhere, not on a shilling pocket money! I'm sixteen a week on Monday, Harry, and I haven't got any of the things most girls my age have. No make-up, perfume, pretty clothes ... nothing!' If Sadie had known what was in Harry's heart, she wouldn't have carried on. But she thought of him as a good friend, someone who had been kind to her. 'If I can get some bloke to take me out, I can spend what little money I've got on trying to make meself look presentable.'

It was on the tip of Harry's tongue to say he'd take her out – she didn't need to date any bloke just because he'd pay for her. But he could hear his mother's words echoing in his head. 'If I see her trying to get pally with you, I'll have something to say to her, believe me.' And she'd do that, his mother, thinking she was saving him from a fate worse than death. He couldn't take a chance on putting Sadie through that. But there was one thing for which he'd throw caution to the winds. 'You haven't forgotten I'm taking you to the pictures on yer birthday, have you? I got in before anyone else, remember?'

'D'yer mean on the Monday?'

'That's the day yer birthday's on, so yes!'

Sadie looked pleased. She'd never been out on her birthday before. In fact, birthdays in the Wilsons' house passed without an acknowledgement of any kind. No cards, no presents and certainly no party. 'Yeah, I'd like that.' Then she touched his arm. 'Can I ask you to take me somewhere else, not the pictures?'

'Of course you can. Where would you like to go?'

'Over to New Brighton on a ferry boat.' Her hands clasped together, her eyes alight with excitement, Harry thought she looked like a child hoping for a treat. 'I've never been on a ferry boat.'

Harry was taken aback. 'Never been on a ferry boat? Never sailed across the Mersey?'

Sadie shook her head. 'No, never. It would be a lovely birthday present, Harry, but only if yer can afford it.'

'I can afford it, Sadie. Me wages are not bad, and me mam doesn't take that much off me.' Harry's mind was running away with him. He couldn't call for her or meet her in the street, that would be asking for trouble. 'We could go straight from work and spend an hour at the fairground.'

'Ooh, that would be lovely.' Sadie was so happy she cupped his face and kissed him. 'Yer a nice bloke, Harry. You and Mary Ann are me very best friends.'

'Aye, well, I don't mind bein' yer friend, but I don't want a friend's kiss. Come here, I want me tanner's worth.'

Sadie smiled. 'Yer still want to pay me for letting yer kiss me?'

Harry's voice was gruff. 'You told me yer'd spent all yer money, so how would yer buy yer pennyworth of chips all next week?'

'I'd go without, Harry.'

'Not while I'm around yer won't. You'll never be short if I've got anything to do with it.'

'If you don't kiss me and get off to see this girlfriend of yours, she'll definitely give you the heave-ho.'

Harry silenced her with his lips. Soft and light, not hard and bruising like Alec's.

Chapter Seven

On the Friday night Sadie ate her sardines on toast without a murmur. She didn't like sardines and Lily knew that, but tonight wasn't the time for complaints. She was meeting Alec at Everton Valley and he was taking her to a dance, but as yet she hadn't plucked up the courage to tell her mother. If they had cross words she'd be told she couldn't go, just for spite, and Sadie wasn't taking any chances. The best thing to do was get ready first, and then ask permission in as humble a voice as she could muster.

There was no mirror in the bedroom so Sadie had to make do without being able to see how she looked. From the neck down she was satisfied with what she could see of her appearance and she'd check her hair in the broken piece of mirror in the kitchen before she went out. That's if she managed to get out. Her mother seemed to have it in for her these days and picked on her for the least thing.

There was no handrail on the steep, narrow staircase – it had been used for firewood years ago. So Sadie put her hand on the wall as she stepped carefully down each stair, her high heels clicking loudly on the bare boards. When she reached the bottom, she stood for a moment before crossing her fingers for luck and taking a deep breath.

The baby was in bed and the other children were out playing in the street, so that was a blessing. Her mother and father were sat next to each other at the cluttered table, reading the *Echo* between them.

'Mam, I'm going to a dance tonight with a boy from work. Will it be all right if I'm a bit late coming in?'

Lily looked up, and seeing her daughter took her back over the years. It was almost like looking at herself. She'd been as pretty as Sadie at her age – with the same colouring, same hair and same lovely figure. But the memory didn't soften her heart because it reminded her of how much she'd let herself go. Not that she placed the blame at her own door. Oh no. In her twisted mind she blamed giving birth to the children for losing her looks and figure, particularly the girl facing her now – a constant reminder of how things used to be.

When her mother didn't answer, Sadie became bold and ventured, 'Shall I take a key with me in case yer in bed?'

'No need for that,' George said, before his wife could answer. 'I'll wait up for yer.'

'You'll do no such thing!' Lily turned on him, angry at the lustful way he was eyeing his daughter. It was his leer that turned the tide in Sadie's favour. 'Go on, get out,' she said, wanting the girl out of her sight. 'We'll leave the back door on the latch. But don't think yer can come sneaking in at all hours 'cos I'll be listenin' for yer.'

'I won't, Mam.' Sadie beat a hasty retreat. 'I'll go out the back way.' After a quick glance in the spotted mirror she was on her way to her first dance.

'Is this it?' Sadie couldn't hide her disappointment as she stood with Alec outside the wooden building. She'd imagined dance halls to be bright fashionable places, not little wooden huts. 'It doesn't look like a dance hall to me.'

'It belongs to the church and it's not so bad inside.' Alec steered her forward. 'If yer want to learn to dance without makin' a fool of yerself then this place is as good as any.'

Inside the door a man sat behind a little card table taking the money and giving tickets in return. It cost fourpence each and the man told Alec to hang on to the tickets because he'd need them to get a cup of tea and biscuit in the interval.

'It's bigger than it looks from the outside,' Sadie said, watching with envy the couples dancing to the tune of a waltz. 'They can't half dance – they're certainly not beginners.'

Alec laughed. 'No, the ones sitting down are the beginners. They won't venture onto the floor until it's packed and no one will notice them tripping over their feet.'

'Aye, well, here's their mate. I don't fancy makin' a fool of meself, either.'

'You'll be all right.' Alec squeezed her arm. 'I'm not much of a dancer but I do know the basic steps an' all you've got to do is follow me.'

'Is that all!' Sadie watched the ease and grace of the dancers as they circled the floor, their steps perfectly matched and their body movements in time with the pianist Sadie could now see sitting in the corner of the room. 'Shall we sit down for a while an' I can watch to get some idea of how it's done?'

Alec glanced around the room and then down at Sadie. She had to be the best-looking girl there. 'We'll wait for the next waltz,' he said as they walked towards two vacant chairs. 'The next dance will be a slow foxtrot an' that's the hardest to learn.'

'I'll be glad if I can learn to just put one foot in front of the other, that'll do me for one night.'

'Yer'll do more than that, Sadie.' Alec slipped his arm across her shoulders. 'There's only three basic steps to a waltz – yer'll learn them by the time yer halfway down the floor.'

He wasn't far wrong, either. Holding her slightly away from him so she could see his feet, Alec kept repeating, '*One*, two, three . . . *one*, two, three.' And in no time at all, Sadie had picked up the rhythm and was grinning all over her face. 'I'll be all right until we come to a corner.'

'There's one coming up, Sadie.' Alec was very patient as he manoeuvred them around the corner. He was also very conscious of the admiring glances coming Sadie's way and he revelled in the fact that he was the envy of half the blokes in the room. But to remind them that she belonged to him, he pulled her close. 'Yer don't need to see me feet now yer've got the steps off.'

'If yer start any fancy footwork, Alec, I'll leave the floor.'

'As if I'd do that to you!' While he was smiling down into her face, Alec took the opportunity of moving his hand sideways from her shoulder blade, just far enough for it to be an easy distance for his thumb to travel to the side of her breast. He casually moved it up and down as he continued to talk. 'Yer've got a natural rhythm, Sadie, it won't take yer long. I bet within a few months yer as good as anyone here tonight.'

'I wonder if I'll be as quick as you, Alec?' Sadie's eyes left him in no doubt of what she was talking about. 'I think you are very quick off the mark.'

Alec kept smiling and his thumb kept moving slowly over her breast. He was quite certain she wouldn't cause a stink in the dance hall. 'If yer not quick in this life, Sadie, then yer get left behind.'

'I'll remember that, Alec.' Sadie let him have his pleasure. After all, it wasn't really doing her any harm and he had paid fourpence for the privilege. He was using her and she was using him; they made a good pair. But she'd make sure that in future the privilege would cost him more than fourpence. And she'd make sure he never got what he was really after.

The interval was over and Sadie waited patiently for the pianist to play a waltz. She'd been on the floor several times and was excited about her progress. 'Will yer bring me again next week, Alec? I'll be practising every chance I get, so I should be a lot better by then.'

'Yeah, okay! But can yer make it Saturday? Otherwise I've got to borrow off me mam.'

Sadie thought of Harry and pursed her lips. 'Can I let yer know through the week? I've half-promised to go somewhere on Saturday.'

'Who with?' Alec felt a pang of jealousy. 'Yer haven't got another feller on the go, have yer?'

'Don't be daft! It's only a neighbour, but I did promise.'

'You can get out of it. Yer would if yer really wanted to.'

'I've said I'll try, Alec, so let's leave it at that, eh? I'll let yer know for sure at the beginning of the week.' When she saw the droop of Alec's mouth, Sadie thought, My God, he's another Brenda. Sulks like a child when he can't get his own way.

The pianist struck up with a waltz and Sadie was on her feet before Alec. 'Come on, I want to get in as much practice as I can.'

An elated Sadie was clapping at the end of the dance when she noticed the clock on the wall. 'Alec, it's half-past ten! I'll have to go.'

'Oh, come on, Sadie, there's only another two dances before the last waltz. Yer can stay till then, surely?'

Sadie shook her head. 'It'll be eleven o'clock by the time I walk home, and if I'm any later than that I'll get a thick ear.'

'Is it always goin' to be like this? You dashin' off and leaving me in the lurch without even a good-night kiss?'

'It won't always be like this, but right now me and me mam are not seeing eye to eye. I'm sixteen on Monday and I think that as long as I tell her where I'm going, and with who, then she should trust me. Anyway, I haven't got time to argue the toss now, so if yer want yer good-night kiss yer better walk me out. Yer can always come back in again – there's plenty of unattached girls.'

Alec had already noted that. There was one in the far corner who'd been giving him the eye all night; she'd probably be generous with her favours. She wasn't in the same class as Sadie for looks, but in a dark doorway he wouldn't see, or care, what her face was like. 'I'll see yer to the top of the street and come back for the last few dances.'

There was an entry before they came to the top of the street and despite her protests, Sadie was pulled into its shadows. Alec wasted no time. His lips came down hard on hers and his hands travelled over her body. It took all Sadie's might to free herself, but she remained in control of her feelings. 'As I said, Alec, yer quick off the mark.'

'Yer don't give me time to be anythin' else!' Alec's desire was roused. 'One of these days perhaps we'll get half an hour alone together.'

'Could be, Alec, could be. But right now I've got to run. I'll see yer in work tomorrow.'

Alec watched her slim legs cover the ground for a while before walking back to the dance hall. He crossed the room to where the girl he had in mind was sitting. When he saw her face light up with pleasure, he knew she was going to be a walkover. Close up, he could see she had a face like the back of a tram, but it wasn't her face he was interested in. If he closed his eyes he could make believe she was Sadie.

Sadie had her shilling pocket money clutched in her hand as she stood looking into the chemist's window. She had to pay Mary Ann the money she owed her, so she was left with sixpence to spend. She was badly in need of a comb, but they were only a penny. It was what to do with the other five pennies that she was deliberating. Did she need scented soap more than a lipstick? It would have to be the soap because there wasn't any in the house and she'd had to swill her face in cold water before she came out. Even if her mother bought a block this afternoon after getting her wages it would be that horrible smelly scrubbing soap. So it would have to be the soap and she could wait until next week for the lipstick.

Sadie had her foot on the shop step when she had a change of heart and went back to looking in the window. All the girls in work wore lipstick but she'd never used it in her life. And Monday was her birthday, she was going on the ferry with Harry. She really wanted to look grown up for that. Oh, dear, what to do? Then with a determined step she entered the shop. The soap was more essential. And anyway, if it was scented she would smell nice.

'Can I have a penny comb, please?'

'What colour would yer like, love?' asked the assistant. 'Black, white, red or blue?'

Sadie lowered her head as she considered the options and there in front of her on the counter was a wicker bowl containing tubes of lipstick. And a sign attached to the bowl read *Lipstick . . . all colours . . . 3d.* They can't be much good, Sadie thought, because even in Woolies a tube of lipstick costs sixpence. She looked at the waiting assistant who was moving from one foot to the other, a bored look on her thin pale face. 'I'll have a blue comb, please. And can yer tell me how much a bar of scented soap costs?'

The girl turned to slip a comb out of the card hanging on the wall behind her. 'All prices from tuppence to sixpence.'

'Do the tuppenny ones have a nice smell?' When the woman nodded, Sadie said, 'Yer see, I've only got sixpence on me and I was just looking at these lipsticks. They're very cheap, aren't they?'

'Yeah, they're a good buy. Me boss is having a clear-out of old stock, that's why they're so cheap. There's nowt wrong with them – I've bought two meself.'

Sadie felt like rounding the counter and giving the girl a hug. 'I'll have a tuppenny bar of soap and a lipstick then.'

The assistant grinned. 'White or pink soap?'

'Pink please, to make the boys wink.'

The woman pulled a bag free of the string it was hanging on behind the counter. She put the comb in, then passed a bar of pink soap over to Sadie to smell before putting it in the bag with the comb. 'Now what colour lipstick d'yer wear?'

'I wouldn't know,' Sadie said truthfully. 'I've never had a lipstick before.'

'There's not many shades to choose from, but there's a pale pink one that would just suit your colouring. Here, I'll get one for you.' The assistant came to the front of the counter. She picked two tubes out of the bowl and took the tops off. 'This bright red one wouldn't suit yer at all, it's too showy. But this pink one, now I think it's ideal for yer.'

Sadie left the shop feeling as though she was walking on air. She'd got the three things she wanted and still had Mary Ann's sixpence. It was by sheer chance she chose that shop to go in, and wasn't she lucky?

The smile was still on her face when she got to Mary Ann's stall. It was busy as usual, and the stall-holder was serving two customers at the same time. Sadie crept up quietly behind her, put her arms around her waist and lifted her up before beginning to sing.

> *'Oh, we ain't got a barrel of money,*
> *Maybe we're ragged and funny,*
> *But we'll travel along,*
> *Singing this song,*
> *Side by side.'*

One by one the customers joined in, linking arms and swaying as the market rang with the sound of happy, laughing songsters.

'In the name of God, girl, what's got into yer?' Mary Ann struggled to find a foothold. 'If I didn't know better I'd think yer'd been on the ale.'

'Oh, don't be such a misery guts, Mary Ann!' a woman shouted. 'I enjoyed that, I did. And the bleedin' song's right! We *ain't* got a barrel of money, and some of us are ragged an' funny, but we can still bleedin' enjoy ourselves.'

Mary Ann grinned at the woman. 'Have yer been goin' to night school, Fanny? I've never heard yer string one sentence together before, never mind six.'

'Ho bleedin' ho!' Fanny folded her arms and hitched up her bosom. 'Listen to brain box talkin'. I bet yer any money yer can't spell encyclopedia.'

'Can you?' Mary Ann asked.

'It's me what asked the question, Mary Ann, so don't be tryin' to wriggle out of it. It doesn't make no difference whether I can spell it or not.'

'It does to me, Fanny.'

'Oh, come off it, yer silly sod. Yer can either spell it or yer can't.'

'Well, it's like this, Fanny.' Mary Ann gave Sadie's arm a squeeze. 'If you can spell it, then I can't. But if you can't, then I can!'

'In the name of God will yer listen to the woman!' Fanny tutted. 'Yer only doin' this to confuse me, Mary Ann, but I'm not goin' to let yer.'

Mary Ann was shaking inside with laughter. 'I'll tell yer what, Fanny, an' this is fair. You spell it first an' then I'll spell it after yer. Yer see, I don't think yer can do it.'

'Oh, that's where yer wrong, Mary Ann, 'cos I can spell it.'

'Okay, Fanny, I'll give yer two bob if yer spell it for us.'

The woman standing next to Fanny gave her a dig in the ribs. 'Oo, er, Fanny! Two bob! Quick, take her up on it before she changes her mind.'

Fanny was lumbered but she wasn't going to go down without a fight. After all, nobody could spell encyclopedia so they wouldn't know if she got it right or wrong. 'It's E N S I K L ...'

A man in the crowd tapped her on the shoulder. 'That's not right, madam. There's no S or K in encyclopedia.'

'Who the hell are you!' Fanny's face was red as she fought down the urge to pull his trilby hat down over his ears. 'An' who asked yer to stick yer nose in where it's not wanted?'

'I was only trying to help,' said the well-dressed man. 'I didn't mean to offend.'

Mary Ann the peacemaker held up her hand. 'Excuse me, sir, but I don't think you come to the market very often so you won't know that Fanny and I go through a funny ten minutes every week. It gives us all a laugh and no harm done.'

The man raised his hat to Fanny. 'Madam, I apologise for spoiling what was a very funny episode. Please accept my apologies.'

Fanny had never been spoken to so politely in her life and didn't know whether to kiss him or thump him one. In the end she gave him her best smile. 'Apology accepted, sir.'

Sadie lifted the sixpence up to show Mary Ann before she slipped it into her apron pocket. 'Can I put this bag in yer special box, Mary Ann? Then I'll serve a few people for yer.'

'Hey! Come back here an' tell us what yer were so happy about!'

Sadie put on a stern look and wagged a stiffened finger. 'Business before pleasure. I'll tell yer when trade slackens off. Right now I can see at least a dozen people waitin' to be served . . . enough to keep your feller in ciggies for a week.'

Mary Ann went back to Fanny with a smile on her face. 'Cheeky little monkey she is, but I'm beginnin' to love the bones of her.'

'She seems a good kid, even if she nearly did start a flamin' war by singin' that song.' Fanny leaned over the counter and lowered her voice, 'Mary Ann, just out of curiosity, an' between me an' you, can yer really spell encyclopedia?'

'Sod off will yer, Fanny! I never got any further than C A T, cat, at school. And since this is just between ourselves, out of curiosity, like, are yer goin' to buy that bleedin' blouse yer've been waving about for the last half-hour? Yer've had more wear out of it than the ruddy owner ever did!'

Fanny tittered. 'Yeah, I'll mug meself seein' as it's only tuppence.'

'Blimey! Pricing me goods for me now, are yer?' Mary Ann held her hand out and took the two pennies. She slipped them into her pocket as she asked in a casual voice, 'Did yer say it was for yerself, Fanny?'

Fanny preened. 'Yeah, it'll go nice with me navy skirt.'

Mary Ann eyed the mountainous bosom and sighed. 'I'll tell yer what, Fanny, I always think of meself as bein' an optimistic person, but I'm not in the meg specks compared to you. If you think yer'll get into that blouse then yer the most optimistic person I've ever met.'

Fanny got on her high horse. 'Of course I'll get into it! Anyone would think I was the size of a house to hear you talk.'

'Have yer got a magic wand at home, Fanny? 'Cos that's the only way yer'll get into it . . . that or with the help of a shoe-horn.'

Fanny held the pink blouse aloft. 'I bet yer I'll get into that with no trouble at all.'

Mary Ann let out a deep pretend sigh. 'Yer must have a very sharp bread-knife at home then.'

Fanny lowered the blouse, her brow creased in a frown. 'What the hell's a breadknife got to do with the ruddy thing?'

' 'Cos the only way that blouse will go near yer is if yer cut off those bleedin' big things that stick out in front of yer. I bet they enter a room two minutes before the rest of yer body.'

Fanny chuckled. 'Yer only jealous, Mary Ann, 'cos you haven't got no bust. Ye're as flat as a bleedin' pancake!'

'Oh, so that's why my feller's always tryin' to eat them.' Mary Ann hit her forehead with the heel of her hand. 'He thinks they're a couple of ruddy pancakes!'

Sadie appeared at her side. 'I've served about twenty customers and you're still with Fanny!'

'Then yer shouldn't be so bleedin' quick, should yer? Anyway, I'll see yer next week, Fanny. Me and my assistant are going to have a quiet five minutes to ourselves.' As her customer turned to walk away, Mary Ann called, 'If I don't recognise yer, Fanny, give me the eye eye. Or, better still, wear the flamin' blouse. 'Cos if I see yer in that I'll know damn well yer've done a hatchet job on yerself.'

Sadie was pulling Mary Ann towards the small box under the table. 'Wait till yer see what I've bought meself.' She brought the paper bag out and emptied the contents on top of the heap of clothes. 'I got all that for a tanner.'

'Yer done well, love.' There was sadness behind Mary Ann's smile. Fancy a girl of sixteen, a working girl, being so excited about a penny comb, a bar of cheap scented soap and a lipstick that would disappear a few minutes after she'd put it on her lips. 'When yer all dolled up in yer finery, there'll be no flies on you, they'll all be bluebottles!'

Sadie put the things back in the bag. 'I wanted to look nice on Monday. I told yer I was goin' on the ferry, didn't I?'

'Yes, yer mentioned it last week, girl.' It was Mary Ann's turn to rummage in the box. 'Don't forget this dress 'cos yer've just given me sixpence for it.' She held up the dress and was delighted when she heard Sadie's gasp of pleasure. In pale beige, the dress had a round neck, short sleeves, a fitted bodice and flared skirt. And setting it off was an inch-wide stiffened belt, slotted through a loop either side of the waist and fastened in the front by a gold-coloured buckle.

'Oh, it's beautiful.' Sadie shook her head, overcome with emotion. 'I don't know how to tell yer how grateful I am.'

'Then don't bother. Yer worked hard for the bleedin' thing, didn't yer? Anyway, it's good for me business to have someone serving who's dressed nice. And the way yer going on, girl, yer'll be needing another wardrobe.'

'Another wardrobe? I haven't got one, never mind another one.'

Mary Ann's eyes widened. 'Yer haven't got a wardrobe?'

'Yer can't turn around in the bedroom I sleep in, it's that small. Me two brothers and me two sisters sleep in a double bed and I sleep on one of those canvas camp beds. There's no room for anythin' else.'

'But yer mam must have a wardrobe in her room. Won't she let yer use that?'

Sadie hesitated. Why did she feel this shame, as though it was her fault their house was so bare? And why should she pretend to a woman who'd been so good to her? 'No, there's no wardrobe in me mam's room, either. Yer see, Mary Ann, she doesn't look after clothes the way most women do. Half the time the kids' things wear out without ever having been washed.'

Now she'd gone so far, Sadie wanted to get it all off her chest. This woman, who she didn't even know existed until five weeks ago, had been the only person who'd offered warmth and friendliness, and the only one she could open her heart to. 'Remember a couple of weeks ago, when I asked yer if I could have that paper bag? Well, that's me wardrobe. Everything I own is in that bag, and I keep it under me bed.'

Mary Ann grimaced as she rubbed her knuckles back and forth across her brow. Not for one second did she doubt the girl's words. But what a way for anyone to live. 'I've told yer what I'd do, girl. I'd start savin' me money and get away from there as fast as I could. They don't deserve a daughter like you.'

Sadie noticed a few people trying to attract their attention and she dropped her belongings into the box. 'Come on, Mary Ann, back to the grind. I'm not goin' out early tonight, so I can stay a bit later an' help yer pack up.'

'If I disappear for a few minutes, girl, don't send a search party out for me, will yer? I'm only goin' to see a mate who has a stall near the entrance. I'll be back before yer can say Jack Robinson.'

'Take as long as yer like, Mary Ann, I can manage on me own.'

The stall-holder was no sooner out of sight than a fresh lot of people crowded the stall to root through the piles of clothes. There was much pushing and shoving but it was good-natured and Sadie enjoyed the challenge of managing the stall on her own. Her face was beaming and her eyes shining when Mary Ann returned. 'I haven't half been busy, Mary Ann – I've taken over three shillings!'

'Good for you, girl. I'll have to leave yer more often, then I'll be able to retire a rich woman.' There was a black handbag swinging from Mary Ann's hand and she held it out to Sadie. 'This is a little birthday present for yer. It's not new, as yer can see, but it's not in bad nick. Yer can put yer bits and bobs in it – save yer carryin' a paper bag with yer everywhere yer go.'

The handbag was in black patent leather with a narrow handle and a gold clasp fastener. The handle was showing signs of wear and there were a few scratches on the surface of the patent leather, but Sadie was over the moon, thinking it would match her high-heeled shoes. 'Mary Ann, yer a lovely woman an' I'll never be able to pay yer back for all the nice things yer've done for me. Just think, I had nothing the first day I came here, now I've got enough clothes to go anywhere I want without feeling dowdy. I can hold me head up with the best of them, thanks to you.'

'Listen to me, girl – even if yer were dressed in a sack, yer'd still outshine everyone. Always remember that yer as good as anyone and a lot better than most.' Mary Ann leaned forward to kiss her cheek. 'Now, while yer putting yer bits into yer new bag, I'm goin' to skate around this lot to prove I can make three bob as easily as you have. If it got out that Mary Ann had been bested by a chit of a girl, I'd never hear the end of it. I'd be the talk of the bleedin' wash-house!'

Harry was waiting in the clearing when Sadie arrived. He'd made arrangements to meet her in the park to avoid being seen by nosy neighbours. 'You're looking very pleased with yerself!' He'd never seen her looking so happy, she was positively glowing. 'Have yer had a good day?'

'I've had a wonderful day, Harry.' Sadie swung the handbag back and forth in front of his face. 'This is me birthday present off Mary Ann. See how it matches me shoes?'

'Yeah, they go together a treat.' Harry smiled but his thoughts were dark. If he had George Wilson there right now he'd strangle him with his bare hands. Out to the pub every night without fail, while his beautiful daughter was left to rummage through second-hand stalls at the market to try and make the best of herself. 'You look lovely, Sadie.' He held out an open hand and she covered it with one of hers. 'And I'm glad yer had a nice day, yer deserve it.'

'I've got another dress, too. I won't let yer down on Monday, Harry, I'll look nice for yer.'

'I'm looking forward to it, Sadie, and I'll be proud of yer.' The thought that had been in Harry's mind for days had to be put into words or he'd have another sleepless night. 'How did the dance go?'

'I only learned the three steps to a waltz, and that was walking round the floor. But I'm goin' again next week, and every week after that, until I can dance proper, like some of the couples there last night. It was a pleasure to watch them.'

'Are yer going with the same bloke every week?'

'As long as he behaves himself. He's a bit of a fast worker an' I've got a feeling he'll go too far one of these days. If he does, then that will be his lot.'

Harry pulled her towards him and put an arm around her waist. 'Sadie, if yer think that, why go out with him?'

'Because he serves a purpose,' Sadie answered truthfully. 'I'd never have him as a proper boyfriend because he reminds me of me dad. And anyway, like I've told yer before, I don't intend settling down with any boy. I'm goin' to stay footloose and fancy free.'

'I don't like to hear yer talking like that, Sadie, 'cos it makes yer sound hard. All men are not bad, yer know.'

'I am hard, Harry, I admit it. And I know all men are not bad because of you. You're me friend and I trust yer.' She fixed her wide eyes on him and smiled. 'Now, I'll have me kiss and you can toddle off to see yer dancing partner. And we won't leave the park together – I'll go out of the far gate.'

Oh dear God, she knows I don't want to be seen with her! She thinks it's because I'd be ashamed, but I'd never be ashamed of Sadie, never! But how could he tell her the truth about his mother's threat without hurting her even more?

It was then the reality of Sadie's life hit him between the eyes like a blow. And he knew why she said she was hard. She'd had to be, because every time she opened her front door and stepped into the street she had to face the hostility of the neighbours – one of them his own mother. And now, in her eyes, he was treating her the same. Someone to kiss in a secluded corner of the park, but not good enough to be seen out with in public. If he was twenty-one and had finished his apprenticeship, he might be in a position to do something about it. But at eighteen he would have to remain a coward.

Chapter Eight

'Haven't yer brought a coat or a cardi with yer?' Harry asked, doubt on his face when he saw Sadie was only wearing the thin summer dress. 'There's always a chill wind blowin' on the Mersey, even when the sun's shining.'

'I'll be all right, honest.' Sadie was too excited to feel the cold. And anyway, she wasn't going to tell him she didn't possess a cardi or a decent coat. They were standing by the rails of the ferry as it filled up at the landing stage, and the sensation of it bobbing up and down in the water was something Sadie had never experienced and she gripped tight hold of the rail. When she saw Harry leaning over to watch the white surf, she pulled him back. 'Be careful, yer might fall in.'

He grinned up at her. 'Will yer jump in and save me if I do?'

'Some hope you've got. I can't swim!'

'Oh, dear.' Harry covered her hand gripping the rail. 'When yer've learned to dance, yer'll have to take swimming lessons. Everyone should be able to swim – yer never know when yer might need to.' He heard the gangplank being raised and told her, 'We're off.'

Sadie was fascinated as the boat moved away from the landing stage and slowly turned in the direction of New Brighton, cutting through the murky waters and leaving a trail of white foam in its wake. A sudden wave of spray came up over the rails to splash on Sadie's face and dress, the coldness of the water making her catch her breath. 'Oh, I'm drenched!'

Harry pulled her away from the rail before any more damage could be done. He handed her a pure white hankie, saying, 'Here, wipe yer face an' we'll sit down. I'll put me coat around yer.'

When Sadie sat on the long wooden seat that stretched the length of the boat, she burst out laughing. 'A fat lot of good me scented soap has done me – it's all washed off! And look at yer hankie – it's got lipstick all over it.' She doubled up with laughter. 'Yer'll have some explainin' to do to yer mam when she finds *that* in the wash.'

Harry refrained from saying his mother was well used to washing hankies with lipstick traces on. But her dislike of the Wilsons was so great, if she knew whose lipstick it was she was more likely to burn the hankie than wash it. He took his jacket off and was handing it to Sadie when he remembered something. 'Oh, hang on a minute.' He took a small packet from one of the pockets, then said, 'Slip yer arms in the sleeves an' yer'll soon warm up.'

Sadie did as she was told, then had a fit of the giggles. The coat swamped her and she had to pull the sleeves up to see her hands. 'Yer could get two of me in this!'

'I'm happy with just one of you, Sadie.' Harry handed the small packet to her. 'Happy birthday, Sadie Wilson.' He kissed her on the cheek, bringing a blush to her face. 'I hope yer like it. I'm not very good at knowin' what to buy a girl.'

There was a lump in Sadie's throat as she stared down at the present. Apart from Mary Ann's, it was the only one she'd got. She'd left the house this morning without her birthday being mentioned by word or deed. She didn't blame the children – they probably didn't know it was a big day for her. But it wouldn't have hurt her parents to give her a penny card and wish her a happy birthday. She should be used to their neglect by now, and she kept telling herself she didn't care, but it still hurt.

She'd bucked up a bit when she got to work and Brenda gave her a card, and then Alec had passed one over to her during the dinner-break. They were in her handbag. But she hadn't expected anything off Harry, not when he was taking her out.

'If you open it, Sadie, I promise it won't bite.'

'I feel terrible.' Her voice was low, her head bowed. 'I've done nothing but take off you since that day in the entry, when you were fool enough to stop and ask why I was crying.' She held the packet in the palm of her hand. 'I can't keep takin' when I've nothing to give back in return. So take this, please, Harry, and give it to the girl yer call yer dancing partner.'

'What! If I gave her a present she'd expect me to marry her!' Harry pulled a face. 'And that would be a fate worse than death.'

Sadie managed a smile. 'Yer givin' me a present and I don't expect yer to marry me.'

'Ah, well, that's different.' Harry was mentally apologising to Clare, the girl he went out with for the lies he was telling. 'You haven't got bandy legs and yer not cross-eyed.'

'Harry Young! You're terrible you are, talkin' about the girl like that! I bet she's as pretty as a picture.'

'Aye, a picture no artist could paint.' Harry winked to let her know he was joking. 'Now, open yer present and give me a kiss for it, 'cos if yer don't, I'll throw it over the side of the boat.'

'Only if yer tell me when your birthday is, so I can buy you a present. That's fair, isn't it?'

'My birthday's a couple of months off, but I'll let yer know nearer the time and yer can take me out for the night.'

'Yeah, okay.' Sadie was secretly pleased. A present was a rare thing for her and she would have been sad if Harry had taken it back. She didn't care if it was only a penny slab of Cadbury's, it was a gift bought with her in mind. But when she ripped the top of the packet and saw what was inside she let out a squeal of delight before kissing Harry smack on the mouth, even though she knew there were amused glances coming their way from the other passengers leaning over the rails. 'Californian Poppy! Oh, Harry, how did yer know this was the best thing in the whole world yer could have bought me?'

Sadie hummed softly as she unscrewed the top and turned the bottle upside down on her index finger. This was a day she would remember for a long time. She checked her finger and found it dry. 'There's none coming out.' Her eyes looked enquiringly at Harry. 'Look, there's none on me finger.'

'Sadie, yer've got to take that little rubber thing out first.' She reminded Harry of a little girl getting her first present off Father Christmas. She looked so happy with her pretty face shining with pleasure, he felt a rush of gratitude towards Clare for using that particular scent, otherwise he would never have heard of it.

Sadie had pulled the little rubber stopper out and was holding the bottle to her nose. 'I've never been in a garden with flowers in, but I bet it would smell just like this.' She dabbed some of the perfume behind her ears like she'd seen Joan Crawford doing. Not that the film star used anything as common as a bottle, she used a spray, but at least she'd shown Sadie where it should go. After holding the small bottle to her nose and breathing a sigh of appreciation, she replaced the stopper and the screw top before leaning sideways towards Harry and putting an ear to his nose. 'Do I smell nice, Harry?'

'Like a garden full of flowers and I'm sitting next to a rose bush in full bloom.'

Sadie was more than satisfied with his answer and she folded her arms across her waist and hugged herself. 'It's me best birthday ever.'

Harry, in all innocence, asked a question that took the smile off her face. 'What did yer get off yer parents?'

'Sweet nothing.'

'Nothing? Yer must have got something off them.'

'Nothing, Harry. Not a present, a card, a birthday greeting or even a smile. It wasn't even mentioned. In other words, what I got off me family was sweet Fanny Adams.'

Harry shook his head in disbelief. What sort of a family were they?

But he wisely kept his thoughts to himself. 'Never mind, they're not worth worrying about.' He reached for her hand. 'We are goin' to have the time of our lives at the fairground.'

But Harry didn't know that just by watching Sadie he really was going to have the time of his life. She had never been to a fairground before and her eyes were wide with wonder at everything she saw. The rifle range, the coconut shy and the stall where you threw darts at cards pinned up at the back of the tent. Harry explained what you had to do to win a prize and asked if she'd like a go on one of the stalls.

'Ooh, no! I'd make a fool of meself! You have a go for me, Harry, on the coconut shy.'

When he knocked one of the coconuts off its perch, Sadie shrieked with delight and clapped her hands. But he was unlucky with his next two throws and so didn't qualify for a prize. But the man on the stall was so taken with Sadie's obvious pleasure, he said, 'Have another go, an' if yer knock one off I'll give yer a prize.' When Harry hesitated he handed three balls over. 'Come 'ed, yer can't disappoint yer girlfriend!'

Much to Harry's relief, he managed to knock a coconut off on his third throw and Sadie walked away holding a tiny teddy bear with a bow of pink ribbon around his neck. 'That was good, Harry. I wouldn't have hit one in a month of Sundays.'

Harry's chest swelled with pride. 'Come on, let's have a look at the rides, see which yer'd like to go on.'

They stood for a while watching the Big Wheel turn and listening to the shrieks of the girls on the ride. 'D'yer fancy that?'

'No, thank you. I'd be terrified on that thing – look how high up those chairs are.'

Harry took her elbow. 'Let's try the Dodgems, then.'

They looked frightening to Sadie at first when she saw the cars whizzing around and bumping into each other. But she got used to it after a while and laughed as heartily as the occupants of the cars when there was a collision. 'Ooh look, Harry, there's four cars bumped into each other and they can't turn around.'

'They'll get out of it, the cars go by themselves.' Harry was eager to show how knowledgeable he was. He was showing off and he knew it, but he did so want to impress Sadie. 'Even if yer were the best driver in the world yer couldn't steer one of those cars, they go on their own.' The ride came to an end and the cars emptied. 'Shall we have a go?'

Sadie nodded, her eyes sparkling. 'You get behind the wheel, though.'

Harry had never had so much fun in his life as he did on that ride. The pretty girl hanging onto his arm like grim death screamed, shouted, closed her eyes when a bump was coming up, and roared with laughter when the car managed to avoid a collision.

'D'yer want to stay on for another go?' Harry asked when the ride came to an end.

Sadie shook her head, already out of the car and trying to walk on legs that felt like jelly. 'Once is enough, thanks, Harry.'

'How about the bobby horses? They should be tame enough for yer.'

Sadie linked his arm. 'Yer don't have to spend any more money on me, Harry. I'm happy just to watch all that's goin' on around me and listen to all the different noises. It's all new to me and I think it's dead exciting.'

Harry wasn't going to tell her he'd been saving up for the last few weeks for this very night. 'I'm all right for money, Sadie.' It was then his eyes lit on a stall selling candy-floss. He steered her towards it. 'I bet yer've never had any of this before.'

Her eyes wide with wonder, Sadie watched as the woman took a thin stick from a can and began to roll it around and around a rotating drum until it had a huge head on it of pink stuff that looked like cotton wool. The woman passed it over to Sadie before going through the process again for Harry.

'What am I supposed to do with this?' Sadie couldn't make it out. She'd never seen anything like it in her life. Then she saw Harry put the concoction to his mouth and take a bite. He grinned as he indicated she should do the same. Timidly, she took a bite. She could feel her teeth closing on the floss but when she went to chew it, her mouth was empty! She took another bite and the same thing happened. She looked at Harry who was chewing away happily and decided she wasn't eating it properly or there was something wrong with her candy-floss. 'Harry, I can't get anything. I take a bite an' there's nothing there.'

Harry could contain himself no longer and doubled up with laughter. 'Oh Sadie, the look on your face!'

'Never mind the look on my face. Yer've paid good money out and I'm not getting anything.'

'You're not supposed to. It's candy-floss, and as soon as yer put it in yer mouth it melts . . . disappears.'

'Well, you seemed to be making a meal out of yours.'

'I was only pretending, just pullin' yer leg.'

'Oh, were yer now.' There was mischief in Sadie's eyes as she put her hand on Harry's arm and pushed it up sharply, so the candy-floss squashed all over his face. 'That's what yer get for makin' a fool out of me.' She gazed at the floss on Harry's nose, cheeks and chin, and it was her turn to double up. 'Oh Harry, look at the state of you!'

Harry fished in his pocket for his hankie and wiped the thick of the sticky pink substance away. 'I'll get you for that, Sadie Wilson.'

'Oh no, you won't. Yer'll not catch me out again, Harry Young.' She saw traces of the sticky floss on the end of his nose and took the hankie from him to wipe it away. When she handed it back to him, she grinned cheekily. 'Your mam's going to think yer've got half-a-dozen girls on the go. Just look at the different shades of pink.'

The dimples in Harry's cheeks deepened when he smiled. 'It'll give her something to think about.'

'I was a bit naughty, though, wasn't I? I really shouldn't have done that to yer.'

'Sadie, I played a trick on yer and you played one back on me. That's only fair, isn't it? Besides, I've never had such a good laugh for a long time. I feel about fourteen again.' Harry's words were carried on in his head. She was a dream to take out. She showed her appreciation and happiness openly, and it rubbed off on anyone close to her. She was so natural – no affectation, no flirting through fluttering eyelashes, no frills or flounces. Her beauty was a joy to behold, and she wasn't even aware of it.

'Come on, let's have a look around before it's time to go.' He cupped her elbow. 'Will yer do me a favour? Yer owe me one for spoiling me handsome face.'

'Yeah, what is it?'

'Come on the ghost train with me.'

'What's the ghost train when it's out?'

'Well, it's like a train and it goes through a dark tunnel. And they have ghosts and all sorts of strange things popping up at yer.'

'Ooh, er! I don't think I'd like that.'

'Don't be such a baby! There'll be lots of other people on the train and yer can close yer eyes if yer don't want to see anything. Do it just to please me?'

So it was with trepidation Sadie sat on the bench seat of the ghost train. Her fear was heightened when the train chugged into action and a door in front of them mysteriously flew open and they found them-selves in complete darkness. She closed her eyes and felt for Harry's hand. 'I knew I wouldn't like it.'

Harry slipped an arm across her shoulder and pulled her towards him. 'Nothin' will happen to you when yer with me.'

Sadie opened her eyes to have a peep just as a white apparition appeared right in front of them. With a skeleton-like face, and making frightening noises, it seemed to be heading straight for the train. Sadie let out a piercing scream and buried her head on Harry's shoulder. She kept it there for the whole ride, missing the ghosts and the other weird things that kept popping up from nowhere. And also missing the smile of happiness on Harry's face as he held her tight.

They stood at the rails of the ferry on the homeward journey, Sadie with Harry's coat across her shoulders to protect her from the cold breeze. 'It's been lovely, Harry, I've never enjoyed meself so much. I've seen and done more in the last few hours than I have in me whole life.' Her laugh had a hollow ring to it. 'I've seen how other girls my age can enjoy themselves. Talk about seeing how the other half live isn't in it! I bet if their mothers gave them a shilling pocket money they'd throw it back at her.'

'Yer'll be getting a rise in yer next wage-packet, yer know.'

'Yeah, I know. The trouble is, me mam knows as well. I've asked her about puttin' me pocket money up but she just fobs me off, tells me to wait and see.'

'She's got to give yer a rise, Sadie. She must know yer can't go many places on a shillin' a week.'

'If I only had to spend the shillin' on pleasure, I'd be made up, but I've got to keep meself on it. I was going to say that half of it goes on me dinner money, but you've been paying for that since that fateful day in yer life. But I've to see to me own clothes and everything. I've tried explaining' to me mam, but I could talk till I'm blue in the face an' it won't make a blind bit of difference.'

'Open yer wage-packet before yer give it to her and take yer money out. I know I shouldn't be tellin' yer to go against yer mam but she's really not a good mother, is she?'

'I don't think there's a worse mother and father in the whole world. And I've thought about what yer've just said, about opening me wage-packet and taking the money out, but if I did that me life wouldn't be worth living. It's not worth living now, not in that house, anyway, but knowing them as I do, it could be ten times worse.'

Harry sighed. 'I don't know what you can do, then.'

'If she turns me down next week I'll just have to hang on until our Dot leaves school in a few weeks. When she starts bringing a wage in, me mam won't be able to plead poverty any more. She'll have no excuse.'

'I can give yer an extra sixpence a week until then,' Harry said. 'That would help yer out a bit.'

'Thanks, Harry, but I scrounge enough off yer as it is. No, I've put up with things the way they are for two years now, I can manage another few weeks until our Dot starts work. With a bit of luck, with her money coming in the kids might even get a few decent clothes.'

'If yer ever in trouble, Sadie, just shout out. I've told yer, I'll always help yer out.'

Sadie could feel the boat slowing down and turned her head to see they were nearing the Pier Head. She handed Harry his coat with a smile on her face. 'The end of a perfect day, and thanks to you it really has been a perfect day. You're a good man, Harry, and a good friend. It's nice to have someone to tell me troubles to and I've no one else except Mary Ann. And I don't tell her as much as I tell you. I just hope I haven't spoiled the day for yer by bending yer ear with all me moans and groans.'

Harry took her elbow as they joined the other passengers in making their way to the gangplank. 'I could stay on the boat and do it all over again; it's been great. But there'll be other days, won't there Sadie?'

'There'll definitely be one more day, and that's on your birthday. It's a couple of months off, or so yer said, and by that time I'll be in the money. It'll be my treat to pay back a little of the kindness yer've shown to me.'

As they neared the gangplank there was such a crush of people trying to get off to dash for trams, the two were separated and didn't meet up again until they were off the boat. Harry was anxiously scanning the crowd and when he spotted her he waved to attract her attention. 'I thought I'd lost yer.'

'You should be that lucky, Harry.' Sadie opened her handbag and took out the tiny teddy bear. 'Thank you for this, I'll never part with it 'cos it'll always remind me of me first trip on a ferry boat, me first visit to a fairground, and the candy floss, the Dodgems and the ghost train. Thank you for all those things, Harry.' She kissed the teddy before putting it back in her bag. 'Now, I think we'd better go our separate ways in case anyone sees us together. There's so many nosy parkers around our way an' I don't want yer gettin' into trouble with yer mam.'

'But we can get on the tram together,' Harry protested. He didn't want the day to end, not like this. He knew in his heart she was right, but why should it be so? You'd have to go a long way to meet a nicer girl than Sadie and he wished his mam wasn't so stubborn. If she'd only give herself the chance to get to know the girl, she'd find out how wrong she was about her. But no, the Wilson family were a bad lot in her eyes and that was the end of it. 'I don't like the idea of you being on yer own, not at this time of night.'

'It's not worth takin' a chance, Harry. You go on ahead and get the first tram and I'll wait for the next. And don't worry about me, I'll be all right.'

'No, I won't do it! We'll get on the tram together and it's just too bad if anyone sees us. If it makes yer feel better we can sit on different seats and I'll get off the stop before. But I'm not leaving yer on yer own down here, Sadie, 'cos there's always drunks hanging around and anythin' could happen to yer. So come on and don't argue.'

'Have it your way, then, but don't say I didn't warn yer.' Sadie held out her hand. 'In case I don't get another chance, I want to thank yer again for me birthday present and a lovely night out.'

Harry looked down at the proffered hand. 'To hell with that, Sadie, I want a good-night kiss. And a promise that yer'll see me in the park on Wednesday night for me usual "two for the price of one".'

Sadie smiled before puckering her lips. 'Yer can have both.'

Sadie tiptoed up the yard so her high heels wouldn't make a sound on the concrete. She was expecting her parents to be in bed and although she was surprised to see a dull glow from the gas-light she just presumed they'd left the light on for her. Carefully she lifted the latch on the kitchen door and stepped inside. She was closing the door behind her when she heard voices and her heart sank. As she'd come in the back way her father had been let in the front door and it was his voice she heard first.

'Where's yer mam?'

It was Dot who answered. 'She's in bed, Dad, so I waited up for yer.'

Sadie was rooted to the spot. With a bit of luck they'd go straight up to bed and she wouldn't have to face them. If they did come out to go down the yard to the lavvy, she'd pretend she'd just come in. Through the narrow gap on the hinged side of the door she saw her father fall heavily into his chair, obviously the worse for drink.

'Dad,' Dot was standing in front of him, 'did yer think about what I asked yer? You know, what I want to do when I leave school?'

George's lips curled into a drunken smile. 'It depends how nice yer are to yer dad, how well yer look after him.'

'I am nice to yer, Dad, an' I do look after yer, don't I? I'll be nice to yer now if yer like, 'cos I know how to make yer happy, don't I, Dad?'

Sadie saw her father nod and noticed the saliva running down the side of his mouth. He's a disgusting, evil man, she was thinking as she saw Dot fall to her knees between her father's legs. And she's no better! She's after something and wants to get it out of him while he's drunk. But when she saw the young girl begin to unfasten the buttons on the fly of her father's trousers, Sadie had to clamp a hand over her mouth to stop the cry of disgust and anger that came to her lips. How in the name of God could a father behave like this with his fourteen-year-old daughter?

Sadie was watching her father's face when he closed his eyes and said in a strangled voice, 'Oh, that's good, that is, girl.'

She moved her eyes to where Dot had undone the trouser buttons, pulled up the front of his shirt and had slipped her hand inside. A wave of nausea swept over Sadie and she knew she had to get out of the house. She opened the door, fled down the yard and into the entry where she bent over and was violently sick.

With her tummy raw with retching, Sadie leaned against the entry wall and tried to think straight. The scene she'd just witnessed flashed before her eyes and she began to sob. No decent loving father would let a fourteen-year-old do what she'd seen Dot doing. But then, he'd never been loving, or decent. And she couldn't feel any pity for her sister because, as she'd known for a long time, Dot was a crafty little bitch. She was the one who'd initiated what was happening inside that dirty little room. Sadie shook her head . . . a dirty room and dirty people.

And what about her mother? Lily had to take some of the blame because Sadie had warned her often enough about what she thought was happening. But never in a million years did she think things had reached the stage they were at now. Did her mother know? She must have some idea but was probably too afraid to do anything about it. Either that or she just didn't care. Perhaps it was a case of anything that kept her husband happy was all right with her.

Sadie sighed. Surely it was against the law for a father to do this to one of his children. But who could she ask for advice? She'd be too ashamed to tell the only two people she trusted, Harry and Mary Ann.

Thinking of Mary Ann made Sadie make up her mind. The best thing she could do was get away from this house as soon as she could and start a life of her own. She'd do it now, tonight, if she could. The thought of having to face her father and sister after what she'd seen brought forth another wave of nausea.

I've got to get away from them, she thought desperately. I know it will take money, but so help me, I'll get that money from somewhere.

Chapter Nine

Sadie's eyes widened in surprise when Brenda took her overall off at the dinner-break. 'My God! You're coming out, aren't yer?'

Brenda smirked as she looked down at the pink jumper she was wearing. It had a low round neck, short sleeves and was tight enough to show her bust off to advantage. 'I got it in Blacker's on Saturday. Three and eleven it cost, but I think it was worth it 'cos it suits me.'

'It does, it looks the gear on yer.' Sadie cast an admiring glance. 'It doesn't half show yer figure off. Yer'll be gettin' loads of wolf whistles when the lads see yer in that.'

This was precisely what Brenda wanted – particularly from a certain lad by the name of Alec. He was smitten with Sadie but she intended to make sure he began to take notice of her. 'Me mam said I can go out with a boy now I'm sixteen, as long as I bring him home first so she can see him to make sure he's the right sort.'

'I don't know how she thinks she can tell if he's the right sort by just lookin' at him.' Sadie said as they linked arms. 'I'm surprised she let yer buy a jumper like that, showing off everything yer've got.'

'Oh, she likes it,' Brenda said, when in fact her mother had nearly hit the roof when she'd seen it. It was only when Brenda swore that she wore her overall all day in work, so no one would see it, that she was allowed to wear it. But she wasn't going to tell her friend that. 'She said the colour suits me.'

But if Brenda thought she was going to attract Alec Gleeson's attention she was to be bitterly disappointed. He was standing in his usual spot, next to Bobby Bennett, leaning against the factory wall. And he only had eyes for the blonde girl by her side. 'All right, Sadie?'

'Oh, can I speak with yer for a minute, Alec?' Sadie gave Brenda a gentle push. 'You go on, Bren, I won't be a minute.'

Alec moved away from the wall and the ears of Bobby. 'What's up?'

'I can't go out with yer tomorrow tonight – I'm sorry.'

'But why not?'

'I feel mean lettin' yer down, Alec, but I saw something I liked in a shop window and the woman put it away for me. I said I'd pick it up on Saturday afternoon when I got me wages, but it costs more than I get in pocket money.' Sadie couldn't look him straight in the face as she lied.

But she'd made a vow on Monday night that she'd get money by hook or by crook and she wasn't going to weaken. 'Me mam won't lend me any money – she says I get enough – so I won't even have the tram fare.'

'Is that all that's stopping yer?' Relief could be seen on Alec's handsome face. 'Blimey, I thought something terrible had happened.'

'No, of course not. It's just that I won't be able to come out with yer. I was looking forward to goin' to the dance as well. But I couldn't resist the underskirt I saw in the shop window. It's beautiful – all pink and lacy.'

Alec grinned. 'I'll give yer the tuppence tram fare.'

As Sadie shook her head, she asked herself how much lying she was going to have to do before she could get away from the house of horror in which she lived. 'No, I couldn't take money off yer.'

'Don't be daft! If I was pickin' yer up from home I'd have to pay yer fare, so what difference does it make?' Alec was thinking of the pink lace underskirt: he intended to catch more than a glimpse of it. 'I want yer to come, Sadie, please?'

She pretended to consider the offer. 'Oh, all right, as long as yer don't think I'm cheap takin' money off yer.'

'Of course I don't!' Alec slipped a hand into the pocket of his navy-blue overalls. 'Here, I've got tuppence on me. Take it now in case I don't see yer in the morning.'

Sadie took the two coins. 'I could pay yer back next week.'

'I wouldn't take it off yer, Sadie, so forget it. Just be on time tomorrow night, eh?'

'I'll be there.' Sadie ran off to catch up with her friend. She hated herself for what she'd done, but part of her was pleased that she'd been able to carry it off. The two coins in her pocket were the start of her bid for freedom. And she knew in her heart that Alec would get his tuppence back in kisses and unwanted caresses.

Sadie sighed as she caught up with Brenda near the chip shop. She was selling herself, whichever way you looked at it, which is what a prostitute did. But a prostitute sold more than kisses and fondling; she sold her body. And Sadie was determined she would never do that.

'Hello, girl!' Mary Ann waved as Sadie approached. 'What with the sun shining and bringin' out the customers, and your smile, what more could a woman ask for?'

'I'll give yer a hand, shall I?' Sadie hid her handbag in the box under the counter. There was a smile on her face, but not in her heart. She'd had a blazing row at home before she'd left because her mam wouldn't

90

give her any extra pocket money. Her wage packet had contained ninepence more than usual because of her rise, but her mother refused point blank to give her a penny more than the usual shilling. She wouldn't even promise an increase when their Dot started work, which angered Sadie even more.

'Here yer are, girl, how much is this?'

Sadie walked across to the old lady called Sarah – the one she'd told Mary Ann she felt like kissing and cuddling. And Sadie was more in need of a cuddle now than she'd ever been. But seeing as how the possibility of her getting one was remote, she decided the next best thing was to give someone else a cuddle. And Sarah was perfect for it. The old lady was surprised when Sadie leaned across the stack of clothes, cupped her wrinkled face in her hands and kissed her on either cheek. Then a smile appeared. 'I don't know what that was for, girl, but it's a long time since anybody kissed me and I enjoyed it.'

'Not as much as I did.' Sadie took the vest old Sarah was holding and gave it a quick glance. It was in good condition and Mary Ann's rule of thumb – tuppence with a hole, thruppence without a hole – came into her mind, but she quickly brushed it aside. 'Is tuppence all right by you, Sarah?'

She was rewarded with a big smile and a wink as Sarah opened her clenched fist to reveal the two pennies nestling in the palm. 'How about that, eh, girl? Yer must be a mind-reader.'

'I'll get a smacked backside off Mary Ann,' Sadie told her. 'But I don't mind that. It's a kick in the teeth I object to.'

Sadie carried the coppers across to Mary Ann. 'I've got a confession to make. I sold old Sarah a vest for tuppence and it had no hole in.'

The stall-holder looked stern. 'That's me bleedin' Sunday roast dinner yer've given away. I don't know, I'll never be a rich woman the rate yer goin' on. Another couple like Sarah and yer'll have me in the workhouse in Belmont Road.'

'Oh, stop yer moanin', Hard-Hearted Hannah, I'll put the penny in meself.'

Mary Ann grinned. 'When yer've been coming a bit longer, girl, yer'll be up to all their tricks. For instance, old Sarah never pays more than tuppence for anything – it's all the money she brings out with her! But I don't mind with Sarah – there's only her and her old man and they're as poor as church mice. But some of the others that come with hard luck stories are in the pub every night knockin' the ale back, and the money's better in my pocket than theirs.'

'Just like my father.' Even saying the word 'father' stuck in Sadie's throat. 'He's in the pub every night without fail.'

Mary Ann saw one of her regulars. 'Hi, there, Nellie, what can I do yer for today?'

'I'm after a nightdress for our Mary's girl, Ruby. The one she's wearin' is falling off her back.'

'How old is she now – about six, isn't she?' Mary Ann walked to one of the side tables. 'I'm sure I've seen a couple in this lot so come and have a root.'

Nellie pushed her way through the crowd. 'Our Mary's feller's out of work and they're living from hand to mouth, so muggins here promised the kid I'd get her one.'

'Well, have a root through that lot while I serve Moaning Minnie over there.'

'Eh, Buggerlugs, I heard that.' A tall woman with a huge bust and round red face shook a fist. 'I've a good mind to come over there and land yer a fourpenny one.'

'Wouldn't do yer no good to come over here, Elsie, 'cos although yer might be bigger than me I can run faster.'

'Are you hinsinuatin' that I'm fat, Mary Ann? 'Cos if yer are I'll break yer bleedin' neck for yer.'

'Now as if I'd say that.' Mary Ann looked suitably surprised. 'Pleasantly plump, perhaps, or of ample proportions, but fat? Never!'

Elsie mulled it over for a while. 'Pleasantly plump' sounded quite nice, even attractive. And 'ample proportions' didn't sound too bad either. In fact, if yer looked at it the right way, the stall-holder was paying her a compliment. So her face creased in a smile, sending the chubby cheeks upwards to cover her eyes. 'I'll let yer off this time, Mary Ann, but only if yer've got a nice blouse for me. My feller's takin' me to the pictures tonight an' I want to look me best.'

Mary Ann spread her arms wide. 'If yer can't find anythin' to suit yer in this lot, Elsie, then all I can say is, yer bleedin' hard to please. But I'll give yer the services of me assistant to help yer, an' I can't be fairer than that, now can I?'

'I'll be glad to help,' Sadie said, ''cos I can look for something for meself at the same time.'

Mary Ann eyed her fondly. 'What are yer after now, girl?'

'Something I don't think I'll find, but there's no harm in trying.'

'If yer tell me I might be able to help.'

Sadie leaned closer and whispered, 'Don't laugh, but I'm after a pink underskirt with lace on it.'

'Don't bother lookin' on the stalls, just have a peep in the box under the table.' Mary Ann smiled as she patted her cheek. 'It could be your lucky day.'

Sadie went to work with a vengeance, eager to get Elsie fixed up with a blouse so she could get to that magical box under the table. She knew Alec would ask if she had her new underskirt on – that sort of thing would be right up his street – and she wanted to be able to lift her skirt a little to show him. After a lot of delving, she came up with three blouses for Elsie to choose from.

'The three of them are nice, Elsie, and all of them would suit yer. But this one,' she held up a pale blue silk blouse with pearl buttons down the front and ragamuffin sleeves, 'is dearer than the others because it's pure silk.' It wouldn't have been Sadie's choice but the woman looked as though she liked showy clothes.

Elsie eyed it with suspicion. 'Are yer sure it's pure silk?'

'Of course I'm sure! Feel it for yerself.'

Elsie fingered the material and looked as though she knew what she was doing, when in actual fact she'd never felt pure silk before. But she wasn't about to say so. 'Yeah, it's pure silk all right. How much is it?'

'It's sixpence that one, but if it's too much the other two are quite nice and they're only thruppence each.'

Elsie dithered. There was pride involved here, loss of face if she said she couldn't afford it. And think how she could show off with a pure silk blouse! She didn't have to tell her neighbours that she got it from the market; as far as they were concerned, she got it from George Henry Lees. 'I'll have the pure silk, I've taken a fancy to it.'

Mary Ann took a fit of laughter when Sadie passed the sixpence over. 'Yer never got that out of Elsie? Well, wonders will never cease! The miserable cow always haggles over the price with me.'

'Ah, but you never sold her a pure silk blouse, did yer?'

Mary Ann's laughter grew. 'No, girl, an' neither did you!'

Sadie's mouth gaped. 'Yer mean it wasn't pure silk?'

'Was it heckerslike! But don't let it worry yer, girl, it was her own bleedin' fault for lettin' yer talk her into it.' The stall-holder was shaking with laughter as she walked away to serve a customer. 'Made my bleedin' day, that has.'

Sadie made straight for the box under the table. She was in such a hurry she missed the glimpse of pale pink and disappointment was beginning to set in. It was during her second search she found it – just what she'd hoped for. Pale pink with white lace around the hem. It was creased and obviusly not new, but no one was going to get that close an inspection. She carried it over to Mary Ann. 'Yer must be me guardian angel 'cos yer've always got exactly what I want.'

'Some angel I am, girl, with the mouth on me! Anyway, that came in yesterday with a stack of other stuff an' I thought of yer right away. It's got no holes in but I'll let yer have it for tuppence, seeing as how yer pulled a fast one on Elsie.'

'Oh, I didn't do it on purpose. I honestly thought it was pure silk.'

'It's to be hoped her neighbours are as ignorant as you, love, otherwise she'll be down next week with a rollin' pin.'

Sadie grinned. 'I'll stand behind you and say you were the one what told me the price.'

'Yer won't stand behind me, girl, 'cos if I see her comin' I'll be leggin' it down Scottie Road as if the devil himself was on me heels. I only argue with people smaller than meself, not someone who's built like bleedin' Man Mountain.'

'I couldn't imagine you being frightened of anyone.'

'There's a few I wouldn't tangle with, sunshine, and Elsie is one of them. I've seen her fell a man with one blow, just because he picked up something on the stall she had her eye on and he wouldn't part with it.'

'Did she get it in the end?'

Mary Ann shook her head. 'No, she couldn't part him from it. What she did part him from, though, was one of his front teeth.'

Sadie jerked her head. 'Yer pulling me leg.'

'If I never move from here, girl, that is the gospel truth. Right in front of me stall it was, an' I thought to meself, Aye aye, Mary Ann, watch out for her in future. Never try an' sell her anything for thruppence that's got a hole in.'

'You're a case, you are,' Sadie said. 'I never know when yer having me on.'

Mary Ann waved to a woman who was calling her over. 'Hang on a minute, Gertie, there's a good girl. That dress yer holdin' has been in circulation a long time, it's not goin' to fall to pieces in five minutes.' She smiled at Sadie. 'How did yer birthday go? Did yer have a good time?'

'Oh Mary Ann, it was wonderful! I saw more in a couple of hours than I've seen in me whole life.' Sadie talked quickly, conscious of the waiting customer. Her eyes shining, she told of her first trip on the ferry boat, the wonders of the fairground, Harry's success on the coconut shy and the episode of the candy floss. 'He's awful nice, Mary Ann, and I don't think we stopped laughing all night. And, on top of all that, he bought me a bottle of Californian Poppy.'

'Ooh,er! Aren't we swanking! Is he serious about yer?'

'No, we're just friends. If his mam knew he was seeing me she'd lay a duck egg. Like everyone else in the street, she hates the Wilson family, me included.'

'Then she hasn't got the sense she was born with. She doesn't know a good thing when she sees one.' Mary Ann patted her arm. 'Don't you take no notice of them, sushine, you'll come off best in the end, you mark my words. Now, I'd better see to Gertie before she has a heart attack. She's nearly blue in the face now with shoutin' at me.'

'I'll stay and give yer a hand for a while,' Sadie said, thinking the less time she spent in the house the better. She hadn't spoken a word to her father or Dot since Monday night; the very sight of them made her feel sick. If it wasn't for her two young brothers and Ellen she wouldn't have opened her mouth at all because her mother didn't even give her the time of day, and the baby was usually in bed by the time she got home from work. 'I'm goin' dancing tonight so I don't have to leave the house till seven.'

'Yer certainly livin' it up these days, what with yer fairgrounds and dancing,' Mary Ann called over her shoulder. Then, as she advanced towards an irate Gertie she muttered under her breath, 'The best dance you could do, would be to dance away from that bleedin' family of yours.'

When it was time to leave, Sadie said, 'I'm not buying anything else today. I'm starting to do what yer told me to do – put a few coppers away each week. With a bit of luck I can put me whole shilling pocket money away this week. I won't be able to do that every time, but no matter how little I save, as you said, it'll all mount up.'

'Yer didn't get any extra, then, out of yer rise?'

'Me mam wouldn't hear of it. But when our Dot starts work, if she still won't give me any, I'll open me wage-packet before I give it to her and take it out meself. I'm not goin' out to work all week so me dad can sit in the pub every night.'

'Good for you, girl. Put yer foot down with a firm bleedin' hand. He's livin' the life of Riley while you're scroungin' through second-hand clothes – well, I'm buggered if *I'd* put up with it.'

'I won't put up with it much longer, Mary Ann, only till our Dot starts work, and that should be in two weeks' time 'cos she leaves school next week.'

'Well, you poppy off now while I serve the few stragglers. Enjoy yerself at the dance an' I'll see yer next week. Ta-ra, girl.' Mary Ann watched until the blonde head had disappeared in the crowd. Then she cursed Sadie's mother and father for not knowing how lucky they were to have a daughter like her.

Alec was waiting outside the dance hall and his first words were, 'Have yer got yer new underskirt on?'

Sadie nodded, lifting her skirt just enough for him to catch a glimpse of lace. She hadn't been able to iron it and it was still very creased, but no one was going to get the chance of seeing that high up. 'I'm over the moon with it.'

Alec took her arm and led her into the hall. 'I'll twirl yer around so everyone will be able to have a dekko.'

'You just dare! It takes me all me time to walk around, never mind doin' anything fancy. So if yer try to make a fool of me I'll walk off the floor and you'll be the one to look a fool, dancin' on yer own.'

'I like a girl with spirit,' Alec said, paying the entrance fee over and pocketing the tickets for tea and biscuits in the interval. 'I like them to put up a bit of a struggle.'

'I should warn yer then that I can put up more than a bit of a struggle, I'm very handy with me feet.'

Alec grinned. 'It's not yer feet I'm after.'

'No, but it's me feet yer'll get if yer try any funny business.' He's another George Wilson, this one, Sadie thought. He'll end up like me dad, a dirty old man. 'I've got a mind of me own, yer know, Alec. If I don't want anything to happen then it won't happen.'

'Don't worry, I'll be nice to yer.' Alec groaned inwardly when he saw the girl he'd taken down the entry last week when Sadie had left early. She'd been very free with her favours, practically throwing herself at him. But it was a stupid thing to have done when he knew she'd probably be here tonight. If she came over and said anything in front of Sadie he'd definitely get his marching orders. She was waving frantically now but he pretended not to see her. And when he heard the strains of a waltz he sighed with relief. If he ignored her she'd soon get the message. 'Shall we dance, Sadie?'

'Yeah, I can't wait. I've been practising in work with Brenda when we've had a slack five minutes and I think I've improved. Only a bit, mind you, but at least I won't be treading on yer toes all night.'

Sadie wasn't as tense as she'd been the week before and she found it much easier to dance to the tempo with her body relaxed. And when they reached the corner of the dance floor and Alec did a little spin, she was delighted when she didn't trip over his feet. 'Ooh, I'm getting good, aren't I?'

'Yeah, yer'll make a good little dancer 'cos yer've got the rhythm.' And she's got the body to go with it, Alec thought, holding her tightly round the waist. If only she was as free with her favours as the girl last week, he'd be quids in. 'We'll have a go at the next quickstep, see how yer get on with that. It's a bit harder but yer've got to learn sometime.'

'Ooh, er.' Sadie looked doubtful. 'I think I should stick to the waltz for now.'

But when they announced an Excuse Me quickstep, he coaxed, 'Come on, have a go. If yer can't manage it we'll sit down. But at least try.'

Sadie was apprehensive but she didn't want to spoil his night for him so she agreed. For the first few minutes her heart was in her mouth, but then she suddenly found her feet were keeping up with Alec's and she really began to enjoy herself. After all, she wasn't the only beginner there, she could see a few who weren't even getting on as well as she was.

Then a man tapped Alec on the shoulder and said, 'Excuse me.' Sadie saw the dark look on Alec's face before he released his hold and then she found herself in the arms of a strange young man. She looked up into his eyes and told him, 'I'm sorry, but I'm only a learner. I can't dance properly.'

'I know, I saw yer here last week. But I was a learner a few months ago – we've all got to start somewhere.' He looked a bit older than Alec, probably about nineteen. Tall, well-built, thick auburn hair, dark eyebrows and lashes and deep brown eyes. 'My name's Geoff, what's yours?'

Sadie hesitated, but only for a second. What harm would it do if that was all he knew about her? 'I'm Sadie.' She could see Alec standing on the edge of the dance floor and he didn't look a bit happy. Do him good to sweat for a change, Sadie decided. He thinks he's God's gift to women. 'I didn't see you here last week.'

'I saw you, though.' When Geoff smiled he showed strong white teeth. 'Yer didn't get up for the Excuse Me quickstep, otherwise I'd have introduced meself then.'

Alec appeared at the side of them and tapped Geoff on the shoulder. 'Excuse me.' Geoff shrugged his shoulders as he made a face at Sadie. 'Sorry.'

'What was he talkin' about?' Alec was none too pleased. 'Yer'd better watch it with him, he's a fast worker.'

Sadie raised her brows. 'Oh? Listen who's talking. He'd have to go some to be faster than you, Alec Gleeson.'

'What was he saying to yer? Was he tryin' to make a date?'

'Holy sufferin' ducks, Alec, I was only with him for two minutes! It seems to me that your mind works a damn sight faster than his tongue, and it's all goin' in the one direction. Everyone's not a ladykiller like you; they don't just have one thing on their mind all the time.'

'That's what you think! With your looks a feller can't help wanting to hold yer in his arms and smother yer to death. Unless he's not normal, that is.'

'Is that all you're after, Alec, to smother me to death?'

'You know what I mean, yer not that innocent.' The music came to an end and Alec led her from the floor with his arm around her waist, as though to say *she's mine so lay off*.

It was after the interval during another Excuse Me quickstep, that Alec felt a tap on his shoulder and there stood Geoff. 'D'yer mind if I cut in?'

'Yes, I do mind.' Alec clung onto Sadie's hand like grim death. 'Go and find another girl and leave mine alone.'

'If you don't want to be excused then yer should sit this dance out. As it is, I'm cutting in.' Geoff stood his ground and his face was set. He took hold of the hand Sadie had on Alec's shoulder and pulled her towards him. 'You can have her for all the other dances, but not the Excuse Me.' With that he moved away, taking Sadie with him and leaving Alec red in the face and fuming.

'Oh dear.' Sadie didn't know whether to laugh or cry. But somewhere deep inside her she felt pleased with having two men fight over her. It showed she could always get somebody else if Alec began to make a nuisance of himself. 'There's a certain person not very happy with you – he's giving yer daggers.'

'I won't let that worry me.' Geoff smiled down into her face. 'The only thing is, he'll be takin' yer off me in a minute so I'll have to be quick. Is he yer boyfriend?'

'No.' Sadie shook her head. 'Not really. I know him from work, but this is only the third time I've been out with him.'

'Would yer come out with me one night? We could go to the pictures if yer like.'

'But I don't know you. I don't know anything about you.'

'You would do if yer came out with me. Please say yes because I think yer friend is about to cut in.'

Sadie saw Alec begin to pick his way through the dancing couples. Geoff seemed a nice-enough bloke, she thought, so why not? It would be another night she didn't have to walk the streets aimlessly rather than be in the house sitting in filth and listening to coarse, vulgar language. 'Okay, how about Tuesday?'

'Where?'

'Outside the pub at Everton Valley – say, half-seven?'

There was no time to say more because Alec was claiming her back. 'If he does that again I'll thump him one,' he glowered.

'Oh, don't be so childish, Alec. It's only a dance, for heaven's sake.'

'He knows yer with me, so why doesn't he find himself a girl instead of pinching mine?'

Her confidence boosted, Sadie said, 'Perhaps he can't find another one he fancies. I feel quite flattered, actually.'

Alec looked sullen. 'I hope yer not leavin' early again. It's not goin' to be worth me while bringin' yer, if yer goin' to dance half the night with another feller and then dash off early.'

'I can't be too late home, Alec, and I've got a long way to go.' Sadie felt a pang of guilt. After all, she wouldn't be here if he hadn't paid for her. Because of him she was able to put all her pocket money away this week. 'You could leave early and walk me halfway home – I'd like that.'

That sounded like a promise to Alec and he cheered up. 'Yeah, okay, we'll leave after the next waltz.'

But Alec wasn't reckoning on Doris, the girl whose favours he'd enjoyed the week before. She'd waited all night for him to acknowledge her but no, he'd looked through her as though she wasn't there. Doris was known in the area as a girl who let any boy have his way with her. Half the lads in the neighbourhood had been down the entry with Doris, and quite a few of the married men. But with her reputation she couldn't get a steady boyfriend. She had a temper, too, and it was reaching boiling point when she decided she wasn't going to be ignored by Alec. He might have got away with it if the blonde he was with didn't look like a film star. But if Doris was good enough for him last week, he wasn't going to get away with ignoring her this week.

'Hello, Alec.' Doris got a lot of satisfaction in seeing the surprise and fear on his face when he turned around and saw her standing behind him with an insolent grin on her face and a hand on her hip. 'I've been waiting for the dance yer promised me last week, remember?'

Alec could have willingly strangled her. But if he insulted her now she'd let the cat out of the bag and he'd be done for. 'Hello, Doris. I didn't know yer were here. Where've yer been hiding yerself?'

'Yer must be bloody blind, Alec, 'cos I've been wavin' to yer all night.' Doris asked herself if she should make him squirm a bit more and decided it was what he deserved. 'I think you've got cats' eyes – yer see better in dark places.'

Alec got the message and the fright of his life. 'I'll finish this dance off with yer, Doris.' He turned to Sadie. 'Yer don't mind, do yer?'

'Not at all, I'm quite happy to sit and watch.' Sadie was having a problem keeping her face straight. The girl looked tough and as common as muck. If Alec had tangled with her then he'd chosen the wrong one to go down an entry with. You could tell by her face she had something on him and was now making him dance to her tune. Serves him right, Sadie thought as she watched them take to the dance floor. He's probably had his fun with her and now he's paying the price.

'Can I have this dance?'

Sadie looked at Geoff's outstretched hand. Why not? If someone better came along, Alec wouldn't think twice about dropping her, so why should she consider him? She smiled and stood up. 'Yer a sucker for punishment, Geoff, 'cos I'll be standin' all over yer toes.'

He grinned as he took her in his arms. 'Looking at your face will ease the pain.'

Sadie was pleased with the compliment because he didn't look the type to flatter a girl because he wanted something from her. She could see Alec glaring at her and she gave him a wave. 'The boy I'm with has met an old friend and is having this dance with her.'

'Oh, aye.' Geoff kept his thoughts to himself. He'd noticed Alec come back in the dance hall last week, minus Sadie. And he'd seen him make a bee-line for Doris, the girl no decent man would touch with a barge-pole. And he'd been behind the pair of them when they turned into the entry at the top of the street. But he didn't know Sadie well enough to warn her that the boy she was with had a reputation almost as bad as Doris. If he said anything she'd think he was telling tales for his own ends. 'It's still on for Tuesday, isn't it? Half-seven at Everton Valley.'

Sadie nodded. 'If I say a thing, I mean it. I will definitely be there.'

'I'll look forward to it.' Geoff spun her around. 'You can think about where yer'd like to go. Where d'yer live, by the way?'

Sadie gave a start. 'I never tell any boy where I live 'cos me parents are very strict. They think I'm out with a girlfriend. But it's somewhere in Toxteth.'

'I live in Wavertree, not that far away.' Geoff looked disappointed when the dance came to an end. 'I'll see yer Tuesday, then.'

'Yeah, okay.' Sadie went back to the chairs they'd been sitting on but there was no sign of Alec. She looked around the room and saw him in a corner talking to Doris, and he seemed to be in a right temper. I'm not waiting for him, Sadie thought, otherwise it'll be midnight before I get home. She skirted the dance floor and came up behind him. Tapping him on the shoulder she said, 'I'll go on, Alec. I can see yer busy.'

'I'm coming now.' He took her arm. 'I'll see yer next week, Doris.'

But Doris wasn't going to let him off the hook that easy. The crafty bugger must think I was born yesterday, she thought. He's put it that way so the blonde he's with thinks he means here, next Saturday. 'Yeah, Alec, outside the Grafton on Wednesday at eight.'

Alec didn't answer. In fact, he never opened his mouth until they were halfway up the street. 'Some hope she's got,' he muttered under his breath, walking so quickly Sadie was panting to keep up with him. 'If she thinks I'm takin' her out she's got another blinkin' think coming.'

'Surely yer wouldn't let the girl down? That would be a lousy trick, Alec Gleeson.'

'Let her down? Have yer seen the face on her – it's enough to curdle the milk.'

'She had the same face when yer took her down an entry, Alec.' Sadie was making a guess but Alec's start of surprise told her she'd hit the nail on the head. 'Now she's makin' yer pay for yer bit of fun.'

'I don't know where yer got that idea from,' Alec said, bluffing it out. 'I'd have to be hard up to be seen with her.'

'That's the point isn't it, Alec? That's what yer go down an entry for – *not* to be seen.'

'I've never been down an entry with her, so for heaven's sake shut up about it.' Alec was not in the best of moods. First that bloody bloke having the nerve to dance with Sadie, and then Doris turning up. He needed something to put him in a better mood, and who better to do that than the girl walking by his side with the face of an angel and a figure to drool over. But he'd have to warm her up first. So he forced a smile to his face and cheerfulness to his voice. 'Yer doing well with yer dancing, Sadie, yer've come on a treat.'

'Yeah, I'm quite pleased with meself. Another couple of weeks and I'm going to try the Grafton or the Rialto.'

'With me, I hope?' They were walking on the main road when Alec stopped, put his arms around her and gave her a kiss full on the lips. 'It will be with me, won't it?'

'Alec, let go of me! Everybody's lookin' at us.'

'Sadie, the road's nearly deserted. But if it makes yer feel any better, we'll do our snogging where we can't be seen.' He pulled a protesting Sadie into a shop doorway. 'There, does that please yer?'

'Alec, what the hell d'yer think yer doing.' Sadie struggled to free herself from his vice-like grip. 'Take yer hands off me!'

Alec's mouth came down hard on hers, stopping her from crying out. He had her pressed back against the side wall of the shop doorway, his body keeping her prisoner while his kiss was rough and bruising. He placed one of his hands on her neck, making it impossible for her to move without being choked. His free hand was fondling her breast, then she felt his body bend and the next thing she knew his hand was up her skirt and on her thigh. It was the feel of his hand on her bare flesh that turned her fear to anger. How dare he do this to her! Who the hell did he think he was! She brought her knee up as hard as she could and was rewarded by his yelp of pain. He fell away from her, his two hands clutching his crotch as he bent double and groaned in agony. 'You little bitch! I'll get you for this!'

Sadie looked down at his stooped figure and felt like kicking him in the face. 'That should teach yer that all girls don't welcome your advances, Alec Gleeson. If I were you I'd stick to girls like Doris who can't get a decent bloke. She's a tart, Alec, and I don't know the word for a male tart, but whatever it is you're one. So you and Doris make a fine pair, two of a kind. She was blackmailing you tonight, or d'yer think I'm too stupid to have figured that out? Well, I hope she puts the screws on yer 'cos that's what yer deserve.'

Sadie left the shadow of the doorway and walked a few steps before turning back. 'I learned a few lessons tonight, Alec, so I suppose the evening hasn't been a complete waste of time. I've always thought most men couldn't be trusted and you have proved me right. Also, I've mastered a few more dance steps which is a good thing. But the best thing that's happened is that you've got yer comeuppance and I'm glad I was there to see it. So on the whole a good night for me but a lousy one for you.'

Once more Sadie walked away, saying over her shoulder, 'I would advise yer to stay out of my path in future.'

Chapter Ten

'What d'yer mean, yer've had a row?' Brenda couldn't keep the excitement out of her voice. With Sadie out of the picture, she could be in the running with Alec. 'You haven't really fallen out, it's just a lovers' tiff.' She managed to add a touch of sympathy to her tone while her heartbeat raced fifteen to the dozen. 'I bet yer.'

'Lovers' tiff? What are yer on about, Brenda? I didn't even *like* Alec Gleeson, never mind love him. He was handy to go out with when I had no money, but that's as far as it went. Anyway, I'll be walking past him today without letting on, so now yer know.'

'But what was the row about?'

'He said something I didn't like, that's all.' This was the tale Sadie had told Harry when she'd met him in the park last night and she intended sticking to it because the truth was far too embarrassing. 'It's over and done with, Brenda, so let's just forget it, eh?'

But Brenda had no intention of forgetting it. Nor had she any intention of walking past Alec without letting on. This was her big chance, and if she had to choose between Sadie and Alec, he would win hands down. So when the bell rang out to announce the dinner-break, she had her overall off before the echo of the clang had died away. She'd bought another new jumper on Saturday and she congratulated herself on having decided to wear it today. It was a summer jumper in a type of knitted rayon which clung to her curves. She pulled at the waistband to straighten any creases, and when she gazed down at herself she was pleased with what she saw. Then the comb came out of her handbag for a quick run though her dark brown hair.

Sadie watched the proceeding with a mixture of amusement and frustration. All this just to attract the attention of a man who wasn't worth the effort. But it wasn't up to her to warn Brenda – she'd have to find out for herself. Anyway, if she did say something her friend would only think it was a question of sour grapes.

Sadie threw her overall on one of the packing crates and reached for her handbag. When she straightened up she was sideways on to Brenda and she thought there was something different about her. 'Have you got something stuck down yer brassière? Yer certainly weren't that size on Saturday.'

Brenda blushed. 'I've put a hankie in each of the cups 'cos yer could see me nipples.'

Sadie shook her head at the lame excuse. The hankies had been put there to make her bust look bigger and for no other reason. 'Come on,' she said, walking towards the door, 'or the chippy will be packed.' Then Sadie's imagination took over. If Alec ever got Brenda down an entry he'd be in for a big surprise and an even bigger let-down.

When they walked out of the factory door the first person Sadie saw was Alec, leaning nonchalantly against the wall, dwarfing Bobby Bennett who was standing beside him. She could feel her heart begin to pound and her tummy was doing somersaults. But she took a deep breath, held her head high and walked on with her eyes fixed straight ahead. She sensed Brenda squaring her shoulders and thrusting her bust forward to make herself look even more voluptuous. Stupid nit, Sadie thought, she's making a fool of herself. The best of it is, if a lad so much as laid a finger on her, she'd scream blue murder and want her mam.

'He was looking at yer, Sadie,' Brenda said as they walked through the gates. 'If yer'd given him the chance he would have spoke to yer.'

'So you were looking at him, were yer?'

'Well, yeah. I couldn't very well pretend I hadn't seen him, could I?' Brenda didn't have the nerve to say that Alec had winked at her and she'd winked back. And he'd given her the thumbs up sign, which meant he thought she looked nice. 'Anyway, Sadie, it's you what's had the row with him, not me. I don't have to fall out with him just because you do.'

'I didn't say you had to. Look, Brenda, you do as you wish. Yer old enough to know what yer doing. Just don't come running to me if you get yer fingers burned.' They joined the line of people in the chip shop. 'Just one last word, though, Bren. I've had enough of Alec Gleeson to last me a lifetime. I don't ever want to hear his name again.'

Geoff was waiting when Sadie got to Everton Valley and she thought how smart he looked in his grey flannel trousers and white short-sleeved summer shirt. And his smile of welcome was so genuine it cheered her heart. He seemed a nice-enough bloke, but if he turned out the same as Alec she'd take to her heels and run.

'Have yer thought about where yer'd like to go?' Geoff's teeth gleamed in his brown, weatherbeaten face. 'It's a bit hot for the pictures, don't yer think?'

'Yeah, it is hot.' Sadie tilted her head. 'You're nice and brown – I didn't notice it at the dance. Have yer been on yer holidays?'

'I should be so lucky! No, I work in the building trade and I'm out in all weathers. I'm an apprentice bricky and I've only got eighteen more months to go before I'm out of me time.'

Sadie was facing the sun and she put an open hand to her forehead to shade her eyes from the strong rays. 'That makes yer nineteen, doesn't it?'

'Nineteen years and seven months, to be precise. And I can't wait to be twenty-one and in the money.' Geoff looked at his wrist-watch. 'What would you like to do?'

'I'll leave it to you.' Sadie's knowledge of where young people went to enjoy themselves was nil. First-house pictures once a week had been her only enjoyment for two years, apart from the one trip on the ferry and two nights at a fourpenny hop. 'You decide.'

'We could nip into Liverpool on the tram and get the train to Southport – how does that appeal to yer?'

'That would be lovely. I've never been to Southport.'

'It'll be nice there in this weather.' Geoff cupped her elbow and led her towards the tram stop. 'We can have a walk around the lake and stop somewhere for a drink.'

'I can't go in a pub, Geoff, I'm only sixteen.'

'We'll have a cup of tea, then, or an ice cream. There's plenty to do and see there so we'll be spoilt for choice.'

The tram ride wasn't a novelty to Sadie, although she didn't use the trams much because she never had any money for the fare. But she'd never been on a train before and she was like a child looking out of the carriage window at the sights. It was mostly factories they passed on one side, and streets of terraced houses on the other. But the further away from the city they travelled, the factories disappeared and the houses became more grand.

'Ooh, look at those houses, aren't they lovely?' Sadie breathed. 'I've never seen anything like them in all me life. And look at the gardens and trees. The people living in them must be very posh.'

Geoff was fascinated by her. He'd travelled this route many times, seen everything before. So he concentrated on the changing expressions on Sadie's face. She wasn't like any other girl he'd taken out before. Apart from a pale lipstick, she wore no make-up at all. But then with her natural beauty she had no need of it. And she was making no effort to impress him. There were no coy smiles, no patting of the blonde hair that owed its colour to nature and not a bottle of bleach, and no crossing of the shapely legs. He'd been immediately attracted to her at the dance where she'd stood out from all the other girls. Now her attitude of complete indifference to him made her all the more attractive to him. 'Is it all right if I talk, Sadie?'

She turned from the window, her eyes and face glowing with pleasure. 'I'm sorry, Geoff, but this is all new to me and I want to get a picture of it in me mind so I can go over it all again when I'm lying in bed tonight.'

Geoff smiled. 'I'd like to have something to think about when I'm lying in bed tonight, too. But unless you talk to me, I won't have anything. I'll think I've been out on me own.'

Sadie giggled. 'Yer've seen the back of me head, what more d'yer want?'

'The back of you is very pretty, Sadie, but not as pretty as the front. So talk to me. Tell me how yer got on with yer "not really" boyfriend?'

Sadie didn't want to talk about Alec. She'd get over what he did to her on Saturday night, but she'd never forget it – nor would she ever forgive him. But she couldn't let it spoil her enjoyment, nor Geoff's. 'He's not even "not really" now. We had a bust-up on Saturday on the way home and I don't want nothing more to do with him.'

'I'm glad, 'cos he's not good enough for yer.' The train was pulling into Southport Station and Geoff reached for her hand. 'Come on, let's paint the town red.'

Sadie's eyes were everywhere as they strolled along Lord Street with its beautiful shops and arcades. She stopped outside an elegant shop to look at a dress that had caught her eye, and nearly fainted when she saw the fifteen-guinea price tag. 'Oh, my God! That's a year's wages!'

Geoff roared with laughter. 'Yer've got to be wealthy to shop in Lord Street, Sadie. It's not for the likes of you and me.'

Sadie was flabbergasted. 'No matter how much money I had, I'd never pay that amount for a dress.' She looked down at the sixpenny one she was wearing and had to stop herself from blurting out how much it had cost. 'I'll make do with TJ's or Blacklers.'

Geoff bought them an ice cream from a 'stop me and buy one' man, and they licked them as they wandered down to the pier. Sadie's enthusiasm and delight in everything was so infectious it rubbed off on Geoff. He'd been to Southport dozens of times, but with Sadie by his side he was seeing things he'd never noticed before. Like the waves gushing around the pier supports and throwing up a white foam. Or the swans on the lake. He'd seen the swans before, but had never noticed how graceful they were until Sadie pointed it out. 'Aren't they beautiful?' she said softly. 'So calm and . . . and . . . I think the word is dignified.'

They were leaning over the railing around the lake when the sun began to set and Sadie thought she'd never forget the sight. The sky was a blaze of colour, from red to gold, and the reflections on the rippling waters of the sea and lake were breathtaking. 'Yer couldn't describe it, could yer, Geoff? No one would believe yer unless they saw it for themselves.' In an impulsive gesture she laid a hand on his arm. 'Thank you for bringing me.'

'Thank you for coming with me, Sadie, and showing me Southport as I've never seen it before.' Geoff thought of the one thing he'd always wanted to do but never got the chance because his various girlfriends didn't want to get their feet wet or their shoes dirty. 'The tide's goin' out now – d'yer feel like having a paddle?'

'Oh, I'd love to!' Sadie clapped her hands in glee. 'I've never had a paddle in me life.'

'Stop pulling me leg,' Geoff said. 'Everyone had a paddle when they were kids.'

'I didn't.'

Geoff could see she was serious so he didn't want to upset her by asking questions. Some other time, when she knew him a bit better, then perhaps he could find out more about her. 'Come on, let's splash in the water together. I'll have to roll me trouser legs up and you'll have to lift yer skirt or yer'll get drenched.'

They were holding hands as they made their way to the railway station and Sadie looked sideways at him. 'I'll have plenty to think about in bed tonight, Geoff.'

'I hope yer thoughts will all be pleasant ones?'

'Oh, yes, they'll be brilliant. If I go over everything, it'll be three o'clock in the morning before I get to sleep. And when I do drop off, I hope I have a lovely dream about that sunset.'

'My dream will be about something lovely.' Geoff showed their tickets to get onto the platform. 'But it won't be the sunset. It'll be about a girl with bright blonde hair, eyes bluer than the sea or the sky, and a smile that would warm the coldest heart.'

'Oh, you, don't be makin' me blush!'

'I don't want to embarrass yer, Sadie, but I just want yer to tell me that yer'll see me again, then I'll sleep a happy man.'

'Ooh, I wouldn't want to be the cause of yer not sleepin', Geoff.' There was laughter in Sadie's voice. 'We can't have that so I'd better say I'll see yer again, hadn't I? Would yer like to make an appointment now?'

'Tomorrow night,' Geoff said quickly. 'And every other night.'

Sadie pulled a face. 'I can't make it tomorrow, Geoff, I'm sorry.'

'Have yer got a date with someone else?'

'No, it's nothing like that. I've promised to go somewhere.' Wednesday night was Harry's free kiss night and Sadie wouldn't let him down. He was the only man she trusted. Never once had he tried to do more than kiss her and she respected him for that. 'Either Friday or Saturday would be the best nights.'

'Friday then, if that's the earliest yer can make it.'

'Look, I'm goin' to be honest with yer, Geoff. I had to walk to Everton Valley tonight from Toxteth, and it's a long walk.' She put her hand up when she saw he was about to speak. 'I did it because I had no money for tram fare. I don't get much pocket money and it's usually all gone by Monday. Then I'm skint until I get paid on Saturday.'

'Sadie, I'll pay yer tram fare. Good God, it's only coppers.'

'This is my night for being honest, so yer might as well get the lot.' Sadie's mind was divided into two camps. One voice was telling her he was too nice to use, like she used Alec, the other telling her to stick to her resolve because the alternative was years of misery at home. 'I let Alec pay me tram fare last week and what he expected in return was too high a price to pay.'

'I'll kill him,' Geoff hissed through gritted teeth. 'I know what he is, he's noted for it, but I didn't think he'd try it on with you.'

'He didn't get what he wanted, Geoff, so don't worry. In fact, he got something he *didn't* want, which must have caused him a lot of pain, apart from denting his pride. I'm only telling yer this because yer offered to pay me fare, like he did, and I don't intend goin' through any capers like that again.' Sadie couldn't resist a grin. 'Many more like Alec an' I'll be breaking me flippin' leg!'

Geoff's face creased in puzzlement. 'I don't understand.'

'I'm not going to draw yer a picture, Geoff. I'll just say that when I left him in the shop doorway that he'd dragged me into, he was doubled up in pain and howling like a baby.'

A slow smile spread across Geoff's face. 'Yer didn't!'

'Oh, but I ruddywell did! So do yer still want to pay me tram fare?'

'I'm not Alec, Sadie, so don't insult me. And why do yer need fare? I can pick yer up from home.'

'No, yer can't. I never take any friends home because me mam and dad are funny with people and I get embarrassed. So I'll meet yer at the Valley on Friday night, as long as I don't have to walk there.'

'If I had a pumpkin and a magic wand, Sadie, I'd turn the pumpkin into a coach and horses and yer could ride in style.'

Sadie's laughter rang out. 'Go on, yer daft nit! Next thing yer'll be having me in a ballgown, and how well I'd look walkin' down our street in a flippin' ballgown!'

They were still laughing when they arrived back at Everton Valley. Geoff waited at the tram stop with her and when he saw a tram trundling towards them he slipped a silver sixpence in her hand and kissed her cheek. 'Good night, Sadie, and thank you for a lovely night.'

'It's me what should be thankin' you, Geoff. I've really enjoyed meself.'

As she stepped onto the platform of the tram, Geoff said, 'I'm looking forward to Friday. It can't come quick enough.'

Sadie smiled and waved before taking her seat. If only everything in her life was as pleasant as the last few hours had been, she'd be the happiest girl in Liverpool.

The next day, as Sadie and Brenda left the factory at dinner-time, Alec was once again leaning against the wall with Bobby beside him. Sadie looked straight ahead and didn't even turn her head when she heard him call, 'Brenda, can I have a word with yer?'

Brenda stopped in her tracks. 'I'll catch yer up, Sadie.'

Sadie closed her eyes but carried on walking. Why couldn't the stupid girl see he was going to use her to get back at Sadie? Still, if that was what Brenda wanted, then good luck to her. But when her workmate caught up with her, all smiles and bright-eyed, and said Alec had asked her to go out with him that night, Sadie tried to warn her. 'He's no good, Brenda, believe me. He's out for all he can get and you won't stand an earthly with him.'

'That's your opinion.' Brenda tossed her head. 'I think he's nice and I'm goin' to the pictures with him.'

'Is he callin' for yer, so yer mam can see him?'

Brenda coloured. 'Not tonight. He said he'll call for me next time and meet me mam.'

'Well, who are yer going to tell yer family yer going out with?' When Sadie saw her friend lower her eyes, she gasped. 'Don't you dare tell them yer going out with me! I don't want them comin' to me if you get yerself into trouble. I've warned yer about Alec but yer won't listen, so leave me out of it altogether.'

'Blimey! I'm only going to the pictures with him, for heaven's sake! What harm is there in that?'

Sadie sighed, thinking, She hasn't the faintest idea what I'm trying to get through to her. She's so innocent it's like leading a lamb to the slaughter. Still, I've done me best, I can't do any more.

As Sadie was walking to the park to meet Harry, she was in a thoughtful mood. Why was it that whenever she was happy, something came along to spoil it for her? She'd been in a happy frame of mind this morning when she went to work, still full of the lovely time she'd had with Geoff in Southport. Now she felt down in the dumps worrying about Brenda. The girl wasn't her responsibility, but still Sadie couldn't get her out of her mind. Shielded from the world by doting parents, Brenda didn't understand how wicked some men could be. It was to be hoped she didn't find out the hard way.

Harry smiled as he walked towards her, happy as always to see her. Then he noted the look of dejection and asked, 'Why so glum?'

'I've just been askin' meself what I ever did to deserve the horrible things that happen to me. I never do no one any harm, but I must be jinxed.'

'Is it yer family again?'

Sadie was silent for a while as she stared down at the grass they were standing on. Then she met his eyes. 'My family are to blame for everything bad that happens to me. If I had a happy home life, things would be so different. But yer don't know what it's like, Harry, to walk into that house every night to be met by the smell of dirt, and listen to your mam and dad coming out with filthy language. And yer don't know what it's like to see yer brothers and sisters dressed in rags, their tummies rumbling with hunger, and yer can't do a thing about it.'

Harry could see tears glistening in her eyes and he put his arms around her. 'You'll get out of there one day, Sadie, and yer'll make a good life for yerself.'

'Oh, I'll get out of there, Harry, that's a dead cert! And the day can't come quick enough for me.' Sadie sniffed up. 'I'm sixteen years of age and I've never once had a friend come to my home because I'm too ashamed. In fact, apart from Brenda in work, I've never had a friend!'

Harry squeezed her shoulder. 'I'm your friend, Sadie.' But even as he spoke he was remembering his mother, not an hour ago, calling the Wilson family every name she could lay her tongue to. She said the whole street was complaining about the smell that was coming from the house, and the state of the children. So while he was sincere in his feelings for Sadie, he knew he was helpless to do anything about it. 'I'll always be here if yer need help, yer know that.'

'No one can help me, Harry, except meself. I can't go on the way I am, afraid to get too close to anyone because I know that as soon as they see the way I live they'd be off like a shot.' The sigh came from deep within Sadie. 'I went out with a nice bloke last night – a decent, respectable bloke. I'm seeing him again on Friday, but when he asked if he could call for me I had to make an excuse. How long can I go on making excuses? That's what my family have done for me, Harry. And it's their fault we're standing here now, hiding in the bushes so no one will see yer with me.'

110

'Oh, Sadie love, what can I say?' Harry pressed her head to his chest, unable to deny that what she said was true. His anger against her parents mounted. They were to blame. He was afraid of being seen with her and it was no good pretending otherwise. And it was all down to her parents. They should never have had children because it was the children who were suffering from their lack of care, love, pride and the responsibility that went with having a family.

Sadie moved away from him and pulled a face. 'Poor Harry, always getting me troubles and me moans. I'm surprised yer keep coming back for more.'

'You need someone to talk to, Sadie, because if yer keep it all bottled up yer'll make yerself ill. And what are friends for anyway if yer can't bend their ear now and again?'

'Now and again?' Sadie managed a smile. 'You get it every time I see yer! But that's because yer the only one I don't have to lie or pretend to. You know exactly what my circumstances are. No one else does.'

'You can't help your circumstances, Sadie, and people should like you for what you are as a person.' Harry put a finger under her chin and lifted her face. 'I think yer as pretty as a picture and one of the nicest people I know.'

'You deserve two free kisses for that, Harry Young, and you can make them two of yer famous smackeroos.'

'Before I do, I want to know who this new bloke in yer life is. If I've got a rival for your affections I want to know all about him.'

'I met him at the dance I went to with Alec. He claimed me in the Excuse Me quickstep. His name's Geoff and that's all I know about him, except he's nice. I don't ask any questions because I'm always afraid they'll ask questions back. And I tell enough lies as it is.'

'Yer not serious about him, then?'

'How can I be, Harry? Can yer imagine me taking a boyfriend home to meet me parents? They'd run a mile!'

Harry sighed with relief. 'That's all right then.' He claimed his first kiss before saying, 'I don't want no competition. It spoils me appetite, puts me off me food.'

The next morning Sadie waited to hear about Brenda's date with Alec. She thought she'd be full of it, but her friend was so subdued Sadie began to wonder whether she'd been told to keep her distance. She wouldn't be surprised because it was the sort of thing Alec would do to get back at her. He was like a big soft kid.

When the dinner-bell sounded, Sadie could keep quiet no longer. 'Are you all right, Bren? Yer've not had much to say for yerself this morning.'

'I'm fine.' Brenda took her overall off, straightened her jumper and combed her hair. 'I was late gettin' to bed and I'm tired.'

'Did yer enjoy yerself?'

'Yeah, it was great.' Brenda gave Sadie a long look, as though she wanted to ask her something, but then changed her mind. 'Yeah, I really enjoyed meself.'

'Are yer seeing him again?' Sadie tucked her arm into her friend's. 'Takin' him home to meet yer mam, are yer?'

'I don't know yet, we'll just have to wait and see.'

But when they were passing Alec in the factory yard, and he called, 'Come here, Brenda!' the girl practically ran towards him, leaving Sadie to carry on on her own.

'My God,' Sadie muttered under her breath, 'that was a flippin' order! He's going to have her dancing to his tune and she's daft enough to do it.'

Brenda was smiling and breathless when she caught up. 'Alec wants me to go out with him tonight.'

'And are yer going?'

'Of course I am. Why shouldn't I?'

'No reason at all, Brenda, so don't be gettin' yer knickers in a twist. I suppose he's calling for yer?'

'No, I'm meeting him outside that dance hall you went to with him. But he said he will come and meet me mam one night,' Brenda said defensively. 'Perhaps on Saturday.'

'That's good.' Sadie was amazed that her friend was so gullible. But the best thing she could do would be to keep out of it. She had enough troubles of her own to contend with.

When Sadie came in from work on the Friday night and sat down at the table opposite her sister, she forced herself not to wrinkle her nose in disgust. The filthy stained oilcloth, the sauce bottle and the opened tin of condensed milk were amongst all the other things that were in the same position on the table as they had been when she had left at half-seven that morning. Her mother didn't believe in making work for herself. I mean, why carry all the things out when you only had to carry them back in?

'How did yer last day at school go, Dot?' Sadie hadn't held a conversation with her sister for nearly two weeks and she wouldn't be doing so now if her own interests weren't at stake. 'Did yer feel sad?'

Dot looked at her in amazement. Through a mouthful of chips she said, 'Yer must be jokin'! I hated school and couldn't get out quick enough.'

'Did they give yer a card to take to the unemployment office?'

Dot took another bite of her chip buttie before answering. 'Yeah, they gave us all one but I won't be needin' mine.'

Sadie's spirits soared. 'Ooh, yer've got a job so soon, have yer?'

There was wickedness in the eyes of her sister as she gloated, 'I'm not goin' to work. Me dad said I could stay home an' help me mam.'

Sadie was stunned. 'Yer not going to work?'

Dot smirked. 'You heard what I said, yer not deaf.'

Sadie looked to her mother. 'Is she tellin' the truth? Did me dad say she didn't have to go out to work?'

Lily lowered her eyes. This was one thing she didn't agree with her husband on, but when she'd told him this he'd lost his temper and was like a raving maniac. So, as always, she gave in for a quiet life. There were a lot of things happening that she was uneasy about, but she was too afraid of upsetting him to speak out. She should have put her foot down years ago; it was too late now. And she was still crazy about him – nothing he did would change that. 'Ask him yerself, he'll be in any minute.'

'I'm asking you, Mam.' Sadie felt like jumping up and slapping the sneer off her sister's face. 'If it's true . . .' They could hear the stamp of heavy footsteps on the bare boards of the hall and the room fell silent.

George came into the room with his usual swagger. He looked at the three people sitting around the table and grumbled, 'What's the matter with youse lot? Yer look as though yer've been to a bleedin' funeral.'

'Dad, is it true that you said our Dot can stay at home, that she doesn't have to go to work?' Sadie was beside herself with anger, and tears weren't far away. 'Yer didn't, did yer?'

'What's it got to do with you if I did? I don't bleedin' have to ask your permission, Miss High and bloody Mighty.'

Sadie stood up so quickly she knocked the chair backwards and it crashed onto the broken-down sideboard that was minus one drawer and one cupboard door. 'Are you expectin' me to go to work every day for a shillin' a week pocket money, while she stays at home lazing around like me mam does?'

'Yer'll do as I bleedin' tell yer!' George's bloated face looked ugly as his eyes blazed and his nostrils flared. 'I'll be buggered if I'll have a scrap of a girl tellin' me what I can and can't bleedin' well do!'

They're so jealous that I can keep meself clean and tidy in this muck midden, Sadie thought, they're trying to break my spirit. Well, I won't let them. She was so incensed by the unfairness, she blurted out, 'Oh no? Yer buggered if yer'll have a scrap of a girl tellin' yer what yer can or can't bleedin' well do, are yer? Well, if I'm a scrap of a girl, what's our Dot? And she's telling yer what yer can or can't do, isn't she? But you and I know, and our Dot, why she can twist yer around her little finger.' Sadie mimicked her sister, saying the words that were imprinted in her mind. ' "I am nice to yer, Dad, an' I do look after yer, don't I?".'

While she watched her father's jaw drop, Sadie heard Dot's sharp intake of breath. 'I want an extra sixpence pocket money tomorrow – and if I don't get it, then if she doesn't go to work, neither do I.'

With that Sadie fled from the room and up the stairs. She'd have to go out without a wash 'cos she wasn't going back in there to face them. She wished she hadn't agreed to meet Geoff, but no matter how bad she felt she wouldn't let him down. And she had to get out of the house, anyway. She wished she could get out for good, never come back. And she'd do that one day, just pack her few belongings and walk away for ever. Let them stew in their own evil and filth.

Geoff took her to the pictures and held her hand in the darkness. 'You're very quiet tonight, Sadie, 'he whispered. 'Do yer feel all right?'

'I've got a headache, that's all,' Sadie whispered back. 'It started in work and has got gradually worse until now it feels like a tight band around me head.'

'Would yer like to go home? It can't be very pleasant for yer sitting here if yer don't feel well.'

If you only knew how much more unpleasant it would be if I went home, Sadie thought. I've got no mother to make a fuss of me and send me to bed with a Beecham's Powder. 'No, I'll stay to the end. I don't want to spoil your night for yer. No good two of us being miserable.'

As he was walking her to the tram stop, Geoff asked, 'Would yer like me to see you to yer front door?'

'No thanks, Geoff, I just want to get home and go to bed. I'll be fine in the morning.'

'Will yer be all right to come out tomorrow night?'

'Yeah, of course I will. I'll be bright-eyed and bushy-tailed to go to work in the morning.'

'Can't we meet in the afternoon and go to Southport again? You enjoyed that, didn't yer?'

'No, I've made arrangements to see a friend in the afternoon and I can't let her down. I'll meet you at seven in the usual place. And Geoff, I'm sorry to have been such a wet blanket. I'll make it up to yer tomorrow.'

'Hello, girl! I was beginnin' to think yer weren't coming.' Mary Ann grinned. 'I thought I'd put the fear of God into yer over Elsie.'

'If I see her coming, Mary Ann, I'll do a bunk.'

'Then yer'd better start runnin', sunshine, 'cos believe it or not she's heading our way. And she's got a face on her like thunder.'

Sadie turned and saw the big woman approaching. She touched Mary Ann's arm and said, 'Just watch this.'

Mary Ann stood with her arms folded. There were customers waiting to be served but they'd just have to wait until she made sure Sadie wasn't going to get a hiding. If Elsie wanted to tangle with her young friend, then she'd have to tangle with her as well. She might only be little but she was good at jumping on people's backs. But the stall-holder got the surprise of her life when she saw Sadie walk towards the big woman with a smile on her face.

'Hiya, Elsie, am I glad to see yer! I've been keeping me eyes peeled for yer, hoping yer'd come.'

That took the wind out of Elsie's sails. She'd come down to demand her money back for the blouse one of her neighbours said wasn't pure silk. And if she didn't get her money she'd throttle somebody. She was spoiling for a fight as she eyed Sadie with suspicion. 'Oh aye, were yer now? Did yer want to see me to tell me the blouse wasn't pure silk and yer were going to refund me money?'

Sadie's vivid blue eyes flew open with surprise. 'No, nothing of the sort, Elsie. I was going to ask yer to sell it back to me.'

Elsie gaped. 'Yer what!'

'Will yer sell it back to me? I was telling me friend all about it an' she said she'd love it. She didn't half tell me off for not keepin' it for her.'

Elsie was flummoxed. 'But one of me neighbours told me I'd been had – that it's not pure silk.'

'I'll buy it off yer in any case, Elsie, 'cos me friend would love it. She's about your size and she's got the same nice colouring, so it would look a treat on her.'

Elsie was in a real quandary now. The much talked-of blouse was lying at the bottom of her shopping bag, waiting to be handed over in return for her money back. But if someone else was prepared to part with sixpence for it, perhaps she'd be daft not to hang onto it. After all, it did look nice on her – her feller had said so. And what the hell did her neighbour know about pure silk anyway? The silly sod didn't know her arse from her flipping elbow!

Elsie looked towards Mary Ann. 'Is she havin' me on? 'Cos if she is, I'll kill her.'

'Ooh, Elsie, I don't think I should interfere because the transaction was between you an' me assistant here, Sadie.' Her two fingers under

115

her chin, Mary Ann wagged her head from side to side as though giving the matter her full consideration. 'The way I see it, though, as an independent outsider, Elsie, yer can't lose. If yer like the blouse then keep it, if yer don't like it then sell it to Sadie for her friend.'

Indecision was plain to see in the eyes Elsie turned on Sadie. 'Why would yer friend want to buy somethin' she hasn't even seen? She must have a screw loose.'

'Ooh, far from it, Elsie. Me friend's got very good taste. As soon as I described it to her and said how nice I thought you'd look in it, what with your figure and colouring an' everythin', she got all excited and asked me to buy it back off yer. Yer see, it's not often yer come across somethin' as pretty as that.'

That did it. 'Your friend, whoever she is, can just sod off.' Suddenly Elsie loved the blouse so much she wouldn't have parted with it for a king's ransom. 'Tell her to find her own bloody bargains!'

Sadie's face took on a look of disappointment. 'Ah, me friend will be dead upset. Still, I'm glad yer satisfied, Elsie, 'cos I enjoyed servin' yer last week. Not all the customers are as nice as you.'

Elsie beamed. 'Thank you, queen, it's nice of yer to say so. Next time I'm in the market I'll make a point of gettin' you to serve me.'

Mary Ann scratched her head. 'I wouldn't have believed it if I hadn't seen it with me own eyes. She came down here to create merry hell an' you've sent her away like a little docile lamb. Well, I never. I thought I was good at bein' two-faced, girl, but I'm not in the meg specks with you. Knock me into a cocked hat, you do.'

'I enjoyed that, Mary Ann.' Sadie's spirits had been lifted by the encounter. 'In fact, if Elsie had taken off on me I'd have flopped her one.'

'I believe yer would 'ave, girl. Me now, I'd have to get meself in a real paddy before takin' anyone like Elsie on.'

'I am in a right paddy, Mary Ann. I could take the whole world on, single-handed.'

'Oh dear, as bad as that, eh? Well, help me clear some of these customers away an' yer can tell me what's ailing yer.'

Mary Ann listened without comment as Sadie poured her heart out. She told the older woman everything exept her father's wickedness. She described in detail the house that was filthy inside and out, how there was never enough to eat and how the children were so cruelly neglected. Her father's drunkenness and her mother's laziness. The neighbours who either ignored or taunted them. Her shame each time she walked down the street and knew that the women standing at their doors with their arms folded, looked on her as they would a piece of dirt. And how she had never had a real friend in her life and never would have until she cut herself free from her family.

Sadie was dry-eyed as she related all this. But when she came to what she called the last straw, tears shone in her eyes. 'Now they want me to go to work while our Dot stays at home. It's so unfair, Mary Ann, and I can't take any more. I've got to get away, find meself somewhere decent where I can have a bit of pride in meself. And I was wondering if you could advise me? Would I be able to get digs somewhere – or would it cost more than I earn?'

'Yer mean yer want lodgings, is that it, girl?'

'I'll have to do something, Mary Ann, even if I end up sleeping on the streets. If I don't get away from that house it will destroy me.'

'I'll have a little think, girl, see what I can come up with. I'd have yer meself but I've only a two-bedroomed house and I've got two kids at home. There must be someone though who would be glad of yer few bob a week. I can think of some who would jump at the chance, but they're not respectable enough for yer. Yer'd only be jumpin' from the frying pan into the bleedin' fire.'

'Will yer have a think for us, Mary Ann? I'd be willing to help with the housework and I am clean.'

Mary Ann kissed her cheek. 'Anybody that gets you would be gettin' a bargain. I'll put me thinkin' cap on and see what I can come up with by next week. But don't be too expectin', 'cos I'll only let yer go where I know yer'll be well looked after.' She nodded to a customer and as she was walking away she said, 'I'll get yer fixed up, girl, even if I have to build yer a bleedin' house with me bare hands.'

Chapter Eleven

'I don't think I like goin' out with boys,' Brenda said, laying sheets carefully in the wooden crate. 'I'd rather go out with a girlfriend.'

'Yeah.' Sadie had enough on her mind without listening to her workmate going on about nothing in particular. Her home life was worse than ever since the row over Dot. Her sister got her own way, she stayed at home with their mother. But as the house looked as bad as ever, it seemed the pair of them sat around all day doing nothing. And Sadie didn't get the extra sixpence pocket money, either. Her mother even had the nerve to say that there wasn't enough money coming into the house as it was, so she was wasting her time complaining.

Sadie hated herself for letting them get away with it, but she didn't give her job up as she'd threatened. Firstly because she decided a shilling a week was better than nothing, and also because she couldn't bear the thought of being in the house all day with her mother and a sister who now seemed to be ruling the roost.

Sadie's train of thought was once again interrupted by Brenda.

'Do you like goin' out with boys, Sadie?'

'It depends upon the boy, Bren. Some are nice, some are not.'

'Do they all – you know – try to touch yer?'

Sadie blew out a deep sigh. 'As I've said, some do and some don't.'

'Do you let them touch yer?'

'Oh, for cryin' out loud, Brenda, grow up, will yer! Yer a big girl now, yer should know what's right and what's wrong, so don't be asking me.' Sadie looked at the serious expression on her workmate's face and was immediately sorry she'd spoken so sharply. Alec was the only boy Brenda had been out with so she could imagine why these questions were being asked. He was a real horror, was Alec, and Brenda couldn't have chosen a worse one than him for her first boyfriend. 'Look, Bren, don't ever let a boy do anything yer don't want him to. That's the best advice I can give yer, so let's drop the subject now.'

Sadie was happy to return to her work and her thoughts. The only bright spots in her life were the times she went out with Geoff, which was three times a week for the last three weeks, her meetings with Harry in the park, and her Saturday afternoon at the market with Mary Ann. If she didn't have those three people in her life she'd have nothing and no one. She was disappointed that Mary Ann hadn't been able to find her lodgings yet, but last week the stall-holder had explained that the person she had in mind hadn't been in the market for a few weeks. But it was better to have a little patience and wait for the right person than dash headlong into something she might regret.

Brenda was speaking again and this time there was pleading in her voice. 'Sadie, if I ask yer something, yer won't bite me head off, will yer?'

'Oh, go on, what is it?'

'Promise yer won't get in a temper, or tell anyone what I'm goin' to tell yer, especially Alec?'

'Brenda, I wouldn't spit on Alec if he was on fire, let alone talk to him. So yer can rest assured that whatever it is, I won't be telling the queer feller.'

'Well, Alec told me all the girls let the lads do things to them. And he said if I didn't believe him to ask you, 'cos you used to let him do things to you.'

Sadie was stunned for a while, then a surge of anger coursed through her whole body. The bloody cheek of him! How dare he! And how many other people had he told that to? She took a few seconds to calm her anger, then said, 'Brenda, Alec did touch me, but it wasn't a case of letting him; he's got roving hands and thinks all girls are there just for his pleasure. Why d'yer think I stopped seeing him?'

Brenda shrugged her shoulders. 'He told me it was him what packed you in, not the other way round.'

'Don't believe a word he says, Bren, 'cos he's a liar. And if yer don't like goin' out with him and what he does to yer, why don't yer give him his marching orders? He'll only bring yer trouble in the end.'

'I've no one else to go out with. I used to have you, but you've got yerself a boyfriend now, haven't yer?'

'I've got a friend, yes, but it's not serious. I have no intention of ever settling down and getting married. I live my life the way I think is best for meself and I think it's time you did the same. Yer can't expect to be pampered and led around by the hand all yer life; yer've got to start making decisions for yerself.' Sadie nodded at the stack of sheets waiting to be packed and said, 'It's about time we got some work done. We don't get paid for jangling.'

Mary Ann could see Sadie scanning her face for clues, so she quickly put her out of her misery. 'Yes, she's been in, girl, but before I say any more I want to have a good talk to yer. So give me a hand to get some of these customers out of the way.'

Sadie started at the opposite end to the stall-holder. She didn't think she could concentrate because her head was racing and there were butterfies in her tummy, but soon she was exchanging jokes with the customers waiting to be served.

'How much is this corset, girl?' Lizzie held the garment out for inspection. 'It can't be much because the tapes are nearly worn out.'

'I don't know, Lizzie, 'cos I've never sold one before.'

The woman standing next to Lizzie said knowingly, 'It's not one, it's a pair.'

Lizzie glared at the stranger. 'I can only bleedin' see one. What would I want with a pair?'

But the woman persisted. 'Yer don't understand what I'm gettin' at. I know it's only one, but when yer buy corsets yer ask for a pair.'

'I don't want a ruddy pair, I don't need a ruddy pair, and I'm not bleedin' well havin' a ruddy pair! Now, will yer mind yer own business an' let me get on with mine!' Lizzie was red in the face when she asked in a loud voice, 'How much is this corset, girl?'

Still the woman wasn't to be silenced. 'It's a pair of corsets.'

Sadie thought it was hilarious and she was laughing fit to burst. But things could turn out nasty so she'd better intervene. 'Before you two come to blows, I'll go and get the price off Mary Ann.'

But the stall-holder had heard the rumpus and was already on her way over. 'In the name of God, Lizzie, what's all the fuss about?'

Lizzie looked astounded. 'I'm not makin' no fuss – it's this know-it-all standin' next to me. She's minding everybody's business but her own. And if she doesn't keep her trap shut, so help me, Mary Ann, I'll clock her one.'

'Now, now, Lizzie, calm yerself down or yer'll be having a touch of the vapours.' The stall-holder took the corset from her to examine it. 'They're not in bad nick, Lizzie, so they're fourpence. Who are they for, anyway?'

'Meself of course, who else?'

'But yer'll never get into them, Lizzie, they're miles too small for yer!'

The stranger had a smug smile on her face when she butted in. 'There yer are, she said "them" not "it", which means they're a pair.'

Lizzie rounded on her. 'Missus, if yer like the shape of yer face as it is, I suggest yer bugger off before I rearrange it for yer.'

Mary Ann held up a hand of peace. 'Knock it off, the pair of yer. Yer should be ashamed of yerselves, actin' like a couple of kids.'

'Then tell her to stop pokin' her nose in where it's not wanted. An' if yer'll tell me the price of the bleedin' corset I can get away before I thump her one.'

'I told yer fourpence, Lizzie, an' I also told yer it's too small for yer. But, if you want to throw yer money away it's no skin off my nose.'

Lizzie was stubborn. After going through all that she wasn't going to let the nosy parker have the last laugh. 'I'll get into it, Mary Ann, I bet yer.'

'Uh, uh, Lizzie.' Mary Ann shook her head. 'Have yer ever heard of an optical illusion?'

'In the name of God, girl, what are yer on about now?'

'Well, an optical illusion is when yer eyes deceive yer brain. Yer seeing something that's not what it seems.'

With a look of scorn on her face, Lizzie reached into her basket for her purse. She rummaged through the loose coins and picked out four pennies. Placing them carefully in her palm, she held out her hand. 'Are these a bleedin' optical illusion? No? Well, I'll take the corset and thank yer for the bloody useless piece of information yer've just given me.' Lizzie stuffed the corset in her basket, glared at the woman next to her, then said, 'See yer next week, Mary Ann.'

'Okay, Lizzie, and don't be doin' anything I wouldn't do.' The stall-holder leaned across the table and patted the woman's arm. 'That's another bit of useless information, Lizzie, 'cos if you do manage to squeeze yerself into those corsets yer'll not be able to breathe never mind gettin' up to any hanky-panky.'

Lizzie cackled. 'Ah, Mary Ann, that sort of thing is just a memory now, and has been for many a long year.'

Mary Ann was just about to say something when her eyes lighted on a familiar figure at the next stall. 'Ay, Lizzie, will yer do us a favour and come and serve for about ten minutes? Yer've been coming here long enough to know the run of things, an' I won't be far away if yer do get stuck.'

There was a look of sheer bliss on Lizzie's face as she elbowed the woman next to her out of the way. 'Excuse me, Mrs Know-all, my experience is required.'

Mary Ann took hold of Sadie's arm and pulled her to the back of the stall. 'This has got to be quick, girl, so listen carefully and think carefully. Have yer thought through all the pros and cons about leaving home? No, don't answer yet, let me spell it out to yer. If yer do leave, it means packin' yer job in because yer family would be down there like a shot to take yer home again. They'll miss yer few bob a week and they'll move heaven an' earth to get yer back again. So it would mean breaking all ties with home and work.'

This was something Sadie hadn't considered and her heart sank. 'But they couldn't make me go back against me will, could they?'

'I don't know anything about the law, love, so I can't answer that. Me own feelings are that if you disappeared completely there's not much they could do about it. I can't see them bringin' the police in if things in the house are as bad as yer say they are. But if yer keep that job on, even if they don't make yer go back, they'll be outside the factory gates waitin' for yer every pay day.'

'I can't stay there, Mary Ann, yer've no idea what it's like, how much I hate it!' Sadie's voice rose as her desperation grew. 'I'll find another job – I wouldn't care what it was as long as I knew at the end of the day I was going home to a clean house where I was greeted with a smile instead of a load of filthy abuse. I want to be treated with respect, Mary Ann, and I want to be able to walk up a street with my head held high, instead of me chin buried in me chest so I don't have to see the disgust on the neighbours faces.'

'I understand, girl, I really do.' Mary Ann had a lump in her throat. 'But I've got to be certain for me own peace of mind that yer know what yer lettin' yerself in for. I care for yer, yer see, and I'm only thinkin' of what's best for yer. Yer won't see yer brothers and sisters again, at least not for a few years, or that boy from next door what's been good to yer.'

Sadie gazed at the woman who had become a mother figure to her – the only person she could pour her heart out to. But there were things she'd kept back from Mary Ann and perhaps now was the time to bring them out in the open. 'When I was a little girl, Mary Ann, about five or six, my father took over the job of bathing me in the zinc bath in front of the fire. Our Dot and Ellen would be done first and put to bed, and me dad would always send me mam out to the corner shop on a message. He used to splash the water on me, laughing and pretending to be playful. But all he time he was touching me in places he shouldn't. I think me mam knew what he was up to because she would be sent out regularly on some stupid message. But she let it go on because she's crazy about the man and I was too afraid to say anything. It went on until I was older and I flatly refused to let him bath me.'

Mary Ann's eyes were wide with horror. 'The swine! The dirty swine!'

'Let me finish, Mary Ann, please. I haven't told yer this before because I feel so dirty and so ashamed. And it's why I have so little self-esteem. Anyway, then he started doing the same thing to our Dot. But he picked on the wrong one with her because she let him get away with it so she could get what she wanted out of him. That's why she wasn't made to go out to work when she left school like everybody else does. And it's still going on with her – I've seen it with me own eyes. She

123

calls it being nice to him and he laps it up. And being nice to him gets her everything she wants. Even me mam daren't say a word out of place to our Dot because of the hold she has over me dad. But I'll tell yer this, Mary Ann, he'll pay heavily for his bit of fun because our Dot is a crafty little faggot.'

Mary Ann grabbed Sadie's arm for support because she thought she was going to faint. She'd heard many things in her life on the market and dealt with some hard knocks. But never had she heard anything so wicked and obscene. She gulped in the fresh air to stem the rising nausea that threatened to black her out.

'Are you all right, Mary Ann?' Sadie felt full of guilt. She wouldn't have said anything if she'd known it would have this effect. But she just wanted her friend to know how urgent it was that she leave home. 'Shall I try and borrow a chair for yer to sit on?'

'No, I'll be all right in a minute, girl, it just knocked me for six.' Mary Ann shook her head in disbelief as she gazed at the concerned expression on Sadie's face. How had such beauty survived in a place of unspeakable evil? Because the girl was beautiful, not only in looks but in her nature. She was kind and caring, and Mary Ann would lay down her life that she was as honest as the day was long. 'Yer'll have to excuse me, girl, but I've got to say it. Your father is one bastard and he needs horse-whipping.' She was feeling stronger now and able to cope with her anger. 'And I'll tell yer somethin' else: I'd like to be the one to do it.'

Sadie hung her head. 'I'm sorry if I upset yer, but I had to tell yer.'

'Of course yer did, girl. But I still can't believe that yer mam let him do those things to one of her children. In my eyes she's worse than yer dad, 'cos most mothers would defend their kids with their life.' Mary Ann waved to someone in the crowd. 'Anyway, yer've got it off yer chest and there's no need to ever go over it again. And I'm not asking yer if yer want to leave home, I'm telling yer yer've got to.'

Sadie looked heavenwards. 'Thank You, God, thank You.'

Mary Ann touched her arm. 'Would yer now like to meet the person I think will give yer a good home?'

Sadie placed her palms on her tummy. 'Ooh, I'm so scared me tummy's in knots. Do I know her, Mary Ann?'

'I think yer in for a pleasant surprise, girl, and that's not before time.'

They were walking towards Lizzie, who was having high jinks with the customers and enjoying every minute of it, when Sadie said, 'Oh, there's old Sarah. Can I go and say hello to her first?'

Mary Ann grabbed her arm just in time. 'I'll come with yer, I haven't seen the old girl for a few weeks.'

Sarah's face was wreathed in smiles when she set eyes on Sadie. 'Hello, girl.'

Sadie put her arms around her and kissed the wrinkled face. 'Where've yer been hiding yerself? I've missed yer.'

Mary Ann prodded her on the shoulder. 'D'yer mind if I get a look in? After all, she is my customer.'

'Oh, no, she's not.' Sadie winked at Sarah. 'She's *my* customer.'

'An' I'm the boss an' I say she's not your customer.' Oh, how Mary Ann was going to enjoy saying these words. 'She's yer ruddy landlady!'

The look of shocked surprise on Sadie's face had Sarah worried. Perhaps the girl didn't like the idea of coming to live with her. She'd be very disappointed if that was the case because she and her husband were looking forward to having a youngster in the house. She rubbed a coarse workworn finger down Sadie's cheek. 'That's only if yer want me to be yer landlady, girl, no harm done if yer don't.'

There was a sob in Sadie's voice. 'Want yer, Sarah? I couldn't wish for anyone better. If I had a million people to choose from, it's you I'd pick. Oh, I'm that happy I feel like singin' at the top of me voice and doin' a jig.' She turned to her friend who was watching with a wide grin on her face. 'Mary Ann, I'll love yer for the rest of me life.'

'There's still a long way to go yet, girl, so don't be jumpin' the gun. But as long as you and Sarah are happy with each other, then that's the main thing and we can take it from there. I'll leave you two to talk things through but don't plan on moving in too quick because Sarah's worrying herself sick because she hasn't got a bed in her spare room. There's a wardrobe and chest of drawers, but no bed and no money to buy one. So that's got to be sorted out. But at least yer know yer on yer way, girl, and yer couldn't be going to a nicer home.' Mary Ann had moved back a few steps, intending to set to and help Lizzie, when she thought of something she thought was important. 'By the way, girl, yer can't call Sarah by her first name when yer go to live with her, it wouldn't be respectful. So that's another thing yer've got to sort out.' With that the stall-holder made her way to where Lizzie was trying to serve three customers at the same time.

'Ooh, yer don't know how happy I feel, Sarah ... Oh heck, I can't call yer that any more.' Sadie was so excited she didn't know whether she was on her head or her heels. A home with this lovely old lady was beyond her wildest dreams. 'Yer won't be annoyed if I ask yer something, will yer? Yer can always say no and I won't mind, honest.'

'You ask away, girl, an' if I don't like what yer askin' I'll tell yer to sod off.' But the smile on the lined face belied her words. 'Go 'ed, out with it.'

'Would yer let me call yer Grandma?' Sadie got the words out quickly before she lost her nerve. This was turning out to be the very best day of her life, and if she could adopt a grandma and grandad, be a member of a real family, she'd be in her seventh heaven. 'Yer see, I haven't got any grandparents and I've always felt sad about that.' The old lady's silence made Sadie think she'd overstepped the mark. 'I'm sorry, I shouldn't have asked that. It was cheeky of me when yer don't really know anything about me. And I suppose yer've got a lot of grandchildren of yer own without me trying to worm me way in.'

There was a trace of sadness in the tired grey eyes. 'No, girl, there's only me and my old man. We did have two children, both boys, but we lost them when they were very young. Joey was only six when he died and Johnny was eight. They were both born with a heart defect and as I said they both died very young. Broke our hearts it did and we've never really got over it. But life must go on, girl, whether we like it or not. We often talk about them, and how different our lives would have been if they'd lived. They'd have been in their late fifties now, so if God had spared them we'd have great-grandchildren.'

Sadie was at a loss. She felt like kicking herself for being so stupid and so childishly selfish. She'd been offered so much in the last hour, more than she'd hoped for – why hadn't she been satisfied with that? 'I am so sorry, I didn't know. If I had I wouldn't have been so thoughtless.'

'It wasn't your fault, girl, how were yer to know? And I'd be tickled pink if yer'd call me Grandma; it would do me old heart a power of good. And as for my feller, Joe, he'd be dead chuffed to have a pretty thing like you call him Grandad.' Sarah grinned. 'I can't wait to see his face when he claps eyes on yer. And God help his cronies in the pub when he goes for his nightly glass of bitter 'cos there'll be no stoppin' him; he'll talk the bleedin' legs off them. Yer see, girl, it's a long time since he had anything to brag about.'

'Ooh, I hope he likes me, Sarah.' Sadie clapped a hand over her mouth. 'If Mary Ann had heard that I'd have got a clip around the ears for not being respectful to yer. But I feel a lot more for yer than respect, and I'm not just saying it to get in yer good books. I fell in love with yer the first time I served yer. D'yer remember?'

'Yes, girl, I remember. But I remember the second time best, when yer gave me a kiss and a cuddle. That was when my feller first got to hear about yer. He asked if he'd get the same if he came down, but I told him yer wouldn't want to kiss a face that's as rough as an emery board. And he's already been warned that if yer do come to us, he's got to keep his false teeth in his mouth and not in a flamin' cup.'

'Oh, Grandma!' Sadie closed her eyes to relish that one word that made her feel part of a family. 'Yer shouldn't have said that to him – he'll hate the sight of me before he's even set eyes on me.'

'No he won't, sweetheart. He's looking forward to yer comin'. He'll be sittin' at home now, in his rocking chair, puffing away at his old pipe and waitin' for me to come back and tell him it's all fixed up.'

'I can't wait to meet him.' Sadie felt delirious with excitement and happiness. 'I hope it won't be too long before I can come to yer.'

'Mary Ann said yer've got things to sort out first, girl, so have a little patience. Rome wasn't built in a day, yer know.'

'I don't want to live in Rome, Grandma.' There it was again, that feeling of belonging, 'I want to live with you and Grandad.'

'Yer've got a good friend in Mary Ann – she'll help yer get yer affairs in order. And see if she'll bring yer to the house one night, so yer can see it for yerself before yer make the break. Me home's nothing posh, but it's comfortable. And the spare bedroom's not a bad size, except that it's short of a bed at the moment.'

'Grandma, I'll sleep on the clothes-line if it comes to the push.'

'It'll never come to that, girl, not when I've got me old horse-hair couch.' Sarah giggled. 'Many's the night I've slept on it to get away from my feller's snores. Honest to God, he makes enough noise to wake the dead.'

'I bet he's lovely, just like you are, and I can't wait to meet him.' Sadie turned to see Mary Ann coping with several customers, all wanting to be served first. 'I'd better give Mary Ann a hand, she's rushed off her feet. I'll see yer next week an' let yer know how I'm getting on, but I am definitely coming to live with yer, so don't you dare let the room to anyone else.'

'No chance of that, girl. I've never had a lodger in me life, and I wouldn't be havin' one now if Mary Ann hadn't told me you were lookin' for somewhere.'

'I'll see yer next week, Grandma.' Sadie leaned across and kissed her on each cheek. 'That's two for good luck. One for you and the other for your feller . . . me brand new grandad.'

It was five o'clock before Mary Ann had any time to spare for serious talking. Sadie was meeting Geoff at seven but she'd have to go straight from the market if it came to the push, because she'd never make that long walk home and then the longer walk to Everton Valley. And decisions about her future life were more important than worrying about what she looked like to go to the flicks or a dance.

Mary Ann kicked her shoe off and rubbed the sole of her foot. 'Me feet are killing me and me bleedin' corn's giving me gyp. I'll be glad to get home and steep them in a bucket of water.'

Sadie was busy gathering clothes together ready for closing the stall for the night. She turned and grinned at the pained expression on her friend's face. 'Yer not leaving here tonight, Mary Ann, until yer've sorted my life out! After all, I'm more important than your feet.'

'Don't start gettin' cocky with me, girl, or I'll throw this bleedin' shoe at yer.' But Mary Ann's thoughts were kinder than her words. She'd never have got through the last couple of hours without Sadie's help; it had been one of the busiest days she'd ever known. It was either that or she was getting older and couldn't take the pace like she used to. Then she pulled a face and shook her head. No, I'm not admitting to getting older so it's simply been a very busy day.

Mary Ann slipped her foot into her shoe and groaned at the pain from the corn on her little toe. 'Now, girl, while we're clearing this lot, let's get you sorted at the same time. Now I understand how urgent it is that yer get out of that home of yours, and I'm happy in me mind about you and old Sarah, 'cos yer can tell by just lookin' at the pair of yer that yer get on like a house on fire, I'll get me thinkin' cap on.' She shook out a large sheet and laid it flat on the ground, and as she was talking she was throwing clothes onto the sheet. 'D'yer have to give one week's notice in, or two?'

'I'm not sure. We work a week in hand, so I suppose it's a week.'

'Well, don't give yer notice in until we work out how yer going to get a bed. Yer'll have to buy it yerself 'cos old Sarah certainly can't afford to.'

'How much will it cost? The Saturday I leave, I'll have me week in hand money as well as me wages, so I'll be picking up sixteen and six. I'll have all that money to meself because I won't be goin' home that day, I'll be going straight to me Grandma's.'

Mary Ann grinned. 'That sounds nice, girl, and yer had a smile on yer face when yer said it.' She stood at one end of the sheet and pointed to the other. 'Pass that corner over to me, there's a good girl, and when I knot these two corners yer can pass me the other.' When the four corners were tied, the stall-holder heaved the heavy bundle to one side. 'That's one lot out of the way, now for another.'

Sadie had never before stayed late enough to see how Mary Ann cleared away and she was amazed that all the clothes were bundled up together. 'Don't yer keep the tuppenny with a hole separate from the thruppenny without a hole?'

'Nah! I couldn't be arsed with all that messing – I'd be here until bleedin' midnight.'

Sadie thought Mary Ann was making more work for herself by doing that, but it was none of her business. 'Back to the bed. I'll have sixteen and six wages to come, and I've got five bob saved up now. That should be enough, shouldn't it?'

'Yer'll not get a decent second-hand bed under thirty bob, girl, unless yer don't mind the mattress bein' full of stains.'

Sadie shivered. 'Ugh, I couldn't sleep on a dirty bed. The one I sleep on now is only a canvas camp bed, but at least no one's ever slept in it but me so I know it's clean. In fact, it's probably the cleanest thing in our house. Me mam got it off the club woman that used to call every week and I remember the poor woman had a terrible time getting the money for it.'

'This isn't solving the problem of where yer gettin' the money from for a bed, does it?' Mary Ann had cleared one table and moved to another. 'Another yer don't seem to have taken into consideration is that yer'll have to pay Sarah out of that money. She'll need the money in advance to buy food for yer, and yer'll need to have some in hand in case yer don't get a job right away.' Mary Ann knew she was dashing the girl's hopes but it was best she knew what was ahead of her. 'Even if yer did get one, and started the Monday after yer left this job, yer'd still have to work a week in hand.'

Sadie's sigh was deep. 'I'm not goin' to make it, am I? I must be stupid not to have thought of all these things. I want me head testing, thinking it was going to be so easy, all plain sailing.'

'Oh, come on, girl, don't be bleedin' lookin' on the black side. Make up yer mind yer'll do it and yer will do, even if it does take a bit longer. A few more weeks isn't going to kill yer.'

'I *will* do it, Mary Ann – I'm determined. I get sixpence a week off Harry, the boy next door, and sixpence a week off Geoff. That only brings me money up to two shillings a week, so I need to get more off them or find a couple more boyfriends.'

There was a look of concern on Mary Ann's face. 'You take money off boys? I hope yer don't do anything yer shouldn't be doing.'

'Don't worry about that; no boy will ever get off me what you're thinking. I can give yer me solemn promise on that. Harry's sixpence started off as a joke. He found me crying in the entry that day me dad lost all his money on the horses and I didn't get me pocket money. He wanted to give me sixpence so I could meet Brenda, but I wouldn't take it off him. So he offered to buy a kiss off me for the sixpence. I was desperate because I didn't want to let me mate down, and I agreed. So for all these weeks Harry has given me sixpence and I've given him two kisses in return. Never once has he asked for more than those kisses, or has he tried to take more.'

'He must be sweet on yer to do that, girl. Sounds like a nice lad to me.'

'Even if he was sweet on me, his mother most certainly isn't. She'd do her nut if she thought her son was associating with one of the awful Wilsons. So apart from the one night, on me birthday, I've never been out with him. I meet him in the park, tell him me troubles, give him his kiss and that's it. And Geoff's sixpence is almost as innocent. I told him I had no money for the tram fare to meet him at Everton Valley, so he gave it to me. He asked why he couldn't pick me up from home and I had to lie and say it was because me parents were difficult. He'd only have to see the outside of our house and I wouldn't see his heels for dust.' Sadie put her face close to her friend's and locked eyes with her. 'And every word of that is the truth, Mary Ann, I swear.'

Mary Ann was thinking that you learn something every day. This young girl had had to claw her way out of a cesspit and had come out with honour. 'I believe yer, girl, and I admire yer for telling me all this. What I want to know now is, where does this Geoff fit into it? Are yer serious about him?'

Sadie gave a very definite shake of her head. 'He's a nice bloke, is Geoff, a real gentleman. But I don't want to be serious with any boy. Me dad has put me off men for life.'

'Oh, dear, what a terrible thing for a young girl to say. You just wait until the right one comes along and yer'll soon change yer tune.'

'I don't want to, Mary Ann! I don't want to get too close to anyone in case they turn out like me dad and I end up like me mam. Oh, I'll go out with boys and I'll use them to get enough money to move from a hell on earth to a nice home. But I won't steal the money from them and I won't lead them on to think they're going to get something they're not. I'll be straight with them all along the line, so they have a choice.'

Mary Ann's heart was heavy. The father and mother of this girl had a lot to answer for. And she hoped that some day they'd be made to pay for their sins.

Chapter Twelve

Sadie anchored a lock of hair behind her ear as she hurried down Everton Brow. She'd tidied herself up as best she could but she still felt grubby. It was amazing how dirty your hands could get handling money. Tony from the shoe stall brought water with him every day which he boiled on a primus stove to keep him going in cups of tea, and he'd given her the drop he had left so she could wipe her face over with a piece of rag. He said she looked good enough to him, so did Mary Ann, but Sadie wasn't happy with her appearance. She wasn't very happy thinking about her financial situation, either. At the rate she was saving now it would be months before she had enough for what she wanted, and the thought of those long months spent suffering verbal abuse from her parents and sister filled her with despair. She'd racked her brains thinking of ways to make money, but ended up none the wiser. The only two people who could help her were Harry and Geoff, and her mind balked at the idea of asking them for more than they were giving now. She had come up with several ideas on how to get money out of them but didn't think she'd have the nerve to go through with it when it came to the push. They were two nice blokes who had been good to her and it wouldn't be fair to play a dirty trick on them.

As Sadie neared Everton Valley her thoughts raced. She couldn't bear to live at home much longer; she'd rather walk the streets. It was bad enough living in filth and having foul language bawled at you, but having to witness the blatant wickedness of her parents and sister was more than she could bear. They didn't even try to hide what they were doing from her or the other children. In fact, Dot seemed to be proud of her new status, strutting around and lording it over everyone like an old married woman of forty, instead of a fourteen-year-old girl.

Sadie spotted Geoff leaning against the wall of the pub and waved. He would give her the money if she explained why she wanted it, same as Harry would. But how could she explain? How would she find the right words without feeling humiliated and ashamed?

'Hello, love.' Geoff wore a broad smile as he took her hand. 'I was beginning to think I'd been stood up.'

'I wouldn't do that to yer. If I didn't want to go out with yer at least I'd have the decency to come and tell yer.'

'Yer face is red, have yer been running?'

Geoff didn't hear Sadie sigh as she told herself that if she was going to lie then now was the time to start. 'I went into town, window shopping, and didn't realise how late it was. I'm sorry if yer've been waiting long.'

'That's all right, we're only going to the Astoria so there's no panic.' Geoff cupped her elbow as they crossed the main road and when her high heel got caught in the tram lines he tightened his grip to save her from tripping up. 'How you girls wear those blinkin' high heels I'll never know. It's a wonder yer don't fall and break yer neck.'

'Oh, come on, now. Yer must admit a girl looks better in high heels than flat ones.'

'You'd look nice in anything, Sadie – even a sack and a pair of clogs.'

'I saw something in town today that I'd look nice in.' Sadie was glad he wasn't looking into her face to see the tell-tale blush. She was getting a dab hand at lying, but she didn't like it. Still, this was a means to an end. 'It was in Etam's window and I must have stood for half-an-hour looking at it with me tongue hangin' out.'

Geoff released his hold to reach into his pocket for money. 'Oh, aye, what was it?'

Don't look at me, Geoff, Sadie said silently, please don't look at me. 'It was a lovely pink underskirt with white lace around the bottom.' It was the only thing she could think of that, if her scheme worked, he wouldn't ask to see. 'I went all dreamy just lookin' at it.'

Geoff left her to go to the ticket kiosk, and when he came back he asked, 'Why didn't yer mug yerself?'

'Mug meself on my money? It cost two and eleven!'

They entered the darkness of the picture house and followed the usherette's torch to seats on the back row. When they were settled, Geoff whispered, 'I'll mug yer to it.'

'Oh, I couldn't let yer do that!' I'm a hypocrite and I'll never go to heaven when I die, Sadie was telling herself when a picture of old Sarah flashed before her eyes. She needed that old lady more than she'd ever needed anyone. Needed the warmth, love, respect and decency. 'No, I couldn't let yer do that.'

'Don't be daft. What's wrong with a feller buying a present for his girlfriend?'

'I haven't known yer long enough to be yer girlfriend. Yer might get fed up with me in a week or two and yer'd have wasted yer money.'

'I won't get fed up with yer, Sadie. It's more likely the other way around. Let me buy it for yer, go on – please?'

Sadie appeared to be considering. 'I'll borrow the money off yer and pay it back when I've saved it up. How about that?'

'Will I heckerslike take money back off yer. What sort of a bloke d'yer think I am? Buy me girlfriend a present and then take the money off her! I may be many things, Sadie, but tight-fisted is not one of them.'

'I know yer not tight, Geoff. I wouldn't have said it if I'd known yer were going to be insulted. I'll let yer buy me the underskirt with pleasure and I thank yer kindly, sir.'

With a smile of pleasure and a sigh of contentment, Geoff settled back in his seat and put his arm across Sadie's shoulders. 'You are my girl, aren't yer, Sadie?'

'Yer only boyfriend I've got, Geoff, but I am only sixteen.' Sadie might lie to him but she wasn't going to lead him down the garden path as well. 'I'm a bit young to be gettin' too serious.'

'I can wait.' Geoff gave her shoulder a gentle squeeze. 'In a year and four months I'll be out of me time and you'll be seventeen and a half. That's not too young to get serious, is it?'

Sadie said the only thing she could say. 'No, that's not too young, Geoff.'

And when they were saying good night, there was more warmth than usual in Sadie's kiss as she tried to make amends for her deception.

Harry was waiting by the park gates for Sadie on the Sunday night. 'There's a courting couple in our speck – let's walk over to the other side.'

As they walked, arms straight by their sides, he glanced at her. 'Did yer go out with that Geoff feller yesterday?'

Sadie nodded. 'We went to the Astoria.'

'I usually see yer going out on a Saturday night, but I didn't see yer last night.' Harry noticed an empty spot between the trees and walked her towards it. His jealousy was so strong it was like a knife being twisted in his heart. 'Were yer out with him all day?'

Sadie shook her head. 'No, I went into town on me own to get away from the house. I needed cheering up so I went window shopping.' She tilted her head and pulled a face. 'I should have known that would make me more miserable. Seeing nice things that I know I'll never be able to afford.'

'You will one day, Sadie, I know yer will.' He was filled with hatred for the family who were not only destroying Sadie's life but his as well. But for them there would be no need to hide in bushes for a stolen few minutes. He could have claimed her for his own, and this Geoff bloke wouldn't be on the scene. With a sigh, he reached for her and put his hands on her waist. 'Tell me what yer saw in town. Did yer go with yer mate, Brenda?'

'Harry, I'm miserable enough without going out with Brenda. She's being a real pain in the neck these days and I'm better off on me own. I just walked around TJ's first, then wandered down to Church Street looking into every shop window.' I should have gone in to be an actress, Sadie thought. I'm getting so good at telling lies I'll be believing them meself soon. 'I spent so long looking in Etam's window it's a wonder they didn't come out and chase me.'

'Why, what caught yer eye?'

'A pink underskirt with white lace around the bottom. It was really beautiful and I fell in love with it.'

'Was it very expensive?'

'Not for some people perhaps, but for me two and eleven is out of the question. A sixpenny one from a second-hand stall at the market is more up my street.' Sadie knew what would come now and she was hating herself even before Harry spoke.

'I'll buy it for yer. I never take yer out, and there's no good beating about the bush because we both know why I don't take yer out. I feel a coward for not standing up to me mam, but yer must admit that where your family's concerned, most mothers would feel the same. So let me make it up to yer by buying yer that underskirt. You'd be doing me a favour because I want to do something to make you happy.'

'I don't deserve a friend like you, Harry, yer know that, don't yer? I've done nothing but take off yer and give yer nothing in return. I can't even say I'll buy you anything to make up for it 'cos I'd only be tellin' lies.' She laid her head on his chest so she wouldn't have to meet his eyes. 'I do tell lies, Harry, I'm sorry to say. They're not big whopping lies that will do anyone any harm or get them into trouble, but I'm not proud of meself. It's just that I've made up me mind to get out of that hell-hole as soon as I can, and I don't care what I have to do to make it happen.'

When Sadie raised her head and looked into his deep brown eyes, it was on her lips to blurt out that she'd be gone in a few weeks. But she remembered Mary Ann's warning about cutting all her ties with home. She'd shed a few tears in bed last night over that. The idea of walking away from her two brothers and Ellen and the baby, without saying goodbye, didn't sit well on her conscience. Only the thought that she could do more for them if she was away from home than she ever could if she stayed, comforted her. On the paltry shilling a week she couldn't keep herself, let alone do anything to put food in their tummies and clothes on their back. With a bit of luck she might get a decent job and be able to buy clothes for them off Mary Ann. She'd have a problem getting the clothes to them but she'd manage it somehow.

Lying in the darkness of her bedroom, the silence broken only by the breathing of her brothers and sisters, Sadie's mind had turned to Harry. She would miss him more than she'd miss anyone because he was always so kind and treated her with respect. She hoped he wouldn't think too badly of her when he found she had gone without so much as a goodbye. Perhaps when she was settled she could contact him and tell him the reason. Then a voice in her head had told her he'd be better off without her. If she wasn't around he wouldn't be able to see her and that meant he wouldn't have to live with the fear of his mam finding out they were friends.

'Hey, Sadie.' Harry put a finger under her chin and raised her face. 'Come back into the land of the living. You were miles away.'

'It's so quiet and peaceful here, I was daydreaming. Yer can't think straight in our house – it's always like Bedlam.'

'I feel like that meself at the moment, so let me daydream with yer. I bet yer mind was on that thingummybob yer saw in the shop window.'

Sadie smiled. 'Something like that. Anyway, can I have me first smackeroo, please?'

'With pleasure. I thought yer were never goin' to ask.'

'A girl shouldn't have to ask for a kiss – it's not ladylike.'

'Shut up, Sadie Wilson, and take a deep breath before yer pucker yer lips ready for one of me famous smackeroos. And I'm warning yer to hang on tight because you an' me are goin' to fly to the moon and back.'

Just before Harry covered her lips with his, Sadie asked, 'Do we have to come back? Couldn't we stay on the moon?'

Harry backed off a fraction. 'You interrupted me there, Sadie Wilson – just when I was gettin' in me stride, as well. So yer not counting that as a kiss 'cos that would be cheating.' He dropped his head back so he could look into her face. 'Now, to answer yer question, when we get up there we'll ask the man in the moon if he's got any rooms to let. Would yer live with me on the moon if we got the chance, Sadie?'

Sadie nodded. 'Yes, I would, Harry.'

Her answer had Harry growing ten feet tall. Unknown to him, his thoughts were identical to Sadie's. Up there they wouldn't have to hide in bushes, they'd be free to do as they wished. 'I'd have to come down now and again, like, to see me family and pay me pools money. Hey, there's a thing! What if I came up on Vernons and won a thousand pounds? You and me could elope to Gretna Green.'

Sadie's brow furrowed. 'Where's Gretna Green?'

'Oh, don't tell me yer've never heard of it? It's a place in Scotland where couples run off to, to get married when their families won't give their consent.'

'Are yer goin' to give me a lesson on general knowledge, Harry, or a kiss?'

'I think a lesson on general knowledge, Sadie, 'cos it would stand yer in good stead for the rest of yer life.' Harry's dimples deepened when he roared with laughter. 'I only know about Gretna Green because one of me mates at work went up there to get married. He lived to regret it though, 'cos when he got back and brought his new wife to his house, his mam chased him up the street, belting him with the sweeping brush. Knocked hell out of him, she did.'

Sadie began to shake with laughter as she pictured the scene. 'What happened?'

'Nothing . . . his mam saw to that. She sent the girl back to her own house and made them wait until they could be married by a priest, "proper like", in church. Me mate never lived it down; he still gets his leg pulled soft over it.'

'Ah, that's cruel to make fun of him. I've a good mind to count that nearly kiss as a full one for bein' so mean to him.'

'I'll tell yer what I'll do to get back in yer good books.' Harry nodded his head while his face wore a serious expression. 'I'll go an' buy his mam a new sweepin' brush, 'cos she broke her one over his head. She's got to bend double now to brush the floor.'

Sadie spluttered with laughter. 'Harry Young, yer in a very funny frame of mind tonight, aren't yer? I bet yer only doin' it so I won't have time to give yer earache with all me moanin' and groanin'.'

'Oh, I've got a much nicer way of shutting you up, Sadie Wilson. Hang on to yer hat 'cos we're off to the moon.'

Brenda was very quiet all Monday morning, barely opening her mouth. When Sadie asked if she felt all right, she said her tummy was a bit off and that's all her friend could get out of her until the bell sounded for their dinner-break.

'I want to have a word with Alec, Sadie, so would you walk on ahead and get in the queue at the chippy?'

'Oh, so that's why yer've got a face on yer like a wet week. Yer've had a row with his lordship.'

'That's where yer wrong, see.' Brenda put her tongue out. 'We haven't had no row.'

'Well, there's something up, Brenda, it's stickin' out a flamin' mile! If he's the one who's making yer so miserable, for heaven's sake pack him in.'

'I'm not miserable, Sadie Wilson,' Brenda snapped. 'Anyway, it's none of your business.'

'Okay, don't bite me flippin' head off. If you want to be miserable then get on with it, but don't expect any sympathy from me.'

Alec was in his usual place, arrogance written all over him. Brenda's welcome to him, Sadie thought as she hurried past. I'm surprised it's lasted so long because she's not the type of girl he usually goes for.

'Sadie, hang on a minute.'

Sadie turned to see Bobby Bennett running after her. 'Hello, Bobby. Goin' to the chippy, are yer?'

Bobby, shy at the best of times, blushed the colour of beetroot. 'No, me mam does carry-out for me.'

'Oh, what can I do for yer then?'

'I was wonderin' if yer'd come out with me one night.' Bobby scraped the ground with the heel of his shoe. 'We could go to the pictures.'

Sadie said the first thing that came into her head. 'Alec's put you up to this, hasn't he?'

'No, honest. I've been wantin' to ask yer since yer fell out with him, but I didn't have the nerve.'

'Does he know yer askin' me now? Is that why he's got that ruddy smirk on his face?'

'Yeah, I told him I was askin' yer.' Bobby's eyes went to the ground. 'He said yer'd laugh at me an' tell me to get lost.'

'Oh, he did, did he? Well, you tell him from me that I think yer more of a man than he'll ever be. I don't know why yer bother bein' friends with him, Bobby, he's always belittling yer in front of people.'

'He's not the only one – I'm always gettin' the mickey taken out of me. I mean, let's face it, Sadie, I'm not much cop, am I?'

Sadie looked at him and her heart filled with sympathy. He wasn't much taller than her, he was as thin as a rake and his ginger hair was sticking out like spikes. His complexion had improved though – he didn't have nearly as many spots as before. 'It's not what yer look like on the outside, Bobby, it's what's inside that counts. And I think yer a hundred times nicer than the queer feller over there.'

'But yer don't want to go out with me?' Bobby said. 'Don't worry, Sadie, I'm used to gettin' knocked back and I should have known a girl with your looks wouldn't want to be bothered with me. What I'll never understand is why Alec packed yer in. He must want his brains testing.'

'Is that what he told yer, Bobby, that he packed me in?'

Bobby shrugged his thin shoulders. 'He told everyone, Sadie, not only me.'

'And everyone believed him, I suppose?' Sadie tutted. Well, there was one way of killing two birds with one stone. She could make Bobby happy by going to the pictures with him, and at the same time give him the opportunity of getting one over on Alec. The arrogant so-and-so would be laughing on the other side of his face when the tables were turned on him. The great Alec Gleeson made a fool of by little Bobby Bennett. And she'd give Bobby enough ammunition to make the big-head the laughing stock of the whole factory. She'd put the record straight once and for all, and have her revenge for the tales he'd spread about her.

'I'll go to the pictures with yer, Bobby. It'll have to be tomorrow night or Thursday because I've got dates on the other nights.'

Bobby's face showed surprise, relief and happiness. 'Oh, thanks, Sadie!' He'd been dreading the sound of Alec's laughter when he went back and said he'd been turned down. 'Tomorrow night will be fine with me. Where would yer like to go?'

'You choose, Bobby, and yer can tell me tomorrow dinner-time. And if yer short of money don't worry, I don't mind goin' in the cheap specks.'

'I'm all right for money, Sadie, I never go anywhere to spend it.' Bobby thought his heart would burst with pride. The prettiest girl in the factory going out with him – well, that was a turn-up for the books. 'We'll go wherever you want to go, money no object.'

Sadie smiled at him, thinking how different he looked when he was happy. If he would only get away from Alec his confidence would grow. His so-called friend only used him because he was so small and thin he made Alec look like a big he-man. 'I'll see yer here tomorrow dinner-time and we'll make arrangements.'

Bobby looked as though he'd lost a tanner and found half-a-crown. 'Thanks, Sadie.'

'Don't mention it, sunshine, it'll be my pleasure.' Sadie was smiling as she made haste to the chippy. Oh, how she'd like to see the look on smart Alec's face when he heard Bobby's news. They say every dog has its day – well, today was hers and Bobby's. And Wednesday would be better still when the whole factory found out how she'd left him doubled up in pain after he'd gone too far with his roving hands.

Sadie was next to be served when Brenda came up beside her. 'Don't get any for me, Sadie, me tummy's really upset.'

'Go and see the nurse when we get back. She can give yer something to settle it down – some of that white stuff that tastes like spearmint.'

Brenda didn't like that idea. 'No, I'll be all right by tomorrow. Me mam said I've got a cold on me tummy.'

Outside the chip shop, Sadie made a hole in the newspaper and offered it to her workmate. 'Are yer sure yer don't want any?'

Brenda wrinkled her nose as the smell invaded her nostrils. 'No, ta, I'll keep me tummy empty for today, see if that helps.'

'They're not half hot.' Sadie pulled a chip out between two fingers and wafted it in the air. 'I'll burn me tongue off if I'm not careful.'

There was a strange look on Brenda's face as her eyes slid sideways. 'What did that drip Bobby Bennett want yer for?'

'Ay, Brenda, get yer eyes tested, sunshine, 'cos you were the one talkin' to the biggest drip walking on God's earth. Bobby is a gentleman compared with Alec. And that's why I've promised to go to the pictures with him tomorrow night.'

Brenda stopped dead in her tracks. 'Yer pullin' me leg, Sadie Wilson. You'd never go out with *him*.'

'I'm not goin' to argue with yer, Bren, 'cos yer like a bear with a sore head these days. So just wait until tomorrow and find out whether I'm pullin' yer leg or not.'

'Ugh, I wouldn't let him do things to me, he's all pimples and blackheads.'

A chip was halfway to Sadie's mouth when she asked, 'What's all this talk about fellers doin' things to yer? It's all yer seem to have on yer mind these days. What sort of things wouldn't yer let Bobby do to yer?'

'You know what I'm talkin' about, Sadie. Yer used to let Alec do it to yer.'

'Oh, aye? And precisely what did I let Alec do to me? Refresh me memory, Brenda.'

'Yer know quite well what it was, Sadie, yer only bein' funny. But I know yer used to let him put his . . . er . . . his . . . thingy between yer legs.'

Sadie gasped as every emotion it was possible to feel sent her head reeling. If this was what was going around the factory, what must everyone think of her? 'A cheap tart' were the words that sprang to her mind. 'He told yer that, Brenda?'

Brenda nodded, a doleful expression on her face. 'Yeah, every time yer went out.'

Oh, my God! If Alec had told Brenda that, he'd probably have told Bobby and all his cronies the same story, bragging about his conquest. 'I'll break his bloody neck for him!' Sadie seldom swore. She'd watched her mother one day, her face twisted into ugliness as she shouted abuse and obscenities at nine-year-old Les. On that day Sadie had vowed never to lower herself to her mother's standards. But she was so angry right at that moment she felt like shouting out every bad word she could think of. Grinding the words out through clenched teeth, she said, 'Brenda, your dear boyfriend never even got his hand between me legs, never mind anythin' else. He's a dirty rotten liar and I'll find some way of making him pay for spreadin' tales about me.' Sadie was so filled with rage she didn't at first notice the pallor of her workmate's face. When she did, the truth hit her like a blow between the eyes. 'Oh Bren, yer haven't, have yer?'

'Well, he told me you did!' Brenda was near to tears as she tried to excuse her behaviour. 'He told me all the girls did and I'd never get a boyfriend if I didn't.' Her eyes were pleading. 'I knew it was wrong but he made it sound like I was a big cry-baby.'

Sadie's mind was racing. How long had Brenda been going out with Alec? It must be six or seven weeks. Oh, dear God, no! 'Brenda, yer do know what can happen when yer do the things you've been doing, don't yer? Yer can get in the family way.' Sadie felt like shaking her friend for not having listened to her, but that wouldn't help. 'Do yer really think yer've got a cold on your tummy, or could yer be pregnant?'

'I don't know!' Brenda wailed. 'I'm too frightened to ask anyone. Me monthly should have started last week and it hasn't. Me mam'll kill me when she finds out what I've been doing. She'll be so ashamed of me.'

As Sadie twisted the chip paper into a corkscrew she was wishing it was Alec's neck. He'd certainly picked his mark with Brenda, in-experienced in the wiles of men like him. He'd fed her a load of lies and must have been laughing himself sick when she fell for them. 'Don't say anythin' to her, just wait and see what happens. I know it's easy for me to talk, I'm not the one in trouble, but don't start worrying yer mam until yer've got to. One thing yer've got to do is keep away from Alec. I told yer he was no good for yer. If yer'd listened to me in the first place yer wouldn't be in this mess now.'

'I thought yer were tellin' me that because yer were jealous of me goin' out with him. That's what he told me and I was daft enough to believe him.'

'Yer've been daft about a lot of things, Brenda, but it's a bit late in the day for regrets 'cos yer can't turn the clock back.' Sadie linked her arm through her friend's and gave it a squeeze. 'Give it another week or two before doing anything; it might be a false alarm.' They were passing through the factory gates when she asked, 'Does Alec know yer worried?'

'Oh no, I couldn't tell him! I wouldn't know what to say!'

'No, well, keep it to yerself for a while. And I think I may be wrong in telling yer not to go out with him again. Perhaps yer should keep on seeing him until yer know for sure that yer not in the family way. But for God's sake, stop him from messing around with yer.'

'Don't tell Bobby Bennett, will yer, Sadie?' Brenda begged. 'I don't want everyone talking about me behind me back.'

'Scout's honour, Bren, I won't mention yer name to Bobby. I will be mentioning Alec's though, I've got a score to settle with him.' Sadie withdrew her arm as they neared the packing-room door. 'Now, put a smile on yer face and keep it there for the rest of the day. I know how worried yer are but goin' around looking like a wet week isn't going to help you or anyone else.' She patted her friend's backside when they reached their bench. 'I'm the one who's got to look at yer clock all day and yer look much prettier when yer smile.'

Sadie went upstairs to change and she'd just reached the landing when she remembered she'd left her handbag at the side of her chair. She tripped lightly down the stairs and opened the living-room door just in time to see Dot pick the bag up and press the clasp back. 'Oh, no you don't!' Sadie dashed forward and grabbed the bag. 'Don't you ever dare to touch anything belonging to me.'

Dot looked defiant. 'I was only lookin' to see if yer had a penny to spare. Yer go out every night and yer must be gettin' paid for by the fellers yer go out with, so it wouldn't hurt yer to pass a few bleedin' coppers over.'

Sadie was clutching the bag with one hand and with her other she seized a lock of her sister's greasy black hair. 'If you want money, then get yerself a job and earn it, like I have to. Don't be stealing it from me like a common thief.'

George Wilson lowered the *Echo*. 'Don't you talk to yer sister like that, and let go of her bleedin' hair before I belt yer one. She was only after a penny, for Christ's sake.'

Sadie yanked on Dot's hair before releasing her hold. 'If it's only a penny she wants, why don't you give it to her? After all, it's you she's nice to, so you put yer hand in yer pocket because I'm certainly not. You were the one who said she didn't have to go to work, so it's only right you should pay her wages.'

'Don't let her talk to yer like that, Dad.' Dot was rubbing vigorously at her sore scalp. 'Take yer belt to her, the stuck-up bleedin' bitch.'

George's eyes went from one to the other. In his sober moments he regretted ever letting Dot get a hold over him. In his drunken lecherous moments he preferred her youth to his wife's now sagging breasts and loose flesh. But of his two daughters he feared Sadie the most. If she went around spouting her mouth off, it would be jail for him. And he had no doubt that, pushed far enough, she wouldn't hesitate to land him in trouble. He rustled the paper. 'I'll give yer a bleedin' penny; it's not worth all the flamin' hassle.'

'Ah, ay, Dad!' Dot was fully expecting her father to stick up for her and wasn't a bit happy about the way things had gone. 'Take yer belt to her, go on!'

'Shut up and let me get on with me readin',' George grunted, keeping his head down. 'Bleedin' kids, should all be drowned at birth.'

Sadie wasn't happy with the outcome either. If she hadn't come downstairs when she did, her own sister would have stolen from her. And for that she should be punished. So she grabbed a lock of the greasy hair again and gave a hefty yank. 'That's for goin' in me bag.' She gave another yank. 'And that's for being so nice to your father.' Sadie put emphasis on the words *your father*. Because never again would she admit to him being hers.

When Sadie made the safety of the bedroom she began to shake all over. One minute later getting down those stairs and Dot would have seen the little bag containing the eleven shillings she'd saved. Money that she'd worked for and lied for. It would have all been taken off her – of that she had no doubt. Nor did she doubt that every penny of it would have been spent over the bar at the pub on the corner. And all her scheming and lies would have been in vain. She'd be further away from escape than she'd been months ago.

Sadie sat on the side of the bed feeling sick at how near she'd come to her dreams being shattered. She'd have to do something with the money. It wasn't safe to keep it in her bag after what had just happened, and there was nowhere in the house to hide it. The only person she could trust, who knew what the money was for, was Mary Ann. So she'd take it to the market with her on Saturday and ask her friend to mind it for her. Until then she'd have to guard it with her life.

Chapter Thirteen

'Shall we go for a walk instead of sittin' in the pictures?' Sadie asked when she met up with Bobby. 'It's such a nice night, it's a shame to spend it inside.' She smiled into his face, making him go weak in the knees. 'The truth is, I was at the pictures last night and yer can have too much of a good thing.'

Bobby was so delirious he didn't care where they went. Sadie looked lovely and he'd be quite happy to stand in the one spot all night just gazing at her. 'Whatever yer want, Sadie, yer the boss.'

'Right,' Sadie took his arm and he thought his legs were going to buckle under him. 'We'll walk into town, sit in St John's Gardens for a while to rest our weary bones, then we'll walk to the Pier Head and watch the ferries coming and going.'

No man could have walked taller than little Bobby Bennett as they strolled along, Sadie's arm linked in his. Nearly every bloke they passed cast admiring glances at her, even the blokes with girls hanging onto their arms. She'd probably never go out with him again, but at least he'd have this one night to remember.

'The nights are pulling in, aren't they, Sadie?' he said timidly. 'In another week or two it'll be dark at eight o'clock.'

'Yeah, the winter will be on us before we know it. I hate the winter 'cos I seem to feel the cold more than most.' Sadie didn't say she never had the right clothes to keep her warm, hardly any covering on her bed or that there was seldom a fire in their grate. 'One of these days I'll get meself a fur coat and I can swank and be warm at the same time.'

'Yer'd look nice in a fur coat, Sadie, like a film star.' Bobby was too shy to add that she didn't need a fur coat to look like a film star. 'When yer ship comes in, eh?'

'Even if me ship did come in I wouldn't look like Constance Bennett did in the film I saw last night. She had this beautiful fur coat on with a big collar to keep her neck and ears warm, and it was right down to her ankles. Ooh, was I jealous, or was I jealous? I'll say I was!'

'I bet yer'd knock spots off Constance Bennett if yer had a coat like that. She probably had thick make-up on her face and false eyelashes. You don't need nothin' like that 'cos yer pretty enough without it.'

'If yer keep that up, Bobby, I'll become so big-headed I won't be able to get in the door.' Sadie tilted her head as she gave his arm a squeeze. 'Ay, it's just struck me, you've got the same name as her! Not related by any chance, are yer?'

'I wasn't going to mention it in case yer thought I was bragging, but yeah, she's me mam's sister,' Bobby said, enjoying the joke. 'But she won't have anything to do with us now she's gone up in the world, thinks we're as common as muck. Me mam said she was always a swank, wouldn't tell anyone she was born in Scotland Road.'

They reached St John's Gardens and Sadie spied an empty bench. 'Come on, let's have a sit-down. High heels might be glamorous but they're no good for walking far.'

When they were seated, Bobby laced his hands in his lap and began to roll his thumbs around each other. 'Sadie, can I ask yer something?'

'As long as it's not for a loan, go ahead.'

'Why did you an' Alec fall out?' Bobby kept his eyes on his rotating thumbs. 'I can't believe he packed yer in, just like that.'

'Alec's story is a load of lies, Bobby, to save his pride. I'll tell yer what really happened and yer have my permission to tell him I told yer. In fact, I'd like yer to spread it around so people don't think I'm what he makes me out to be.'

Sadie began at the beginning, and as her story progressed Bobby's hands became still and he was totally absorbed in what he was being told. He didn't utter a word, but his shaking head told of his disbelief. Sadie finished her tale by repeating her parting shot to Alec as he was doubled up in pain outside the shop doorway. 'And that is the plain, unvarnished truth, Bobby. Right from the horse's mouth.'

'The blackguard! The dirty lying blackguard!' There were other things he felt like calling Alec but he wasn't going to say them in front of a lady. And Sadie *was* a lady. 'Yer should have heard his version of why he packed yer in. He's said some terrible things about yer, Sadie, and he deserves a good hidin' for it.'

'I have heard some of the things he said, Bobby, and that's why I want you to know the truth. And I want yer to spread the word, take him down a peg or two. Yer'll only need to tell one or two men and it'll be round the factory in no time. They say women like to gossip, but men are just as bad when they've got a juicy bit of scandal.' Sadie leaned forward to look into his face. 'Just out of curiosity, if yer believed what he'd told yer about me, why did yer ask me out?'

'Because I didn't really believe him. I've found him out in so many lies I take what he tells me with a pinch of salt. But I never thought he'd stoop so low as to say such terrible things about you. He was so serious when he was telling me, and half-a-dozen other blokes,he must have convinced himself that what he said happened really did happen. I can see now he only believed what he wanted to believe.' Bobby's face looked troubled when he asked, 'I hope yer didn't think that was why I asked yer out? That I was hoping yer were like, you know, like he said yer were.'

'The thought never entered me head, Bobby, an' that's the truth. I'm goin' to tell yer something that I've never told anyone, even Brenda. My father is a rotter through and through, and because of him I'm wary of all men. Oh, I know they're not all like me dad and Alec Gleeson, but I keep me guard up against them just in case. You an' Alec Gleeson are poles apart, an' the sooner yer realise that and get away from him, the sooner yer'll begin to get some confidence in yerself, be your own man. I think yer a smashin' feller, Bobby, and I bet lots of other girls would if yer came out of yer shell. As long as yer hang around with Alec yer'll have an inferiority complex because that's the way he wants it. He can't stand competition – he's always got to be the big cheese.'

'Would yer come out with me again, Sadie?'

Oh dear, Sadie thought, I don't want him getting ideas because I'll be gone in a couple of weeks. But she didn't want to disappoint him either, 'cos he was a nice lad and she'd like to help him become more sure of himself when it came to asking a girl for a date. If going out with her went a little way to achieving that end, she couldn't refuse. 'I've got a boyfriend, Bobby, and I see him three times a week. But it's not serious 'cos I've no intention of settling down at my age, so I'll go out with yer again if yer like.'

'If I like! I'd be over the moon! Didn't yer say yer were doin' nothing on Thursday?'

Sadie grinned at him as she stood up. 'Yer a fast worker, Bobby Bennett! Now get off yer backside and we'll walk down to the Pier Head. We can talk about it as we walk.'

'If yer do come out with me, I want to take yer somewhere. I haven't spent a penny on yer tonight.'

'You will before the night's over, Bobby, 'cos I'm goin' to ask yer for the tram fare home.I haven't brought any money out with me and I couldn't face that long walk home, not in these flamin' shoes.'

'I'll take yer, Sadie. I couldn't let yer make yer own way home late at night.'

'No, yer won't, Bobby. I never let any boy take me home.'

Bobby's mouth drooped. He wouldn't be gettin' a kiss, then. Still, she had promised to go out with him again, which was more than he'd dared hope for. 'Okay, Sadie, I'll give yer the fare and make sure yer get on the right tram.'

* * *

Bobby was alone the next day when the girls came out for their usual walk to the chippy and Brenda's eyes searched the yard for sight of her boyfriend. 'Where's Alec?'

'Yer'll never believe it, Bren, but the funniest thing happened. Alfie Duncan was stretching his arm out to put his overalls on and, blow me, didn't Alec walk straight into his fist! I know I shouldn't laugh but I've never seen anythin' so funny in all me life. If Alfie had been aiming at a target he couldn't have been more spot on. Poor Alec is sporting the biggest black eye yer've ever seen.'

Sadie managed a straight face but couldn't keep the sarcasm out of her voice. 'Aah, the poor lad. Fancy a thing like that happening.'

Brenda gave her a withering look before asking, 'Why hasn't he come out for his dinner, like he always does?'

'Oh, I don't think yer'll be seeing Alec for a few days, not until the swelling and the colouring dies down. He's sittin' by a machine with a cold-water cloth to his face to try an' get the swelling down, but I can't see it meself. I'm running to the shops for him now, to see if there's any cream that would help.' The smile Bobby gave Sadie had more than a hint of mischief in it. 'Don't you girls use somethin' called vanishing cream? I think I'll get him some of that to try.'

'Bobby Bennett, yer as thick as two short planks!' Brenda didn't think the subject was being treated with the sympathy it deserved. 'Yer can't get him vanishing cream – it's only for girls 'cos it smells nice, like scent.'

'Oh, that's no good then. Here was I thinking it would make him vanish.'

Brenda clicked her tongue and rolled her eyes towards heaven. 'I'm not standin' here wasting me time talkin' to someone who's as soft as a brush. I'll walk on and get in the queue.' She started to move away, saying over her shoulder, 'Ask Alec to come out tomorrow will yer, 'cos I've got somethin' to tell him.'

'I'll tell him, but I can't guarantee he'll take any notice,' Bobby called. 'I wouldn't hold me breath if I were you.' He waited until Brenda was out of earshot before confiding to Sadie, 'I've got a feeling Alec will take a few days off sick. Yer know how vain he is – he'll not be wanting anyone to see him with the shiner he's got. Honest to God, Sadie, it's a belter of a black eye, a real corker.'

'Did he really walk into Alfie's fist, or did the fist come to meet him?'

'The fist came to meet him, and what a wallop it was, too! I was havin' a go at Alec over the lies he told about you, and Alfie must have overheard. I didn't even know he was there, I just heard him roar like a bull before his fist connected with Alec's face. And he doesn't half pack a wallop, does Alfie. He was as mad as blazes, told Alec he had a daughter the same age as you and if anyone blackened her name, like Alec did yours, he'd kill the bastard.' Bobby sighed. 'I almost felt sorry for Alec 'cos there was a gang around by this time and everyone witnessed his humiliation. And I can tell yer he didn't get any sympathy from the men; they just looked at him with disgust and walked away. It'll be a long time before me laddo lives that down.'

'I'm glad everyone knows the truth, Bobby, thanks to you. But I didn't mean to be the cause of him getting hurt. I wasn't expectin' that.'

'He got what he deserved, Sadie, so don't be feelin' sorry for him. There's many a girl had her reputation ruined through his bragging. Anyway, we'd better move or we'll get nowt to eat.'

As they walked towards the factory gates Sadie was thinking Alec might be in for more than a black eye if Brenda was in the family way. Her mother would have him hung, drawn and quartered. And she'd have him walking down the aisle whether he liked it or not. She wouldn't have her daughter disgraced.

'Still on for tomorrow, Sadie?'

'Yeah, but I'll see yer in the dinner-break to make arrangements.' Before they parted outside the factory gates to go in opposite directions, Sadie made a suggestion. 'Get some Vaseline to rub on Alec's bruises,that should soothe the pain. But I don't think they sell anything for bruised vanity.'

'My God, girl, have yer robbed a bank?' Mary Ann stared down at the money in Sadie's hand. 'How much is there?'

'Thirteen shillings,' Sadie told her proudly, 'and I didn't have to rob no bank. I just told a few fibs, that's all. Two of me boyfriends think they've bought me a present. I didn't tell them what the money was really for.'

'As long as yer haven't done nothing wrong to get it, girl, then good luck to yer. I'll mind it for yer with pleasure.' Mary Ann looked with fondness at the pretty face.'Yer'll soon have enough to get a bed and pay yer ways.'

'I reckon with that thirteen shillings, and the seventeen I'll get from work the day I leave, countin' me week in hand, that'll be enough for the bed. All I need to save now is the money to pay Sarah for me keep.'

'There's a second-hand furniture stall at the other side of the market, and I know the bloke what runs it. I asked him to keep his eye out for a single bed in good nick, and he came over this morning to tell me there's one come in that's almost like new. Nice oak headboard and a spotlessly clean mattress.'

'Mary Ann, that's all the money I've got.' Sadie looked stricken. 'I won't have enough to buy a bed until I leave work and get me two weeks' money. Would the man keep it for me, d'yer think, if you asked him for us?'

'I wouldn't have the cheek to ask him, girl. The poor bugger's goin' to have to sell it to the first buyer 'cos he needs the money . . . he's got a family to keep. He's forked out for it and he can't afford to be out of pocket for a few weeks.'

'And I bet when I've got the money I won't be able to get a decent bed anywhere.' Sadie felt disappointed. 'Just my luck, that is.'

'Nip over and have a look at it. See what yer think, then ask him to keep his eye open for one like it the week after next.'

'How much does he want for it?'

'I didn't bother askin' him 'cos I was too busy servin', and that's what I should be doin' now, not keepin' me customers waitin'. Go an' ask him yerself – yer've got a bleedin' tongue in yer head, girl. His name's Andy – tell him I sent yer.'

Andy was a tall, well-built man with a mop of unruly black hair and a grin that spread from ear to ear. 'Mary Ann sent yer, did she, queen? Well, this is the bed I was tellin' her about. It's as good as any yer'll get in Buckingham Palace – in fact, I wouldn't be at all surprised if the King himself hadn't slept in it. If I could prove he had, I'd slap another bleedin' five bob onto the price.'

Sadie was smiling as she listened to his patter. Andy was a typical market trader whose personality sold his goods rather than the quality of the merchandise. But he wasn't exaggerating about the bed, it really did look like new. 'It's just what I want, but I can't buy it off yer 'cos I won't have enough money for two weeks. But could yer tell me how much yer want for it?'

'Twenty-seven and sixpence, queen, and that's practically giving it away. One like that in the shops would knock yer back a fiver, and that's givin' the shops the benefit of the doubt. But if yer haven't got the money, queen, then yer haven't got the money, that's all there is to it. I'll keep me eye open for yer when yer give me the nod, but I can't promise one in this condition again.'

'Thanks.' Sadie tried to hide her disappointment. 'I'll nip over and see yer next week.'

When she got back to the stall, Mary Ann was busy serving three customers while having a good gossip at the same time. It was her friendliness and willingness to talk to all her customers, old and new, that brought them back week after week.

'Mary Ann, d'yer mind if I sort some of these clothes out?' This was something that Sadie had always wanted to do. There were some really good clothes mixed in with the 'tuppence with a hole, thruppence without a hole', and she was sure Mary Ann could charge more for the good stuff. 'If yer get busy, give us a shout.'

'Yeah, okay.' Mary Ann raised her eyebrows at Lizzie. 'She's wastin' her bleedin' time sortin' that lot out. They'll be as bad as ever in five minutes. Still, when I was her age I always thought I knew best too – an' many's the clout I got off me mam for it.'

Sadie was busy sorting the clothes out, putting the ones she thought were in good condition to one side, when Mary Ann sidled up to her. 'Here comes yer mate, Elsie.'

Sadie looked up, a smile covering her face. She waved and called, 'Hi, Elsie, come over here a minute. I've got some things to show yer.'

Elsie's head went up with pride and her magnificent bust seemed to shoot out even further. It wasn't everyone who got special treatment and she revelled in it. 'What is it, Sadie, love?'

Mary Ann folded her arms and looked on with a smile on her face. Making sure no one could overhear, she whispered to Lizzie, 'The girl has certainly tamed that one. She's changed her from a tiger to a pussy cat.'

Sadie was busy with her sales talk. 'Seein' as yer one of me favourite customers, Elsie, I wanted yer to see these before they go out on the table. They're far superior to anything that's on show and I know how yer like good quality clothes. They're sixpence each, and while I'm not expectin' yer to buy one, I wanted yer to have first choice.'

Lizzie touched Mary Ann's arm. 'I didn't know yer had superior clothes, girl.'

'I didn't know me bleedin' self, Lizzie. And if Sadie gets a tanner off her for one of those, I'll eat me flamin' hat.'

Sadie was busy holding different coloured blouses up for Elsie's inspection. They were all in excellent condition and in Sadie's opinion well worth sixpence. 'They're all nice, aren't they, Elsie? But as soon as I saw this pale green one I thought of you.'

'Yes, it is nice,' Elsie fingered the blouse, 'but I like the beige one as well.'

'Yeah, they're both nice,' Sadie said diplomatically, 'but yer can't afford two in one week, Elsie, or yer feller will have yer guts for garters.'

'My husband let's me have everythin' I want, and he likes to see me

149

all dolled up.' Elsie looked from the pale green to the beige. 'He's got a decent job and he doesn't keep me short.'

A customer attracted Sadie's attention. 'Excuse me, but could I have a look at that beige blouse, please?'

That quickly decided Elsie. 'I'm sorry, missus, I'm buyin' both of these. But there's plenty more nice ones if yer come over here.'

Lizzie showed her toothless gums when she grinned. 'Did yer say yer'd eat yer hat, Mary Ann?'

Mary Ann was flabbergasted. 'She sold her two! I can't believe it!' The stall-holder didn't utter the words she was thinking. Sadie had made sixpence more for those blouses than she would have done. 'D'yer know what, Lizzie? I've a good mind to buy a bleedin' hat, just so I can eat it!'

Sadie's new customer also bought a blouse and the girl was as proud as Punch. 'There yer are, Mary Ann, one and sixpence.'

The stall-holder looked at the money in Sadie's outstretched hand. 'Yer did good, there, girl, and I'm proud of yer.' She narrowed her eyes. 'D'yer really think there's a call here for sixpenny stuff?'

'Definitely! I've thought that since the day I came. Those dresses yer sold me for a tanner – yer could easily have got a shillin' for them.'

Mary Ann thought hard before she spoke. 'How would yer like to work on the market when yer pack in the job yer've got?'

There was a gleam in Sadie's eyes that was as bright as the hope in her heart. 'Doin' what, Mary Ann?'

'Working for me, of course – what d'yer bleedin' well think? With your talent, I'm not likely to let yer go to one of the other stalls, am I?' If Mary Ann had wanted to say more, she didn't get the chance because Sadie was hugging her so tight she could hardly breathe.

'Oh, yes please! Thank you, thank you, thank you! Ooh, I love the bones of yer, Mary Ann, I really do.'

'In that case, yer wouldn't want to kill me, would yer? Let go of me, for God's sake, I can't get me breath.'

Lizzie was watching from a distance. 'Hey, Mary Ann. Tell the girl about yer eatin' yer ruddy hat . . . that's if yer had one, of course, which yer haven't.'

Mary Ann pulled a face as she smoothed her bright red hair. 'I said if yer sold Elsie one of those blouses for sixpence, I'd eat me ruddy hat. And Tilly Mint over there is staying to see if I keep to me word.'

'Do yer really mean it about giving me a job?' Oh, wouldn't it be wonderful, Sadie was thinking. Seeing Mary Ann every day, and the customers she'd grown fond of. And leaving the market each night to go home to Sarah . . . Oh, it all sounded too good to be true. 'Tell me I wasn't hearing things, Mary Ann, please?'

'Yer weren't hearin' things, girl. I said it and I mean it. But we'll have to take more money than we do now to pay yer wages. So let's hope your superior quality, sixpence-a-go clothes find favour with the customers. But I've got a feeling that they will, and that you an' me will make a good team.'

Sadie was thrilled. 'I'm goin' to give me notice in on Monday and tell them I'm leaving the week after. I'm over the moon at the thought of getting away from that house and goin' to live with Sarah, but I'm also nervous. I've only got a few friends, but I'm going to feel lousy telling them lies. I've known Harry all me life and he's the best friend I ever had. And Brenda at work. She gets on me nerves sometimes, but we've been mates since the day we started at the factory together. And there's a boy at work, his name's Bobby – he's been good to me as well. I'm going to tell them I've got a better job, but I can't tell them where in case they come down and see me. And as I've never told them about me family, they wouldn't see any harm in telling them where I am. So I'll have to tell more lies . . . It seems to be all I do these days.'

'Yer'll make new friends, girl, yer only young. But I noticed yer never mentioned the other boy yer see a lot of – Geoff.'

'I don't know what to do about him.' Sadie's eyes looked troubled. 'I suppose I could go on seeing him because he knows nothing about me at all – where I live or where I work.' She let out a deep sigh. 'I'll think about that over the next week. At the moment I'm going to dwell on the nice things that are happening for me. Like coming to work for you and living with Sarah. I won't know I'm born, will I?'

'Talking about old Sarah, how did yer get on about the bed? Was it a good one?'

'Almost brand new – and he only wanted twenty-seven and six for it, so it's a real bargain. I explained to Andy that I didn't have the money now, so he's going to keep his eye open the week after next to see if he can pick up another good one.'

Mary Ann made a quick decision. 'I'll lend yer seven bob to put to what yer've given me, that'll make it up to a pound. Take it to Andy and tell him to hang on to the bed until next week and I'll make sure he gets the difference.' She saw the doubt on Sadie's face. 'He'll do it for yer, girl, 'cos once he's got the pound in his hand he can't lose, can he? If yer don't come up with the rest of the money, he hangs on to what yer've paid him, *and* the bed. But he knows I won't let him down, so go and see him and take the pound. Oh, and yer can tell him he won't have far to go to deliver it.'

'Yer mean he'll take it to Sarah's? How will he do that? It's very heavy.'

'How d'yer think he'll get it there? On his bleedin' back? He's got a big handcart, yer daft ha'porth.'

'Ooh, that's handy, isn't it?'

Mary Ann looked at Sadie with amusement twinkling in her grey-green eyes. 'Dyer know when yer stayed late last week and helped me bundle all the clothes up? And when yer left I had all those bleedin' big bundles around me feet? Well, what did yer think I was goin' to do with them?'

Sadie pursed her lips, a frown on her face. 'I don't know – I didn't think about it.'

'Well, I'm sure yer didn't expect me to carry that lot home on me head, so I'll tell yer. I was waitin' for my feller to bring our handcart so we could pile everythin' on it and push the ruddy lot to a little wooden hut we rent off some man who lives at the top of our street.'

Sadie grinned. 'I'm learning, Mary Ann, and I learn fast. I promise I'm not as thick as yer seem to be thinking.'

'Ay, sunshine, anyone that can sell two blouses to Elsie is definitely not thick. And to get sixpence each for them – well, that puts yer in the genius class.'

'Will I get to meet yer husband, Mary Ann? I've often wondered about yer family.'

'Where d'yer think I get all these clothes to sell?'

Sadie shook her head. 'I imagined yer bought them off people.'

'No, my feller goes around the streets with his cart. He goes to the posh districts like Allerton, Orrell Park and Mossley Hill – that's where he gets your superior quality goods from. The other stuff he collects locally. He comes every morning to give me a hand to set up and then at night to clear away.' Mary Ann grinned. 'Yer gettin' me whole story in one go instead of gradual. But before I go an' see to Tessie, who's callin' me for all the lazy bastards under the sun, I'll rattle the rest off quick. I've got two kids, a boy of twelve and a girl of eight who yer'll meet when yer come to work here. They don't come on a Saturday because I'd never get anythin' done with them under me feet.' Mary Ann walked away, saying, 'Second instalment next week, girl.' She had a wide smile on her face when she approached the customer. 'For God's sake, Tessie, keep yer ruddy hair on! Even a slave is allowed a five-minute break!'

'Five minutes? More like flamin' fifteen, if yer ask me. There yer were, yer hands goin' as quick as yer ruddy mouth, and me standin' here, gormless, willin' and waitin' to spend me hard-earned money with yer.'

152

'Ah, yer poor thing! Why don't yer buy yerself a violin, Tessie, an' yer could really tug at me heartstrings.'

'Heartstrings? What ruddy heartstrings? It's not a heart you've got, Mary Ann, it's a bloody brick!' That was a good answer, Tessie thought, considering I didn't have much time to think. I must remember to tell my Jack when I get home – he'll enjoy that. 'D'yer want me to prove yer've got a brick where yer heart should be, Mary Ann?'

'Yeah, go on, Tessie, baffle me with bleedin' science.'

'Well, see this man's shirt I've got in me hand? I'll bet yer goin' to ask me for thruppence for it when anyone with half an eye can see it's only worth tuppence. That's because yer've got no heart, yer see, Mary Ann.'

Sadie was in a happy frame of mind when she came back from seeing Andy. He'd agreed to take the pound and keep the bed for her until next week. She was in time to hear the latter end of the teasing exchange and decided to join in. After all, she'd be working here permanently in two weeks and she wanted to be on friendly terms with all the customers. 'Excuse me, but that shirt should be on our sixpenny superior-quality stall, over the other side. I can't imagine how it got mixed up with these.'

Tessie's jaw dropped. 'What the bleedin' hell is she on about? Sixpenny superior-quality! I've never heard nothin' like it in all me born days. Yer can sod off if yer think I'm goin' to give yer sixpence for a shirt what's got two buttons missin'.'

'Now be reasonable, Tessie,' Mary Ann said. 'The missing buttons are at the very bottom; no one will notice when your feller's got it tucked in his trousers.'

Tessie raised her thick bushy eyebrows and adopted what she thought was a haughty stance. 'I'll thank you not to be so personal about what my feller keeps in his trousers, Mary Ann.'

The stall-holder was ready as usual with a quip. 'Now, Tessie, yer should know me better than to think I'd talk about a little thing like that.'

The two women looked at each other and burst out laughing. 'Ooh, I enjoyed that, Mary Ann.' Tessie wiped at the laughter tears running down her cheeks. 'But just wait until I tell my feller yer insulted his manhood.'

'Tessie, all is pure to the pure. I can't help it if you've got a dirty mind. And before we lose track of what started all this off, I can't take less than thruppence for the shirt because I've got a husband and two kids at home that happen to like the taste of food.'

Tessie clicked her tongue as she opened her purse. 'Does that brick yer've got beat like a proper heart, Mary Ann?'

'Yeah, it's just like a normal heart, Tessie.' Mary Ann pocketed the coins. 'The only thing is, it sometimes gets a bit heavy.'

'So yer took me money off me with a heavy heart, did yer?' Tessie was delighted and amazed at her own wit. Her Jack would be in stitches when she told him. 'That's a bit of consolation for me, girl. Makes parting with me money that much easier.'

Mary Ann leaned across the table. 'Yer in fine form today, Tessie, I'll say that for yer. But will yer bugger off home now an' let me get on with me work?'

'Yeah, okay, Mary Ann, I'll see yer next week.'

Mary Ann turned to see Sadie busy at one of the far tables. She shouted across, 'How did yer get on with Andy?'

Sadie smiled and lifted a thumb. 'Just like you said.'

'Yer doin' well if yer not caught, girl. A good day all round for yer.' Mary Ann was smiling when she attended to another customer. She was happy things were working out for the girl, God knows she deserved something better out of life than she'd been getting.

Sadie was on pins when it was time for her to head for home. She was meeting Geoff at half-seven and she had to go home and get changed first. But she couldn't leave without airing her fears. How to do it though, after Mary Ann had already done so much for her? There'd come a time when the stall-holder would get fed up and tell her to sort her own problems out, but Sadie hoped it wouldn't be today.

Mary Ann threw a bundle of clothes onto the sheet spread out on the ground then came to stand in front of Sadie. 'Yer like a cat on hot bricks, girl. If yer've got somethin' to say, spit it out.'

'It's about the bed, Mary Ann. How am I goin' to pay the seven and six to Andy? The most I'll have next Saturday is half-a-crown.'

'I've got it all under control, girl, so yer can rest easy, I'll put five bob to what you'll have, which means yer'll owe me twelve shillings altogether. Yer can pay me that when yer draw yer two weeks' wages.'

Sadie gave a sigh of relief. 'I'll be able to do that, and pay Sarah me keep. But if I have to work a week in hand for you, I'll be stuck the following week.'

Mary Ann laughed. 'Yer don't work no week in hand here, love. Yer'll get paid on a Saturday as per usual. If I pay yer the same wage as yer getting now, will that do yer while we see how things go? If your high-class superior-quality clothes stall does well, yer can have a rise. How does that sound to yer?'

'It sounds like music to my ears,' Sadie said. 'I thank God every night for sending you into my life, Mary Ann. He was certainly lookin' after me that day.'

'Just wait until I'm yer boss, girl – yer might see a different side to me. I get a right temper on me sometimes.' She patted Sadie's cheek. 'When God gave me this red hair, He gave me the temper to go with it.'

'I'll take me chances,' Sadie said. 'Anyway, I'm very quick at ducking.' She cupped the stall-holder's face in her two hands. 'When I come to work for yer, I'll work like a demon to pay yer back for all yer've done for me.' She kissed both cheeks. 'And that's a promise.'

'You're looking very bright and cheerful tonight, love,' Geoff said as they swayed from side to side with the rocking of the tram. 'What's happened to make yer so happy?'

During the long walk to Everton Valley Sadie had changed her mind half-a-dozen times over Geoff. First she was going to cut him off completely, as she was her other friends. Then she changed her mind because she needed one friend, someone to go out with, and she wouldn't find anyone better than Geoff. And as he didn't know anything about where she lived or what her family was like, he couldn't cause her any trouble. She could tell him she was going to live with her grandma for a while – he wouldn't see anything strange in that. He could even call for her if Sarah and her husband didn't mind. So she could safely tell him part of the story and leave the rest a secret.

'I am feeling pleased with meself – very pleased, in fact.' Sadie bestowed a beaming smile on him. 'I might be goin' to live with me grandparents for a while and I'm made up. I've told yer I don't get on very well with me mam and dad, they're not easy to live with, but I get on smashin' with me grandma. She's lovely, like an angel.'

'Perhaps when yer've settled in, I'll be able to meet her and her husband.' Geoff couldn't understand why Sadie wouldn't let him take her home – not even to the end of the street, never mind her front door. But perhaps this move might see him meeting some of her family. 'They don't mind yer going out with boys, do they?'

'No, I shouldn't think so. They'll probably be delighted to meet yer.' Sadie crossed her fingers for good luck. She hadn't told him any big lies, just left out the whole truth. 'Anyway, it won't be for a few weeks yet. I'll see yer loads of times before then.'

'Where do they live?'

'I'm not telling yer no more in case it doesn't come off.' Sadie told herself it had to come off or she'd die of disappointment. She'd just come from a house that wasn't fit for any human being to live in and if she didn't get away she'd lose her sanity.

Chapter Fourteen

As soon as Sadie saw Brenda on Monday morning, with her bright smile and clear eyes, she knew her friend's fears had been groundless. 'If you put yerself in that position again, Bren, then yer've only yerself to blame an' yer'll deserve everything yer get. Yer lucky, yer've had a warning so heed it. Keep away from stinkers like Alec or yer'll get yerself a bad name and no decent feller will touch yer with a barge-pole.'

'Don't worry about that – I'll be steering well clear of Alec Gleeson,' Brenda said, nodding her head for emphasis. 'I heard how he got that black eye, and why. And I want yer to know, Sadie, that I was stupid to believe what he said about yer and I'm sorry.'

Sadie's voice was high with surprise when she asked, 'Who told you?'

'Sylvia Black from the sewing room. She said everyone in the factory had heard about it and they're all givin' Alec the cold shoulder.'

'Well, at least it'll put paid to him ruining your reputation, or anyone else's. He'll be afraid to open his mouth in future. But for God's sake let it be a lesson to yer, Brenda, and keep any other boy at arm's length. Nice girls don't let boys do what you let Alec do, so bear that in mind.'

Sadie was silent for a while, deep in thought. Then she decided that as she'd have to go to the office today to give her notice in, it would be mean not to tell her workmate first. 'Bren, I've got meself another job an' I'll be givin' me notice in today. I'll be leaving a week next Saturday.'

Brenda looked stunned. 'Oh, yer not, Sadie. Please tell me yer not.'

'I'm sorry, Bren, but it's true.' Sadie took one look at her friend's face and was filled with guilt. And when the lies started she felt even worse. 'I've got the chance of a job in a sweet shop in Aigburth and I'm takin' it.'

Brenda had always shown signs of being selfish and childish, and it came out now as her eyes filled with tears and she wailed, 'But what about me? We've always worked together, yer can't leave me just like that!'

Sadie's guilt evaporated when she saw the tears of self-pity roll down Brenda's cheeks. 'Oh, but I can! I've found meself a better job and I'm taking it. And if you were any kind of a friend you'd show some interest in the job and be happy for me. But the only person you're interested in, Brenda, is yerself. Let's hope the girl they put in my place will be as soft with yer as I've been for the last two and a half years. I can't see it meself 'cos there's not that many fools around. Not in this factory, anyway. Most of them would make mincemeat of yer if yer tried to come the little innocent with them.' She thought back over the years to the number of times Brenda had pleaded an upset tummy or a headache for being so slow filling a crate that Sadie had given her a hand so she wouldn't get into trouble. 'If I were you I'd start right now learning how to do the job properly. Try moving yer arms and legs a bit quicker and with a bit of luck yer'll be able to keep up with the new girl when she comes.'

The rest of the morning passed in stony silence. Sadie knew it was a ploy on Brenda's part to fill her with such remorse she'd change her mind about leaving, so she let her get on with her sulking. There was as much chance of the sky falling down as there was of her changing her mind. When the dinner-bell sounded, Sadie grabbed her bag and made for the door, saying over her shoulder, 'I want a word with Bobby, so I'll see yer at the chippy . . . that's if yer intend going.'

The smile dropped from Bobby's face when he heard the news. 'Ah, blimey, Sadie, just when I was gettin' to know yer! But it won't stop yer comin' out with me, will it?'

'No, I shouldn't think so. Anyway, it's two weeks off – I'll be goin' out with yer four times before then. And I can come and see yer in me dinner-hour because it's only about six stops on the tram.' May God forgive me, Sadie thought, for telling lies to someone as nice as Bobby Bennett. If only Brenda could have seen the goodness in him, he'd have been an ideal boyfriend for her. Then she had an idea. It was worth a try, and if it worked out, it would salve her conscience. 'Bobby, on the Thursday before I leave, would yer mind if Brenda came out with us? Just a little farewell thing, nothing spectacular. I've worked with her since the day I started, so it would be nice to ask her . . . that's if yer don't think I've got a cheek for asking?'

'If that's what you want, Sadie, I'm willing.'

'Bobby Bennett, yer one of life's gentlemen, yer really are.'

'And you, Sadie Wilson, are a real little lady.'

Sadie giggled. 'Shall we stand here all through the dinner-break and starve while we pay each other compliments?'

'Lookin' at you is better than a corned-beef sandwich any day, Sadie.'

'It won't stop yer tummy rumbling, so I think we'd better eat. And I don't have a lot of time 'cos I have to go to the office to hand in me notice. So I'll see yer tomorrow, Bobby.'

Sadie was waiting to be served when Brenda walked into the chippy. She handed a penny over, saying, 'Get mine, will yer, Sadie?'

When they were walking back to the factory, eating their chips in silence, Sadie decided it was time to break the ice. She had another two weeks to work with Brenda, and she didn't want those two weeks to be miserable; she wished to part as friends.

'Me and Bobby were wondering if yer'd like to come out with us next Thursday? It'll only be to the pictures but it might be the last chance we get of all goin' out together. And we've been friends for a long time, so it would be nice. There's really only you an' Bobby that I'll miss. I haven't made any other friends.'

Brenda had had time to reflect and come to the decision that Sadie was much more sensible for her age than *she* was. And that was all the fault of her mother for insisting upon treating her like a pampered child. But the time had come to put away childish things and grow up, like Sadie said. 'Doesn't Bobby mind me comin' out with yer?'

'Not at all. He'd be over the moon having a pretty girl hanging on each arm.'

'I'm surprised at you goin' out with him, he's not handsome or anything.'

'Brenda, how many times do I have to tell yer that it's not the wrapping yer look at, it's what's inside the parcel. Next time yer see Bobby, open yer eyes and yer ears, and yer'll be surprised. As far as I'm concerned, I'd rather have him a hundred times over than the likes of Alec Gleeson.'

'It'll be nice for the three of us to go out together.' Brenda said. 'When I tell me mam she'll be made up. She worried that I never took Alec home, but every time I asked him he made an excuse.'

'It's a pity about that, 'cos your mam would have seen through him in no time, like I did. I had him pegged from the word go. I only went out with him because I had no money an' I needed someone to pay for me.'

'I should have taken notice of yer, Sadie, then I wouldn't have let him do those horrible things to me. I'll watch out for every boy in future.'

'All boys are not the same, I'm fed up tellin' yer! Bobby Bennett is a real little gentleman, he respects girls.'

'I'm goin' to look for a boy like that – someone who respects me.'

Sadie smiled as she heard the words. Brenda was very childish for her age, there was no getting away from the fact. But, please God, she'd have enough sense to see that Bobby was just the kind of boy she was looking for.

* * *

Sadie couldn't wait for Saturday to come. The time seemed to pass so slowly. In work she'd be willing the hands of the clock to go faster while smiling and nodding her head in response to Brenda's constant chatter. There was no sadness in her heart about leaving, no feelings of sentiment. It had been a job, nothing more. The floorwalker was a good bloke, he'd always been cheerful and helpful. But apart from him, and Brenda, she'd never made friends with anyone else in the packing room. How could you have friends when you couldn't invite them to your home? Even on the nights she was out with Geoff or Bobby, her mind wasn't with them, it was at the market with Mary Ann, Sarah and her own, very first proper bed. Only on the night she met Harry in the park did she feel sad. He was the only one who knew about her family and the conditions in which she lived, and yet he'd stuck by her. In Sadie's eyes that made him a true friend and she'd miss him. She had never let herself think of him as anything but a friend because she knew it could never be otherwise. He'd settle down one day with a nice girl from a decent family, someone his mother would approve of.

When Saturday finally came, Sadie hurried home from work to pay her wages over and have a bite to eat before going to the market. She found Jimmy sitting on the front step looking very depressed. There was nothing in his life to be happy about, but today he seemed more miserable than usual. 'Have yer had yer dinner, Jimmy?'

'No.' Jimmy gazed down at his hands, clasped between his knees and with the dirt still on from the day before. 'I've only had a round of bread all day an' I'm starvin'.'

'Why isn't the dinner ready? Isn't me dad home yet with his wages?'

'Yeah, he's home. Me mam sent our Dot out to get the messages.'

'And she hasn't come back yet?'

'Oh yeah, she came back!' Jimmy stood up and dug his hands into pockets that were ripped to pieces like the rest of his trousers. His young face dark with anger, he looked at Sadie. 'They're dirty they are, and I hate them! I wish they were dead! When I'm a bit older I'm goin' to run away from home an' I'll go away to sea. I'll go where they'll never, ever, find me.'

Sadie was shocked to the core. 'What on earth's happened? I've never heard yer talk like this before, Jimmy. What's upset yer so much?'

Near to tears, the lad shook his head. 'They're bad, they are. They're wicked an' I hope they go to hell when they die.'

'Tell me what's happened to get yer in such a state. Come on, Jimmy, yer know yer can talk to me.'

Jimmy cast his eyes down. 'Yer know how me dad always drags me mam upstairs to the bedroom on a Saturday? Well, when our Dot came back from the shops and found out they were up there, yer should 'ave heard the carry-on out of her! She started screamin' and shoutin', and the bad words she used were terrible. Everyone in the street must 'ave heard her.' The lad's eyes looked sad and troubled. 'Our mam and dad are not like a real mam an' dad, are they, Sadie? They don't look after us proper.'

Sadie was raging inside. This was a twelve-year-old boy talking. He should be dressed in decent clothes, his tummy should be full and he should be out playing footie with his mates. Instead he was dressed in rags, his tummy was empty and he didn't have any mates. And because she'd suffered all these things herself, she knew exactly how he felt. And from next week he wouldn't even have her to tell his troubles to . . . But even if she stayed, cast aside her dream – what could she do to improve the quality of Jimmy's life? And that of Ellen and Les and baby Sally? Nothing – because she was too young in years and too short of money. But she wouldn't abandon them; she'd find some way of helping them.

'Jimmy, I want yer to know that whatever happens I love you and the other kids. Not our Dot, I'm afraid, I'm not goin' to be a hypocrite about it, I can't stand her. But I'll always be there to help when I can. And keep tellin' yerself that yer won't be a kid forever. The day will come when yer grow into a man and can choose the life yer want to live.' Sadie held her hand out to him. 'Come on, let's see if your dear sister's got yer dinner ready.'

'She's upstairs in the bedroom with me mam an' dad.' Jimmy's voice was choked. 'I told yer, she took off like a ravin' lunatic. Threw all the messages on the table and ran up the stairs shoutin' her head off.'

Sadie ground her teeth together. 'Oh, she did, did she? Well, we'll soon see about that!' Rage had Sadie taking the stairs two at a time. She banged on the bedroom door with a clenched fist, shouting, 'If yez are not out of that room pronto, I'm goin' for the police. And don't think I won't, 'cos it would give me great pleasure to see yez all behind bars, which is where yer should be.'

She could hear scuffling behind the closed door and banged again. 'I want me dinner on the table before yer can say Jack Robinson or I'll take the kids with me to the chip shop and buy them a dinner out of me wages. Then I'll go to Blackler's and spend the rest of me money on meself.' After one last bang on the door, Sadie tripped down the stairs, beckoned to Jimmy to come in, and they sat side by side on the couch, watched with awe by Ellen, Les and the baby.

Dot was the first to show her face and the look she gave Sadie was one of hatred. 'I don't know who the bleedin' hell yer think yer are, but yer not ordering *me* around. If yer want any dinner, make it yerself, smarty pants.'

'Right. That suits me fine.' Sadie stood up and stared back into the hard face of her sister. 'I'm sure the kids would rather have somethin' from the chippy than the muck you serve up.'

Dot was having second thoughts. 'I'll do the kids' dinners, but I'm not doin' anythin' for you, so yer can bugger off to the chippy.'

Lily Wilson came through the door in time to hear her daughter's words. She swiftly crossed the room and delivered a stinging slap to Dot's face. 'Yer'll do as yer told, yer hard-faced little madam! And don't you dare back-chat me or I'll give yer more than a slap across the face. Get in that kitchen and see to some dinner for the whole family.'

Lily didn't meet Sadie's eyes as she picked up the baby. What was happening in the house was getting out of hand but she was powerless to stop it. She was being usurped by her own daughter and blackmailed into silence.

Jimmy tugged on Sadie's skirt and patted the seat next to him. When she was seated he winked at her and braved his mother's wrath by saying, 'I wish it was you at home all the time, our Sadie, instead of our Dot. She's a dirty, lazy thing, and mean. She's always hittin' us for nothing.'

Lily shook her fist at him. 'You keep yer trap buttoned.'

'Oh Mam, yer should never stop anyone from telling the truth.' Sadie's voice dripped with sarcasm. 'After all, it's you who's got yerself in a hole; it's no good takin' it out on the kids 'cos ye can't dig yerself out of it.'

There was venom in Lily's eyes but she wisely kept her mouth shut.

'Sarah's been waitin' ages for yer, girl, she was beginnin' to think yer weren't coming.' Mary Ann eyed Sadie's flushed face. 'Been rushin', have yer?'

'Me dinner wasn't ready an' I had to wait.' Sadie wasn't going to tell the truth. Apart from the shame, she was afraid the stall-holder would be so incensed she'd take the matter further. If that were to happen, the children would be split up and put in institutions and Sadie might never see them again. It was the fear of that happening that had stopped her from ever going to the police or telling her teacher when she was at school. 'Where is Sarah?'

'She may have gone to see Andy, to give him the address for delivering the bed.' Mary Ann grinned. 'Anyone would think she was expectin' royalty to move into her spare room, she's that excited.'

'Ay, I'll have you know I'm as good as royalty any day.' Sadie had used the time it took to walk from home to calm her emotions. Devastated by the state of affairs at home and the plight of her brothers and sisters, she'd made a vow to spend some of her weekly pocket money on buying clothes for them off Mary Ann's stall and finding a way of getting them to the children without disclosing where she lived. She would keep in touch with them until she was old enough to offer them a home where she could take care of them. But she was starting a new life for herself and that must take priority. From next Saturday Mary Ann would be her friend and employer, the market would be her work and Sarah and her husband would be her family. These people were giving her the chance of a new beginning; they didn't want to take her problems on as well. So Sadie's smile was wide when she told the stall-holder, 'I've never mentioned it before 'cos I didn't want to sound big-headed, but me real title is, wait for it, Princess Sadie of Sefton Park.'

'I'm glad about that, girl.' Mary Ann's face was as straight as a poker. 'It will add a touch of class to yer superior-quality clothes stall. Which, incidentally, has been in great demand. Your friend Elsie has been spreadin' the word an' we've had several requests. I had to tell them my supervisor in superior-quality clothes hadn't arrived but would be here later to show them her wares.' The stall-holder dropped her pose and, jerking her head, said, 'So yer'd better get crackin' and sort some of the clothes out, girl, 'cos once a customer is let down they don't come back again.' She began to shake with laughter at the thoughts running through her mind. 'If I were you, girl, I wouldn't tell Elsie about yer bein' Princess Sadie of Sefton Park. 'Cos yer see, girl, I think she'd be after yer for the job of lady-in-waiting.'

'If she brings customers to me stall then she can have the job of lady-in-waiting. In fact, if she brings enough customers, and the money starts rolling in, I'll let her have a go at bein' Princess Elsie of Paddy's Market.' Sadie tutted at the expression on Mary Ann's face. 'Yer only jealous! I'll tell yer somethin' else, as well. Andy said it's quite possible that the King has slept in that bed I'm gettin'.' She poked her tongue out. 'So there!'

'Oh, anything's possible, girl, but it doesn't often happen. I was picked to be Queen of the May once, dressed up like a dog's dinner in a procession. I thought I was really somebody that day, me head was so big they couldn't get the crown of roses to fit. And it didn't do me no bleedin' good because the next day at school I got me hair pulled that much by the girls who were jealous, me head was really sore. Put me off being a Queen, I can tell yer. One girl, Bella Ingham, she said I

163

looked like a witch, and another one, Josie Roberts, she said me dress didn't fit an' I looked a mess.'

'But they couldn't take that day away from yer, could they? Yer'll always have it to look back on, which is more than Bella Ingham an' Josie Roberts have.'

'It still did me no bleedin' good, girl, and neither is standin' here talkin' to you! The longer yer leave setting up yer superior-quality clothes stall, the more money yer costing me. So get a move on, kiddo – let's see yer do yer stuff.'

'Shall I take the half-a-crown to Andy's first, in case he thinks I'm not coming?'

'I'm not paying yer wages yet, girl, so I can't tell yer what to do. But Andy can wait for half an hour until yer've got the stall set out. I've put a bundle of new stuff under the table so yer can have yer pick of the best before I put it out.'

'Right, I'll get cracking on that and go and see Andy later.'

In between serving customers, Mary Ann watched with interest as Sadie selected the best blouses, skirts and ladies' underwear. Then, as she was serving Maggie, she said, 'She's got talent, has that girl. Look at the way she's arranging those blouses – they look as good as anythin' yer'd see in Bunny's. In fact, Maggie, I can see one there I'd buy for meself, and give her a bleedin' tanner for it!'

'Now, Mary Ann, don't do anythin' rash.' Maggie's teeth clicked back into place. 'Tell her yer won't give her more than fourpence for it.'

'Take a leaf out of your book, eh, Maggie? Well, don't be comin' those tricks with me, sunshine, 'cos that pullover yer hanging onto like grim death is thruppence, and I'll not take a penny less.'

Maggie already had the threepenny joey in her hand and she passed it over. ''Tis a hard woman yer are, Mary Ann.'

'Hard and poor, Maggie, hard and poor. But I've got a feeling in me water that me luck is about to change, with the help of me new assistant . . . the Princess of Sefton Park.' And Mary Ann chuckled as she walked away leaving Maggie with her mouth hanging open.

It was half an hour before the stall-holder had time to visit her young assistant. There'd been quite a rush on and the weight of coins in Mary Ann's pocket gave her a warm glow. She knew Sadie was doing well because she'd kept an eye on her. Not just to check how she was doing, but to make sure no one was giving her any trouble. It wasn't unusual for a fight to break out between two people wanting the same article; this didn't worry Mary Ann, to whom it was all in a day's work. But Sadie was new to the game and might not know how to handle two irate women who were in danger of ripping the blouse with which they were playing tug-of-war. 'How's it going, girl?'

Sadie was radiant with pride and success. 'I've sold eight things!'

'Go 'way! Well, I never,' Mary Ann gushed to add to the girl's pleasure. 'Yer've got a business head on yer shoulders, girl, no doubt about that.'

'And they've all said they'll be back next week. Ooh, I'm dead excited, Mary Ann. I can't wait until I'm working here proper – like, when it's me proper full-time job.'

'I know what yer mean, sunshine, and I'm looking forward to it meself. I believe that yer going to bring me lots and lots of good luck.'

'I don't know about that, Mary Ann. I haven't had much good luck in me own life. In fact, the only good luck I've ever had was meeting you. It was through you I've got meself a real live grandma and grandad, a nice place to live in and me own bedroom.'

'Listen to me, girl, yer don't have to keep thankin' me for what I've done for yer. I did it because I wanted to. And yer've already paid me back by being here every Saturday to give me a hand. Plus, and this is the very best, plus creatin' our superior-quality clothes stall. Now, d'yer want me to keep me eye on things while you go an' see Andy?'

'There's no need, I gave the money to me grandma an' she's taken it for me.' Oh, what a lovely feeling it was to have someone of her own to talk about. 'Andy's delivering the bed tonight, on his way home from the market.'

'Not with the King still in it, I hope?'

Sadie's laugh rang out. 'Mary Ann, I suppose yer know that yer two sheets to the wind?'

'I know, girl, but don't tell the woman that's waiting for yer to serve her. Word gets around the market like wildfire an' I don't want the whole world to know I'm doolally pop.'

'Your secret is safe with me, have no fear.' Sadie smiled before turning to the customer. 'Can I help you, madam?'

Mary Ann's face was a picture as she walked away. 'Madam? Blimey O'Riley. If I'm not careful she'll have us comin' to work in navy-blue frocks with little white lace collars.'

'Ay, Mary Ann, they put yer away if yer go around talkin' to yerself.' Lizzie grinned. 'They send men in white coats an' they put yer in a strait-jacket and take yer to the loony bin.'

'Go 'way!' Mary Ann wagged her head from side to side. 'Did they hurt yer when they put that strait-jacket on yer before they carted yer off to the loony bin?'

Lizzie had been leaning on the stack of clothes, but the stall-holder's words had her stretching to her full height, bust standing to attention. 'What are you hinsinuating, Mary Ann?'

'Nothing, really. It's just that yer seem to be very knowledgeable about the procedure, and yer must admit that yer do go missing for a few weeks every now and then.'

'Go missing? I've never gone missin' in all me life! If you don't see me for a week or two, it doesn't mean I've flamin' well gone missing, it means I've had no bleedin' money to spend with yer, yer stupid cow!'

'Oh, is that what it is? I apologise for having had evil thoughts about yer, Lizzie, and I won't never have them no more, even though me takings might be down a couple of coppers. So shall we pretend this conversation never took place an' start again, eh? I'll walk away an' when I come back I'll act as though I've never seen yer before.' Mary Ann turned on her heels and walked a dozen paces away, all the time willing herself not to laugh. 'Right!' She turned and walked towards Lizzie with a false smile pinned on her face. With her hands folded neatly in front of her, and bowing her head slightly, she asked in a refined voice, 'Is there anything I can interest you in, madam? Some lingerie perhaps, or hosiery?'

'Stupid cow!' Lizzie turned to the woman at the side of her who was highly amused. 'Didn't I say she was a stupid cow? Well, that just proves me point.'

'Is Andy goin' to carry the bed upstairs for yer, Grandma? You an' Grandad mustn't attempt it, d'yer hear?'

'It's all arranged, darlin', so don't be worryin' yer pretty head. Andy is not only goin' to carry it upstairs, he's goin' to put it together for us.' Sarah O'Hanlon was even more excited than Sadie, if that were possible. To have a youngster in the house was something she and Joe had stopped dreaming of many years ago, and even the thought of having Sadie live with them had given them a new lease of life. 'Wouldn't yer like to come and see the room before yer move in? It would give yer a chance to meet my Joe, as well.'

'I'd love to. Mary Ann did say she'd take me, but I know she's got enough on her plate without worrying about me. I could come tomorrow afternoon, would that be all right? Say about two o'clock?'

'Why don't yer come earlier an' have a bite to eat with me and Joe? It won't be a feast, but we do manage a roast on a Sunday.'

Sadie was dying to accept but she wanted to spend as much time as she could with her brothers and sisters. Sunday was really the only day she saw much of them and this Sunday was special because it would be her last one at home. 'I'd like to, Grandma, but I think I should have me dinner at home tomorrow. So I'll call in the afternoon.'

'Yer know where to find us, do yer, sweetheart?'

Sadie smiled into the lined face that was already so dear to her. 'Mary Ann told me where yer live, just off Scotland Road. It's going to be me home, so don't worry, I'll find it. And tell Grandad I'm really looking forward to meeting him. Tell him I hope he's going to like me, and that I'm going to love both of yer and spoil yer to bits.'

Chapter Fifteen

Sadie stopped outside the two-up two-down terraced house that had a pure white step, polished red-raddled window sill, and white net curtains hanging behind gleaming windows. It was just like the house in her dream, except that this wasn't hers so she had no key to fit in the lock. Her heart was thumping and the hand she raised to the brightly polished brass knocker was shaking. What if they'd changed their minds? Or say Joe didn't like her?

The door was opened so quickly Sadie knew Sarah had been watching out for her. 'Come in, sweetheart, and set my feller's heart at rest. He's been a bundle of nerves all day.' Sarah opened the door wide, and as Sadie stepped inside she was enveloped in two frail arms. 'Welcome to yer new home, sweetheart.'

'I don't know about your husband being a bundle of nerves.' Sadie's teeth were chattering. 'I'm shakin' like a leaf – I can't stop!'

Sarah closed the door then walked ahead of Sadie down the hall. 'Yer new granddaughter has arrived, Joe.'

As soon as Sadie walked through the door she fell in love with the old man sitting in his rocking chair, an unlit pipe in his mouth. He looked frail, like his wife, with sparse white hair and deep wrinkles. He had a white silk knitted scarf around his scraggy neck, knotted neatly over his Adam's apple, and was wearing a navy-blue cardigan and dark grey flannel trousers. Sadie took all this in, in the second before she caught his eyes on her. They were kind eyes, holding a hint of mischief and more than a hint of apprehension. The little love's as scared as I am, Sadie told herself as her heart went out to him. 'Hello, Grandad.'

'Hello, queen, I'm really glad to meet yer at last.'

'Oh, me too!' Sadie ran across the room and dropped to her knees at the side of his chair. She put her arms around him and hugged him gently before kissing his cheek. 'I think you and me are goin' to get on like a house on fire.'

His faded blue eyes twinkling, he said, 'My Sarah said yer were pretty, but I wasn't expectin' a film star. A sight for sore eyes, yer are, queen.'

'I can see I'm goin' to have to keep me eyes on you two,' Sarah said,

169

her face beaming. 'Otherwise yer'll be runnin' off together, leavin' me all on me lonesome.'

Sadie noticed the special look in Joe's eyes when he smiled across at his wife. 'When you were Sadie's age, yer were just as pretty. And that's how I see you today, and always will see yer. Yer've never aged in my eyes, Sarah O'Hanlon.'

Sadie could feel a lump forming in her throat. She'd seen more signs of love in this house in five minutes than she'd seen in a lifetime at home. 'Can I call yer Grandad?'

'Yer better had, queen, 'cos I'm counting on it. It's a proud man I'll be when I introduce yer to the neighbours, proud as Punch.'

'Neighbours be damned,' Sarah said, bending down to take some cups and saucers from a cupboard in the highly polished sideboard. 'Don't yer mean yer cronies in the pub?' She put the crockery down on a small table set under the window that looked out onto the yard and smiled at Sadie. 'He'll be swankin' his head off tomorrow night, sittin' in the snug with his half of bitter in front of him and his mates around him. They'll not get a word in all night.'

'Well, if I'm goin' to do so much talking, I won't be drinking, will I, love? So I won't be coming rolling home like I usually do.'

'The day you come home drunk, Joe O'Hanlon, is the day I take the fryin' pan to yer. That would teach yer a lesson.' Sarah pulled on Sadie's arm. 'Come and sit down, sweetheart, or yer'll be getting housemaid's knees.'

Sadie sank into the fireside chair facing Joe. 'How long have you and me Grandma been married, Grandad?'

'Over sixty years, queen. We've had our share of trouble, as me wife has told yer, but me an' Sarah have stuck together through it all. We love each other, yer see, and that helped us through the bad times.'

Sadie was too full of emotion to answer so she let her eyes travel the room. It was so clean and tidy it was a credit to two people in their eighties. The ornaments, mirror and fireplace were spotless, and even the leaves on the aspidistra plant looked as though they'd been polished.

'Yer room looks nice, Grandma,' Sadie shouted to Sarah who was standing by the kitchen sink filling the kettle. 'I'll be able to give yer a hand when I'm here to stay.'

'I manage all right when the weather's fine, sweetheart, but I'll be glad of a hand when the cold weather sets in. Me bones are old, yer see, and they think I've got a cheek for expectin' them to work when it's cold and icy.'

'I can help yer before I go to work. Yer won't have to go down the yard for coal, I'll fill the scuttle before I go out. And any messages yer want, I can bring in with me.'

'I can see we're goin' to get spoilt.' Sarah poured the boiling water into the dark brown earthenware teapot. 'But don't think we want yer for a skivvy, sweetheart, 'cos yer only young and yer must have plenty of friends to go out with.'

'I've never had a lot of friends, Grandma, and the ones I do have I won't be seeing after I leave work. I don't want me family to find out where I am so it's best to make a clean break. Except for one boy – I'll probably go on seeing him 'cos he doesn't know me family.'

Joe leaned forward, his elbows resting on his knees. 'Don't yer get on with yer family, queen?'

'I get on with me two brothers and two of me sisters, but me mam and dad are no good. I know I shouldn't say bad things about them, but they should never have had children 'cos they don't look after them. Me dad spends all the money down at the pub while the kids go around like tramps and don't get enough to eat. There's no love or affection shown to any of the children – that's why I'm leaving. I can't take any more.'

Sadie gave a deep sigh. 'I don't want yer to worry that I'm hard to get on with, 'cos I'm not. I just want to live in a clean house, be liked and treated with respect. One day I might tell yer about me family and the sort of life I've had, but not now, Grandad, 'cos I'd only start getting upset. I will tell yer one thing, though, which might help yer understand why I have to get away. I'm sixteen years of age, I go to work six days a week, and I've never taken a day off all the time I've worked there. And for that I get a shilling a week pocket money, which I'm expected to buy all me own clothes out of and pay for me dinners.'

There was tenderness and sympathy in Joe's eyes. 'I'm sorry, queen, yer deserve better than that.'

'And she'll get better than that.' Sarah bustled in with the teapot and sugar and milk on a wooden tray. She'd delayed bringing them through because she didn't want to interrupt the girl. It would do her good to share some of her heartache. 'You an' me will make sure she does. And yer've got a good friend in Mary Ann, too. She'll be watching out for yer all the time, yer can bank on that.'

Sadie's face brightened. 'It's hard to believe how it all came about, isn't it? I only had one dress to me name and I'd scrounged sixpence to buy meself a second-hand one. And of all the stalls in Paddy's market, I picked on Mary Ann's.' She began to giggle. 'I'll tell yer sometime who I scrounged the tanner off, an' who I've been scrounging off since. But the first boy is the one I'll miss most of all. He's been a real good friend.'

'It's hard walkin' away from a life yer've been used to, queen; yer bound to be homesick for a while.'

'I won't be homesick, Grandad, 'cos yer see, I've never had a home. I lived in a house, that was all. I'll pine for me brothers an' sisters, I know that. But I intend keeping in touch with them. I don't know how, but I'll do it.'

Sarah didn't want the girl to leave feeling sad, so she quickly changed the subject. 'I bet yer never thought, the day yer met Mary Ann, that one day yer'd be working for her?'

Sadie shook her head. 'I've had a lot of dreams in me life, Grandma, dreams that I knew would never come true – like a knight in armour charging towards me on a white horse to sweep me off me feet and carry me away. I used to laugh at meself, the far-fetched things I dreamed about. But even in me wildest fantasies I would never have imagined Mary Ann offering me a job. And not only a job, but a whole new life.'

'Ah, well now, sweetheart, it cuts both ways, yer see. And Mary Ann would be the first to tell yer. She's gained as much from that first meeting as you have. I mean, she would never have thought up a superior-quality clothes stall, would she?' Sarah made a trip to the kitchen to pick up a plate of fairy cakes she'd baked that morning specially for Sadie's visit. She was chuckling when she came back in the room. 'If I tell yer somethin', yer must promise not to tell Mary Ann, or she'll have me guts for garters. Promise?'

Sadie nodded, 'I won't breathe a word.'

Sarah handed her the plate. 'Here, eat one of these while I'm tellin' yer, otherwise my feller will scoff the lot.'

Sadie reached out with both hands and took two off the plate. 'One for me and one for me Grandad.'

'I'll have one after,' Sarah said, 'I can't talk with me mouth full. Now, to get back to what I was saying – and yer won't half laugh when yer hear this. Mary Ann was tellin' me that when yer asked her if yer could sort through the clothes and pick out the best, she said to herself, "Oh well, she's only a kid and kids do like to play, so let her enjoy herself. She's not doin' no harm".' Sarah laughed at the memory of the stall-holder's face. She was a one for telling a tale was Mary Ann, you got all the actions to go with the words. 'Then she said, "I didn't half get me bleedin' eye wiped when she sold that blouse to Elsie for a tanner, I can tell yer! I'd have been lucky to have got thruppence out of her without a flamin' argument. And now, thanks to that kid who I thought was only messin' around, I'm the proud owner of the only superior-quality clothes stall on the bleedin' market!".' Sarah was satisfied with the smiles on the faces of her audience. 'So yer see, girl, you are very much appreciated by yer future boss.'

'I think I'll ask for a rise to go with me status,' Sadie grinned. 'After all, superior-quality clothes need a superior-quality salesgirl to sell them, don't you agree?'

Joe was sitting back in his chair thoroughly enjoying the company. Young Sadie was a right bonny girl, there were no two ways about it, and she had a ready smile and a sense of humour. All in all, it appeared that he and his Sarah had found the family they had always longed for but had given up hope of ever having. In the winter of their lives they had been granted a sunbeam.

'Would yer like to come up an' see yer room, sweetheart? I had a bit of beddin' that will do yer while the weather's mild, but before the winter sets in we'll have to get yer another blanket and a quilt.'

'I'll keep me eye out,' Sadie said, following in the slow footsteps of her new grandmother. 'Mary Ann gets bedding in sometimes, so we shouldn't have any trouble finding something decent.' Mentally she added, I'll have to get meself some warm winter clothes, too. It'll be bitter standing in that market in the cold weather.

'Here yer are, sweetheart.' Sarah opened the bedroom door and stood aside to let Sadie go in first. 'It's only a small room, I did warn yer, but it's cosy.'

'Oh!' Sadie clapped a hand to her mouth. The room was the same size as the bedroom at home, but there were five of them sharing that. This one was just for her. There was a single wardrobe, a small chest of drawers with a mirror hanging over it, a wooden kitchen chair and the bed that the King himself might have slept in. Oh, the luxury of it! A wardrobe all to herself and even a mirror! 'Grandma, it's beautiful. I won't know meself having such privacy. And yer've got the bed nice – I like the knitted cover.'

'I made that meself, many years ago. In fact, I made it when my Joe was still working so yer can tell how old it is. I could afford the wool then, with his money coming in.'

'Talkin' about money, Grandma, can yer tell me how much yer'll need for me keep?'

Sarah pursed her lips and frowned in concentration. 'I don't know, sweetheart, I've never had no lodger before. What had you in mind?'

'I honestly don't know. You'll have to tell me 'cos you know how much more food yer'll have to buy.'

'How about four bob a week, would that be too much?'

'Yer can't keep me on four bob a week!' Sadie's voice rose. 'Yer'll not get far on four shillings.'

'Sadie, four bob will go a long way in this house, believe me. It's only a case of a few more potatoes and a bit more of this an' that. When yer making a dinner, one extra is neither here nor there. Those few shillings will be a great help to me and Joe, I can tell yer.'

'All right then, Grandma, we'll start off with me givin' yer five bob, and I'll give yer extra when I can. Will that suit yer?'

'It's more than ample, sweetheart, if yer sure yer not leaving yerself short?'

'I'll have more in me pocket than I've ever had,' Sadie told her honestly. 'So I'll buy the bedding and I need some warm clothes for meself. I also want to try and get some warm clothes for me brothers and sisters or they'll freeze all through the winter.'

'Yer takin' a lot on yer shoulders for a young girl, sweetheart. Don't leave yerself skint every week – get out and enjoy yerself.'

'I do get out, Grandma, but I don't pay for meself. If a boy asks me out then it's only right that he should pay. If I had to fork out meself I'd never go anywhere 'cos I've never got the money.'

'But yer'll be better off after next week,' Sarah said. 'Yer'll have a bit more in yer purse each week.'

'I still won't pay for meself, not if I can help it, anyway.' Sadie had a determined look on her pretty face. 'Mary Ann told me to put a few coppers away for a rainy day an' I'm goin' to follow her advice. I'll buy all the things I've just mentioned, but after that I'm goin' to save up an' get a bit of money behind me.'

'You can cross my feller off yer list, then, sweetheart, 'cos he wouldn't be able to afford yer. He's never got more than a few coppers in his pocket, just enough for his half-pint of bitter a couple of times a week and his ounce of baccy.'

'I'll mug both of yer when I'm in the money, Grandma.' Sadie put her arm across Sarah's shoulders. 'I'll be tight-fisted with me boyfriends but never with you and Grandad.'

'Listen to me, lass, by just coming to live with us yer have given us something that no amount of money could buy. We'll have a reason for living now, with someone coming in from work every night and telling us all that's happened during the day. Someone to sit at the table and have a meal with us instead of me an' Joe sitting lookin' at each other with nothing to say. We love the bones of each other, but when yer get to our age and never go anywhere, there's nothing to talk about only the old days, and that makes us sad.'

'Yer'll not be sad when I'm here, 'cos I won't let yer be. I'll talk the hind legs off yer with all the goings-on at the market. There's some funny things happen there, I can tell yer. I'll have you and Grandad laughing yer socks off every night.'

'We'd better get downstairs or all me fairy cakes will be gone. He's got a very sweet tooth, has my Joe – can't resist a cake. And the sight of a slab of Cadbury's has him watering at the mouth.'

Sadie turned for a last look at the room that was to be her very own. She wanted it imprinted on her mind so she could dream it up if she started to get cold feet towards the end of the following week. She brought a smile to Sarah's face when she whispered, 'Goodbye, room, see yer next Saturday.'

Sadie stayed and had some tea with Sarah and Joe, then when she was leaving at half-seven they both came to see her off with a hug and a kiss. When she reached the corner of the street she turned to see them still watching her, Joe's arm across his wife's shoulders. She blew them a kiss before turning into Scottie Road, thinking how wonderful it was that two people still loved each other so much after sixty years. They would have made marvellous parents and it must have broken their hearts when their sons died so young.

Sadie was in high spirits as her long slim legs covered the ground, taking her to her meeting in the park with Harry. In her mind she went over every little detail of the house that was to be her new home. Sarah had it like a little palace and it would be a treat to come back to it every night after work. And the bedroom, well, she couldn't find the right words to describe how she felt about having a bedroom all to herself so she shivered with delight. But best of all were the two lovely people who had agreed to share their home with her. If she'd had a million people to choose from, they were the two she would have chosen.

As she neared her destination, Sadie's happiness dimmed. After tonight she'd only see Harry one more time. One more time to feel his gentle embrace and his tender lips on hers. No other boy kissed her like Harry did, even Geoff. There was nothing demanding about him, he was just, well, just nice. She would miss him, but with the passing of time she'd get over him. As he would get over her. Just a memory to be recalled with affection.

Harry was waiting inside the park gates and his face lit up at the sight of her. 'Yer look as lovely as ever, Sadie.' He reached for her hand and squeezed it as they walked towards their favourite spot, both hoping it wasn't taken over by a courting couple. 'The best-looking girl in Liverpool, bar none.'

'Flattery won't get yer nowhere, Harry Young. Yer probably have the same patter for all yer girlfriends.'

'I might say it to them,' Harry laughed and his dimples deepened, 'but I don't mean it, not like I do with you.'

'You'll fall for a girl one of these days, Harry, and yer'll be asking yerself what yer ever saw in "that Sadie Wilson from next door".'

'Never in a million years, Sadie.' He gave a sigh of relief at finding their speck empty. Reaching for her other hand, he held them both in his. 'To me you will always be the beautiful girl next door. Even when we're both old and grey, you will always be that.'

It's funny he should say that, Sadie thought. Me grandad said practically the same thing about me grandma. But me and Harry will never grow old together like they have; my family have made sure of that.

'The nights are drawing in pretty quick now,' Harry said, his head tilted slightly. 'In another couple of weeks it'll be dark at eight o'clock. How would yer fancy meeting me straight from work one night and we can go for a trip on the ferry? We could go to New Brighton and spend an hour at the fairground. You enjoyed it last time.'

'Yeah, okay.' Sadie had to force the words past the lump in her throat. 'I'd like that.'

Harry leaned forward and kissed the tip of her nose. 'That's not counted as a kiss, don't forget. I'm workin' me way up to one of me smackeroos so it'll last longer. It's got to see me over until Wednesday, and that's a long time.'

'Yer a soppy article, Harry Young. So soppy I'll let yer have two smackeroos tonight. That should keep yer going until Wednesday.'

When he dropped her hands and pulled her into his arms, Sadie laid her head on his chest and wished she could be straight with him and tell him there was no chance of her going on the ferry with him, because she would be long gone out of his life. But she knew she couldn't tell him that without also telling him where she was going and why.

She lifted her face and her blue eyes gazed into his deep brown ones. 'Can I have me first of the two kisses, please?'

Harry felt a tingle run down his spine. She was the only girl who had that effect on him. 'I'm always willing to oblige a lady. And seeing as you asked for this one, it doesn't count.'

When they parted half an hour later to make their way home by different routes, Sadie was clutching Harry's sixpence in the palm of her hand. It would be the last one she'd ever get from him and she vowed never to spend it. She'd keep it, no matter how hard up she was, so she'd always have something to remember him by. There was a sadness in her heart that took away some of the joy she'd felt earlier. Grandad was right – it was hard to walk away.

Harry was whistling as he neared home and there was a spring in his step. A night out with Sadie, hours in her company instead of a stolen half-hour, was really something to look forward to. He grinned as he remembered the ride in the ghost train, when she'd clung to him in fear. They'd definitely have another go on that!

Bobby proved himself the perfect gentleman by sharing his attentions between Sadie and Brenda. And while Sadie was grateful to him, Brenda was delighted to be treated with such courtesy. He sat between them in the picture house and handed them each a small box of Cadbury's chocolates. He would have preferred to be on his own with Sadie, holding her hand in the darkness of the cinema, but she'd asked him not to leave Brenda out or she'd feel like a gooseberry. And he had to admit that the girl sitting on his left was a lot more pleasant to him than she had been on the night they were out in a foursome. And with a smile on her face instead of a frown, she was really quite pretty. Not in the same class as Sadie, mind, but then very few girls were.

When the picture house emptied, the threesome stood on the pavement outside and waited for the crowds to disperse. 'I enjoyed that,' Brenda said. 'I think the Three Stooges are a scream.'

'Yeah, it was a good laugh.' Bobby grinned at Sadie. 'Did yer like the picture, Sadie?'

'It was hilarious,' Sadie lied. In fact, if they asked her she couldn't have told them what the film was about because her mind had been elsewhere. Everything she did these past few days was in the knowledge that it would be for the final time. Like last night with Harry – it was almost more than she could bear when he said he'd see her on Sunday as usual. It took all her willpower not to blurt out the truth. She was surprised he didn't notice the change in her, how she'd kissed him as she never had before and held him as though she never wanted to let him go. And when she drank in his features, his mop of dark hair, deep brown eyes, strong white teeth and attractive dimples, she really didn't want to let him go. But even if she stayed he would never be hers, there would always be a barrier between them.

Tonight was the same. This was the last time she'd go out with Bobby. But while she was fond of him, there wasn't the depth of feeling there that she had for Harry.

'Look, Bobby, you don't live far from Brenda, why don't yer see her home?' Sadie hoped her attempt at matchmaking wouldn't be in vain. 'I'll be all right on me own.'

Bobby didn't like that idea one little bit. Blimey, he hadn't objected to the girl tagging along because that was what Sadie wanted, but to be expected to see her home was taking things a bit too far. 'I'm not leaving yer here on yer own. We'll see Brenda safely on the tram, then I'll walk yer part of the way home like I always do.'

'Bobby, that's a crazy idea! You get the same number tram as Brenda, yer may as well travel together.' Sadie could see his forlorn expression, and as she leaned forward to kiss him on the lips she told herself that was another thing she was doing for the last time. 'It's only for tonight, Bobby.'

A kiss in public from Sadie raised his spirits. She wouldn't have done that if she didn't like him. 'Oh, okay, as long as yer sure yer'll be all right.'

'Go on, poppy off, I'll see yer both tomorrow in work.'

Sadie watched them walk away, thinking that her disappearance would bring them together. They were bound to wonder why she didn't come to see them as promised, and the more they talked and wondered, the closer they'd become. At least, that was Sadie's hope.

On the Saturday morning Sadie sat on her bed waiting for her father to leave for work. When she heard the front door close behind him she carefully pulled the paper bag from under her bed. In that bag were all her worldly possessions: a dress, blouse and skirt and a change of underwear. The small things – her purse, comb, lipstick and soap – were in her handbag. She crept to the door, avoiding the floorboard that creaked, then turned to look at the four sleeping children in the double bed. Last night, before she went out to meet Geoff, she'd kissed each of them and said a silent goodbye. It wasn't goodbye for ever, she would definitely see them again as soon as possible. But that thought wasn't enough to stop her tummy from turning over with nerves, guilt and sadness.

Downstairs, Sadie made herself a jam buttie and poured out a cup of the tepid tea left over from her father. Then as she sat at the table eating her meagre breakfast, her eyes raked the room. The broken-down side-board that her father had been too lazy to ever fix, the cluttered table that her mother and Dot never thought of clearing, the floor which was so dirty your feet stuck to the lino, and the tattered and torn couch with the springs sticking up through the filthy moquette. But worse than the sight of the filthy room was the smell. Dirt mixed with urine, soiled nappies and sweat. It was so strong it was nauseating and Sadie screwed up her face as she forced herself to eat the bread and drink the tea. She'd get nothing else to eat now until she got to Sarah's, and she couldn't go all day on an empty tummy.

Sadie got to her feet and picked up the paper bag and handbag. She took one last look around and compared this room to that of her new home. Regrets? Not in a million years.

Chapter Sixteen

'Ah, ay, Elsie, it's easy worth sixpence.' Sadie held up the blue jumper which had a round neck, long sleeves and was knitted in an attractive open-work pattern. 'If yer don't want it I'll have it me blinkin' self!'

They both looked down at their busts, then at each other's and burst out laughing. Elsie's breasts were the shape of footballs, and four times the size of Sadie's. 'Come off it, kid, it would be down to yer flippin' knees,' Elsie said. 'Talk about once round you and twice round the gasworks, wouldn't be in it. Little Orphan Annie would have nothin' on you if yer went out in that.'

'Well, perhaps if I looked like Little Orphan Annie yer'd take pity and buy it off me.' Sadie giggled as she imagined herself in the jumper. It was so big she could wear it as a nightdress – it would keep her feet warm in bed. 'Anyway, Elsie, everything on this stall is sixpence an' I can't do anything about it. Buy the flamin' jumper and I won't charge yer anythin' for the laugh.'

Elsie had every intention of buying the jumper but had been hoping to get a copper knocked off. She could see now that Sadie wasn't to be shifted and gave in, but not gracefully. 'I'll buy the bleedin' thing, if only for yer bare-faced cheek.'

The woman standing next to Elsie said in a quiet voice, 'I'll have it, Elsie, if you're not really fussy on it.'

'Sod off, Dot. I brought yer here to buy somethin', but not something I had me eye on. Sadie will find a nice bargain for yer, seein' as yer a friend of mine.'

'Hello, Dot.' Sadie smiled at the woman who was as tall and generously built as Elsie. She looked about the same age, too, but her hair was snow-white. 'Did yer have anythin' particular in mind? Blouse, jumper, skirt or underwear?'

'No, girl, just something that takes me fancy.'

'What about Tony, the bloke on the shoe stall opposite?' Over the weeks Sadie had learned that the more you talked, the more you sold. 'Does he take yer fancy?'

Dot grinned. 'That begs the question, would *he* fancy *me*?'

'Ay!' Elsie gave her friend a dig in the ribs. 'This is supposed to be a superior-quality clothes stall, not a ruddy knocking shop.'

'We aim to please our customers, Elsie,' Sadie said. 'If Dot fancies Tony then I'm quite prepared to oblige and go and ask him what price he puts on himself.'

'Well, while yer at it, ask if he's got a friend for me,' Elsie said. 'But tell him mine must have a few bob in his pocket and all his own teeth.'

'Okay, but hang on to yer sixpence until I've been over in case yer owe me more. Yer see, fixing yez up with fellers is an extra service and we charge tuppence for it.'

'Blimey, it is a knocking shop!' Elsie pushed the jumper into her basket and handed sixpence over. 'Hurry up an' serve me friend, I don't want to be seen associating with such disreputable people. That's how yer get yerself a bad name. There's an old saying, and it's a true one, that yer can tell a person's character by the company they keep.'

Dot winked at Sadie while jerking her head sideways at Elsie. 'If that's true, what the hell am I doing with you? Doesn't say much for my character, does it?'

While Sadie was showing a variety of blouses to Dot, a lilac-coloured one took Elsie's eye and that went into her basket and another sixpence was passed over. Not to be outdone, her friend also bought two items, bringing Sadie's takings up to seven shillings for the few hours she'd been there. She felt as though she was walking on air when she took the money to Mary Ann.

'That's good, isn't it, Mary Ann? Just think how much it'll be next week when I'm here for the full day.'

'Yer've done well, girl, but don't be expectin' sales like that every day. There'll be times when yer standin' on yer feet for hours on end, blue with the cold, and only take a couple of bob the whole bleedin' day. Especially in the winter when folk won't brave the cold unless they've got to. So learn to take the rough with the smooth, sunshine, and don't let anythin' get yer down 'cos it ain't worth it.'

'Okay, I'll remember that when I'm shiverin' with the cold. I'm good at imagining things, so when the snow's coming down I'll pretend the sun's crackin' the flags.'

'Yer'll have to teach me that trick some time, girl, 'cos I've got to admit I'm not at me best when it's raining or snowing,' Mary Ann said. 'It's me chilblains, yer see. They affect me something chronic when the weather's bad.'

'Will it be all right if I clear me stall away now?' Sadie asked. 'I told Grandma I'd be home for tea and I've got a date with Geoff at half-seven.'

'Yeah, go 'ed, there's not much doing now. By the way, did yer have enough money left after paying me to give Sarah something for yer keep?'

Sadie nodded, giving a smile of satisfaction. 'I'm straight with everyone, don't owe no one a penny. I'm what you would call skint and happy.'

'I can lend yer a couple of coppers if yer stuck, girl – yer only have to ask.'

'Thanks, Mary Ann, but I don't want to borrow. If I start straight from next week, I'll know exactly where I'm working and can spend accordingly.' Sadie put her hand on the stall-holder's arm. 'There is somethin' yer can do for me, though, Mary Ann.'

'Oh aye, here it comes! Navy blue dresses with white lace collars!'

Sadie looked mystified. 'What navy-blue dresses with white lace collars?'

'Nothing, girl, it's just that sometimes I have a good imagination, too. Not often, like, just perhaps once every blue moon. Anyway, whatever it is yer've got on yer mind, spit it out before it chokes yer.'

'Well, it's like this yer see.' Sadie clasped her hands together and held them to her chest. 'I wondered if yer'd think I was cheeky if I asked yer to let me call yer Auntie Mary?'

Mary Ann swallowed hard as she stared into the beautiful, flawless face. The face that had the power to reduce her to tears. 'I don't know what good yer think it'll do yer.' She held her chin in her hand and gave a weak smile. 'But if yer daft enough to want me for an auntie, then by all means be my guest.'

'It'll give me something to talk about when I go out with Geoff.' Sadie's face was aglow. 'I can say me grandma said this, or me grandad said that, and me Auntie Mary told me so-and-so. I've never been able to mention me family before, but I can now.' A big hug had Mary Ann gasping for breath. 'Thank you, Auntie Mary, that's a better present than selling those two blouses to Elsie's friend. In fact, I'm so happy, if we'd had this conversation before they came I'm sure I could have talked her into buying three.'

'Yer ambitious, girl, I'll say that for yer. Now poppy off and let me get some of these stragglers served. And tell yer grandma and grandad that yer Auntie Mary sends them her best wishes. Ta-ra, sunshine.'

'Ta-ra, Auntie Mary.'

'Hey, hang on a minute, girl, I've just thought of something.' Mary Ann was shaking with mirth when Sadie turned back. 'Yer know this imagination of yours, where yer able to think the sun's crackin' the flags when it's snowing? Well, yer wouldn't let yer imagination run away with yer, would yer? What I mean is, yer wouldn't stand in six inches of snow with a parasol over yer head to keep the sun off yer face, would yer? After all, not everyone's been blessed with this vivid imagination and if me customers thought me young assistant from the superior-quality clothes stall was doolally pop, they'd stay away in droves and I'd end up in the poor house.'

Sadie adopted a dramatic pose. With the back of an open hand across her brow, she sighed deeply before saying in a posh theatrical voice, 'Alas, an auntie of mine in the poor house – never! As long as I've got breath in my body, Auntie Mary, and me superior-quality clothes stall, the wolf will never darken your door. So have no fear, 'cos Sadie's here.'

'My God, you haven't half come out in the few months I've known yer,' Mary Ann said, keeping to herself the pride she felt at having, in a small way, helped bring this girl out of her shell and given her the confidence she was sadly lacking. 'Frightened of yer own bleedin' shadow, yer were, an' now yer giving me all the old buck yer can think of.' She waved her hand in dismissal. 'Go on, bugger off. And don't you dare turn up on Monday mornin' and say yer didn't enjoy yerself tonight or I'll want to know why.'

'I'm goin', I'm goin', I'm goin'! But first I want to put yer mind at rest, over me imagination an' yer customers leaving in droves. I promise that if I do have the urge to put a parasol up to keep the sun off me face, I'll be standin' in the snow with a pair of wellies on me feet. That way, yer customers will think I'm only half-doolally pop.'

'Sadie, if yer don't bugger off, so help me I'll flop yer one! Yer gettin' to be a right ruddy nuisance.' But the tenderness on the market woman's face was in contrast to her words, and when Sadie walked away there was a smile on her face. She had three people in her family now and she was a very happy girl. Better to have three friends that you loved and who loved you in return, than a mother and father who didn't give a toss for you. After all, you could choose your friends; you couldn't choose your parents.

There were three lads standing on the corner when Sadie turned into Penrhyn Street, and she blushed when they whistled after her. They looked about eighteen years old and one, who seemed very sure of himself, walked beside her with a cocky swagger. 'Where've you been hiding yerself, Blondie?' He wasn't put off by her silence. 'Where yer off to? How about comin' to the flicks with us?'

Sadie quickened her pace, furious with herself for blushing. 'Not that it's any of your business, but I'm going to me grandma's and then I'm goin' out with me boyfriend. Are yer satisfied now, nosy poke?'

It wasn't often such an attractive girl came down their street, and Peter Townley wasn't going to give up so easily. 'Where does yer grandma live?'

When Sadie came to a halt and faced him she got the shock of her life. He was so like Harry! Same build, same dark hair and brown eyes, the same lopsided grin. Only the dimples were missing. Even in her embarrassed and angry state she couldn't help but grudgingly admit he was a handsome lad. Clean and nicely dressed, too. But he wasn't Harry and he had no right to upset her by looking like him. 'It's none of your business where me grandma lives, so on yer bike and stop pestering me or I'll be late for me date.'

'Does she live in this street?'

Sadie huffed and shook her head impatiently. 'How many times do I have to tell yer that it's none of your business. Now just vamoose, will yer?'

'I'll soon find out,' Peter grinned. 'I'll follow yer.'

'What a pity yer've got nothing better to do with yer time.' Sadie took to her heels and pelted hell for leather down the street. She stopped outside Sarah's house and banged on the knocker as she fought for her breath. He had some cheek, that bloke!

Sarah opened the door with a smile of welcome on her face. 'Hello, sweetheart.' She looked over Sadie's head. 'This is a surprise, Peter. I didn't know you and me granddaughter knew each other.'

Sadie gasped and spun around. 'I don't know him from Adam! He's followed me an' I've never seen him before in all me life. And another thing, I wouldn't know him again if I fell over him.'

Sarah chuckled as she wagged a finger at the now sheepish-looking lad. 'I'm glad to see yer know a good thing when yer see one, Peter, but will yer please not frighten the life out of me granddaughter? She doesn't want to be accosted every day when she walks down her own street.'

Peter stood to attention at this news. 'Yer mean she's living with yer, Mrs O'Hanlon?'

Sarah nodded. 'I'm happy to say that she is, Peter.'

'I didn't know yer had a granddaughter, Mrs O'Hanlon. Where've yer been hidin' her?'

'Excuse me!' Sadie had been looking from one to the other; now she stood with her hands on her hips, her eyes flashing. 'Don't be talkin' about me as though I wasn't here. I have got a mouth of me own, yer know.'

Peter looked at the kissable lips and grinned. 'I had noticed.'

'I don't know who yer are, but yer a cheeky beggar,' Sadie said, wishing he didn't look so much like Harry. 'And in future when yer standin' on the street corner with yer mates, hoping to pick up girls, don't bother trying it on with me 'cos I'm not interested. Have yer

183

got that into yer big head, Peter who-ever-yer-are?'

'Peter Townley's the name, and I live next door.' There was merriment glinting in his brown eyes. 'It would be nice if you returned the compliment and told me your name, don't yer think? I mean, like, it wouldn't be nice if I just called yer "Mrs O'Hanlon's granddaughter", would it? Doesn't sound very neighbourly at all.'

Sadie snorted before pushing her nose in the air and stepping into the hall. 'I really couldn't care less what you call me.' She kissed Sarah's cheek. 'Grandma, tell him to leave me alone, please.'

As she watched Sadie stalk down the hall, Sarah bit on her bottom lip to keep a smile at bay. 'I'll try, sweetheart, but he's a very stubborn lad is Peter.' She gave him a broad wink. 'Still, I'll do me best, Sadie.' She put stress on the name and was rewarded with a thumbs-up sign. In a low voice she told him, 'I'd go now if I were you, Peter, it won't do yer no good to rub her up the wrong way. And it's not as though yer won't see her again – yer'll be bumping into each other every day.'

'I'll make sure of that, Mrs O'Hanlon. And may I congratulate yer on having a very lovely granddaughter . . . even if she can get in a right paddy?'

'It's spirit she's got, son, not a paddy. And what sort of a girl would she be if she let herself be picked up by a total stranger? Not the sort of girl yer mam would like yer to get mixed up with, I'm sure. Take a little bit of advice from an old woman, Peter, and next time yer see Sadie just say hello and walk on. She's a very happy, pleasant girl, as yer'll find out if yer give her time to get to know you. But I've got to tell yer she does have a boyfriend. She's seeing him tonight, so I'd better get in and make her tea.' Sarah was about to close the door when curiosity got the better of her. 'What on earth possessed yer to try and pick up a strange girl, Peter? I've never known yer do anythin' like that before. If yer mam found out, she'd box yer ears for yer.'

'I've never done it in me life before, Mrs O'Hanlon. Me and me mates were just discussin' where we should go tonight, and along comes this dream of a girl. I don't know what came over me; it all happened so quick – on impulse, like. I felt I wanted to get to know her and if I didn't do anythin' about it I'd never see her again. I didn't know she was livin' next door to me, or I wouldn't have dared.'

'No harm done, Peter, it'll all come out in the wash. Good night to yer, son.'

Sadie was standing by the sideboard waiting for her. 'That's a good start to me first day, isn't it, Grandma, fallin' out with yer neighbour's son. But I'm not taking the blame for it; he frightened the life out of me.'

'He took a fancy to yer, sweetheart, that's all.' Sarah went into the kitchen where Sadie's dinner was being kept warm on top of a pan of hot water. She brought it through and set it on the table. 'Here yer are, my girl, get that down yer. I bet yer've had nothing to eat all day and that won't do yer no good.'

Sadie sat down, and as her nostrils were invaded by the aroma wafting up from the plate of stew, she sighed with pleasure. 'Ooh, that doesn't half smell good, Grandma.' She could vaguely remember when she was a toddler her mother making dinners like this. But when the babies started to arrive at regular intervals, Lily lost interest, serving up whatever was quickest, easiest and cheapest.

Sadie picked up her knife and fork and licked her lips. 'Oh boy, am I going to enjoy this!' She tucked in with relish, watched by Joe and Sarah. The old couple were amazed and delighted at her appetite – little realising it was the first real meal she'd had in years. They didn't speak until Sadie's plate was empty and she was rubbing her tummy. 'I'm full to the brim . . . me eyes are bigger than me belly.'

'Lass, it was a treat just to watch yer,' Joe said. 'Took me back to when I was your age and could empty me plate in five minutes flat. I remember me ma used to leave me until last because I was such a glutton, but I still managed to clean me plate before the rest of the family.'

'The appetite of youth and energy, love,' Sarah smiled at him with love in her tired eyes. 'At sixteen yer hungry for everything in life, and hunger is good sauce.'

Sadie sat back in her chair feeling overwhelmed by the goodness in her life now. 'I was hungry, Grandma, but I'd have eaten that even if I wasn't 'cos it was delicious.'

'I hope yer've left a little spot in yer tummy for rice pudding?'

'What! You mean there's more to come? Oh Grandma, don't be spendin' extra money just because I'm here.'

Sarah scraped her chair back and stood up. 'Your extra five bob has made a hell of a difference to us, sweetheart. It means me and Joe can enjoy a few luxuries. And don't worry, I'm a good manager. I won't spend what we haven't got.'

When Sarah put the dish of rice pudding in front of Sadie, all milky and browned on the top by a sprinkling of nutmeg, the girl didn't know whether to laugh or cry. She had never tasted rice pudding in her life and it was all too much for her. This day would stay in her memory for ever, with the other eventful days in her life. Like the day Harry gave her the first sixpence, collected his first kiss, and the day he took her on the ferry to New Brighton. Then there was the day she first met

Mary Ann, and through her, Sarah and Joe. All these events would never be forgotten, no matter how long she lived.

Sarah waited until Sadie was halfway through the pudding before saying, 'With regards to Peter, from next door, I'd hate yer to have the wrong impression of him. Me and Joe have known him since the day he was born, haven't we, love? In fact, we used to mind him when his mam wanted to go anywhere. He's a good lad, honest as the day's long and he'd always do yer a good turn, never a bad one.'

The spoon stayed halfway to Sadie's mouth as she gave the matter some thought. Then, wanting to please Sarah, she smiled. 'We just got off on the wrong foot, Grandma, that's the top and bottom of it. I'll say hello to him next time I see him but, I've got to be honest with yer, if he tries to get fresh I'll thump him one.'

Joe was having trouble keeping his false teeth in place. They were a bloody nuisance and as soon as Sadie went out they'd be back in the cup of water. He'd had them twenty years and God only knows how he had persevered, but he just couldn't take to them. Like now, he couldn't enjoy a good belly-laugh. He opened his mouth and it came out like the cackle of a hen. 'That's right, queen, don't you stand no messin'. Tell them where to get off and make no bones about it.'

'I'll do that.' Sadie leaned across the table and winked at him. 'And I'll tell them me grandad said I had to do it.'

Sarah had her eye on the clock. 'I don't want to rush yer, sweetheart, but if yer don't make a move yer'll be late. I know they say it's a woman's prerogative to keep a man waiting, but I've never held with that view meself.'

'Well, that's news to me!' Joe's raised white eyebrows nearly touched his hairline. 'If I had a penny for every time I've stood outside the Rotunda for half an hour waiting for you, I'd be a rich man.'

Sadie touched his hand. 'I think yer a very rich man, Grandad. Yer've got Grandma an' that's worth more than all the money in the world.'

He moved his hand to cover hers. 'And now we've got you, me and my lovely Sarah are both lucky and rich.'

'Will you two cut it out?' Sarah reached for Sadie's plate. 'You go and make yerself pretty for yer young man, sweetheart. Five minutes late is acceptable, half an hour is not.'

'Geoff's not my young man, Grandma, he's just a friend that happens to be of the opposite sex. We're not going steady or anythin' like that, I'm too young to be thinkin' of settling down.' Sadie tried to stop Sarah from taking her plate. 'I'll wash up first, Grandma. It won't take me long – I'm a quick washer-upper.'

'Another night, perhaps, when yer've got more time, but not tonight.

Me an' Joe will have it done in no time, then we'll sit and listen to the wireless.'

'How will I get in, Grandma? We're going to the pictures and second house doesn't let out until half-ten. It'll be eleven before I get home.'

'Me an' Joe would stay up for yer, but we'd need matchsticks to keep our eyes open until that time of night. So we'll let yer have a spare key.'

'I'll be as quiet as a mouse when I come in.' Sadie gave an impish grin. 'I'll even stop breathin' until I'm in bed.'

Ten minutes later, standing in front of the mirror in her very own little room, Sadie pinched her arm to make sure she wasn't dreaming. All those years she'd longed and prayed for a better life, and now it was here. She raised her eyes to the ceiling and whispered, 'Thank You, God, for giving me all these things. I haven't forgotten me brothers and sisters, I'll do what I can for them, but in the meantime would You keep an eye on them, please, and see they come to no harm?'

Sadie pulled the front door closed behind her and started up the street. She was outside next door when who should appear on the front step but Peter. Oh dear, she thought, trust him! Another minute and I'd have been well away. Then she remembered her promise to Sarah and nodded curtly. 'Good evening, Peter.' Without giving the lad time to reply, she walked on quickly, her high heels tapping the paving stones. She'd got that over with, now he couldn't tell her grandma she'd ignored him.

But Sadie hadn't reckoned on the resilience of Peter. In a few strides of his long legs he was beside her. 'Good evening, Sadie.'

Sadie's jaw dropped and her step faltered. What was she going to do about him? Surely he wasn't going to pester her every time she left the house? If she thought he was getting fresh with her she'd thump him one, like she'd said. But all he was doing was walking beside her and if she told him to get lost he was cheeky enough to remind her that the pavement was public property.

'Got a heavy date, have yer, Sadie?'

She would have liked to look down her nose at him, but seeing as he was over six foot that was physically impossible. So she settled for what she thought was a look of scorn. 'I did tell you I had a boyfriend and was seeing him tonight. But perhaps yer a bit deaf, so as I've always been told not to mock the afflicted, I'll tell yer again, this time louder.'

Peter's hearty laugh rang out as he put a hand on her arm. 'There's no need to, I heard yer the first time.'

Sadie looked down at his hand. Now that was what she called getting fresh. 'If yer don't take yer hand away, I'll thump yer one.' Peter's laughter riled her even more. 'I mean it, yer big soft dope! Get yer hand off me or yer'll be seeing stars.'

Peter looked down on the small slender figure, one he could pick up with one hand, and his whole body shook with laughter. 'Mrs O'Hanlon said yer had spirit, and she never spoke a truer word. This street will never be the same again, Sadie what-ever-yer-name-is.'

'My name is for me to know and you to find out.' Sadie knew she wasn't going to win with this boy and the knowledge didn't please her. So she decided it was better to retire undefeated than lose altogether. 'My boyfriend will be getting worried, so if you don't mind I'd like me arm back. And I'm sure there's some daft girl waiting for you. I don't like pulling people to pieces, especially if I've never met them, but any girl that would go out with you must have a screw loose.'

'I can tell by yer eyes that yer dying to know, so I'll tell yer. Me and me two mates are meeting three girls at the Rialto. All the girls have a head, two arms and legs, and all the other oddments attached to the human body. And although I know yer won't believe me, I'll tell yer anyway – they've all got a fairly good brain box.'

Sadie jerked her arm free. 'All very interesting, I'm sure. But if yer'll excuse me, I'll be on me way before me boyfriend gets fed up waiting.'

'Oh, he'll wait for yer, Sadie. I know *I* would.'

'That is one occasion that will never arise, Peter I've-forgotten-what-yer-name-is, so if I were you I wouldn't lose any sleep over it.'

'Yer'll have to come dancing with me one night, Sadie. I'd really enjoy havin' the last waltz with you.'

Sadie hurried away without answering, but she knew a moment's sadness when he mentioned dancing. She hadn't been to a dance since the episode with Alec and she was sorry because she'd enjoyed it. She was beginning to get the hang of the different dances, had more confidence on the dance floor, and even had ambitions to become as skilled as some of the couples she'd seen spinning and twirling so effortlessly. How she had admired them. But whenever Geoff suggested going to the Grafton or the Rialto, she always found an excuse not to because she was afraid of bumping into Harry and embarrassing him. It was even more out of the question now. Tomorrow night he'd be waiting at the park for her as usual, and it grieved her that she'd deceived him so. And at the back of her mind she admitted that the instant dislike she'd taken to Peter was because he reminded her of Harry, and that was the last thing she wanted.

'I was beginning to think something terrible had happened to yer,' Geoff said, relief written on his face as he rushed towards her. 'Yer've never been this late.'

'I'm sorry, Geoff. I've moved in with me grandparents today and it's been all go. We'll still make the pictures in time, won't we?'

'Second house has probably started, but we'll be in time for the big picture.' Geoff cupped her elbow, thinking he didn't care where he went as long as she was by his side. 'When am I going to meet your grandparents?'

'Oh, give us a chance, Geoff! Let them get used to having me in the house first, before I start bringing visitors. They're old, yer know, over eighty.'

'They do know about me, don't they?'

'Of course they know about yer! Who d'yer think I told them I was going out with? Icky the fire-bobby?'

'Yer don't seem to be in the best of moods tonight, Sadie. I hope it's got nothing to do with me.'

'I'm just tired, that's all, Geoff. So much has happened today it seems like an eternity. But I can have a lie-in tomorrow and a nice quiet, lazy day.'

'There's no one buying tickets, it must be later than I thought.' Geoff pressed on Sadie's arm to urge her forward. 'I hope the kiosk isn't closed, or we've had it.'

They were lucky, the attendant was just about to close the window. 'Yer'd better hurry, the big picture's starting.'

They were shown to their seats as the credits were rolling, and Sadie was glad to take the weight off her feet. The film opened with a scene showing Victor McLaglen lumbering across a room with his familiar gait, and later that was all Sadie could remember about the picture because at that point she lost her concentration. She was dead tired, emotionally and physically, and the events of the long day had left her drained. It was a big step to leave home; even if it was what you wanted, it was still a big step. And saying goodbye to Brenda, knowing she'd never see her again, that had affected her. After that it had been one big rush . . . flying to her new home to hand over her five-shilling keep in case the old lady didn't have enough money to buy the extra food in, refusing to stay even for a cup of tea, then legging it to the market. It had been hard going, and if the truth were known she would have preferred to stay in tonight and spend a quiet night in her new home, getting to know her new family. But she couldn't let Geoff down, so here she was, tired out and with a splitting headache and sore feet.

Geoff glanced at Sadie's face as he reached for her hand. Her eyes were closing and she was having difficulty holding her head upright. Poor love, he thought, she looks dead beat. 'Here, put yer head on my shoulder and have forty winks.'

Sadie's eyes blinked rapidly as she tried to keep them open. 'I might snore.'

'I'll wake you if yer do. Go on, have half an hour.' Geoff watched her eyes close and within seconds she was sound asleep. He could feel her breath on his neck as he slipped his arm around her waist and held her close. He was crazy about her and wished she would show some sign that she felt the same way about him. But he couldn't get close to her; she kept him at arm's length. He'd been going out with her for months, but never once had she suggested taking him home to meet her family. He didn't even know where she lived; she was very secretive about her home life. Still, she'd half-promised to invite him to her grandparents' house – that would show she had some feelings for him. He wouldn't bring the subject up again tonight, she was too tired, but he would press her the next time they met. He had to know where he stood with her.

'D'yer fancy a game of rummy, queen?'

'What's rummy when it's out, Grandad?'

Joe looked surprised. 'It's a card game . . . surely yer've played cards, queen?'

Sadie shook her head. 'Never in me life, Grandad, honest! But yer can teach me – I'm quick at picking things up.'

'It's an easy game – so yer'll pick it up in no time,' Sarah said. 'A couple of hands and yer'll be knockin' spots off me and Joe.'

'It'll pass an hour away,' Joe said, opening a drawer in the cupboard built into the recess at the side of the fireplace. 'There's nothin' on the wireless that would interest a young girl like you.'

'I'll have a bash, Grandad, but yer'll have to be patient, me being a learner, like.'

'He's a one for cheating, is my Joe.' Sarah winked broadly. 'But I'll keep me eye on him until yer've got the hang of it.'

Sadie glanced at the clock, as she'd been doing every few minutes for the last hour. It was five to eight. 'I think I'd better nip down the yard first, save goin' in the middle of a game. I'd hate to give me Grandad a chance to cheat on me.'

Sitting on the scrubbed wooden bench-like seat of the outside lavatory, Sadie wrung her hands. Harry would be waiting for her outside the park gates right this minute. Oh, she should have told him; it was a lousy trick to play on him. Perhaps she could write to him and explain, say how sorry she was. If she did that, at least he'd know she cared. And she didn't have to tell him where she was – she could leave the address off. Yes, she'd do that tomorrow. She'd buy some paper and an envelope, and write it in the privacy of her bedroom tomorrow night. She knew she'd never see Harry again, but she couldn't bear the thought of him thinking ill of her.

Her heart a little lighter, and a smile on her face, Sadie walked back up the yard to be introduced to her first game of cards.

Harry paced up and down outside the park gates. He'd been waiting for half an hour and was now beginning to lose hope. Perhaps she didn't feel well and wasn't able to let him know. There must be a good reason; Sadie wouldn't let him down unless it was something important. But he couldn't help feeling depressed. His whole life revolved around his twice-weekly meetings with her, and right now he felt so disappointed he could cry. He'd have to try and catch her coming home from work tomorrow night to ask why she hadn't turned up. And he needed to see sight of her; he couldn't wait until Wednesday – that was a lifetime away.

Harry didn't whistle on his way home, he felt too miserable. He'd have to bring his relationship with Sadie out into the open; he couldn't carry on like this. He knew his mother would go mad, but it was his life and the one thing he was certain of was that Sadie was the only girl with whom he wanted to spend it.

Chapter Seventeen

Mary Ann stood shaking her head as she watched Sadie going through the bundle of clothes she'd just opened. It was a ritual with her now, checking each bundle for clothes that would suit her brothers and sisters. This was her sixth week working at the market and once or twice a week she'd find something suitable and it would be put away until the weekend when she got her wages and could pay for them.

'It's none of my business, girl, but surely to God yer've got enough clothes now to kit the bleedin' army out! Isn't it about time yer started getting some gear for yerself? It's nippy this morning, yer could do with something warm on.'

'I'm only young, Auntie Mary, and young ones don't feel the cold like you oldies.' Sadie grinned. 'Anyway, I'm saving up until a fur coat comes in.'

'Huh! Yer'll have a long ruddy wait, sunshine. If a fur coat comes in . . . and it's a big flamin' "if" . . . yours truly will be first in line. I don't mind yer havin' the superior-quality clothes stall, even if it does make yer sound more posh, but when it comes to yer havin' a fur coat, well, I draw the line at that.'

Sadie handed her a boy's grey shirt that had obviously been worn as part of a school uniform. 'Will yer put it away for me, Auntie Mary, please? I can pay yer for that today and that'll keep us straight.'

Mary Ann huffed as she took the shirt. 'I think it's bloody ridiculous that yer spendin' yer hard-earned coppers on clothes when it's yer mam's place to buy them.'

'I know she should buy them, Auntie Mary, but the trouble is, she doesn't. And I don't spend all me money on them – I always put at least one and six away every week. And don't forget I've bought some beddin' for meself, as well, so I haven't done too bad. And now I've got enough clothes for the kids I'll start to see to meself.'

'Now yer've got all this gear, what d'yer intend doin' with it? Have yer thought of a way to get it to them without yer mam and dad seein' yer?'

Sadie nodded, 'Yeah, I've got it all figured out.' She was looking very pleased with herself. 'If you'll let me have an hour off one afternoon, I can be outside our Jimmy's school when he comes out.'

Mary Ann looked suitably impressed. 'Ay, that's a good idea. Yer not just a pretty face, are yer, girl?'

'No, I do have a few loose brains rattling around in me head.' The grin slipped from Sadie's face. 'Can I go tomorrow, Auntie Mary? I'm dying to see him, and to find out how all the others are.'

'Of course yer can, girl, it's only natural yer want to see him. Are yer goin' to tell him where yer live, and that yer work here?'

'No, it wouldn't be fair on him. He's only ten, and me mam and dad would easy get it out of him. I'm not goin' to ask him to lie, so it's best if he doesn't know. What he doesn't know, he can't tell. I've been the biggest liar on God's earth for the last two years – I don't want to turn him into a liar as well.'

'The lies you told never hurt anyone, girl, so don't be losing no bleedin' sleep over it. If yer parents had been halfway decent it wouldn't have been necessary.'

'There was someone I hurt with me lies.' Sadie eyes were on the ground. 'I hurt the one person who'd been more kind to me than anyone.'

'Yer talkin' about Harry, the boy next door?'

Sadie nodded. 'God will punish me for what I did to him.'

'Are yer still hankering after him, sunshine?'

'I do miss him,' Sadie admitted. 'But I wouldn't feel so bad if I could have told him to his face that I was leaving.'

'I was under the impression that yer'd written and explained.'

'I did, but words on a bit of paper are cold; I would rather have said it to his face. We could at least have parted as friends.'

'Don't be getting yerself all upset,' Mary Ann said. 'Just think of what yer've got to look forward to tomorrow.'

Sadie hugged herself. 'Yeah, I'm really looking forward to seeing our Jimmy. I bet he's grown a lot in the last six weeks. I wish it was tomorrow now.'

'Well, the time passes slowly when yer hands are idle, girl,' Mary Ann said, her face as straight as a poker, 'so why don't yer sort that bundle out and take whatever yer think is suitable for yer superior-quality clothes stall? It's not that I don't like standing jangling with yer, 'cos I'd go as far as to say I'm quite partial to it. Unfortunately, I'm also quite partial to eating, an' the way we're going on there'll be no bleedin' money to satisfy me partiality.'

Sadie feigned a frown as she tilted her head. 'I don't think that's very good English, Auntie Mary.'

'What's not good English, girl?'

'What you've just said. I've never heard anyone say "satisfy me partiality".'

'Of course yer have!'

'I have not!'

'Yer've just bleedin' well heard *me* say it, yer daft ha'porth! If I hadn't said it, why would you have said yer'd never heard of it?'

Sadie raised her hands in a gesture of surrender. 'You win, Auntie Mary, I know when I'm beat.' She went back to sorting the clothes out but could not stop her laughter from erupting. 'Yer know, Auntie Mary, if the customers that come to my superior-quality clothes stall heard the language out of you, they'd be decidedly highly indignant.'

'What does that mean, girl?'

'What does what mean, Auntie Mary?'

'This decidedly highly indignant lark. Haven't never heard that before.'

'Yes, you have.'

'Oh yeah, silly me, of course I've heard it before – from you! Honestly, I've got a head like a bleedin' sieve.' Mary Ann clapped a hand over her mouth. 'There I go again with me bad language. Oh, woe is me, I'll never get promoted to the superior-quality clothes stall. I'm destined to remain forever on the tuppence with a hole, thruppence without a hole.'

The two of them burst out laughing before attacking the bundles with a vengeance to make up for the time spent jangling.

Sadie stood with her hand gripping one of the bars of the school railings, the bundle of clothes at her feet. She'd heard the school bell go a short while ago and knew that any minute now, swarms of children would pour out of the doors screaming and shouting, rejoicing in their freedom from the fear of a rap on the knuckles with a ruler or, horror of horrors, three strokes of the cane. And if they went home and complained that they'd had the cane just for turning around in the middle of a lesson, they'd be told they must have deserved it and get a cuff on the ear for good measure.

The double doors burst open and the stampede began. Sadie's breath was coming in short gasps and her tummy was turning over as her eyes scanned the faces of the boys. There were so many she began to fear she'd miss her brother, and when the crowd petered out and he still hadn't appeared, her heart sank. She'd either missed him or he wasn't at school. She had almost given up hope when a lone figure emerged through the doors.

'Jimmy!' Sadie waved her hand through the railings. 'Over here!'

The boy stopped and screwed up his eyes as he tried to make out who was calling his name from the other side of the high railings. Then, when recognition dawned, his face broke into a smile and he dashed across the playground and through the gates. 'Sadie!'

Sadie held her arms wide and he ran into them. As they hugged each other, tears streamed down his face and for a brief second he felt ashamed in case any of the other boys in the class saw him. Then when he looked into his sister's face and saw how happy she was to see him, he stopped worrying about being called a cissie. 'Are yer coming home, our Sadie?'

Sadie held him away from her. 'Yer've shot up since I last saw yer. The way yer going on, yer'll be head and shoulders over me soon.'

Jimmy seemed to grow in stature at her words. But he wanted an answer to his question. 'Are yer comin' back home?'

'No, Jimmy, I'm not ever going back home. But I've missed yer and I think about yer all the time.' Sadie touched the bundle with her toe. 'I've been saving up an' I've brought some clothes for yer. There's things there for you, some for Ellen, Les and the baby. So yer see, although I might not be there, yer always in me mind.'

Jimmy looked crestfallen. 'It's terrible at home without yer. Me mam and dad do nothin' but shout at us and our Dot's a holy terror. Nobody smiles any more, not since you left. Won't yer come home, our Sadie, please?'

Sadie's heart went out to him. His clothes were dirty and torn, he had no socks on and his shoes were falling off his feet. It was such a shame because he was a nice-looking boy and dressed decently would be a credit to anyone. 'I'm sorry, Jimmy, but I couldn't live in that house any more. And I'll never live with me mam and dad again, nor our Dot. You know I had no life there. I was sixteen and didn't have a friend because of them. I used to be ashamed walking down the street because of them. Frightened to have a boyfriend because of them. No, Jimmy, I couldn't face living like that again.'

'Where are yer livin', our Sadie? Couldn't I come and live with yer? I wouldn't be no trouble, honest, I'd be as good as gold.'

'I haven't got a place of me own, Jimmy, I live with someone. And I'm not goin' to tell yer where it is in case me dad belts it out of yer. But I promise yer this, and it goes for Ellen and Les, too, that as soon as I'm old enough to get a house of me own, I'll have yer all to live with me. And that's a promise.'

'I'd like that, our Sadie, livin' with you. We'd have a nice clean house, wouldn't we, like Mrs Young next door.'

Sadness wrapped around Sadie's heart. 'Yes, Jimmy, like Mrs Young.'

'Her son stopped me one day – you know, the one called Harry. He asked me where yer'd got to, said he hadn't seen yer around.'

'And what did yer tell him?'

'I couldn't tell 'im nothin', could I? I said we didn't know where yer were, that yer'd just left home.'

Sadie sighed. For a brief moment she thought of giving Jimmy a message to pass on to Harry, but she quickly dismissed the idea. 'I had to be underhanded, Jimmy, otherwise I wouldn't have got away with it. But tell me what happened on the Saturday I did leave. What did me mam and dad say?'

'There was ructions! Me mam sent me down to the factory to see if yer were working late, but the place was closed. She was ranting about what she'd do to yer when yer got in, for leavin' her without money. Then when it got to night-time she said she was goin' to the police, but me dad wouldn't let her. I'll leave out the bad swearwords he used, our Sadie, 'cos they was terrible. He said, "Can't yer get it through yer thick head that the so-and-so has left home, yer silly old cow?".'

'Are things still as bad, Jimmy?'

'Well, our Dot's had to go out to work.'

Sadie gasped. 'Go 'way! When was this?'

'The week after yer left. There was murder over it. Our Dot was dead hard-faced with me mam, said she had no intention of findin' a job and that was that. But me mam gave her the hidin' of her life, belted her all around the room and said if she didn't get out the next day and find herself a job she'd break her so-and-so neck.'

Sadie's eyes were wide. 'What did me dad have to say about that?'

'He agreed with me mam that they needed the money. So our Dot now works at that tobacco factory, and she hates it. She's hard, is our Dot, as hard as nails. She goes out with fellers now an' sometimes it's turned twelve when she comes in.'

'What about the others, Jimmy; Ellen, Les and the baby? Does me mam look after them proper?'

Jimmy scraped the ground with the toe of his shoe. 'Nah, the house is a tip and we don't get fed proper. An' yer can see by the state of me that she still doesn't buy us anythin' to wear, even though our Dot's working. Me dad spends all the money down at the pub.'

There were lots of questions Sadie would have liked to ask, but not of a ten-year-old boy. 'Well, I've brought yer some decent clothes so yer'll be all right for a few months. And yer can tell me mam I met yer outside school, but I wouldn't say where I was living.'

'I will see yer again, though, won't I? I don't half miss yer, Sadie.'

'Yer'll see me again, I promise. I can't tell yer when, but I'll be waiting here for yer one day when yer come out of school. But let it be our secret – don't tell me mam in case she takes it into her head to keep watch on yer. Give our Ellen a big kiss from me and say I hope she likes the clothes. And our Les and Sally.' Sadie pulled a face. 'I bet I wouldn't know the baby, she must be walking by now.'

'Yeah, she's into everythin',' Jimmy said proudly. He idolised his little sister. Many's the clout he'd had off Dot because he'd stopped her from hitting the baby. 'She looks like you, our Sadie. Me mam said she's the spittin' image of you when you was a baby.'

'Oh, so me name does get mentioned in the house, does it?'

Jimmy nodded. 'Yeah, me and Ellen, and Les, we're always talkin' about yer. And the day me mam was givin' our Dot that hiding, she told her that it should have been her what left home 'cos you'd make ten of her.'

'She's left it too late in the day to be thinkin' that,' Sadie said. 'She can't rub sixteen years away with a few words. But I haven't let it ruin me life for me, I've got out and I'm learning what it's like to be normal. To live in a house that's clean, with people who love each other and don't even raise their voices, never mind shouting and cursing. And I've made some good friends, Jimmy, real friends that are kind and who help yer when yer in trouble. When you're older, you can do that, too. Don't let me mam and dad ruin yer life like they tried to ruin mine. Just keep thinking ahead to when yer old enough to break away. I'll be there for yer, I'll always be there for you and the other kids. Tell our Ellen and Les that for me, will yer? And tell them I love you all very much. I know Sally's too young to understand, but will yer mention me name to her now and again, so she won't forget me?'

Jimmy looked down at the bundle. 'Yer said there were some things in there for Sally, so I'll tell her it was you what sent them. And every time she's got somethin' on that you sent, I'll remind her they were a present from you.'

Sadie sighed. 'I'd better go, I only got an hour off work. But I feel heaps better now I've seen yer. I feel so proud of me handsome brother.'

'Which way are yer goin', Sadie? Are yer goin' the same way as me?'

Sadie shook her head. 'No, I'm goin' up to the main road to hop on a tram. Can yer manage that bundle all right?'

'If you can manage it, then it should be easy-peasy for me.' Jimmy moved from one foot to the other, feeling uncomfortable. Wanting to say so much but not knowing quite how to say it. 'Thanks, our Sadie, for not forgetting us. I told our Ellen and Les that yer never would, not in a million years, but when the weeks went by I was beginnin' to think we'd never see or hear from yer again.'

Sadie held her arms wide again and he walked into them. 'I love yer,

Jimmy, yer big daft ha'porth! And when yer love someone, yer don't forget them. I'll be down to see yer again in a couple of weeks, I promise.'

Words of love didn't come easy to a boy who lived in a house where they were never used. But this beautiful sister of his had been the only one who had ever shown affection to him and the other children. She'd given them the love their mother wasn't capable of. He couldn't let her go without telling her. 'We all love you, yer know, our Sadie.' He was close to tears. 'I don't half wish we could live with yer, we'd be a real happy family then.'

'So do I, Jimmy, so do I. And although it's only a dream now, I'll do my damnedest to make the dream come true.' She kissed his cheek. If she didn't get away right now she'd burst out crying. 'I'll see yer in a couple of weeks. Don't forget to give my love to the others.' With that she took to her heels and fled, leaving the young boy gazing at her retreating figure. He watched until she was out of sight, then, with a deep sigh, he picked up the heavy bundle. He didn't often say his prayers, but from now on he'd say them every night to ask God to help Sadie find a way of making the dream come true.

There was a look of anxiety on Mary Ann's face. 'Well, did yer see him, girl?'

Sadie nodded. 'I've cried all the way back, I couldn't help it. The tram conductor asked me if I was all right and that made me cry even more.' She wiped her eyes with the back of her hand. 'And d'yer know what? He wouldn't take me fare off me.'

'Go 'way! My God, girl, yer flamin' face would get yer the parish! If I sat on the tram cryin' me eyes out, the conductor would probably lend me his bleedin' hankie! *And* he'd ask for it back when I was gettin' off.' The market woman was trying to cheer Sadie up and was relieved when she was rewarded with a faint smile. 'Mind you, if he did, I'd blow me blinkin' nose on it first an' it would serve him right.'

Sadie stretched out a hand to stroke the bright red hair. 'I love you, Auntie Mary, I really do. Yer cheer me up when I'm down in the dumps, an' yer shoulder is always there for me to cry on. I don't know what I'd do without yer – I'd be completely lost.'

'No yer wouldn't, girl, 'cos yer a fighter. But I wouldn't want yer to get on without me, not now. I've grown used to yer an' we make a good team. An' as I've told yer before, it cuts both ways. Or, as my feller would say, you scratch my back an' I'll scratch yours. If it wasn't for you I wouldn't be the envy of every stall-holder in the market, not just for me superior-quality clothes stall, but also because of me young assistant looking like a bleedin' film star!' Mary Ann folded her hands across her tummy and nodded her head with a pleased and knowing look on her face. 'Before you came to work here, girl, the only men who ever came to the stall were with their wives, or maybe every other Pancake Tuesday we'd get a bloke on his own, but that's about it. Now, suddenly all the blokes workin' the market are showin' an interest in what their wives are wearing! Take Tony from over yonder – he'd never bought a thing off me before, but I bet his wife's got enough superior-quality blouses and jumpers now to open her own bleedin' shop. And the same goes for Andy and Bill and the rest of them. And the young ones that aren't married, they're buyin' them for their mams! What the womenfolk think is anyone's guess.' Mary Ann's green eyes twinkled as she gave a broad wink. 'They're probably wonderin' what brought on this sudden rush of generosity but, like me, they know when they're on to a good thing so they keep their traps shut.'

'That was a very long speech, Auntie Mary,' Sadie said. 'And it's done what yer wanted it to do, stop me from bawling me eyes out.'

'Well, I mean, girl, yer've got to see it from my point of view. If you were to stand here sheddin' yer tears over all the goods, it wouldn't do me business any good, now would it? Like I keep sayin' to Maggie when she gets herself all het up, it would be very inconsiderate of her to have a heart attack in front of my stall. Customers don't like it, yer see, girl – it puts them off buying.'

'Yer can knock it off now, Auntie Mary, I've decided to leave me crying until I'm in bed tonight. I can't cry in peace when yer making me laugh all the time.'

'That's my girl.' The stall-holder rubbed her hands together. 'Now yer can tell me how yer got on with yer brother. Was he pleased to see yer?'

'He was as pleased to see me as I was to see him. He said he thought I'd forgotten them and they'd never see me again. By them I mean Jimmy and our Ellen and Les. He gave me all the news from home, which wasn't very much. The house is still filthy and he said there's nothin' but fighting and swearing. But there was one piece of news that surprised and pleased me; our Dot was made to go out and get a job. Jimmy said she hates it and that pleased me even more. It's about time somebody put their foot down with her, she's too cheeky by far. She's just fifteen now, and our Jimmy said she goes out with boys and doesn't get in until after twelve o'clock.'

'Well, yer mam's to blame for that. Fancy allowing your Dot to come in at that ungodly hour. When I was her age I had to be in by half-past nine or me da would be waitin' behind the door for me with his belt in his hand.'

'Huh! Me dad would never hit our Dot, she's his blue-eyed favourite and gets away with murder. Me mam might hit her, but not me dad.'

'Makin' a rod for their own backs, they are. They'll be lucky if she doesn't bring trouble to their door, you mark my words.' Mary Ann shook her head so vigorously a lock of her red hair came loose from the tortoiseshell comb and dropped to cover her eyes. 'The best thing yer ever did was get out of that house, girl, and that's a fact.'

'Yeah, but I had to leave the other three behind, that's what saddens me. Our Jimmy asked me to go back again and I felt really mean when I said I couldn't. Then he asked if he could come and live with me, and that's what made me cry. They shouldn't have to live in those conditions, Auntie Mary, it's just not fair.'

'And it's not fair that you should have the bleedin' worry of them on your shoulders, neither. There's not a thing yer can do about it, sunshine, only help them where yer can. Those clothes today are serving two purposes. They'll rig them out so they look decent, and they'll also remind them that yer haven't forgotten them and yer love them enough to spend yer hard-earned money on them.'

'I'm goin' to make sure they have something for Christmas, too.' Sadie's chin was set with determination. 'I know it's a long way off yet, but it'll give me time to save up. They'll not have any more Christmases without new clothes or even a little present.'

Mary Ann shook her head. 'No presents under the tree?'

'What tree, Auntie Mary? We didn't even have a fire in the grate. But me mam and dad didn't feel the cold; they had a bottle of whisky to keep them warm and me dad had enough ciggies in to last over the holiday.'

'It's bloody unbelievable.' Mary Ann ground the words out with anger. 'I can't make up me mind what I'd do to your parents if I could get me hands on them. Should I slit their throats, strangle them or have them hung, drawn and quartered? I sound real bloodthirsty, don't I, and I've never been one for fighting – I'd walk away first. So what I would do is to shame them. Stand them in a cart with a placard round their necks and drive them through every street in Liverpool. That's what they should do to all the people who are cruel to children. Show them up and let their neighbours know what they are so they can punish them every day by treating them like lepers.'

'They'll get paid back, Auntie Mary, God will punish them. I don't care what happens to them, it's just the three kids I'm concerned about. Well, four really, but the baby's too young for me to cope with. I'll do what yer said, keep in touch and take clothes to them. And for Christmas I'll buy them games, 'cos if I bought them sweets our Dot would pinch them and I wouldn't give her a drop of water if she was dying of thirst. I know it's terrible to talk about me own sister like that when I've been taught to forgive them that trespass against us, but I'll never forgive her for some of the things she's done, never.'

'Forget about her, sunshine, put her out of yer mind 'cos she's not worth the space she's taking up. Just concentrate on the other three – that's more than enough for a young girl like you.' Mary Ann tutted with frustration as she anchored the wayward lock of hair behind her ear. 'Anyway, girl, I've got some news that should cheer yer up. Will yer promise to put a smile on yer face if I tell yer?'

'Is it good news?'

'I should bleedin' well think it is! D'yer remember when yer started to work here, I told yer if yer did well I'd give yer an increase in wages?'

'I remember, Auntie Mary, but yer didn't make any promises so don't worry about it 'cos I manage all right.'

'Oh, what am I goin' to do with you! You can be as daft as a brush sometimes, girl, yer drive me to distraction. Yer've got to be more pushy in this life or yer'll never get on.' Mary Ann raised her eyes to the heavens and said softly, 'God give me strength.' Then she pushed her face close to Sadie's. 'Yer know how well yer superior-quality clothes stall does, so why don't yer ask me for a rise?'

Sadie stared back. 'Because I know I don't have to ask. If you can afford it I know yer'll give it to me.'

Their noses were almost touching now. 'In that case,' said Mary Ann, 'I'll put yer wages up to ten bob a week from this Saturday.'

Sadie's jaw dropped and it was several seconds before her eyes began to sparkle. 'Ten bob a week? I don't believe it. Ten whole shillings a week! Oh, you wonderful, wonderful woman!' She grabbed Mary Ann around the waist and twirled and twirled until the stall-holder begged for mercy.

'That's the last bleedin' time you get a rise,' Mary Ann gasped when she found her feet. 'I'm glad I didn't have no dinner, otherwise it would have come back again.'

Tony had been watching with interest from the shoe stall opposite. He liked Sadie; in fact, all the stall-holders liked her, you couldn't help it. She was always happy and polite and would run an errand for anyone. And she was a joy to look at. 'Hey, what's the celebration? If there's to be a party then I want an invite.'

Sadie beamed across. 'I've just had a rise in me wages, Tony, isn't that the gear?'

'It sure is, kiddo. And yer deserve it, too.'

'Ay, Tony Henshaw, don't you be fillin' her head, now.' Mary Ann wagged a finger at the laughing market man. 'She'll be askin' me for a rise every week if yer keep tellin' her how good she is.'

'No, I won't, Auntie Mary.' Sadie was over the moon. She'd have five whole shillings for herself every week. No she wouldn't, she'd give an extra shilling to her grandma for her keep. Or, better still, she'd buy her and Grandad a little present every week, a little luxury they wouldn't otherwise be able to afford. Oh, she'd be rich with all that money in her pocket every week.

Mary Ann snapped her fingers in Sadie's face. 'Wake up, girl, it's time to clear away. For all the business we've done today we may as well have stayed at home.'

'Are yer sure yer can afford to give me that rise, then?' Sadie's spirits had dropped; she'd rather manage on what she was getting than take money that Mary Ann couldn't really afford to give her.

'Of course I can! Don't take any notice of me moanin', it comes natural to me. And a good moan does yer a power of good. We always have slack days through the week, but we make it up at the weekend.'

'Would yer think I'm cheeky if I make a suggestion on how I think yer could take a bit more money on the stalls? Yer can tell me to get lost if yer like, but I think it's worthwhile talkin' about it.'

'If it's another superior-quality clothes stall yer've got in mind, girl, then yer can sod off because we don't get that many good clothes in.'

'No, it's not that. Yer know Rita, the one who has the second-hand clothes stall just further down? Well, it was looking at her things that gave me the idea. She has everything in piles on the ground and the people have to bend down and rummage through them. Some of her stuff is quite good but it's mixed in with all the tatty stuff and people aren't going to root through a pile of rags.'

Mary Ann put a hand over her mouth to stop a chuckle from escaping. 'Don't tell me, yer in the money now and yer going to buy Rita out?'

'Stop messin' around, Auntie Mary. It's nearly going home time and I don't want to be late 'cos I'm seeing Geoff. So will yer just listen to what I've got to say, think it over in bed tonight, and tell me tomorrow what yer think?' She waited for her friend's nod before going on. 'Sometimes when I'm going through the bundles to pick out the gear for my stall, I come across a blouse or a jumper that I hum-and-haw about. It looks too good for thruppence but not quite good enough to charge sixpence for. So why don't we have a fourpenny stall? It would bring a few extra coppers in every week to help to pay my wages, and we wouldn't be doing the customers; we'd only sell a thing for what we think it's worth.' Sadie put up her hand when Mary Ann looked as though she was going to speak. 'Don't say anything now, just mull it over in yer mind. We're luckier than Rita, we've got all these tables to spread the things out on and make them look nice. The customers appreciate that, yer can tell by the way the clothes on my stall sell.'

'I don't need to think it over, girl, we'll give it a try. Nothing ventured, nothing gained. But I'm going to leave it to you to sort the stuff out, okay?'

'Auntie Mary, yer a little love. And if I've got anything to do with it, yer'll get that fur coat one of these days.'

Mary Ann grinned. 'There's a woman in our street got a fur coat an' it would be the price of me if the neighbours said the same about me as I say about her. "Oh aye, look at the state of her. All ruddy fur coat and no knickers!" I don't say it to her face, of course. I'm not that brave or that daft 'cos she's about twenty stone. I know me limitations, girl.'

Sadie was deep in thought as she hurried home. It was only a five-minute walk from the market, much easier than the half-hour or more it used to take her when she lived in Toxteth. It had been quite a hectic and eventful day, what with seeing their Jimmy, getting the unexpected wage rise and having Mary Ann agree to rearranging the stalls. She hoped she was right about the fourpenny stall – she'd hate it if her idea turned out to be a flop.

Sadie sensed someone walking beside her and turned her head to see Peter Townley keeping in step with a huge grin on his face. It was getting to be a regular thing now, and Sadie was convinced it wasn't just accidental. She was about to ask him if he had nothing better to do than lie in wait for her every night, but Peter got in first.

'I think you must be following me, Sadie.'

Taken by surprise at his audacity, for a second Sadie was at a loss for words. Then she raised her dark eyebrows and threw him a look of scorn. 'What did you say?'

'I said yer must be following me 'cos we keep bumping into each other.'

'Just how big-headed can yer get, Peter Townley? If yer think I've got nothin' better to do than follow you, then yer've got another think coming.'

'I did wonder about it,' Peter said, his face straight but his eyes dancing. 'I keep asking meself why yer would follow me when yer courting strong.'

'Well, next time yer havin' a conversation with yerself, try and remember what I'm going to tell yer. I have never had any interest in Peter Townley, I have none now and I never will have. Can yer remember all that or shall I write it down for yer?'

'I'll keep repeatin' it in me head so I won't forget.' The grin on his face told Sadie he was really enjoying himself. 'But seein' as we have accidentally on purpose bumped into each other, I'll mind me manners an' ask how yer are.'

Sadie was mentally giving him ten out of ten for perseverance. No matter how rude she was to him, it didn't put him off. She slowed down as they reached Peter's house. 'I'm very well, thank you, Peter. And how is yerself?'

'Fit and well, thank you, Sadie. And just out of neighbourly interest – nothing else, mind – are yer still courting strong?'

'Yes, Peter, I'm still courting strong.'

'Yer will let me know if there's ever a change in yer courtin', won't yer? Like if the strong becomes a bit weak and yer feel like givin' him the elbow?'

'I'll write and let yer know immediately.' Sadie knew she'd burst out laughing as soon as she got behind her own front door. He was a comic, no doubt about it. 'I might even send yer a telegram.'

'I'd rather yer just knocked on the door, Sadie, 'cos me mam would die if the postman turned up with a telegram in his hand. She'd think the worst, you know, like maybe our dog's been run over.'

'I didn't know yer had a dog.'

'We haven't, but she wouldn't remember that with the shock. People have been known to die when they receive a telegram, yer know, and that's before they open it!'

Sadie just couldn't keep the laughter back. 'Peter Townley, you are a real head-case. Do yer ever talk sense?'

The smile dropped from his face. 'I'm talking sense when I say I think yer a real nice girl, Sadie. Yer look nice, yer talk nice and yer act nice. Me mam was only saying the other day what a difference yer've made to the old couple next door. Yer've brightened their lives up no end.'

'And they've done the same to mine. I love the bones of them.' Sadie moved away. 'I'd better get me skates on, I'm going out in half an hour.'

'Just before yer go, when we were talking about yer we got to wondering how yer came to be their granddaughter? With them having no children, like, it seems unusual that they should have a grand-daughter!'

Sadie's heart flipped. 'I think if yer want to know any of me grand-parents' business, yer should ask them instead of discussing it behind their backs. I certainly have no intention of telling yer anything.' With a toss of her head she walked the few steps to the next door. Inserting the key in the lock, she said coldly, 'Ta-ra, Peter.'

Peter stood rooted to the spot. What had he said to change her mood so quickly? He felt like kicking himself. They'd been getting on so well and he had to go and put his foot in it. Now they were back to square one and he didn't know why.

Chapter Eighteen

Sadie closed the door and leaned back against it, her heart in her mouth. If people were starting to ask questions it was bound to come out about her past. Was she never going to get away from it? Was it going to haunt her for ever, no matter where she went?

'What's up, sweetheart?' Sarah had seen Sadie pass the window and had come out to see what was keeping her. 'Are yer feeling all right?'

'Yeah, I'm fine, Grandma.' Sadie put a smile on her face as she walked down the narrow hall. 'I was just catching me breath.' She kissed the wrinkled face as she did each day, and gave Sarah a gentle hug. 'Something smells nice.'

'I made a steak and kidney pie, I know it's yer favourite.'

Sadie entered the living room and put her bag down on the sideboard before crossing the room to give Joe his kiss and cuddle. 'You two are spoiling me. I'll be as big as a house the way yer feed me.'

'It's good to have someone to spoil, queen.' There was tenderness in Joe's eyes. 'It makes a nice change for me an' my Sarah.'

'Here yer are, sweetheart.' Sarah carried a steaming plate through and put it on the table. 'Get it down yer while it's nice and hot.'

Sadie pulled out a chair and sat down. She hadn't had anything to eat all day and had been ravenous until she'd met Peter. What he'd said had taken her appetite away. She looked up at Sarah who was standing beside the table and the love she felt for the old lady brought tears to her eyes. 'I'm not really all right, Grandma. I was fine until I bumped into that clown from next door and he said something that upset me. And I think you an' Grandad should know what people are saying.'

Sarah seated herself opposite Sadie. 'I don't think for one moment that Peter would knowingly say something to upset yer, sweetheart, he's not the type. And what are people saying that yer think Joe and me should know about?'

'He didn't say other people were saying it, only his family. But if they're talking, then yer can bet yer life the rest of the neighbours are, too.'

'But I've known these neighbours for years, love, they're not going to talk beind me back. If they had anything to say, they'd say it to me face. I can't imagine what Peter's said to upset yer so much.'

Sadie was close to tears. 'He said I'm not yer granddaughter.'

Sarah tutted. 'I'm sure he didn't say it like that, Sadie.'

'Well, those weren't his exact words; he said because you didn't have any children then yer couldn't have a granddaughter.'

Joe leaned forward to tap the bowl of his pipe against the top bar of the grate. 'Well, that's true, isn't it, queen? I mean, all the neighbours know that, it's no secret.'

'But who do they think I am, then?'

'Our granddaughter once removed.' Joe smiled to try and ease the hurt in eyes that were as blue as the sky on a summer's day. 'Me and Sarah knew there'd be questions asked, so we were ready for them. We said yer were her sister's granddaughter, and when her sister died you adopted us. I'm surprised that Peter mentioned it because his mam was the first one we told.'

'He said it to make a liar out of me and I hate him. Just because I won't go out with him, that's all.'

'Yer should never say yer hate anyone, child, because the day might come when yer regret it. And once a word is spoken yer can never take it back.' Sarah pointed to the plate that was still untouched. 'Eat some of yer dinner, sweetheart, I made it specially for you. I'll be upset if I have to throw it on the fire.'

Sadie picked up her knife and fork. Rather than upset her grandma she'd eat it even if it choked her. 'I don't hate Peter, Grandma, I just don't like him. And being yer adopted granddaughter is just as good as being a real one, isn't it?'

'I would have thought it was better,' Joe said, filling his pipe from the battered tin he'd had since he retired. He could afford to buy his Golden Virginia by the tin then, but now he had to buy it loose, half an ounce at a time. 'Yer can't choose yer family, queen, yer have to take what comes. But when yer adopt, yer've got the pick of the best. And that's what we got when we got you . . . the best.'

Suddenly the steak and kidney pie tasted good. Grandad was right, Sadie thought. You *can't* choose your family – and she should know that better than anyone. And she felt a warm glow inside, knowing she was here because they wanted her.

'You and Peter have never hit it off from the word go, have yer, sweetheart?' Sarah was heartened to see the girl tucking into her dinner. 'I can't understand the reason for this 'cos he's the easiest-going person I've ever known. D'yer think it might be your fault? That yer made up yer mind not to like him from the start and so he can't do anything right in your eyes?'

'No! That's not true!' Sadie licked her lips and put down her knife and fork. She stared at the plate for a while then met Sarah's questioning eyes. 'Yes, it is true, Grandma. I wouldn't pass the time of day with him if it wasn't for him being one of yer neighbours.'

'But why, sweetheart? Yer can't look at a person for the first time and make up yer mind there and then that yere not goin' to like them! Yer not doing justice to them or to yerself.'

Sadie pushed her plate out of the way and leaned her elbows on the table. 'I told yer about Harry, didn't I? The boy who lived next door and was so good to me? Well, Peter is the spittin' image of him, except that Harry has dimples. At first I didn't want to know Peter because he reminded me of Harry and it upset me. Later, I didn't want to get too friendly in case he started asking questions and found out about me background. That's how my life has always been, afraid to get too close to anyone because I knew when they saw where I lived they'd run a mile. And I couldn't bear the shame of being hurt and rejected. Better not to get involved with anyone, then I couldn't be hurt.'

'But what about Geoff? Yer've been going out with him for a long time and he hasn't rejected yer.'

'I think Geoff and I will be parting company soon, Grandma. He keeps asking me why I won't take him home to meet me parents, and I can't keep putting him off. I promised him weeks ago that I'd bring him to meet you and Grandad, but what's the use? Some time or another he's going to find out the truth and that'll be the end of it.'

'You can't be sure of that. If he loves yer enough he'll not let yer family stand in his way, no matter how bad they are.'

'Ah well, yer see, Grandma, I don't love him. He's as nice a bloke as yer'll find in a month of Sundays, but he's not the boy for me.'

'Then yer should tell him that, sweetheart. Yer shouldn't let him be living in hope when there is none.'

'That's right, queen, yer shouldn't string him along.' Joe's pipe was drawing nicely and he had the look of a contented man. 'Wouldn't be fair to the lad.'

'I've never strung him along, Grandad. I've told him a few fibs about me family, but I've never told him I love him, nothing sloppy like that.'

'Maybe not, queen, but if yer keep going out with him, that's the impression he's going to get.'

Sadie sighed. 'I'll tell him tonight, but I don't relish the idea. I'm a bit of a coward, but I will tell him.'

It was Sarah's turn to sigh. 'Think it over carefully, sweetheart. Make sure yer know what yer doing 'cos he's the only friend yer've got.'

'That's not a good enough reason to lead Geoff on, is it, Grandma? And I could have plenty of dates if I wanted them. There's loads of young lads working at the market and I think every one of them has asked me out.'

Sarah leaned across the table, a smile on her face. 'And there's always Peter to fall back on.'

'No, Grandma, don't be matchmaking me with Peter. It wouldn't be long before he started askin' me where I come from and why I wasn't living with me family. He lives too close for comfort. If I fell out with him it would only cause unpleasantness between you and his family. I'll stick to the odd date here and there, a case of love 'em and leave 'em.' Sadie scraped her chair back. 'I'd better get meself ready, but I'm not looking forward to tonight. In future I won't go out with nice boys then it won't be so hard to say goodbye.'

'Geoff, could we go to that little dance hall, you know, where I first met yer? It would make a change from going to the pictures.'

'Yeah, that's a good idea.' Geoff looked pleased as he tucked her arm in his. 'It's been ages since I went to a dance, I'll probably be rusty.'

'I hope yer are, then yer won't notice how bad I am. If yer rusty, and I'm as stiff as a board, we should make perfect partners.'

'I won't be that bad,' Geoff laughed. 'Once yer learn to dance yer never forget. And anyway, even if you couldn't put one foot in front of the other, Sadie, yer'd still be the perfect partner for me.'

Sadie groaned inwardly. She didn't want him to be too nice to her, she felt bad enough as it was. If he was all lovey-dovey she wouldn't have the heart to tell him she wasn't seeing him again. It was a shame really, because she enjoyed going out with him. He always treated her well and never expected anything more than a good-night kiss. But she knew his intentions towards her were getting more serious with each passing week, and it wasn't fair to lead him on. No matter how long they courted, she knew she would never grow to love him because the spark was missing. She'd never been in love but she felt there had to be more to it than the feelings she had for Geoff.

The dance hall was quite crowded and Sadie scanned the room nervously for sight of Alec. He wouldn't come near her, not with Geoff by her side, but nevertheless she'd die of humiliation if she came face to face with him.

'D'yer want to try this slow foxtrot?' Geoff's dark brown eyes were appealing. 'All yer've got to do is follow me.'

'I'll make a holy show of yer.'

'I'll take a chance if you will. Yer'll never learn if yer don't try.'

'On your own head be it.' Sadie allowed herself to be led onto the dance floor and it was so crowded her nerves soon disappeared. Who was going to notice her in amongst this lot? Anyway, she could see several couples who were more or less just walking around; at least she was making an effort to keep up with Geoff.

When the dance was over, Geoff kept his arm around her waist as they walked from the floor. 'I think yer did very well. Yer've got the makings of a good dancer, Sadie – yer've a sense of rhythm and yer body movements are nice and easy. We should come dancing at least one night a week instead of going to the pictures.'

Sadie smiled and nodded, not trusting herself to speak. He was so nice, why couldn't she feel more for him? Was she capable of loving any boy, or had her twisted father poisoned her mind against all men?

When Geoff heard the strains of a waltz he grinned and held his arms wide. 'I believe this is your favourite?'

Sadie grinned back. 'If yer see me lips moving don't think I've flipped me lid, I'll just be counting, one-two-three, one-two-three.'

They danced every dance, with Sadie gaining confidence in response to Geoff's whispered words of encouragement. He told her she was coming on in leaps and bounds and she felt very proud of herself. In fact, she was enjoying herself so much she was sorry when the evening came to an end. She was laughing with pleasure when they stepped into the street. 'I am delighted with me little self! I think I did very well, even though I say it as shouldn't.'

Geoff pulled her close and his handsome face was a picture of happiness as he smiled down at her. 'I don't want yer to think I'm bragging, Sadie, but I deserve some of the credit for that. After all, the pupil's only as good as the teacher.'

'You've got a nerve, Geoff Barnes. The best teacher in the whole world is no good if the pupil's as thick as two short planks, an' I'll have you know I'm not as thick as two planks, long or short.'

'Okay, let's say that because you were such a good pupil, yer made me look good. How does that suit yer?'

'That's more like it.' Sadie turned her face away from him. She couldn't finish with him tonight, not when he looked so happy; it would be cruel. She'd have to leave it until another night when he was in a more serious mood. If he wasn't so easygoing she could try and pick an argument with him and walk off in a huff, but it would be a waste of time because he wouldn't argue with her. Anyway, that would be a cowardly way out and he deserved better than that.

Sadie sighed inwardly. She'd have to be honest with him and tell him to his face. While he was taking her out, under the impression they were courting, he was missing the chance of finding a girl who was right for him. One who would really love him as Sadie knew she never could. But she couldn't bring herself to do it tonight, not when his spirits were so high. On Friday night, she vowed, I'll definitely do it then.

'Good morning, girl.' Mary Ann's smile was radiant. 'Or, as they say in dear old Ireland, "the top of the mornin' to yer, me darlin' ".'

Sadie grinned, thinking what a pleasure it was to come to work these days. 'Yer looking very pleased with yerself, Auntie Mary. If yer licked yer lips yer'd look like the cat that got the cream off the top of the milk.'

'I've got to admit that I am in a happy frame of mind, sunshine, and so will you be when yer get a dekko of the gear my feller picked up in Woolton yesterday. He had a real good day, the best he's ever had.'

'All good stuff is it, Auntie Mary?'

'Good? I'll say it is! It'll give yer an idea of how the other half live when yer see what they've thrown out.' The stall-holder removed a strand of hair from the corner of her eye. 'Not that they threw them out exactly, 'cos my feller has to fork out for them. But there's good winter coats here that must have cost about six or seven guineas when they were new, and all they got for them was the price of a pair of lisle stockings.'

'Yer not complaining, are yer, Auntie Mary? As long as they're satisfied, why should you worry?'

'I ain't worried, sunshine, I'm over the moon. And yer should have seen my Tom's face – as pleased as Punch he was, right proud of himself.'

'I hope yer gave praise where praise was due, Auntie Mary? There's nothing worse than thinking yer've done well and someone comes along and puts a damper on it. I hate it when someone does that to me.'

'Oh aye, girl, are yer by any chance tellin' me how to keep my feller sweet? Go an' teach yer grandmother how to milk ducks, sunshine, 'cos I know exactly how to make my man happy, and I can assure you he was amply rewarded.'

Sadie waited for her blush to spread after that last remark, but thankfully it didn't put in an appearance. 'Shall I begin sorting it out? It'll take a bit longer with us starting the new fourpenny stall.'

Mary Ann was keeping her patience with the greatest of difficulty. She'd hardly slept all night, tossing and turning as she tried to imagine the expressions on Sadie's pretty face when she saw the contents of the two big bundles. They were under one of the tables and she now pointed to the nearest. 'Start on that one first and put to one side anything that yer fancy for yerself.'

Sadie now had an idea why her friend looked so happy. 'Yer know there's something in there that I'd like, don't yer? What is it this time, Auntie Mary? A jumper for me or something for one of the kids?'

'Yer've only just given them a pile of clothes.' Mary Ann tutted loudly. 'I don't begrudge them anything, sunshine, honest I don't. If the truth was known I feel heartily sorry for them. But it's time yer started looking after yerself and there's a few things in there that'll look a treat on yer. And it's not as though yer don't need them, 'cos yer do. I've warned yer what it's like here in the winter. Yer need some warm clothes or yer'll bleedin' freeze to death.'

Sadie stood to attention, clicking her heels together as she saluted. 'Aye, aye, sir! Right away, sir!'

'Ay, I'll have less of that lip, yer cheeky little monkey! You just lift that bundle up and get cracking. And seein' as yer've just promoted me to Captain, I'm going to stand and watch every bleedin' move yer make.'

Sadie chuckled. 'Captains don't swear, Auntie Mary.'

'Not usually they don't, girl, I'll grant yer that. But I'm not just any old run-of-the-mill Captain, I'm more yer Long John Silver type.'

'Auntie Mary, Long John Silver had a wooden leg.'

'What d'yer think I wear a long skirt for, sunshine, if it isn't to hide me wooden leg?' Mary Ann made a fist and shook it in Sadie's face. 'I'll be takin' it off and hitting yer with it if yer don't get a move on.'

Sadie swung the bundle onto the empty table. There must be something special in here, she thought, as she untied the knots in the top of the sheet. Mary Ann seldom gets excited about clothes that are brought in, but she's all keyed up right now. The knots untied, Sadie let the sides of the sheet fall away, and there on the very top of the pile, all neatly folded, was the cause of the stall-holder's sleepless night.

'Don't stand there gawping, girl, lift it out! Honest to God, yer've got me bleedin' nerves shattered. I won't be a bit of good all day after this.'

Sadie lifted the coat out and held it up, the delight spreading across her face more than compensating Mary Ann for her loss of sleep. The coat was in navy-blue velour with collar and wide revers in navy velvet. She'd agreed with her Tom that it was the finest item of clothing he'd ever had the good fortune to pick up on his cart. It was almost brand new, not a mark on it and no sign of wear around the button holes or deep pockets.

'It's beautiful, Auntie Mary.' Sadie found her voice at last. 'Really beautiful.'

'Well, don't be wearin' the bleedin' thing out by just looking at it. Try it on before me heart gives out on me.'

Sadie didn't need telling twice. As she was slipping her arms into the silk-lined sleeves, she was telling herself she had to have this coat – she'd fallen in love with it on sight. But she wouldn't wear it to work in the market, it was too good for that. Besides, she'd stand out like a sore thumb in anything so grand. She'd find another one for work – one that had been well worn and wouldn't cost so much.

'Oh girl, it looks the gear on yer.' Mary Ann tilted her head and narrowed her eyes, a habit she had when inspecting something. 'Anyone would think it had been made for yer – it fits yer like a glove. Remember when yer told me, in a joke, like, that yer were Princess Sadie of Sefton Park? Well, yer certainly look the part in that coat. Talk about being proper posh isn't it in it.'

Sadie was stroking the soft material, a faraway look in her eyes. The mention of Sefton Park had brought back memories of Harry. She could imagine the look of admiration in his eyes if he saw her in this coat. His dimples would deepen as he smiled and took her hand, telling her how nice she looked.

'Hey, come on, girl.' Mary Ann was getting impatient. There were lots more surprises for Sadie in that bundle. 'Have I got a sale, or haven't I?'

'Oh, definitely, Auntie Mary. I love it. No matter how much it—'

'Two bob,' the stall-holder interrupted. 'And cheap at half the price.'

'It's worth more than that.' Sadie's voice rose. 'Yer can't keep giving me things on the cheap, it's not fair!'

'I said two bob and I meant two bob. Anything else yer want, yer can pay me a fair whack for, but I'm standing firm on the price of the coat, so don't argue. It's my own little way of saying "thank you" for working so hard and bringin' more business to me stall.'

Sadie threw her arms around her friend. 'I love you, Auntie Mary, I really do.'

Mary Ann snorted, 'Stop bein' so sloppy, yer daft ha'porth.' But deep down she was pleased. She couldn't have cared for Sadie more if she'd been her own daughter. 'Get the rest sorted out on the double, girl, 'cos yer never know, we might even get a bleedin' customer before the day's out.'

Sadie picked out two jumpers that would have gone on the new fourpenny stall, and two warm cardigans that would have found their way to the superior-quality stall. 'That's just on four bob I owe yer, Auntie Mary.' She was smiling with pleasure. 'I'll bring the money in with me tomorrow and we'll be quits.'

'The weekend will do, girl, I'm in no hurry.'

Sadie shook her head. 'Tomorrow, Auntie Mary. I can be just as stubborn as you.'

'I'm not stubborn, girl, just bloody-minded.'

'It's funny you should say that.' Sadie slipped out of the coat and began to fasten the buttons before folding it neatly away. 'I did hear that as well as having a wooden leg, Long John Silver was bloody-minded.'

'Will yer tell me his life story some other time, girl, like next year? Right now I'd like yer to sort those clothes out and get the stalls looking a bit more inviting than they are now. The way we're shaping it'll be time to pack in before we've even started!'

Mary Ann was wiry, quick of mind and movement. But Sadie left her standing. With a quickness of eye and a deft hand, she sized each garment up for price and had them on the appropriate stall in no time, and arranging them to attract the eye of passing potential customers. 'How's that, Auntie Mary? All present and accounted for.'

'Talk about the hand being quicker than the eye, girl, I missed half of what yer did. Yer make me look as though I'm standing still, like a bleedin' statue.'

Sadie laughed as she rubbed her hands together. 'All we need now are the customers.'

'I'll see to any customers, girl, don't you worry. They won't get past me 'cos I've brought me big hook to pull them in. You see to that other bundle, there's a good girl.' Mary Ann had deliberately left the second bundle till the last for a reason. It was all good-quality children's clothing and she knew Sadie would have pounced on some of the items for her brothers and sisters. It didn't matter now because the girl had bought things for herself, things she badly needed, and Mary Ann had no intention of letting her change her mind. She admired Sadie for caring so much for her family, and for her generosity. But enough was enough and she had to start thinking of herself.

'Good morning, girl.'

Mary Ann spun round at the sound of the familiar voice. 'Maggie! Thank God for that. I was beginning to think the whole of Liverpool had emigrated to Australia. The bleedin' market's deserted, like a flippin' ghost town.'

'It's hard-up day, girl.' Maggie put her basket on the ground between her feet and rested her elbows on the clothes piled on the tuppence with a hole stall. 'It's two days to pay day, everyone's skint and happy.'

'I hope yer haven't come just to tell me yer've no money, Maggie? Yer know I love the bones of yer, being as yer one of me best customers, but I've got a living to make. If yer want to feel sorry for someone, then feel sorry for my feller 'cos he's gone to work this morning with the arse hanging out of his kecks.'

Maggie's top set of false teeth dropped when she laughed. 'That'll be the day, Mary Ann!' She straightened up, folded her arms across her tummy, hoisted her ample breasts and, feeling more comfortable, settled herself once again to rest on the clothes. 'If yer trying to tell me yer skint, don't bother wasting yer breath 'cos I wouldn't believe yer. I bet yer a pound to a pinch of snuff that yer've got a long stocking stashed away somewhere.'

'Maggie, if I had a long stocking stashed away, d'yer think I'd waste me time standing here nattering to someone who has no intention of buying anything? Not on yer bleedin' life I wouldn't.'

'Yer wrong there, Mary Ann, 'cos I have come to buy. So you just be careful how yer treat me or I'll walk down to the next stall.'

Mary Ann laced her fingers together and held them out as though begging. 'Forgive me, Saint Margaret, I make myself humble before you. Your wish shall be my command.'

The table was pushed forward a few inches as Maggie's tummy shook with laughter. 'Yer a head-case if ever there was one, Mary Ann. That's the first belly laugh I've had since I was here on Saturday.'

'Right! That laugh is goin' to cost yer an extra penny on whatever it is yer goin' to buy. And if yer don't hurry up and tell me what yer after, I'll add another penny on for me time.'

Maggie was unmoved by the threat. 'Yer can add on what yer like for all I care, girl, it won't make no difference to me 'cos all I've got in me purse right now is sweet Fanny Adams.'

'I wish yer'd make up yer mind, Maggie. First yer want something, now yer don't. Yer've got me fair flummoxed trying to keep up with yer. And while yer going through this "I will, I won't" lark, Sadie's had to leave what she was doing to serve a real live money-in-the-hand customer.'

'The bloody cheek of you! I'm a real live money-in-the-hand customer, Mary Ann, so you just mind yer manners. I've come on a message for the old lady who lives next door to me. She can't get out herself 'cos she's crippled with rheumatism. She wants a nice thick cardi to keep her warm; she feels the cold something chronic.'

'What size is she, Maggie, and how much does she want to pay.'

'It'll have to be one without a hole 'cos she can't darn. I'd say she was about your size, near enough. Do what yer can for her, Mary Ann, she's a nice old soul.'

'Let's see what we've got on the thruppenny stall.' Mary Ann moved to the next table and Maggie left her comfortable perch to follow. 'How about this one? It's in pretty good nick, not a break in it.'

'Nah!' Maggie's chins moved in the opposite direction to her head.

'Pale blue is not a good colour for her. She needs a dark one that won't show the dirt.'

'We've got a fourpenny stall now, Maggie, with a better selection. Could the old lady run to fourpence?'

Maggie looked doubtful. 'She only gave me a thruppenny joey and I wouldn't like to ask her for more 'cos she's as poor as a church mouse.'

Mary Ann raised her eyes to the heavens. 'Tell me, God, why do I get all the sob stories? Have I got a sign on me forehead with "sucker" on it?'

'Don't you be taking off on me, Mary Ann Worsley! I only came for a thruppenny cardi, like I've been doin' for years and never had this malarky before.'

'And yer won't be having any malarky today, Maggie, me old friend. I see Sadie has finished with her customer so I'll call her over. Two heads are better than one.'

Sadie was told the story of the little old lady who was so crippled with rheumatism she couldn't walk, was as poor as a church mouse and wanted a nice warm cardi for the winter to keep body and soul together because she could only afford to buy half a bag of coal a week. And as Maggie listened to Mary Ann, her face showed real concern, as though she'd never heard the tale before and didn't know the old lady from Adam. In fact, so convincing was the stall-holder, if she'd asked for a whip-round to help the poor old soul, Maggie would have been the first one to get her purse out.

'I think we've got just the thing for her, Maggie,' Sadie said. 'It only came in today and hasn't been put out yet.'

'What's that yer say, girl?' Maggie's eyes blinked rapidly as realisation began to dawn. 'Oh yeah, that would be champion.'

The cardigan was a thick woollen one in black cable stitch. It buttoned up to the neck and had two deep pockets. It had obviously been worn a lot 'cos it had that lived-in look, as though someone had found it comfortable to wear. But there was still plenty of life in it. 'That should keep her nice and warm, Maggie,' Mary Ann said. 'Just the job for the winter.'

Maggie was highly delighted but had no intention of letting it show until they'd told her the price. 'How much?'

Sadie looked at Mary Ann for guidance. 'What d'yer think, Auntie Mary?'

'Well, it was goin' on the fourpenny stall, but seeing as it's for Maggie's neighbour she can have it for thruppence. But only on one condition, Maggie.'

'What's that, Mary Ann?'

'That yer promise to come and visit me when I'm in the bleedin' workhouse.'

'I'll visit you any time, any place, girl.' Eager to be off to show her neighbour how clever she'd been, Maggie pushed the cardigan into her basket and backed away. 'Even in Walton Jail.'

'You cheeky sod!' Mary Ann shouted after her. 'That's the last favour I'll do for you.'

Maggie turned and waved. 'See yer on Saturday, Mary Ann.'

'Okay, Maggie. You look after yerself now.' The stall-holder was smiling when she turned to face Sadie. 'She's gone home as happy as Larry, thinking she's pulled a fast one on us and got herself a bargain.'

'She has, Auntie Mary. That cardi was going on me sixpenny stall.'

'Yer what? Why didn't yer open yer flamin' mouth an' tell me?'

'I did ask yer, but yer sounded so sorry for the old lady I wasn't going to argue with yer. Anyway, why worry? We'll make up the difference on the new stall, so yer haven't really lost anything.'

'No, yer right, girl, I'm getting ahead of meself. Too greedy, that's my trouble.'

'No, yer may be many things, Auntie Mary, like Long John Silver, but never greedy.' Sadie looked around to make sure there were no customers waiting before asking, 'Can I buy some of the children's clothes that were in the other bundle?'

Mary Ann shook her head vigorously. 'No, you can not. We agreed a sale over the other stuff and I'm keeping yer to it. On no condition am I going to let you change yer mind, so put it out of yer head.'

Sadie looked puzzled. 'I haven't changed me mind, I still want the clothes I picked for meself. But I'd like some of the kids' things because we don't often get them in such good condition, and there's a strong pair of boots that would fit our Jimmy.'

'You can't afford to clothe four children, sunshine.' Mary Ann's face was sad as she took a deep breath. 'You're sixteen, love, only a child yerself. With your looks yer should be dressed in all the latest fashions, and God knows yer work hard enough to deserve to.'

'I've got the money to buy them, Auntie Mary – I'll use me savings.' Sadie saw the troubled look in the green eyes and hurried to reassure her. 'I'll make it up in the next few months 'cos I'll have nothing else to buy. I'd give our Jimmy the boots for him to wear in the bad weather, but I'd put the other clothes away to give them as Christmas presents. Please, Auntie Mary?'

Mary Ann was in a dilemma. She'd encouraged Sadie to put some money away each week in case of emergency. Anything could happen to Sarah and Joe at their age, and Sadie would find herself out on the streets because no landlord would rent a house to a sixteen-year-old who only earned ten bob a week. But she'd never voiced her fears because she knew how much the girl loved her adopted grandparents and she didn't want to mar her happiness. For the first time in her life, Sadie was enjoying a warmth and love she'd never known before, in a house that was truly a home.

Mary Ann sighed. 'Yer can have the clothes by all means, girl, but I want yer solemn promise that from this Saturday yer'll put a certain amount aside every week, without fail, come what may.'

'I'll do better than promise yer, Auntie Mary, I'll give yer half-a-crown out of me wages each week to mind for me. How about that?'

'I'm goin' to be strict with yer, sunshine, but it's for yer own good. I'll mind the money for yer on the understanding yer add to it every week, and not ask for it back, until yer've got a little nest egg behind yer.' Mary Ann wouldn't rest easy until she knew Sadie had a few pounds at the back of her. Then, if anything did happen to Sarah and Joe, God forbid, she'd be in a position to find decent lodgings. 'If I hang onto the money yer won't be tempted to spend it, and mark my words, yer'll be surprised how quick it mounts up.'

Sadie grinned. 'First yer were me friend, then me boss, after that me Auntie, and now yer me banker.' Her smile faded. 'I wish most of all that yer were me mother.'

'I'm as good as yer mother, aren't I?' Mary Ann decided to keep the tone light, otherwise they'd both be as miserable as sin all day. 'Who else but a mother would look after yer financial affairs, now tell me that?'

Sadie's smile reappeared. 'Yeah, yer do look after me like one of yer own, and I love yer to bits.'

'Just don't start calling me "Mam", that's all. Otherwise I'll be doing an inspection on yer every morning like I do with my two, making sure they've washed behind their ears and haven't got a tide mark around their necks.'

'Ay out, Auntie Mary, we've got two customers. You take Lizzie and I'll see to Florrie.' Sadie winked broadly as she walked away. 'Yer see, things are picking up. I bet we have a good day after all.'

'Huh!' Mary Ann grunted. 'Forever the bleedin' optimist, you are. Two swallows do not a summer make, sunshine – have yer never heard that old saying?'

'I have that, Auntie Mary, and I've also heard the one that goes "Laugh and the world laughs with you; weep and you weep alone".'

'Well, I never! Did yer hear that, Lizzie? She's gettin' too big for her boots is that young assistant of mine from the superior-quality clothes stall. I've a good mind to put her back on the tuppence with a hole stall. That would put her in her place, bring her down a peg or two.'

Lizzie caught Sadie's eye and winked before saying, 'Go on, Mary Ann, yer'd be lost without her and you know it.'

'Keep yer voice down, Lizzie, or she'll be asking me for another bleedin' rise.' Mary Ann's tummy was shaking with laughter at what she was going to say. 'Now, Lizzie, before we start, have you got a neighbour who is very old, who is so crippled with rheumatism she can't walk, is as poor as a church mouse and can only afford to buy half a bag of coal a week?'

Lizzie scratched her head and frowned in bewilderment. 'I haven't got no neighbour like that, Mary Ann.'

'Thank God for that, Lizzie! You and me are very lucky women that you haven't got a neighbour like that. So what can I do yer for?'

Chapter Nineteen

Sadie was laden down as she walked home that night. All the clothes she'd bought were wrapped in a sheet Mary Ann had lent her, and her arms were aching as she carried the heavy load in front of her. But she was so delighted with her purchases she kept herself going by saying it wasn't that much further and a few aches and pains were neither here nor there. She couldn't wait to show off her new coat to her grandparents, and in her mind's eye she could picture herself posing by the sideboard, all dressed up to the nines.

'Here, I'll carry that for yer, Sadie.'

Sadie was so startled she missed a step and nearly went flying. 'Oh, not you again, Peter! Will the day ever come when I can walk in this street without seeing your ugly mug?'

'There's only one way I can help yer there, Sadie, and that's to ask me mam to move to another street. She wouldn't take kindly to the idea, seeing as she's lived here for over twenty years and likes it, but I'll see if she'll discommode the whole family just so you won't be inconvenienced.'

Sadie smiled in spite of herself. He really was very funny. 'I can't stop to argue with yer, Peter. As yer can see, I've got me hands full.'

'Let me take it off yer, don't be so flippin' stubborn.'

Sadie knew she'd be cutting her nose to spite her face if she refused, because her arms were nearly dropping off. 'Thank you, Peter,' she said primly. 'I could have managed but I appreciate your offer and accept.'

Peter took the bundle from her and when he felt the weight, asked, 'What on earth have yer got in here?'

'Mind your own business.' Wild horses wouldn't have dragged the truth from Sadie. She had visions of herself walking down the street, nose in the air and dressed to kill. How soft she'd look if he knew everything she had on had come from Paddy's market! She'd die of shame. 'Because I'm letting you help me, it doesn't mean I want to be pally with yer.'

'I was hoping to see yer, Sadie, to apologise for what I said the other night about yer grandparents. I didn't mean to upset yer, and I only said it to keep yer talking a bit longer. We were getting on great, then I had to go and put me big foot in it and you stormed off in a huff. I kicked meself all the way down our hall, honest I did. In fact, I'll show yer the bruises if yer'll hold this bundle for a minute. Black and blue me shins are, and even a bit of yellow in parts.'

Sadie threw her head back and her laughter rang out loud and clear. 'Yer tuppence short of a shilling, you are, Peter Townley. As soft as a blinking brush.'

Peter turned his head to look at her. God, but she was beautiful. 'Are we friends again, then, Sadie? I know yer courting strong, yer don't have to keep telling me that, but I'd still like to be friends with yer.'

Sadie had no intention of going into detail about Geoff, so she let it pass. 'Okay, Peter, we'll call a truce.'

He let out a loud exaggerated sigh of relief. 'I'm glad about that, Sadie, 'cos I'm a growing lad and I need me sleep. You've been stunting me growth since yer moved into the street. I can't get to sleep for thinking about yer.'

'Peter Townley, if you lose any sleep because of me then yer need yer bumps feeling because I'm not worth it.'

'I have given that very subject a great deal of thought, Sadie. And after much soul-searching and deliberation, I have reached the conclusion that you are worth losing sleep over. And to prove how much confidence I have in the outcome of my deliberation, I lie awake every night just gazing at the cracks in me bedroom ceiling. Twenty-four there are, by the way; I counted them.'

They were outside Sadie's house by this time and she stared at him, open-mouthed. 'Have you swallowed a blinkin' dictionary, Peter Townley?'

'Yeah.' He rested his chin on the top of the bundle, his face smiling and his brown eyes dancing with mischievous laughter. 'The pages weren't that bad to swallow, but the hard back cover was murder. Couldn't get it past me Adam's apple, yer see.'

Sadie doubled up with laughter. He might be a blight on her life but he was a comical one. There'd be no miserable faces in his company. 'Wait until I knock on the door, then I'll take that load off yer.'

But the door opened before her hand reached the knocker. 'I saw yer passing the window, sweetheart.' Sarah looked surprised when she saw who her companion was. 'Are you two on speaking terms again?'

'He's a nutcase, Grandma, a real head-the-ball.' Sadie grinned. 'But he's been very good carrying me bundle for me, so I'll not insult him by saying more.'

'She won't tell me what it is I'm carrying, though.' Peter rolled his eyes. 'Must be ill-gotten gains.'

'No, I won't tell yer what it is, and neither will me grandma. So I'll thank yer kindly and take it off yer hands.'

'I've carried it this far, I may as well finish the job off properly and put it on me Auntie Sarah's table for yer.'

Sadie gaped. 'Auntie Sarah? She's not yer Auntie!'

'She's been me Auntie Sarah since the day I was born, and she'll always be me Auntie Sarah whether you like it or not.'

Sarah could see a fight brewing and decided she wasn't having any. They could play silly beggars if they liked, but not in front of her. 'Can't we have one night where you two say good night as friends? Every time yer see each other yer end up fighting! Behave yerselves, the pair of yer, and act yer age.'

Peter grinned while Sadie looked shamefaced. 'I will if she will, Auntie Sarah.'

'Oh, all right, we'll be friends,' Sadie said. 'So will you take me bundle inside, Peter, please? And then I'll say ta-ra and let yer get about yer business. I've taken up enough of your time as it is.'

Peter nodded and grinned at Sarah. 'She has too, yer know. If it wasn't for her I wouldn't know we had twenty-four cracks in me bedroom ceiling.'

The old lady looked puzzled. 'Yer've lost me there, son. I don't know what your bedroom ceiling's got to do with anything.'

'Take no notice of him, Grandma, or we'll be here all night. Just let him put the bundle on the table and I'll stand here until he comes out.'

Sadie was waiting when Peter came out of the house minus the bundle. 'Good night, Peter, and thank you.'

'Are we friends then, Sadie? I'm only asking so I'll know whether to speak to yer next time we just happen to bump into each other. It makes things awkward when yer don't know whether to say "hello", or just pull tongues.'

Oh, he really was the limit, Sadie thought. But she couldn't help smiling. 'Don't you dare pull tongues at me, Peter Townley!'

'So we're on speaking terms, I take it, Sadie?'

'Yes, Peter, we're on speaking terms.'

'Thank God for that! Those twenty-four cracks can look after themselves tonight, I've stood guard long enough. It's a good night's sleep I'll be having tonight, and I bet I'll have grown another two inches by the time I get out of bed. Me growth will no longer be stunted.'

'Good night, Peter, enjoy yer sleep.'

'Good night, Sadie. At least yer can't fall out with me when I'm asleep.'

Sadie was chuckling when she closed the front door. That was one bloke you couldn't fall out with – he wouldn't let you!

'Oh, sweetheart, yer look absolutely beautiful.' There were tears in Sarah's eyes. 'A lovely coat for a lovely girl.'

Sadie did a little twirl. 'I thought yer'd like it, Grandma. What about you, Grandad? Could yer fall for me in this rig-out?'

'I could fall head over heels for you in anything, queen, but in that I'd do a double somersault.' Joe couldn't have been more proud of Sadie if she'd been of his own flesh and blood. In fact, there were times when he forgot she wasn't. 'If yer were old enough I'd take yer down to the pub with me, to show yer off to me mates.'

'Over my dead body, you would.' Sarah's eyes flashed. 'Nice girls don't go in pubs, Joe O'Hanlon, so don't you be leading her astray.'

'Before you two come to blows, can I show yer me coat properly?' Sadie took Sarah by the arms and sat her down. 'It's not often I get the chance to swank, so let me enjoy meself.'

Sarah smiled and clasped her hands in her lap. 'We're all eyes and ears, sweetheart.'

'See how these lapels, or revers, are lying flat, Grandma?' Sadie ran the back of her hands down the soft velvet, liking the feel of luxury. 'Well, when the weather's cold I can fold them over and they'll fasten up to me neck to keep me nice and warm. It's a shame to hide the velvet, but when it's fastened up it doesn't half feel good next to me skin.' She smiled and hugged herself. 'I wonder if the girl who it was bought for loved it as much as I do?'

'That's something we'll never know, queen,' Joe said, 'but one thing's for sure, it couldn't look any better on her than it does on you.'

'She must belong to a monied family.' Sarah spoke softly, as though to herself. 'It cost a pretty penny, did that coat.'

'These must have been hers, too.' Sadie held one of the jumpers aloft. 'I wonder if she knows how lucky she is?'

'She's made you a very happy girl, so yer can thank her for that.' Sarah pushed herself up from the chair. 'Now, young lady, if yer don't shift everything off the table, yer dinner won't be fit to eat. Yer can show us the rest after yer've had yer meal.'

'Oh, the rest of the things aren't for me, they're for me brothers and sisters.'

Sarah's eyes widened. 'But yer've just given them a stack of clothes, sweetheart. It's your mother's place to see to them, not yours.'

'Grandma, I've had one lecture off Mary Ann, so don't you start on me, please! I know everything yer saying is true, but neither you nor Mary Ann know just how bad things are at home. And none of it is the fault of the kids. Believe me, their life is like a hell on earth, and they're too young to do anything about it or help themselves. I know exactly how they feel because I had to go through it, too. All I ever thought about was the day I would be old enough to walk away from it. But I can't just abandon the other kids, put them out of me mind as though they don't exist. I couldn't live with meself if I did that.'

'All right, sweetheart, don't be getting yerself all upset. Clear the table and I'll bring yer dinner through.'

'I'll nip upstairs with some of these, get them out of yer way.' Sadie grabbed an armful of clothes and made for the stairs. On her way down again the smell of liver and onions assailed her nostrils and the hunger pangs began. 'Ooh, that smells delicious, Grandma, me mouth's watering.'

'It's nice and tender, sweetheart, just the way yer like it.'

There wasn't a word spoken as Sadie tucked in with an appetite that was envied by Sarah and Joe. They used to eat big meals like that right up until Joe finished work. But as they grew older their need for food diminished. They still had a hot dinner every day, Sarah insisted on that, but their plates were no longer piled high.

'Grandma,' Sadie rested her knife and fork, 'yer won't tell Peter what was in the bundle, will yer? I'd hate him to know all me clothes are cast-offs.'

'Not a word will cross my lips, sweetheart, I promise.'

'He will ask, yer know. He's cheeky enough for anything. No matter what I say to him, how rude I am, he won't leave me alone.'

Sarah bit on her lip to keep a smile away. 'Will yer give yer tongue a rest and finish that dinner before it gets stiff? With the weather getting colder yer'll need plenty of nourishment inside yer to stand in that market all day.'

'So me Auntie Mary keeps telling me.' Sadie was thoughtful as she pushed her fork through the mound of mashed potato. 'Has Peter Townley got a girlfriend? He's old enough to have one, and if he has why is he pestering me?'

'From what I saw, Sadie, he wasn't pestering yer tonight, he was helping yer. And as for him having a girlfriend, well I wouldn't know. And he's not that old, yer know, only a couple of months older than you. I've seen him with plenty of girls – they hang around the top of the street waiting for him. After all, he's a nice-looking lad. But as to whether he's got a regular girlfriend, well, yer'll have to ask him that yerself.'

'I wouldn't be bothered doing that.' Sadie pushed a fingernail between two bottom teeth to dislodge a piece of liver. 'He'd think I was

225

interested if I asked him something personal like that.'

'Yer've just asked me, sweetheart, so yer must be a bit interested in him.'

'I am not!' Sadie sounded indignant. 'I only wondered because he seems to be always following me. He's like me blinkin' shadow.'

Joe wasn't due for a smoke, but with the excitement of Sadie's new clothes and everything, he decided this was a special occasion that called for a treat. It would mean one less tomorrow, he told himself as he rubbed the tobacco between his palms, but he'd worry about that when the time came. 'This situation with you and Peter, queen, it's like one of these serials yer see at the pictures where yer have to go back the next week to see what happened. It just gets to an exciting part when it says "To be continued".'

Sadie raised her brows. 'Excitement, Grandad? I would have thought nuisance was more like it.'

Joe drew on his pipe and a look of contentment settled on his lined face. His old briar was one of the few pleasures left in life. The other two were looking at him now, his beloved wife and the young girl who'd come into their lives and brought a ray of sunshine. She'd given them so much. The days didn't seem so long now they knew she'd be home at six every night with her bright smile lighting up the room. But on the matter of young Peter, he didn't agree with her. 'Me and Sarah have known Peter since he was a babe in arms, queen, and I think she'll bear me out when I say he's a good lad. One of the best, eh, Sarah?'

His wife nodded. 'They don't come any better than Peter. But then it wouldn't do for us all to be the same, would it? We each have our own likes and dislikes, and that's the way of the world. If Sadie doesn't like Peter that's her business; she's entitled to her own opinion, Joe, even if we do think she's wrong.'

Sadie gazed from one to the other. 'I don't dislike him. In fact, I'd think he was a smashing bloke if he'd just leave me alone. I mean, if it was only now and again, and we could have a good laugh, I'd get on well with him. But never a night goes by that he doesn't pop up from somewhere like a blinkin' Jack-in-the-box.'

'I think he's taken a shine to yer, sweetheart,' Sarah said, 'and yer should be flattered, not annoyed. But let's forget about Peter now. Tell us how yer got on with Geoff last night. Yer were in such a rush this morning I didn't get a chance to ask yer.'

Sadie pulled a face. 'I didn't tell him, I didn't have the nerve. We went dancing and we had such a really good night, I just couldn't do it. He's one helluva nice bloke and I don't know why I can't fall for him. I'm beginning to think I'm not made right.'

Sarah's wise old eyes were serious. 'Don't stay with him just because yer feel sorry for him, sweetheart, that wouldn't be fair to him or to you. If yer let it go on too long yer'll end up marrying him because that's what he'd expect, and, child, yer'd regret it for the rest of yer life. Yer can't turn love on like a water tap; it's something yer feel inside of yer when real love comes along. Yer'll meet the right boy some day, the one that's meant for yer, and believe me, sweetheart, yer'll know him right away. Yer heart will beat faster and sing every time yer see him and your tummy will feel as though there's a million butterflies flying around in there. There's no other feeling like it in the world, sweetheart, and it's worth waiting for.'

'Oh Grandma, that was lovely, what yer said.' Sadie pushed her chair back and rounded the table to hug the old lady. 'It sounded real romantic.'

'And every word was true,' Joe said. 'I can vouch for it. I still feel the same way about yer Grandma as I did the day I met her. I never look at her without me heart turning over.'

Sarah's look was tender. 'Yer an old softie, Joe O'Hanlon, but if Sadie gets one as good as you she won't go far wrong.'

'I'll tell Geoff next time I see him.' Sadie gave the frail shoulders a gentle squeeze before returning to her chair. 'And I'll wait for that special Mr Right to come along. Someone like Grandad, so we can live happy ever after, like they do in fairy stories.'

'It's a Prince Charming yer after, is it, queen?'

'No, Grandad, just an ordinary bloke will do me fine, as long as he loves me. That's all I ask.'

Sadie's heart sank when she saw the pleasure on Geoff's face as he came to meet her. Oh dear, she wasn't looking forward to this at all. All day she'd been rehearsing what she'd say to him, but the real thing was going to be much harder than the rehearsal. It would be best to get it over with right away, otherwise she'd be on pins all night.

'Where d'yer want to go, Sadie?' Geoff cupped her elbow. 'Shall we go dancing again, or would yer rather go to the pictures?'

Sadie swallowed hard to try and get rid of the lump in her throat. 'Can I have a word with you, Geoff, before we go anywhere?'

The tone of her voice told him that all was not well and his smile changed to a look of concern. 'Why, what's wrong?'

'There's nothing really wrong.' Sadie could feel her inside shaking. 'It's just that I worry sometimes about us going out together so often. I don't want yer to get serious about me because I'm too young to be courting seriously with anyone. I'm only sixteen and that's too young to know me own mind. And while yer going out with me it's stopping yer from meeting someone who's ready to settle down, someone a bit older.'

'Don't yer like going out with me, Sadie?' Geoff's voice was low. 'Is that what it is?'

'No! I like going out with yer, Geoff,' Sadie said honestly. 'I always enjoy meself with yer and yer always treat me nice. But I know I'm not ready to settle down yet and I don't think it's fair to let yer keep on spending yer time and money on me without me telling yer how I feel.'

'Don't stop seein' me, Sadie, please. I like going out with yer and I'd miss yer.'

'But yer'd soon meet another girl, Geoff. Yer've got everything going for yer! Yer've got good looks, a smashing personality, a caring nature and a happy disposition. The girls will be falling all over yer, pushing each other out of the way to get to yer first.' She managed a weak smile. 'And yer can't half dance.'

'But I'm not the one for you, am I?' Geoff kicked at a piece of paper that had been blown along by the wind. 'Is there someone else, Sadie?'

Sadie shook her head. 'I'd tell yer if there was, Geoff. I'd been out with a few boys before I met you, yer know that, but none since.'

'Then there's no reason why yer can't come out with me now and again, is there?' Geoff coaxed. 'We can just be friends, if that's what yer want. Or we could even be dancing partners, there's no harm in that.'

'Yer'd have to teach me to dance first.' Sadie's heart was feeling lighter now the worst was over. She wouldn't mind going to a dance with him now and again, in fact she'd enjoy it. It would mean she had something to look forward to without the worry of him having the wrong ideas about her. 'I'd like that, Geoff, as long as yer know how I feel.'

'I'll teach yer to dance, Sadie, and when we're good enough we'll go to all the big dance halls and go in for competitions.'

'Ah, ay, Geoff, don't be getting any big ideas. I'm not Ginger Rogers, yer know!'

'Yer will be when I've finished with yer.' The tension had lifted and Geoff smiled. 'How about going to the dance tonight and beginning our partnership?'

'As long as you understand how I feel, Geoff, 'cos I don't ever want to let yer down. If you meet a girl that yer like, or if I meet a boy, then we part company the best of friends. Is that okay with you?'

Geoff nodded. 'Purely a dancing partnership.'

Sadie smiled as she took his arm. 'I think we'll concentrate on me learning the slow foxtrot first, eh? And in a couple of weeks we'll be able to show the others how it should be done.'

* * *

Sadie rubbed her arms briskly. 'Yer were right about it being cold here, Auntie Mary. I'm freezing! I've got goose-pimples on top of me goose-pimples.'

'Just wait until it gets really cold.' Mary Ann nodded her head knowingly. 'It's only November now, the worst weather has yet to come. When the snow and sleet come down it gets cold enough to freeze the you-know-what off a brass monkey. It's half-a-dozen vests yer'll want on then, girl, and fur-lined bloomers.'

'I'll borrow me grandma's fleecy-lined ones with the elasticated legs. No one will see them and they'll keep me really warm.'

Mary Ann grinned. 'Just remember not to bend down in them, girl, 'cos the legs will come down to yer knees and yer'll not look so glamorous with half a yard of pink fleecy-lined bloomers showing.'

'Warmth comes before vanity, Auntie Mary, I'm finding that out.' Sadie looked down at the shapeless brown coat she was wearing. 'I look like Granny Grunt in this thing, but I'd be lost without it. It was a blessing it came in, otherwise I'd have to wear me nice navy-blue one and I don't want to do that, 'cos I keep that for best.'

Mary Ann was looking over Sadie's shoulder and she jerked her head when she saw one of the young stall-holders approaching. 'Ay out, sunshine, here comes Romeo.'

'Good morning, Mary Ann, is it cold enough for yer?' Tommy Seymour worked on a second-hand tool stall further down the market. He managed it alone through the week while his dad went out with a cart collecting old tools and any scrap he could get. Tommy was seventeen and had had his eye on Sadie since the day she came. He'd asked her for dates and been turned down so many times Mary Ann wondered how he had the nerve to keep coming back, but she admired his perseverance.

'Is it me yer've come to see, Tommy?' Mary Ann asked. 'Or have yer come for yer daily refusal from Sadie?'

Tommy grinned, not in the least put out. 'Yer a mind-reader on the quiet, Mary Ann. I think yer should make a career out of it, yer'd do well. People pay a tanner to have their fortunes told, did yer know that?'

'I'm sure you wouldn't pay me a tanner just to tell yer what Sadie's answer will be, would yer, Smart Alec?'

'Auntie Mary!' Sadie blushed. She didn't like to see anyone made a fool of, especially when she was involved. 'Leave the lad alone, yer embarrassing him.'

Tommy threw his head back and roared with laughter. He was a tall, lanky lad with a mop of ginger hair and wide grey eyes. His face was weatherbeaten with being outside all the time and he looked the picture

229

of health. 'It would take more than that to embarrass me, Sadie. I've got the skin of a rhinoceros.' Then he narrowed his eyes. 'But yer could stop her from embarrassing me if yer wanted to.'

Mary Ann pulled a face and rolled her eyes. If Sadie fell for that one she'd fall for the flaming cat. But no, she wasn't that daft. She was naive for her age, granted, but she wasn't that blinking naive.

'What d'yer mean, Tommy?' Sadie asked. 'I couldn't stop Auntie Mary from doing anything she wanted to do.'

'Yer could, yer know.' Tommy crossed his fingers for luck. 'Yer could say yer'd come to Blair Hall tonight with me an' Spike.'

There was no immediate refusal like there usually was, as Sadie pursed her lips in thought before saying, 'Yeah, okay. But I'm not paying for meself.'

Mary Ann's eyes and mouth were wide open. 'Well, I'll be buggered!'

'I never knew the meanin' of that saying, Mary Ann, it never made sense to me before. But now I think I've got the general idea.' Tommy was jubilant, his grin stretching from ear to ear. 'Me and Spike will pay for yer, Sadie – it's only right when we asked yer to come. Shall we pick yer up from old Sarah's about half-past seven?' He waited for Sadie's nod before hurrying back to his stall, whistling with delight. Patience had certainly paid off in this instance. It just went to show that you should never give up if you really want something.

'Don't look so surprised, Auntie Mary. I'm only goin' to a dance with them.'

'Surprised? Yer could knock me over with a bleedin' feather! An' I'll tell yer this, sunshine, I'm not half as surprised as Tommy is. He must think it's his birthday. After all the times he's asked yer, what made yer agree to go with him this time?'

'A couple of reasons, really,' Sadie said. 'First, Spike will be with us so I won't be on me own with him. Second, because I like dancing and never get the chance to dance with anyone but Geoff. I want to find out if I can manage the steps with someone else.'

'Are you and Geoff still just dancing partners?'

Sadie nodded. 'Always will be, Auntie Mary. I've cut our dates down to two a week now, hoping he'll go dancing on his own and find himself a nice girl.'

'Well, yer'll enjoy yerself with Tommy and Spike, they're good lads. Even if they can't dance it'll be worth it for the laugh.'

Sadie shivered. 'The only part of me that isn't cold are me feet. And that's because Grandad put a couple of layers of newspaper in me shoes. It hasn't half made a difference.' She tilted her head. 'I should get those boots to our Jimmy, he could do with them in this weather. Would yer let me have an hour off one afternoon, Auntie Mary, and I can meet him coming out of school?'

'I've been having a little think about time off, girl, and there's no reason why we couldn't both have a day off. There's nothing doing on a Monday and Tuesday, only sorting the clothes out, so we could have one of those days each. I managed the stall on me own for years so I could do it again, and I know you could manage on yer own standing on yer head.' It was Mary Ann's turn to tilt her head. 'How does that sound to you?'

'It sounds marvellous, Auntie Mary, but yer the boss, not me.'

'Yeah, I am, aren't I? Lucky old me! So, in that case, if yer want to scoot off home now, and pick up those shoes for yer brother, yer can do. Yer'll have plenty of time to get a nice warm by the fire and have something to eat before it's time to go to the school. Then after yer've seen yer brother there'll still be a couple of hours spare for yer to titivate yerself up for yer big date tonight.' Mary Ann struck up a pose, licked each of her thumbs in turn, then lifting her skirt and humming a fast tempo song, she gave a very good account of herself in a demonstration of the Charleston. Tony from the shoe stall saw her and began to clap, joined within seconds by other stall-holders.

'Atta girl, Mary Ann,' Tony called. 'Show a leg there, love, give us all a treat. There's nothing better to warm a feller up on a cold day, than the sight of a pair of garters.'

'Don't you be looking at me Auntie's garters,' Sadie said, shaking a finger at the laughing stall-holder. 'Keep yer eyes to yerself.'

Mary Ann stopped, red in the face and gasping. She turned her back on the watching eyes and bent from the waist down, as though trying to catch her breath. But when she stood up and Sadie saw the shaking shoulders she knew Mary Ann had a trick up her sleeve. And she wasn't wrong.

Mary Ann spun around and lifted one of her arms high in the air. In her hand she had a pair of home-made elastic garters which she waved at Tony. 'Here yer are, sunshine, put these on yer stall and yer'll be warm all day.'

Tony's laugh was the loudest. 'Thanks, Mary Ann, I appreciate the gesture. Give them to Sadie to bring over, there's a good girl. Oh, and will yer do us a favour, Mary Ann?'

'For you, Tony, my love, anything.'

'Then before yer send the garters over, will yer put yer legs back in them?'

'Get away with yer, yer cheeky sod! I pity your poor wife, I really do. Sex mad, that's what yer are.'

231

'Mad for the want of it, Mary Ann, mad for the want of it.'

'Oh, get about yer business, Tony Henshaw, and don't be chasing me customers away, either.'

'What customers? Yer haven't got no customers.'

'I know that, yer daft article. That's because yer've chased them all away. Now keep yer evil eye off me and I might have a bit more luck.' Mary Ann winked at Tony before she bent down and slipped the garters over her feet and up to her knees, making sure her long skirt covered her actions. 'You get off now, sunshine, otherwise the day will be wasted if yer hang around.'

'I'm glad I was still here to see that little exhibition.' Sadie grinned. 'Yer can sure shake a leg, Auntie Mary.'

'That was nothing, girl – yer should see me do the Black Bottom. I know yer think I'm ancient, but I can still dance with the best. Especially on a Saturday night when I've had a couple of jars, there's no stopping me then. My poor feller's stopped trying. He said it's easier to halt a twenty-two tram between stops than it is to try and stop me when I've had half-a-dozen bottles of milk stout.'

'I bet yer had all the lads running after you, when yer were a young girl, Auntie Mary.'

'Oh, I had my moments, girl, no doubt about that. Now, will yer please get yer skates on and skedaddle before I change me mind.'

Sadie hesitated. 'Auntie Mary, if I have a day off, will I be docked a day's pay?'

'Of course not, soft girl. I'm having a day off too, so will I be docking me own pay? Not bloody likely I won't! We'll just have to work harder on the other days to make it up.'

Sadie breathed a sigh of relief. 'I was a bit anxious, with Christmas not being far off. I want to buy some presents this year, for the first time in me life. And I want to surprise Grandma and Grandad by buying a Christmas tree. They were saying the other night they'd never bothered about Christmas since their two boys died, so I want to make this one a happy one for them.'

'I'm glad about that, girl, and I'm glad you'll be able to do it. I never thought yer'd stick to giving me half-a-crown a week, but yer have and I'm proud of yer. Two pounds yer've got saved now, so yer can cut down a bit on yer saving if yer want to buy things to put away for Christmas.'

'I will after this week, then I'll start again the first week in the New Year.' Sadie kissed the tip of Mary Ann's nose which was bright red with the cold. 'And behave yerself when I'm gone; don't be showin' yer garters off to strange men.'

'Oh, so I have your permission to show them to Tony, do I? 'Cos he's not a strange man, I've known him for years. Mind you, come to think of it, I've always thought he was a bit strange.' Mary Ann pushed Sadie's shoulder. 'On yer way, sunshine, and I'll promise not to lift me skirt for anyone unless it's Cary Grant.'

Jimmy spotted Sadie as soon as he came through the door, and he elbowed his way through the groups of boys in front of him. 'I look out for yer every day, our Sadie.' His joy at seeing her was written all over his face. 'I've been dying to see yer.'

Sadie gave him a hug. 'It's good to see yer, Jimmy. I think of yer all the time and say a prayer for yer every night. And for our Ellen, Les and Sally. Look, I've brought yer a present.' She handed him the parcel wrapped in newspaper. 'They should keep yer nice and warm.'

Jimmy tore at the paper in his excitement. Nice surprises didn't come his way very often. When he saw the boots his eyes were like saucers. 'Boots! Ooh, our Sadie, I've never 'ad a pair of boots before, not like this anyway. Feel the weight of them, they're not half strong.'

'They'll stand yer in good stead for the winter, Jimmy. The snow and rain won't get through those thick soles.'

'Thanks, our Sadie. I wasn't expectin' nothing like this. I'm glad me dad's got bigger feet than me, otherwise he'd have them off me. He's not half greedy, Sadie, even worse than when you were at home. He's not like the other dads in the street – they take their sons to the match or fishin', and they all get pocket money so they can go to the Saturday matinée if they want. But not our dad. He doesn't even talk to us except to bawl his head off if we don't get out of his way quick enough.'

'Does he still drink as much?'

'Every night he comes home paralytic, that's what gets up my nose.' Jimmy became emotional at the unfairness. 'D'yer know what he did last night? This will just show yer how cruel he is. He sat at the table tuckin' into bacon and two fried eggs, while all we had was bread and drippin'. And he was laughing at us, dipping his bread into the egg yolk and holding it out for us to see. Sally asked for some and he held a piece out to her, but when she went to take it he pulled it back and laughed his head off when she started cryin'. Honest, our Sadie, if I'd been older and bigger, I'd have landed him one last night for what he did to Sally. I mean, she's only a baby, he had no right to do that to her.'

'Just hang on in there, Jimmy, and remember what I've told yer about it not lasting for ever. Our Ellen will be fourteen in May and starting work, and there's only ten months between yer. So if yer look at it that way, yer haven't got long to wait.'

Jimmy hung his head. 'I wish you could see our Ellen and have a talk to her, Sadie. She's not like she used to be, gabbing all the time, she hardly says a word now. And when I ask her what's wrong, she won't tell me. But she'd tell you, I know she would, 'cos she told me she wished yer were at home.'

Sadie shivered at her thoughts. Surely to God their father wasn't up to his old tricks? 'Jimmy, am I too late to catch our Ellen now, before she gets near our street?'

Jimmy didn't hesitate. He worried about his sister and wasn't going to miss the chance of getting help for her. He had an idea what was making her the way she was, but he was too shy to ask her and too young to do anything about it. But their Sadie would help, he knew she would. He thrust the parcel into her arms and was sprinting away even as he spoke. 'I can run faster than you. Just stay where yer are and I'll bring 'er to yer.'

Sadie got a shock when she saw Ellen. Her shoulders were drooped, the lovely dark hair lank, her pretty face devoid of colour and her eyes listless. The girl was either sickening for something or worried to death. 'Here, Jimmy, take the boots and get off home. Yer can tell me mam I was outside school again, but don't mention that I've seen Ellen. Go on, there's a good boy.'

However Jimmy wasn't going without something to look forward to. 'Yer will come again soon, won't yer, our Sadie?'

Sadie nodded. 'Yeah, I'll be here in a couple of weeks, but don't let on to me mam or dad. And I'll see yer again Christmas week 'cos I'll have presents for all of you, with the exception of our Dot.'

Jimmy tucked the parcel under his arm and pulled a face. 'I wouldn't give our Dot a spot if I 'ad the measles. She's horrible to us.'

Sadie gave him a quick peck on the cheek. 'Go on now, love, I want to have a talk to our Ellen and it's girl talk.' She waited until he was out of earshot before facing her young sister. 'You don't look very happy, Ellen.'

The girl shrugged her thin shoulders. 'I've nothin' to be happy about, Sadie, but I am glad to see yer.'

'Same here, Ellen, I'm made up about it. But yer don't look well and I'm worried about yer. I know yer've not got much to be happy about, but is there something making you unhappy? Something at home, perhaps?'

Ellen lowered her eyes. 'No more than usual. Yer know what it was like in our house when you were there – well, it's ten times worse now.' Her voice stronger, she met Sadie's gaze. 'Couldn't yer come home again, Sadie? You looked after us when yer were there, stopped me dad and our Dot from hitting us and made sure we got something to eat.

You were like a mother to us; now we've got no one.'

'I'm sorry, Ellen, but I had to run away, I couldn't take any more. You were too young to understand, but I'd been a skivvy in that house since I was about four years old. I got out to make a life for meself, meet nice people and make friends. And I've done it, Ellen, I've got meself a job that I love and I live with wonderful people. And the time will come when you and Jimmy can do the same. You'll be better off than I was, because I had to do it on me own while you'll have me to help yer.'

Interest flickered in the brown eyes. 'Yer mean if I run away I can come and live with you in yer friend's house?'

'I'm not making any rash promises over that, Ellen, it wouldn't be fair to yer. The people I live with might not want another lodger. But I will make one promise that I swear I'll keep. The week you leave school I'll help yer find a job and somewhere to live. And when our Jimmy leaves school and starts work, we should be earning enough between us to rent a house of our own.'

'I wish it could happen tomorrow, Sadie, 'cos I hate living in that house and I hate me mam and dad.'

Sadie was thoughtful for a while, seeking words that wouldn't upset her sister. 'Me dad's a dirty man, isn't he, Ellen?'

Her eyes on the ground, Ellen nodded. 'I hate him.'

'Shall I tell yer how to stop him pestering yer?'

'I've told him to stop, our Sadie, but he just laughs at me.'

'Well, next time he comes within a yard of yer, just tell him that I'll be keeping in touch with yer and if he doesn't leave yer alone I'm going to the police. And if he gets mad with yer and goes to hit yer, tell him I said yer had to scream the place down. And don't be frightened of him when yer say it, Ellen, let him know that yer mean it. Me dad's a bully in the house but a coward outside. He'd be terrified of his cronies finding out he's a dirty old man 'cos they'd kill him.'

A smile crossed the pale face. 'I'll do it, our Sadie, I really will.'

'I know yer will, Ellen, because that's what I did to stop him.'

Ellen's jaw dropped. 'Yer mean he used to . . . used to . . .?'

'Yes, he did, Ellen, but I put a stop to it, and that's what you've got to do. I'll be down to see yer in a week or two and I want to see a smile on yer face when yer telling me how yer told our dad to go jump in a lake. Okay?'

'Oh, I'm glad you came today, our Sadie, I feel so much better. I will stick up for meself, I promise. Now I know it won't go on for ever, I won't mind so much. At least I'll have something to look forward to.'

'Yer've got a whole lifetime to look forward to, Ellen – a lifetime of happiness. Yer'll soon put the old life behind yer, and that's another promise I'm making yer.'

Chapter Twenty

Florrie Young left her warm speck by the fire to close the gap in the curtains where she would swear there was a draught coming through. As she was pulling the curtain across, a figure passed the window and she grunted in disgust. 'There he goes again, same time every night, Mr Moneybags himself. The house is a dump, inside and out, the mother goes around like a gypsy wearing dirty clothes and the kids look half-starved.' She took her seat and picked up the shirt of Harry's she was sewing a button on. 'Doesn't stop him from goin' out boozing every night though; come hell or high water he's in that pub knocking the pints back. Beats me how she lets him get away with it. If he was a husband of mine I'd have taken the rolling pin to him years ago.'

Jack lowered the paper he was reading. 'It's a good job yer married a soft touch like me, then, isn't it?' He glanced over to the table where Harry was sitting with his head bent over the inside pages of the newspaper, but it was obvious he was listening rather than reading. It was to be hoped his wife didn't carry on about their neighbours because it only ended up with mother and son arguing. Perhaps if he gave her something to take her mind off the subject. 'Put the kettle on, love, and let's have a cuppa.'

'After I've finished sewing this button on.' Florrie, wearing a brass thimble on her forefinger, pressed the needle through the hole in the button and pulled it out the other side. 'It's a mystery about that daughter of theirs, the blonde one. It must be nearly six months since she just disappeared without trace. Neither sight nor sound of her since. It seems fishy to me.'

Harry raised his head. 'Mam, I've told you that the girl you call "the blonde one", had a name. Her name was Sadie, she was a nice girl and I liked her.'

Jack lowered the paper to his knees. He'd never mentioned it to anyone because he knew his wife would throw a fit if she found out, but twice on his way home from working overtime, he'd been sitting on the top deck of a tram and seen Harry standing at the gates to Sefton Park. And the first time, when he'd turned his head to make sure it was his son, he'd seen Sadie walk up to Harry, saw them join hands and stroll into the park. On the second occasion his son had been alone, but within seconds the tram had passed Sadie on her way to meet him. And Jack had to admit he could understand his son falling for her; she was as pretty a girl as you were ever likely to see.

Florrie broke the cotton with her teeth before answering. 'Then I'm glad she's gone, Harry, 'cos I wouldn't want no son of mine mixing with the likes of them.'

Harry's face was flushed and his eyes blazing. 'I wasn't mixing with "the likes of them". I was friendly with a nice girl, that's all. And considering you never even passed the time of day with her, I don't see that yer in a position to know what she was like.'

'I know the family, and that's enough for me. I want no truck with them.' Florrie was angry now. 'Have yer seen that sister of hers? Only just left school and she's actin' like a twenty-year-old. Out every night, she is, tottering along on high heels and made up like a tart. If she was my daughter I'd have her across me knee and tan her backside for her.' She took a deep breath, her nostrils flared in anger. 'I'm stuck with them as neighbours, more's the pity, but don't expect me to offer them the hand of friendship because I'd just as soon give them a dose of arsenic.'

Harry pushed his chair back. 'I'm going out for a walk to get some fresh air in me lungs. The atmosphere in this room is stifling me.'

Jack groaned inwardly as he heard the door slam. He loved his wife dearly but once she got a bee in her bonnet there was no shifting her. Stubborn as a mule she was. What he couldn't understand was why she hadn't noticed the change in her son since the girl next door disappeared. Florrie adored the two boys and was usually quick to sense the slightest hint of unrest. But she seemed not to have noticed the change in Harry. She had commented on the fact that he didn't go out as often, but readily accepted his excuse that he didn't feel like it.

'You were out of order there, Florrie,' Jack said. 'There was no need for some of the things yer said. And Harry was right when he said yer weren't in a position to know what the girl was like when yer'd never even spoken to her.'

'Oh, I get it – it was all my fault, was it? I've got it all wrong, have I? Well, I'll tell yer what, I'll invite all the Wilson family to dinner on Sunday, shall I? Make them a big roast dinner and be all "hail fellow well met", is that what yer want?'

Jack shook his head. It probably would have been better to let the matter rest, but now they'd gone this far he might as well say what was on his mind. 'Florrie, do you trust Harry?'

Florrie gaped in surprise. 'That's a daft question, isn't it? He's me son, I love the bones of him and would trust him with me life.'

'Do you trust him enough to believe he knows right from wrong, good from bad?'

'What's got into you, Jack Young? Of course our Harry knows right from wrong and good from bad. That's the way we've brought up him and our Paul.'

'Then why don't you believe him when he says young Sadie was a nice girl?'

'How can she be?' Florrie blustered. 'Coming from a family like that.'

'So, what yer telling me is that every one of the kids next door are no good – is that it, Florrie? When they go around with clothes hanging off their backs and no shoes on, it's their fault, is that what yer think? If it is, then I'm on Harry's side. If he says Sadie was a nice girl, then I believe him.'

Florrie was flabbergasted. Never in all their married life had Jack taken sides against her. She regretted what she'd said to Harry about the girl, had regretted it even as the words were coming out of her mouth because she knew that for some unknown reason it would upset him. But she wasn't going to take anything back that she'd said about the father and mother, or that the house was a dump and they were lousy neighbours. So if Jack wanted to get a cob on over it, then let him get on with it. 'Suit yerself, Jack Young. What you think is no skin off my nose.'

'Well, unless yer've fallen out with me, can I have that cuppa now?'

Without a word Florrie went into the kitchen, and as she leaned against the sink waiting for the kettle to boil she let her mind go over what had been said in the last half-hour. Had she been unreasonable with Harry? Was she so incensed because the state of the house next door made a show of hers, that she hated everything about it, even innocent children?

Florrie carried the two cups in and handed one to Jack. 'Here's the cuppa yer've been moaning about, yer grumbling old fogey.'

Jack grinned, knowing by her tone of voice that she bore no grudge. 'I'm sorry, lass, but I had to say what was on me mind. You went too far and it grieves me to see our Harry so upset.'

'I know, and it won't happen again. But I can't understand why he feels so strongly about the girl. After all, he never went out with her, did he?'

'That is something we'll never know.' Just a little white lie that will harm no one, Jack thought. 'But he seems to be upset about her leaving, so he must have liked her. I'm surprised you haven't noticed that he seldom goes out now, only once or twice a week.'

'Of course I've noticed, yer daft thing! But I didn't say anything because I thought he'd fallen out with Clare, the one he used to go dancing with. I didn't want to interfere.' Florrie jerked her head to the ceiling. 'I've interfered good and proper now though, haven't I?'

'When he comes in, just pretend it never happened. He'll get over it.'

At that moment Harry was turning the corner into the street after a brisk walk around the block. His head was down, chin on chest and eyes on the ground as, for the umpteenth time, his mind went over what his mother had said. He had to admit she had reason to dislike the Wilsons. She was so houseproud herself, you could eat off her floor; it must get her down having to pass next door every time she went out. And she was right about Dot, too; she was really hard-faced for a girl of her age. She'd stopped him a few times, brazenly asking if he'd like a date with her, but he'd sent her packing. It was hard to believe she and Sadie were sisters.

Harry's thoughts were miles away and he didn't see Jimmy Wilson coming out of the corner shop until they'd collided. 'Sorry, mister.' Jimmy bent to pick up the bundle of firewood that had been knocked out of his hands. 'I didn't see yer.'

'It was my fault,' Harry said. 'I wasn't looking where I was going.' He stared into the young boy's face and couldn't stop himself from asking, 'Have yer heard anything from Sadie?'

Jimmy hesitated. The bloke had always been friendly with him, not like some of the others in the street. Surely it wouldn't hurt to say he'd seen his sister? After all, he couldn't tell him where she was because he didn't know himself. 'Yeah, I've seen her, She came down to the school to see me. Twice, she's been.'

'How is she?'

'She's all right. She told me she's got a job that she really likes, an' she's got somewhere nice to live.'

'Oh, aye?' Harry's heart was beating fifteen to the dozen but he tried to keep the eagerness out of his voice in case he frightened the kid off. 'Where's she living, then?'

Jimmy shrugged his shoulders. 'I dunno, mister. She won't tell me anythin' in case me mam and dad get it out of me. She doesn't want them to know nothin', see?'

'I was a friend of Sadie's, yer know, she wouldn't mind yer telling me where she is.'

'Honest, mister, I don't know. I wish I did, then I could go and visit her.'

Harry could tell the boy was speaking the truth so there was no point in pushing him. 'Will you be seeing her again?'

240

'Oh, yeah,' Jimmy said proudly. 'Our Sadie said she loves me an' the other kids, an' she'll never forget about us.'

'If I wrote a letter to her, would yer give it to her for us?'

Oh dear, Jimmy hadn't been expecting this. Perhaps he should have kept his mouth shut. 'I don't know when I'll see her again, mister – it could be ages. An' I haven't got nowhere to hide a letter an' me mam would find it an' I'd be in trouble. So I'll just tell our Sadie that yer were askin' after her an' see what she says.' Jimmy lifted the bundle of firewood. 'I'd better get home with this or me mam'll kill me. She wants to light the fire to have the room warm for me dad comin' in.'

Harry narrowed his eyes. 'Yer mean yer haven't got a fire lit now?'

'No, mister, we don't have a fire during the day, only at night for me dad comin' in from work. He didn't half take off when he came into a cold house tonight – yelled the blinkin' place down. That's why me mam wants to get the place warm now for him comin' in later, so there'll be no trouble.'

'But he's only in that pub across the street. By the time he gets home it'll be time for him to go to bed.' Harry shook his head in anger and disbelief. 'The fire should be lit during the day to warm the house through for the children, not at ten o'clock at night when they're in bed.'

'I know, mister, but me dad's the boss in our 'ouse and what he says goes. An' If I don't get back with this wood smartish, I'll be gettin' a thick lip off me mam.'

'Okay, but don't forget what I said about Sadie, will yer? Give her my regards and say I'd like to see her some time.'

'Yeah, I'll do that.' Jimmy took off like a shot. It was all getting too involved for him; he'd land himself in trouble if he didn't learn to keep his mouth shut. Sadie had warned him to be careful and he would be from now on. He wouldn't even tell her he'd spoken to the bloke from next door.

Harry watched the boy running like the wind, as though the idea of a thick lip held no attraction for him. But what a stroke of luck he'd bumped into him. At least he knew now that Sadie was keeping in touch with the children, and that meant there was the possibility of him finding out where she was. And to think he wouldn't have that knowledge if it hadn't been for the argument he'd had with his mother. He'd walked out of the house in a right temper, but he was going home with hope in his heart.

Sarah insisted that Sadie invite Tommy and Spike in when they called for her. She knew both the lads from the market, and knowing they

241

were a pair of jokers she thought they'd cheer her husband up. And it was nice for them to know the company Sadie was keeping.

'You two look after our girl, d'yer hear?' Sarah sat on a straight chair, a clean pinny on and her hair neatly combed for the occasion. 'If yer don't, it's me and my feller yer'll have to answer to.'

Tommy grinned. 'We'll treat her like the crown jewels, Sarah, cross me heart and hope to die if we don't.'

'Like a piece of Dresden china,' Spike said, nodding his head for emphasis before turning to his mate. 'That's what they call that dear stuff, isn't it? What all the posh people use with their little finger stickin' out.'

Tommy tutted. 'Yer dead ignorant, you are. I can't take yer anywhere without yer makin' a show of me. Stuff is what clothes an' curtains and that sort of thing are made of. Yer can't call china "stuff".'

'Oh.' Spike was given his nickname because his hair was always standing up like spikes, and when he ran his hand through it now, it made him look like Stan Laurel. 'What d'yer call it then?'

'Huh! You're not soft, are yer? Talk about act daft an' I'll buy yer a coal-yard isn't in it!' Tommy spread his hands and appealed to Joe. 'Now, I ask yer, Mr O'Hanlon, wouldn't I be a mug to tell him? I've already taught him his two times table, and how to count up to a hundred. If I keep passin' all me knowledge on to him, he'll soon be as clever as me an' I don't fancy that at all.'

Spike laughed with the rest of them. 'I'll tell yer what, Tommy, even if I was an idiot I'd still be cleverer than you.'

Sadie picked her handbag off the sideboard. 'Come on, you two, or we'll just be in time for the last waltz.' She grinned at Joe. 'They're like this all the time, yer know, Grandad, there's never a dull moment when they're around. I don't know how they ever sell anything at the market, the way they fool about.'

'It's better than being miserable, queen, any day – *and* it's good for business. While their customers are laughing their socks off, it's easier to get them to part with their money.'

'I wish me dad saw it that way, Mr O'Hanlon. He's always tellin' me to grow up an' stop clownin' around.'

Sadie punched Spike on the arm. 'Will yer shut up and let's get going? I hope yer not going to gab all night, I'd like to get some dancing in.'

Tommy gave a cheeky grin. 'I bag the first dance.'

Spike pulled a face and snapped his fingers. 'I'm foiled again. We haven't even got out of the door yet an' I've been knocked back already.'

'Ah, yer poor thing,' Sadie said. 'Never mind, yer can have the second dance.'

They were laughing as they walked down the hall, Sarah and Joe following so they could wave them off. 'Enjoy yerselves,' Sarah called after them. 'And you boys make sure that Sadie gets home safely.'

'She'll be escorted right to her front door, Sarah, by two of the bravest, strongest men in the city of Liverpool. If we come across a dragon, like that Saint George feller did, we'd slay it with our bare hands rather than let it get to the fair maiden.'

'You speak for yerself, Tommy Seymour,' Spike said. 'First sight of a dragon an' I'll be off; yer won't see me heels for dust. You can be a dead hero if yer like, but me, I'll be a live coward.'

They were passing under a street-lamp when Sadie turned to wave. 'Don't worry, Grandma, they're not as daft as they make out. Now you two go inside before yer catch yer death of cold. Good night and God bless.'

'Good night and God bless, sweetheart.'

'Good night and God bless, queen.' Joe put his arm across his wife's shoulders and led her back into the house. 'Sadie won't be short of a laugh with them two.'

'No, they're good lads, she's in safe hands with them.' Sarah began to chuckle. 'She better had be! Any shenanigans out of them and Mary Ann will have their guts for garters. She'd think nothing of giving them a good hiding, big and all as they are.'

The strains of a tango greeted them as they climbed the stairs to Blair Hall. 'I'm good at this,' Tommy bragged. 'Everyone says I knock George Raft into a cocked hat with me tango. He's not in the meg specks.'

'In that case yer'd better find yerself another partner.' Sadie pulled a face. 'If yer that good, I'd only cramp yer style.'

Spike held the door to the ballroom open, and as Sadie walked through he said in a loud whisper, 'Take no notice of him, Sadie, he can't tango to save his life.'

'He can't be any worse than me. So if yer want to have a bash, Tommy, I'm game.'

Spike was right: Tommy *was* hopeless. But he was so funny he had Sadie in stitches. Holding her arm straight out, as stiff as a broom handle, he marched her down the centre of the dance floor, his body and head movements deliberately exaggerated and the expression on his face dead serious. And he gave way to no one. Any other couples unfortunate enough to cross their path had to swerve to avoid a collision because Tommy was determined to get to the other end of the dance floor if it killed him. And once there, with a little corner to themselves, he decided to be daring and try a movement he'd never tried before. He'd watched other blokes do it and it looked as easy as falling off a bike. So, with his hand pressed firmly in the small of Sadie's back, he bent his body forward, forcing her to bend backwards until she was nearly bent in two. The trouble was, while Tommy had been busy watching the blokes' bodies, he hadn't bothered watching their feet. Instead of being firmly on the floor to take the weight of Sadie's body, his feet were both turned in. Too late, he tried to right them. The consequence being, he stumbled and let go of her, and she ended up sprawled out on the floor.

His face the colour of beetroot, and hoping that no one had seen what a fool he'd made of himself, Tommy bent down to try and help Sadie up, only to find she was so helpless with laughter she couldn't move. A small crowd had gathered around them and Tommy's embarrassment grew. 'Come on, Sadie, everyone's lookin' at us.'

Sadie ignored his outstretched hand and scrambled to her feet, convulsed with a fit of the giggles. 'Oh dear, oh dear, oh dear! Just wait until I tell Mary Ann, Tommy Seymour – yer'll never hear the end of this.'

'Hello, Sadie.'

Sadie spun around and surprise replaced the smile on her face. 'Geoff! What are you doing here?'

'I could ask you the same thing.' Geoff still had his arm around the waist of the girl he'd been dancing with. 'I've been coming here every Wednesday for the last few weeks. Who are you with?'

'I'm with Tommy here, and another boy, Spike. They, er, they live in the same street as me grandma.'

The music came to an end and the crowd dispersed. 'We'd better get back to Spike, but I'll see yer later, Geoff.'

'Yeah – save me the next slow foxtrot, will yer?'

'Okay.' Sadie watched them walk away and noticed that Geoff not only escorted the girl back to her seat, he stayed with her. She wondered whether there was anything in it, but she wasn't allowed to dwell on her thoughts because Spike joined them and began to tease Tommy without mercy.

'I remember yer tellin' me once, Tommy, that yer ambition in life was to be an exhibition dancer. Well, I can honestly say yer've fulfilled yer ambition tonight, me old mate, 'cos yer've just made a right exhibition of yerself.'

'Leave him alone, Spike,' Sadie said. 'He slipped, that's all. It could happen to anyone.'

'I bet it doesn't happen to George Raft.' Spike wasn't going to let an opportunity like this pass. 'D'yer know this dragon yer said we might meet on the way home? Well, I hope he doesn't want to do the tango with yer, Tommy, 'cos those things breathe fire, yer know. If he ended up on the floor like Sadie, he'd burn the backside out of yer kecks while yer were leggin' it hell for leather up the street.'

Tommy took it all in good fun. 'Now yer've had yer money's worth, Spike, d'yer mind if I have a laugh at meself? I mean, there's not much point in makin' a fool of yerself if yer not going to get a laugh out of it.' A cheeky grin spread across his face. 'I told meself it would be as easy as fallin' off a bike. But me memory failed me, 'cos I fell off a bike once and it wasn't a bit easy, or funny.' He turned to his friend. 'You should remember 'cos you were with me when I pinched the loan of Bobby Hyland's bike. We were about ten, and he'd left it propped up outside the corner shop while he was on a message for his mam. In fact, now I come to think of it, you were the one who dared me to have a ride on it! I'd never been on a bike before but you egged me on, saying it was a doddle. It was a doddle all right – I fell off before I'd gone two yards and I scraped all me knees.' He nodded his head as he remembered more of that sorry episode. 'It's all comin' back to me now, yer little twerp. When Bobby went home crying because I'd buckled one of the wheels, and his mam came out and chased me down the street, you told her yer knew nothing about it! A fine friend you turned out to be. As well as gettin' a clip around the ear off Mrs Hyland, I got another one off me mam when I got home.'

Sadie shook her head. 'You two take the biscuit, yer know that, don't yer? Yer've gone from exhibition dancing to dragons, from pinchin' a kid's bike to buckling the wheel on him, from his mam comin' out and chasing yer, and you getting a clip around the ear off her, then another one off yer mam! Yer've covered some ground there all right. And what started it all off, pray? I get pushed to the floor, that's what started it. And neither of yer have even bothered to ask if I'm dead or alive.'

The two boys exchanged glances. They'd been pals for so long, since infant school, they could practically read each other's mind. 'She's touchy, isn't she?' Spike said. 'Just like a blinkin' girl.'

'Yeah,' Tommy agreed. 'I mean, it's not as though she's broken anything. She's still in one piece, so I don't know what she's got to moan about.'

'That's where yer wrong, yer see,' Sadie said, keeping her face straight. ''Cos I did hurt meself.'

Tommy's grin disappeared. 'Yer didn't, did yer? Where did yer hurt yerself?'

'All over. Me backside, me elbows and me pride.'

'Ah well, we can't do anything about yer pride, Sadie,' Spike said. 'But me an' Tommy would be more than happy to rub the other two better for yer.'

Tommy's shoulders started to shake and Sadie knew he was going to come out with something outrageous. 'When I was little and I hurt meself, my mam used to kiss it better. That's where the saying comes from, "kiss me backside".'

Sadie feigned shock, even though she was laughing inside. 'You just wait until I tell me Auntie Mary on you, Tommy Seymour. She said, "You tell me, girl, if they say one wrong word out of place and I'll marmalise the pair of them".'

'That's mean, that, Sadie.' Spike shook his head sadly. 'Especially after he's promised to slay the dragon for yer.'

Tommy gave her a dig. 'Ay, Sadie, here's that feller comin' to claim yer for the slow foxtrot.'

'He's an old friend – I go out with him now and again.'

'Why did yer tell him we lived in the same street as yer grandma?'

Sadie saw Geoff was almost upon them. 'I'll tell yer later.'

After a brief nod at the two boys, Geoff led Sadie onto the floor. 'I never expected to see you here.'

'I never expected to see meself here,' Sadie laughed. 'Tommy and Spike were coming anyway, so when they asked me I thought I might as well. I had nothing else to do and they're a good laugh.'

'A good laugh? That ginger-haired one yer were dancing with is an idiot! He can't dance for toffee an' shouldn't be allowed on the floor. He's lucky you didn't break a leg.'

'He's not an idiot, he's just a young lad that enjoys life.' Sadie stared into Geoff's eyes and it struck her suddenly why she'd never been able to feel more for him than liking. He was a nice, decent, steady bloke, and they'd had many a laugh together. But it had never been a side-splitting belly laugh because he had no sense of the ridiculous. He could never make her laugh like Harry used to, or Tommy or Spike did. And Peter Townley, he was another who could make her giggle even when she was telling him to get lost! It wasn't Geoff's fault that he didn't have a good sense of humour, Sadie didn't know she had one herself until she'd met Mary Ann. And coming from a home where laughter was rare, she appreciated it more than most. It was an added bonus to the quality of life she now enjoyed.

'You don't mind me not sitting with yer, do yer?' Geoff asked. 'Only for the last week or so I've been staying with Ruby in between dances an' she'll expect it.'

'Of course I don't mind – I don't own yer. We agreed to do our own thing, didn't we? And anyway, I couldn't leave Tommy and Spike, not after they brought me.' Sadie looked to where Ruby was sitting, her eyes watching their every move. 'She looks a nice girl, Geoff, very pretty, too.'

'Yeah, she is nice. She's a good dancer, too.' He slowed down to a walk. 'She's not as pretty as you, though.'

'Looks aren't everything, Geoff. In fact, they can be very deceiving. And I don't think you should dance with me any more tonight, it's not fair on her. Besides, I've already got two partners.'

'Some partners. The first dance and you ended up on the floor!'

'I saw the funny side of it, Geoff. In fact, I thought it was hilarious. They're as crazy as two coots but I'm not half enjoying meself with them.' The music was coming to an end so Sadie spoke quickly. 'Look, d'yer want to skip seeing me on Saturday night so yer can take Ruby out?'

Geoff shook his head. 'No, I've got a date with you an' we'll leave it at that.'

'Don't be daft, I wouldn't mind. Give the girl a chance, Geoff. She's never taken her eyes off yer since we started dancing, so she must like yer. You take her out on Saturday, I'll see yer here next Wednesday and yer can tell me how yer got on. I'll come with the boys so I won't have to play gooseberry.'

Geoff walked her back to where Tommy and Spike were standing. 'Are yer sure that's what yer want, Sadie?'

Sadie smiled at him. 'I'm sure, Geoff. You an' me are good mates and I want to see yer getting the best out of life.'

Apart from an odd wave as they passed on the dance floor, Sadie had no more contact with Geoff that night. But she didn't miss him because she was too busy enjoying herself. Spike's dancing was on a par with Tommy's – atrocious. But what they lacked in experience on the dance floor, they made up for with their constant chatter and joke-telling. Sadie did have a passing notion that she could perhaps teach them what little she knew, but she dismissed the idea before it could take root. It would take a better one than her to teach these two scallywags how to trip the light fantastic. Unless it was the Sailor's Hornpipe or an Irish jig – they'd be brilliant at throwing their arms and legs about. Even on their way home they didn't let up. Down every entry they passed lurked a huge green monster, just waiting to pick Sadie up. But the lads vowed to protect her even if it meant being slain themselves. Their acting was so over-dramatic, by the time they reached her front door her face was stiff with laughing and she was pressing at the stitch in her side.

'Well, we didn't get much done in the way of dancing, but I've had a whale of a time. Thanks very much, boys.'

247

'Yer enjoyed it, then, Sadie?' Tommy asked. 'I mean, yer not going to close the door on us and breathe a sigh of relief, saying, "Thank God that's over"?'

Sadie laughed. 'No, Tommy, I really did enjoy meself.'

'Come with us again next week, then?'

'Yeah, okay, but I'm not paying for meself. How soft I'd be to fork out good money just to be thrown on the floor! I'd have to be a head-case, like you two.'

'Oh, we'll pay for yer, Sadie, with pleasure.' Spike jerked his head at Tommy. 'I'll have a word with one of the fellers in the band and ask him not to play a tango, then this madcap can't repeat tonight's performance.'

'There's no fear of that, I've learned me lesson.' It was dark in the street so Sadie couldn't see Tommy's face clearly, but she'd bet he was wearing a grin. 'No, I thought I'd try that other thing next time – you know, where the feller holds the girl's arm high in the air and she spins around and around while he stands watching her? I mean, I couldn't come to no harm just standin' there, could I?'

'Uh, uh,' Sadie grunted as she shook her head. 'The tango is off-limits for you from now on, Tommy Seymour. Yer not the only one who's learned a lesson.'

'I'm cut to the quick, Sadie, I really am. Me pride's been dented.'

'Well, will yer go home to mend yer pride, Tommy, 'cos I'm going in now, it's way past me bedtime. I'll see yer both in the morning, and thanks again for takin' me out.'

'Will yer practise that spin in the meantime, Sadie?' Tommy didn't want the evening to end, he liked being with Sadie. 'An' I'll practise standing like one of the dummies in Burton's window, with me arm in the air and pretending to hold yer fingers while yer spin around.'

'Spike, will yer take him home, please? I'm dead beat.'

'Anything to oblige.' Spike took his friend's arm. 'Come on, an' no messing 'cos we've got to be up early.'

Tommy sighed. 'The night's still young, I'm not a bit tired.'

'On yer way, pal.' Spike dragged on his arm. 'It doesn't mean that because yer not tired everyone else has to be full of the joys of spring. Good night, Sadie.'

'Good night, Spike, good night, Tommy.'

'Ta-ra, Sadie, see yer tomorrow.' Tommy waved before turning on his friend. 'Yer like a ruddy wet week, you are. A real misery guts.'

'Anything you say, pal, I'm too tired to argue.'

Sadie was just about to close the door when she heard Tommy say, 'No, yer definitely look more miserable than a wet week. More like it's rained every day for a month and yer shoes are lettin' in and yer haven't got an umbrella.'

Spike thought it was time to retaliate. 'D'yer know who yer a dead ringer for? Boris Karloff as Frankenstein's monster . . . only he had more brains than you.'

'Nah! Yer need yer eyes testin', you do. Boris Karloff hasn't got ginger hair! And he's got a whopping big screw sticking out of his neck an' he walks funny, as though someone's wound him up.'

Spike nodded. 'Just as I said, yer a dead ringer for him. In fact, yer could be twin brothers.'

Sadie turned into Penrhyn Street the following night and was immediately confronted by Peter Townley. 'In the name of God, Peter, yer frightened the life out of me, I nearly jumped out of me skin!'

'Oh, I wouldn't want yer to do that, Sadie, 'cos yer skin suits yer. It fits yer that well anyone would think it had been made for yer.'

'Don't make me laugh, Peter, 'cos the muscles in me face are sore from laughing too much last night.'

'Funny yer should say that, Sadie, 'cos that's what I want to talk to yer about.'

Sadie's eyes widened. 'What is it yer want to talk to me about?'

'Don't look at me like that with those big blue eyes of yours. It makes me go all weak in the knees.'

'Peter, will yer get on with it, please? Me grandma will have me dinner on the table an' she'll go mad if I'm late and it goes cold.'

'Where did yer go last night that made yer muscles sore?'

'Pardon? What's it got to do with you where I went?'

'It was only a friendly enquiry, Sadie. If you wanted to ask me a question, as a friend, like, I wouldn't bite your head off.'

Sadie gave this some thought before saying, 'I went to a dance, if yer must know.'

Peter nodded, his face solemn. 'I thought as much. Now, when I ask me next question I want yer to remember that yer still in the witness box an' yer've sworn on the Bible to tell the truth, the whole truth and nothing but the truth.'

'Peter, what am I going to do with you? If my dinner's ruined I'll clock you one.'

'This matter is very serious, Sadie, so think on. It's so serious I was back last night to counting the cracks in me bedroom ceiling.'

'Oh dear, oh dear, oh dear.' Sadie resigned herself to eating a cold dinner. 'What is it now?'

'Who were those two strapping lads yer went out with last night?'

Sadie gasped at the cheek of him. 'As I said before, what's it got to do with you?'

'Well, it got me thinking that it was naughty of yer to go out with two strange men when yer supposed to be courting strong. I didn't think yer were the type of girl to two-time a bloke. And if yer are that type of girl, then why can't yer two-time him with me? I'd be perfect to two-time somebody with.'

Sadie bit so hard on the inside of her mouth she could taste blood, and the smile she was trying to keep back turned into a grimace. 'Seeing as me life seems to have become a hobby with yer, I'll bring yer up-to-date. I mean, I'd hate yer to miss out on anything. First, me and the boy I was goin' out with have decided not to see each other so often. I'm too young to be going serious with anyone. So I'm not two-timing him, see? I'm fancy free and can go out with who I like, when I like. And now you can answer me a question. How did yer know I went out with two blokes last night?'

'Because I watched yer,' Peter grinned. 'I saw them passing, heard them knocking on yer door, then I went up to me mam's bedroom and kept watch through the window. I sleep at the back of the house, yer see, so it wouldn't have done me no good to look out of my bedroom window. I'd have sat there all night and seen nothin', only the woman who lives in the house at the back getting undressed and putting her red flannelette nightie on.' He pretended to shiver. 'And I can tell yer that's not a pretty sight. It's enough to put yer off women for life.'

'It doesn't seem to have put you off.'

'Ah well, yer see, you don't look like the woman who lives at the back.' He leaned forward and gazed into her eyes. 'Please tell me that yer don't wear a red flannelette nightie, Sadie – I couldn't bear it.'

'Yer a cheeky beggar, Peter Townley, and nosy. I've a good mind to go and see that woman at the back and tell her she's being watched by a Peeping Tom.'

'Yer could do better than that; yer could do her a big favour by putting a stop to it. If I was taking you out I wouldn't have time to spare, would I? So do Mrs Thingamajig a favour an' say yer'll come out with me?'

Now was a chance to get her own back on him. 'Can you dance, Peter?'

'Can I dance? Yer'd have to see it to believe it, Sadie.'

'I'm going to Blair Hall on Saturday night if yer interested.'

'If I'm interested – I'll say I am! What time shall I pick yer up?'

'The two strapping lads you saw, they're calling for me at half-seven.' Sadie's eyes were pools of innocence. 'Is that all right with you?'

'Sadie,' Peter groaned. 'Don't do this to me. I want to take yer out on me own.'

'What yer want in this life, and what yer get, are two different things, Peter. Yer have to settle for what's offered. But don't worry if yer not interested, it was only a thought.'

Peter didn't take long to decide. After all, it was better than nothing and at least he'd be in her company. 'Would I get a dance with yer?'

'Of course yer would.' Sadie hesitated for a second. 'Any dance except a tango. I'm hopeless at that.'

'Ah, what a shame. I'm better at a tango than anything.'

Once bitten twice shy, Sadie thought. Tommy had said the same thing last night and he was a disaster. 'There'll be plenty of girls for yer to dance with, don't worry. Give us a knock at half-seven on Saturday an' we'll be ready. That's if me grandma doesn't throw me out tonight for being late for me dinner. I'll tell her it was your fault for keepin' me talking.'

'Wouldn't Auntie Sarah like to go to Blair Hall with those two strapping lads, and me and you could go to the pictures?'

'I seem to have gone deaf, Peter, can't hear a thing. I can see yer lips moving, but that's all. So I'll say ta-ra for now.'

Chapter Twenty-One

Sadie sat at the table wrapping Christmas presents in the coloured paper she'd bought at sixpence for twenty sheets. It was the first time in her life she'd ever bought presents, and her excitement and pleasure were shared by Sarah and Joe who watched with smiles on their faces. It was as much a treat for them as it was for Sadie.

'Have yer got all yer presents in now, sweetheart?'

'All except Auntie Mary's – I don't know what to get her.' Sadie laid her hand on the parcels already wrapped. 'Ludo for our Les, gloves for Ellen and Jimmy, and the doll for the baby, Sally. She won't know what's hit her, Grandma, she's never had a doll before. And it looks lovely in the clothes you made for it; they don't half make a difference.'

'Why don't yer buy a tortoiseshell comb for Mary Ann? You wouldn't go far wrong with that because she's always got one in her hair.'

Sadie pursed her lips and wagged her head from side to side. 'I have thought of that, then I couldn't make up me mind between a comb or a scarf. I don't mean a scarf for work, but a pretty one that she could wear when she goes out.'

'I'd settle for the scarf, queen, she'd be over the moon.' Joe offered his suggestion with a knowing nod. 'It's something she'd think twice about buying for herself because of the money, so it would be a nice surprise.'

'There speaks the man of the house.' Sarah ran a finger gently down her husband's wrinkled cheek. 'And I think he's right. Mary Ann would be delighted with a pretty scarf.'

'Right, that's settled then, yer've made up me mind for me. I'll get it this afternoon on me way to meet Ellen comin' out of school. This is me last day off before Christmas 'cos Auntie Mary said we'll be mad busy next week.' A frown creased Sadie's brow. 'I don't know how I'm goin' to get the things to the children. I won't be able to take time off to meet them outside school, and I don't want to give them to them now, it's too far off Christmas and it wouldn't be the same.'

Sarah and Joe exchanged glances. 'Me and Joe have been talkin' about that, sweetheart, and we wondered if yer wouldn't like one of them to come here and pick them up? It would save yer a lot of worry.'

'But I don't want them to know where I'm living, Grandma, in case me mam and dad find out. I could trust our Ellen and Jimmy to keep a secret if it wasn't for me dad being such a wicked article. If he found out they knew where I was, he'd belt it out of them.'

Sarah sighed. 'It was only a thought, sweetheart, but you know best.'

There was a loud rat-tat at the knocker and Sarah made to rise. 'That'll be the rent man.'

'You stay where yer are, Grandma, I'll go.' Sadie scraped her chair back and picked up a rent book off the sideboard. 'Is the money inside?'

'Right to the penny, sweetheart, as usual. Give George my regards.'

George Scott was turning the page in his ledger when he looked up and saw Sadie standing on the top step, holding the rent book and money out to him with a huge smile on her pretty face. It was the first time she'd been home when the rent man called so they were strangers to each other.

'My God, Sarah, yer don't half look well.' George stepped back and feigned surprise. 'What have yer been taking, rejuvenating pills or something?'

Sadie chuckled. 'Yeah, but I went overboard. It said on the bottle to take one every morning, but I thought I'd speed the process up and took six.' She waved a hand downwards. 'This is the result.'

'Well, I'll be blowed.' George ran his fingers through dark hair which was showing signs of white at the temples. He was a portly man in his forties, with a ruddy complexion and a happy disposition. 'Whatever will they think of next? You don't happen to have the bottle handy, do yer? I wouldn't mind a tanner's worth of those pills.' He threw his head back and his roar of laughter could be heard the length of the street, causing heads to turn. 'On second thoughts I'd better make it a shilling's worth; there's no point in me going back to me childhood if the missus doesn't come with me.'

Sarah's voice floated down the hall. 'I'm listening, George Scott! Don't you be leading me granddaughter astray, d'yer hear? Yer get paid to pick up the rent money, not pretty young girls.'

'Ah, if only I could, Sarah. The only thing I can pick up is a heavy cold.' George dropped the money in the large leather bag which hung from a strap on his shoulder and handed the book back to Sadie. 'So, you're a granddaughter? Are yer staying with Sarah?'

Sadie nodded as she folded her arms and hugged herself. It was a bitterly cold day and her jumper gave little protection from the wind. 'Me name's Sadie, and yer haven't seen me before because I go out to work. Today's me day off.'

'Well, it's been nice meeting yer, Sadie, and yer've brightened me day.' He closed the ledger and tucked it under his arm. 'Pity about those pills, though. I had visions of being twenty-one again.'

'If yer were, would yer change anything about yer life?'

'No, I suppose not. I'm a lot better off than some.'

'There yer are, then.' Sadie grinned even though her teeth were chattering. 'I'm happy, you're happy, God's in His heaven and all's right with the world.'

Sadie did the last of her Christmas shopping on her way to meet Ellen coming out of school. She chose a voile scarf with a pretty floral design on for Mary Ann, a pair of warm slippers and an ounce of tobacco for Joe, and a pair of gloves and a slab of Cadbury's for Sarah. She'd have to sneak them in and hide them in her wardrobe until she had time to wrap them properly. The presents for her grandparents would be going under the tree on Christmas Eve. She'd already ordered the tree off one of the men at the market but hadn't said anything at home because she wanted to surprise them.

Sadie's happiness gave her a warm glow inside as she walked towards the school, but after standing outside the gates for ten minutes she was dithering with the cold. There was nowhere to shelter from the wind, only the entry on the opposite side of the street, but she was afraid to move in case she missed her sister. Ellen didn't know she was coming so wouldn't be watching out for her. It seemed ages before the doors finally burst open and a stream of noisy girls poured out, pushing and elbowing each other out of the way to be first across the playground and out through the gates.

'Ellen!' Sadie waved frantically, afraid she wouldn't be seen or heard above the din. But her sister had spotted her, and with a look of determination on her thin face she barged her way through the heaving mass.

'I had a feelin' yer'd come today, Sadie.'

Sadie hugged her tight. 'I'm like an iceberg standin' here; let's go in that entry out of the wind.'

Ellen linked her arm. She had so much to tell her sister she couldn't wait to get it out. 'Me dad said if yer send any more clothes for us, he'll put them on the fire. He went mad over those boots yer gave our Jimmy. He was on his way out to the bin with them but our Jimmy stood in front of the door and wouldn't let him out. Me dad was like a raving lunatic, he would have killed our Jimmy if me mam hadn't stopped him.'

'What happened to the boots?' Sadie asked, her voice tight with anger.

'Me mam calmed me dad down and took the boots off him. She gave them to Jimmy and told him to take them upstairs out of sight. He's wearing them, but yer can tell by me dad's face that he's still blazing over it. He's just dead jealous that he hasn't got a pair of boots as good as those.'

'He would have if he didn't spend all his money in the pub.' Sadie tucked her hands into the sleeves of her coat. 'So, I can't give yer any more clothes, eh?'

'That's what me dad said, that he'd burn them. And he would, too, Sadie, 'cos he's a bad, wicked man.'

'Has he been leaving you alone?'

Ellen lowered her head. 'I told him everything yer told me to, Sadie, but he said I could go to the police if I wanted, he didn't care. He said they'd put me in a children's home and they'd keep me there until I was eighteen.' Her face flushed, she faced her sister. 'I was frightened, Sadie. I don't want to go in no home.'

'Is he still doing things to yer?'

'When he gets the chance he puts his hand up me knickers.' Tears were threatening as she went on. 'Our Jimmy doesn't leave me alone with him if he can help it. And I go to bed at the same time as him every night so I'm not on me own with me dad.' A tear trickled down her pale face. 'I hate him, our Sadie. When he touched me the other night I almost picked the poker up to hit him with.'

Sadie ground her teeth in anger. 'I've got Christmas presents for you and the others, Ellen, and I'm bloody determined that yer get them and yer keep them.' It was so unusual for Sadie to swear, Ellen's eyes flew open. 'I'll think of something, don't you worry. Even if I have to bring them meself, you'll get them.' Sadie's mind was whirling. She had no idea how she could manage it, but with her anger came determination. 'Don't say a word to anyone except our Jimmy. I want both of yer to stay in the house on Christmas Eve, don't go out under any circumstances. It's important, Ellen, do you understand?'

'What are yer goin' to do, our Sadie? Me dad will kill yer if yer come to the house.'

'That's my worry, Ellen – I'll sort something out. Come hell or high water, you and the other kids will get yer Christmas presents. And I promise yer they won't be put on the fire by our loving father.'

When Sadie saw the worried looks on the faces of Sarah and Joe, she was ashamed that she was the one who had put them there. 'I wasn't going to tell yer, but I had no one else to talk to. I can see I was wrong now. I've no right to be bringing trouble to yer door after yer've been so good to me.'

'Nonsense, child! We're family now and families stick together through thick and thin. I don't know that me and Joe can be much help to yer, but we'll do our level best.'

'I only want some advice, Grandma. I've gone over and over it in me mind and there's no way I'm going to let the kids down. I'll take all the stuff up meself on Christmas Eve. I don't mind doin' that, I'm not frightened of me dad. But I need somebody with me just in case he tries to take it out on the children after I've gone. I need someone to put the fear of God into him. Not only about the clothes and presents, but also for the way he treats the kids.'

Joe puffed on his pipe, wishing he was fifty years younger so he could sort the bugger out himself. 'What had yer in mind, queen?'

'I was wondering what yer thought about me asking Tommy and Spike to come with me? It would mean me telling them me business, which I never have – they don't know anything about me. But I'm desperate and can't afford to feel ashamed of me home and me parents. The lads wouldn't have to come in the house, as long as they stood outside and me dad knew they were there. He thinks nothing of belting a child, it makes him feel brave, the great "I am". But a big strong man would be a different proposition. He'd grovel before he'd stand up to someone his own size.'

'It sounds a good idea, sweetheart, and I'm sure the boys would jump at the chance to help yer. But I'd be worried about yer putting yerself at risk by goin' in the house on yer own. If the boys were outside they wouldn't know what was going on inside. Yer father could be belting hell out of yer.'

Sadie grinned. 'Grandma, I've got a good set of lungs on me. If he so much as raised his hand they'd hear me screams down at the Pier Head.'

'Well, have a word with Tommy tomorrow an' see what he says.'

'I won't have time tomorrow, it's Auntie Mary's day off and I won't be able to leave the stall. Besides, it's not the best place to have a private conversation. And I won't be able to mention it on Wednesday when we go to Blair Hall 'cos Peter will be there. I don't want him knowing.'

Sarah shook her head and tutted. 'He'd be the first one to offer to help yer, sweetheart. He thinks the world of yer.'

'I know that, Grandma, and I think he's a smashing lad. But I don't want him to see where I've come from. Yer should hear me dad's language when he starts, it's enough to make yer hair curl. And me mam's no better. I don't mind Tommy or Spike, they're more rough and ready, but not Peter.'

Joe leaned forward and tapped the bowl of his pipe against the grate. 'Why not ask them to come here, then? Yer'll feel more at ease in yer own home, and yer'll have me and Sarah at hand for moral support.'

'That would be the best thing all round,' Sarah agreed. 'And yer've no need to make a big issue out of it, just give them the bare details. You ran away from home because yer dad's a drunken bully, and yer worried now that he won't let you in to give the children their Christmas presents. That's all they need to know and yer wouldn't be telling them no lies.'

'You make it sound so easy, Grandma. I just hope yer right.'

'Listen to me, queen,' Joe said, a twinkle in his eyes, 'if those two lads are prepared to slay a dragon for yer, then facing up to your dad should be a piece of cake.'

'I hope they don't have to stand up to him, Grandad. I'm banking on the size of them frightening the living daylights out of him.'

'Well, Tommy and Spike are big strapping lads, queen, they don't come much bigger. You and I know they're as harmless as kittens, but yer dad doesn't.'

'Don't you believe it.' Sarah squared her shoulders, folded her arms and set her lips in a thin line – all signs indicating that she was going to say something of great significance. 'I'll have you know that young Tommy can handle himself. I was standing by their stall one day when a bloke insulted his father, and before yer could say Jack Robinson, Tommy had the bloke by the scruff of his neck. There was a crowd around in no time 'cos this feller was a known big mouth and trouble-maker, and they were all egging Tommy on to belt him one. He would have done, too, if his dad hadn't stepped in. Even then Tommy wouldn't leave go of the bloke until he'd apologised to his dad.'

Sadie's mouth gaped in surprise. 'Go 'way, Grandma! Well, yer do surprise me.'

'Doesn't surprise me,' Joe said, his nod saying that his mind agreed with his mouth. 'Yer can tell by lookin' at him that he can take care of himself. Him and Spike might act daft but, believe me, they're nobody's fools.'

Sarah tilted her head, her eyes tender. 'Joe O'Hanlon, will yer stop giving that empty pipe the glad eye and put some tobacco in it? Yer look like a fish out of water when yer not puffing away at the ruddy thing.'

'I can't do right for doin' wrong, can I, queen?' Joe gave Sadie an over-the-top wink. 'If I light up I get accused of burnin' money and filling the room with smoke. If I don't light up I look like a ruddy fish! There's just no pleasing this wife of mine.'

Sadie sighed with pleasure as she laced her fingers and laid her arms flat on the table. Her eyes travelled the room and she told herself that this was what you called a home. A fire crackling in the grate, comfortable lived-in furniture and a kettle keeping warm on the hob. And most importantly of all, the two wonderful people who had made this place what it was with their love and warmth. They had taken her into their home and into their hearts. She idolised them, and for herself asked nothing more of life than to stay in the shelter of their love.

The market was crowded, as it had been every day that week. It seemed everyone wanted something new for Christmas, even if it was secondhand. Sadie had never seen anything like the mass of heaving bodies as they jostled for position near the stalls. She was worried at first, as the tables were pushed further and further back, but the crowd were so good-natured, so full of the festive spirit, she left her worries behind and began to enjoy herself. The Christmas tontines had been paid out and the women were eager for bargains on which to spend their hard-saved money. All year they'd been passing over coppers they could ill-afford to a collector, now they were reaping the benefit and thanking God they'd persevered with those weekly payments.

'Have yer got anythin' for me, Sadie?' Elsie pushed her way between two women who were arguing about which jumper to buy for their mother. 'I'm relying on yer, girl, for somethin' nice to wear to a party me and my feller have been invited to.'

Sadie winked. 'Can yer hang on a minute, Elsie, until I've served these two customers? They won't be long, will yer, ladies?'

'It's not me, queen, it's me sister here what's being long-winded. She wants to buy this green jumper for me mam when she knows bloody well me mam thinks green is an unlucky colour. Me Auntie Fanny bought a green coat once, and didn't she go and die the very next day? Me mam's refused to have anythin' green in the house since, and soft girl here knows that.'

'Ooh, I feel the same way as yer mam, girl.' Elsie thought she'd hurry the proceedings along. 'My neighbour says that it's unlucky to say that green's unlucky because God made all the trees and the grass green. But me, I wouldn't take no chance. Best to be on the safe side, that's my motto.'

The doubting sister gave in, but not gracefully. 'Oh, all right, have it yer own way or I'll never hear the end of it. If anyone in the family pegged out I'd get the blame.'

Sadie gave a sigh of satisfaction as she pocketed their sixpence. The two women had been so long making up their minds anyone would think they were in George Henry Lees and debating about jumpers costing pounds instead of coppers. 'Thank heaven for that, Elsie. I was beginning to think they were here for the day.'

Elsie grinned. 'It was sad about their Auntie Fanny dying the day after buying a new coat, though, wasn't it? Poor woman never even got the chance to put it on her back. I was goin' to ask them what happened to it 'cos I rather fancy a green coat meself, but I thought it might sound a trifle indelicate.'

'Especially when yer'd put them off buying green. I only hope they don't pass when I'm showing yer the blouses I've put away for yer to look at. Two of them are green.'

Elsie eyed the stall. 'Yer don't seem to have much left, Sadie. Have yer been busy?'

'That's putting it mildly, Elsie – we've been rushed off our feet. But I've got a few nice things put away for me best customers, so will yer keep yer eye on the stall for us while I fetch them?'

'Bring whatever yer've got, Sadie, 'cos I'll have a couple of things off yer, and me neighbour said if yer had anything exciting to get it for her.'

On her way to the box under the back table, Sadie stopped by Mary Ann. 'How's it going, Auntie Mary? Busy enough for yer, is it?'

'Best week I've ever had.' Mary Ann patted her cheek. 'It'll be a ten-pound turkey we'll be having this year.' She looked at the customer she was serving and narrowed her eyes. 'Yer didn't hear that by any chance, did yer, Milly? I don't want you turning up on me doorstep on Christmas Day with your gang.'

'That's charming, that is! Yer a cold-hearted cow, Mary Ann Worsley, so yer are.' Milly stretched herself to her full height. 'I wouldn't lower meself to come where I'm not wanted. Me and me husband, and the six kids, will make do with a quarter pound of corned beef for our Christmas dinner. We may be poor but we've got our pride.'

'I didn't know yer had six children, Milly,' Sadie said. 'I thought yer only had two.'

'She has only got two, she's pullin' yer bleedin' leg.' Mary Ann thought Sadie had come a long way in the last six months, but it was still easy to pull the wool over her eyes. 'And don't be losing any sleep over her havin' corned beef for her Christmas dinner, either. She's just been braggin' about how well off she is. The turkey's paid for, she's been in a club at the greengrocers, the corner shop and the sweetshop. She'll be havin' a better Christmas than any of us. Isn't that right, Milly?'

'It is right, Mary Ann, but would yer mind letting me do me own bragging? Yer see, I hadn't finished! On top of all the things yer've mentioned, we've also got a bottle of port wine and a bottle of sherry.'

'My God, Milly, there's no flies on you, they're all ruddy bluebottles! But I hope yer have a lovely time and I apologise for doing yer braggin' for yer. I don't know what came over me, stealing yer thunder like that.'

'That's all right, Mary Ann, I'm not about to take the huff when it's a time of peace on earth and good will to all men.'

'Bloody hell!' Mary Ann turned to Sadie. 'Twenty years I've known Milly, an' she hasn't noticed I'm not a flamin' man.'

'Now, now, Auntie Mary, peace on earth and all that, remember?' Sadie grinned. 'Anyway, I've left Elsie minding the stall. I'd better scarper.'

There were six blouses in the bag Sadie took back to her table. One, in pale blue with long sleeves and a tie neck, she hung over her shoulder. 'I put this one away for meself to wear on Christmas Day. These others are all in your size, Elsie, and yer goin' to have a job to choose 'cos they're all nice.'

Elsie took all five. 'I'll have three and me mate will have the other two.' She passed three shillings over. 'Keep the tanner change as a Christmas box for yerself. Yer've been good to me and I appreciate it. All the best to yer, Sadie, an' I'll see yer in the New Year.'

Sadie felt quite choked. Next year she'd make sure she gave each one of her regular customers a greetings card. Just a small token to thank them for their continued support and for making a friend of her. She filed the idea away in her mind as she served the never-ending stream of customers. At three o'clock her stall was nearly empty and she had nothing to display.

'Auntie Mary, can I get some more stuff out? My table's as bare as Old Mother Hubbard's cupboard.'

Mary Ann shook her head. 'If yer put any more out, sunshine, we'll have nothing left for tomorrow, and it's going to be busier than it's been today. We can't have people coming first thing to find we've nowt to sell. So just clear yer table and come give me a hand.'

That suited Sadie down to the ground. There was nothing she liked better than working alongside her friend. Moving between the tuppence with a hole and thruppence without a hole, laughing and joking with the customers, her excitement began to mount. This was going to be her first year for celebrating Christmas and she felt like a child again.

'I'm collecting the tree when we've finished, Auntie Mary. Tommy picked it out for me and he said the branches are nice and thick and it's four feet tall.'

'That's nice, girl. Sarah and Joe are in for a big surprise, aren't they?'

Sadie felt as though her heart would burst with happiness. 'I've got

261

some tinsel and some silver balls hidden in me wardrobe, and a little fairy to go on top of the tree.'

'Yer could have sat on top of the tree yerself, girl, and saved yerself a few coppers. Yer'd make a good fairy.' Mary Ann's brow creased. 'I suppose yer have got something to stand the tree in, haven't yer?'

Sadie looked puzzled. 'How d'yer mean, stand the tree in?'

'Well, yer not expectin' the bleedin' thing to stand on its own, are yer?' The stall-holder raised her eyes to the sky. 'Yes, that's exactly what she is expecting.' She looked at Sadie. 'I hate to burst yer bubble, sunshine, but yer need a bucket of sand or something like that to keep it standing steady.' She spun around. 'Maggie Malone, will yer stop yer coughin' and sneezin' all over me good clothes? I've got to sell them, yer know.'

Maggie wiped the back of her hand across her nose. 'I didn't have no cold when I left our house, Mary Ann Worsley. It's only come on me since I've been standin' here freezin' to bleedin' death while you two are nattering away as though it was a summer's day and folk like me have got nowt else to do but wait around until yer decide to favour us with yer assistance.'

'My God, Maggie, for someone who's pretending to be dying of pneumonia, yer can't half talk. I'll be with yer in two shakes of a lamb's tail, but in the meantime don't be coughing all over me customers, if yer don't mind. They're me bread and butter, and if you put them in a sickbed I won't be gettin' any bread and butter.'

Mary Ann put a hand on Sadie's arm. 'You run and see the man who's selling the trees and ask if he's any suggestions, while I see to Moaning Minnie before she lays a duck egg. And will yer just look at the gob on the one standing next to her? In the name of God, Vera, yer face would stop a ruddy clock! Anyone would think yer were in agony.'

'Ooh, I am, Mary Ann.' Vera turned her head from side to side to make sure no one was listening over her shoulder. After all, it was a very delicate problem, not one to be discussed in front of strangers at a stall in Paddy's market. 'It's me bleedin' piles – they're torturing me something chronic.'

Chapter Twenty-Two

Sadie turned the corner of the street and set the tree down on the ground. She'd struggled this far with it, but if someone had paid her to, she couldn't carry it another yard. Her arm was tired and her hands and legs tingling from the sharp pine needles. Anyway, Peter had promised to meet her so she'd stand here until he came. The tree hadn't felt heavy when she'd tried it, but since Spike had set it firmly in a block of wood it weighed a ton. Mind you, it was a good idea of Spike's, she would never have thought of it.

'Need a hand, do yer, Sadie?' Peter grinned. 'Yer look all-in.'

'Then I look as I feel.' Sadie smiled back, happy to see him. 'D'yer know, this is the one time I'm really glad to see that ugly mug of yours. I could manage meself if it wasn't so awkward, but me hands are scratched to blazes with it.'

'Because yer've been doin' it the wrong way, soft girl. Yer need a man on the job, that's the top and bottom of it. Women are hopeless.'

'There's only one way to carry it, Peter, so don't be so blinkin' big-headed.'

'No, there's two ways to carry it – the right way and the wrong way. You, of course, being a woman, were doing it the wrong way.' Peter rubbed his hands together then pushed up the sleeves of his donkey jacket. 'Now, stand aside and watch an expert at work.' He bent down and gripped the tree at the very bottom, between the block of wood and the branches, and after lifting it effortlessly he let it tilt forward so the tree was horizontal and away from any part of his body. 'See, Sadie, it's the way yer hold yer mouth.'

Sadie lifted her hands in mock surrender. 'Okay, I give in, I'm stupid.'

'You are not stupid!' Peter was quick to defend her. 'Yer just didn't think.'

'I am stupid, Peter, so don't argue with me. I've struggled all the way home with it, cutting me hands and legs in the process and laddering me stockings into the bargain. Then you come along, clever clogs, and with a "hey presto" yer make it look as easy as wink.'

'Well, let's get it down to yer grandma's so I can go home. Me mam was putting me dinner on the table when I came out to meet yer, and she'll skin me alive if I let it get cold.'

'Will yer stand it in front of the door for us? Me grandma doesn't know anything about it, and I want to surprise her. So when I've knocked on the door we'll both hide.'

'I can't play hide-and-seek, Sadie, not when me dinner's gettin' cold. One thing me mam's got no sense of humour over is spending her time making a nice dinner for us and then seeing it wasted. If yer think I'm pulling yer leg, ask me dad. He got his dinner on top of his head once, just for letting it cool down.'

'Now I don't believe that, Peter Townley, not of your mam. Yer having me on again, aren't yer? Trying to wind me up.'

'I told yer to ask me dad if yer don't believe me. All over his head she tipped it. He said it didn't taste nearly as nice as it would have done in his mouth. And the best of it was, he'd only nipped down the yard to the lavvy to spend a penny.' Peter puckered his brow and scratched his head. 'Me dad must have been put off goin' to the lavvy for life 'cos I haven't once seen him go down the yard since.'

'You don't half tell some tall stories, Peter Townley. It's to be hoped that when yer get a girlfriend you'll have the decency to warn her that she can't believe a word that comes out of yer mouth.'

'Well, seeing as it was you brought the subject up, and it was on me mind anyway, when are yer going to come out with me on yer own? It's not that I object to Tommy and Spike, but I don't want to spend me life going out with them, there's no future in it. When me mates in work ask if I've got a girlfriend, I have to tell them I've got a third share in one.'

'Peter, I've told you over and over that I don't want a steady boyfriend.'

'There's nothing steady about me, Sadie – I'm the most unsteady bloke yer ever likely to meet. So unless yer can think of another obstacle to put in the way, I can't see why yer won't come out with me.' Peter could see she was giving it some thought so he went on to press his point. 'Come on, Sadie, give me an early Christmas present and say yer'll come out with me one night, without the bodyguards in tow.'

'I'll come if yer promise there's no strings attached. No tellin' anyone that we're courting or going steady.'

Peter beamed. 'I'll be that unsteady, Sadie, yer'll have to link me to keep me upright. And when we go to the pictures I won't even try to hold yer hand. If there's a girl sittin' the other side of me, I'll hold her hand instead. Unless she's got a face like the back of a tram, in which case I'll have to content meself with holdin' me own hand.'

'Peter, will yer go home now, before yer dinner ends up on yer head?'

'Just tell me when the big night is and I'll go home a happy man.'

'One day next week, will that suit yer?'

'I'll say it will.' Peter leaned closer and grinned into her face. 'Can yer guess what I'm going to do on Christmas Day to pass the time away?'

'I haven't the foggiest idea, Peter, and I'm not really interested. Just go home, please!'

'I'll tell yer anyway 'cos I know that deep down yer dying of curiosity. I'm going to fill in the cracks on me bedroom ceiling 'cos I won't need them no more.'

'I'm going to knock on the door now, Peter, so will yer vamoose and I can flatten meself against the wall to hide from Grandma? When she opens the door I only want her to see the tree.'

'Sadie, can I flatten meself against the wall with yer? It sounds far more exciting than the ham shank me mam's got for our dinner.'

'Peter Townley, if yer don't make yerself scarce right now, yer needn't bother filling in those cracks in yer ceiling 'cos yer'll need them more than ever.' As Sadie stretched up to the knocker, she hissed, 'Scram!'

'Hang on a minute, Sadie.' Peter stayed her hand.' I don't think it's a good idea to give me Auntie Sarah a surprise, 'cos surprises aren't always good for old people.'

'Don't be daft, she'll be made up to see the tree.'

'Yeah, if you're with it! But if she opens the door, sees the thing, and then you jump out on her in the dark, well, that's not goin' to do her old heart any good.'

Sadie studied his face for a moment. 'I should have thought of that without you having to tell me. So I'll thank yer for being concerned about me grandma's health, but I've got to warn you that yer beginning to get on me nerves for always being right.'

They didn't hear the door open and Sadie looked up in surprise when she heard Sarah ask, 'If Peter's right, why would he get on yer nerves, sweetheart?'

'Because I'd like to be right for a change, Grandma. It's enough to give a girl an inferiority complex, being with someone who knows all the answers.'

Sarah's eyes were becoming accustomed to the dark and she spotted the tree standing between the young couple. 'That's a bonny tree, Peter – are yer taking it home?'

'No,' Sadie said quickly. 'He only helped me carry it. It's a present for our house, for you and Grandad and me.'

'Oh, sweetheart, what a lovely surprise! Joe will be delighted – we haven't had a Christmas tree in the house for I don't know how long. Oh, I am pleased.'

'Sadie's been in a very generous mood today, Auntie Sarah.' Peter lifted the tree to carry it into the house. 'A tree for you and the promise of a date for me.'

'Don't push yer luck, Peter Townley. Yer only caught me in a weak moment.'

'Take no notice of her, son. If she's made a promise she'll keep it.' Sarah turned to walk down the hall. 'Bring it through for us, there's a good lad, and Sadie can say where she wants it to go.'

'On the little table by the window, Grandma, it would look nice there.' Sadie walked behind Peter, her hand on his back pushing him forward. 'Hurry up, slow coach, your mam will have yer life.'

Joe's face was a mixture of surprise and pleasure. 'This is goin' to be the very best Christmas we've had for nearly fifty years.' He coughed to clear his throat. 'And it's all down to you, queen.'

'I'll have to be off,' Peter said, 'but if yer need any help to put the fairy on the top, just knock on the wall.' He whispered in Sarah's ear, 'I'm having me dinner on me head tonight, Auntie Sarah.'

'Are yer, son?' Sarah smiled at him fondly. She knew him too well to be surprised at anything he came out with. 'Well, we all have our own little peculiarities; it wouldn't do for us all to be the same. Wherever yer have yer dinner, I hope yer enjoy it.'

Sadie sat back on her heels to admire her handiwork. She'd gobbled her dinner down in her haste to decorate the tree, and had spent the last hour draping tinsel over branches and tying on silver balls. The blonde fairy with a wand in her hand took pride of place on the very top. 'D'yer think it looks a bit bare? I wish I'd bought some coloured tinsel instead of all silver, and a few chocolate animals. It needs a bit more colour.'

'It looks a treat, sweetheart, it really does.'

'I've got an idea.' Joe pushed himself out of his chair. 'Remember those soldiers, love? Would it upset yer if I got them out?'

Sarah's eyes clouded for a second, then she shook her head. 'No, it wouldn't upset me. I think I'd like to see them again after all these years.'

Joe came downstairs with a shoe box tucked under his arm. 'I painted these for the boys. They've been lying in the wardrobe for fifty years now.'

Sadie crawled across the floor to sit in front of his chair. When he took the lid off the box she gasped, 'Oh Grandad, they're lovely! Can I touch them, please?'

As Joe handed her one of the lead soldiers, Sadie noticed that each figure in the box was different. Some were standing to attention with their rifles by their side as though on guard, others were standing or kneeling with their rifles aimed ready for firing. And each figure had been painted with great attention to detail, in the colours of various regiments. It had been a labour of love for the two sons whose lives had been cut short.

Sadie held the lead hussar in her hand while tears rolled down her cheeks. 'I'm sorry, Grandad, I can't help it, it's so sad.'

'Don't cry, queen, I'm sure the two boys will be looking down at us and they'll be happy to see that their toys are being used to brighten our lives. If we tie a piece of cotton around the necks of the soldiers, they'll hang from the tree and brighten it up.'

Sadie sniffed. 'Are yer sure it won't upset yer to see them?'

Sarah leaned forward and cupped Sadie's chin. 'Sweetheart, me and Joe grieved until we could grieve no more. Now we talk about the boys and think of the good times we had with them. We didn't have them for long, but they were with us long enough to leave us with memories. So don't be getting yerself upset, child. Leave us with our happy memories.'

Sadie was tying one of the figures on the tree when she said, 'Our Jimmy would love to see these.'

'Well, take a couple with yer tomorrow night and he can put them on their tree.' Joe held out the shoe box. 'Come on, choose a couple.'

'Grandad, there won't be a Christmas tree in our house. There won't be any decorations, or a turkey, presents or cards. It will just be an ordinary day in the Wilson household, with little to eat and the house cold and filthy. The only thing there'll be plenty of is shouting and bad language.'

Joe looked across at his wife. 'It's hard to believe, isn't it, love? People like that don't deserve to have children.'

'Couldn't you invite them here to see our tree?' Sarah asked. 'We haven't got much, but we'd be more than happy to share what we've got with them.'

'There's only our Ellen and Jimmy; the baby and our Les are too young to find their way here. And as for our Dot, I want nothing to do with her 'cos she leads the children a dog's life.' Sadie swivelled around on her bottom. 'I'd love our Ellen and Jimmy to come, so they could see how happy I am and know that they can get out themselves one day. But if I call there tomorrow night, and our Ellen and Jimmy say they're going out on Christmas Day, me dad's crafty enough to put two and two together and I'd lay odds on him following them. It's not worth the risk. I'm not bringing trouble to your door.'

'What about Boxing Day?' Sarah asked, eager now to help the children. 'We could lay a little spread on for them, and when I go to the shops tomorrow I could buy a present to hang on the tree for them. It wouldn't be much, just a slab of chocolate or something.'

Sadie gazed at the flames flickering in the grate. She'd love the children to meet Sarah and Joe, to let them taste, just for a couple of hours, the happiness of being with good people in a home filled with love. 'I'd give anything for them to come here, Grandma, but I'm worried about you and Grandad, in case yer ever have cause to regret it.'

Joe gave a low chuckle. 'If Tommy and Spike do a good job tomorrow night, from what yer've told us about yer father, I don't think he'll have the guts to come looking for trouble.'

'If he did, I'd take the broom to him.' Sarah nodded to say she meant what she said. 'You invite them, sweetheart, and if trouble comes we'll meet it head on.'

Sadie grinned. 'I'll do it! I'll tell our Jimmy to bring Ellen to the Rotunda and I'll meet them there. He won't know where it is, but if he asks the way to Scotland Road, he'll soon find the Rotunda.' She sprang to her feet and hugged them both. 'They say everyone has a guardian angel watching over them – well, mine must have been asleep for sixteen years and is now trying to make up for lost time, 'cos in the last six months I've been happier than I ever thought possible.'

'They've been good months for me and Joe, too, sweetheart, so your guardian angel must be looking after us as well.' Sarah squeezed her hand. 'Hadn't you better start making a parcel of the things yer taking with you tomorrow night? Yer don't want to leave it until the last minute.'

'I'm going up to start on them now. Tommy and Spike are coming here with me straight from work, so don't do me dinner, Grandma, 'cos I probably won't get back until nine.' Sadie turned at the door for one more look at the tree. 'It looks lovely. Those soldiers have made all the difference, Grandad.'

When she'd gone upstairs, Joe smiled at his wife. 'D'yer know, I'm enjoying all this excitement. I almost hope that Sadie's dad does come and cause trouble. If he does, I'm having the broom and you can have the rolling pin.'

Sadie came down with the tiny teddy bear Harry had won for her at New Brighton fair when he'd taken her out on her birthday. 'I found this in me drawer, so I'll put him on the tree and he can watch us all having a good time.'

Sarah raised her brows. 'Didn't the boy next door win that for yer? I think yer said his name was Harry.'

'Yeah.' Sadie sat the teddy on one of the branches. 'Harry won it for me.'

'Yer liked him, didn't yer, sweetheart?'

'I did like him, Grandma, and if I never see him again for the rest of me life I'll always think of him as the best friend I ever had. Not that you and Grandad aren't me best friends, or me Auntie Mary, but it was different with Harry, if yer know what I mean.'

'I understand, sweetheart, there's different ways of liking people. From what yer've told me of Harry, he was special to yer.'

'Anyway, I've got everything into two parcels.' Sadie didn't want to talk about Harry. Every time she thought about going back to the street tomorrow night, he came into her mind. She'd love to see him again. Just one five-minute meeting in the park, to hear his voice and see his dimples when he smiled. But what was the use? He'd probably forgotten her by now and had a steady girlfriend. 'The boys can take turns carrying the clothes, I'll carry the presents.'

'What's the scarf in aid of, Sadie?' Tommy's eyes slid sideways to where Sadie was walking with her head bent, her blonde hair covered by one of Sarah's black woollen headscarves. 'Yer look like Orphan Annie.'

'I don't want anyone in the street to see me. I just want to go straight to our house, leave the presents, say what I've got to say, then get out again as quick as I can.'

'We'll come in with yer, if yer frightened,' Spike said, relieving Tommy of the parcel so he could have a turn at carrying it. 'Might be better if we're with yer.'

'I'm not looking forward to it, I'll be honest. Me nerves are shot to pieces, I'm shakin' like a leaf inside. But I doubt me dad would raise his hand to me. He'll rant and rave, swear like a trooper, but he won't touch me, not when he knows you two are outside. It's after we've gone that worries me, in case he takes it out on the children.'

'D'yer know what I think would be the best thing to do?' Tommy asked, swinging his arms and walking with his usual swagger. 'I think me an' Spike should carry the parcels in, so he gets a good look at us and knows we're with yer. We'd go straight out again if that's what yer wanted, and wait in the street for yer.'

The last thing Sadie wanted was for them to see the inside of her home. Both boys were rough and ready, but they were spotlessly clean, and she knew their mothers were houseproud. She'd never be able to look them in the face again if they set foot in the hovel she'd lived in for sixteen years. It was bad enough them seeing the outside, but she was hoping they wouldn't be able to see it clearly in the dark. The nearest lamp-post was six houses away, thank goodness. 'Our Jimmy will be lookin' out for me, he can help me carry the things in. And he'll give yer a shout if I need help.'

'We'll fall in with whatever yer want, Sadie, just give us the nod.' Spike's voice was gruff. 'We just don't want yer gettin' hurt, that's all.'

'I won't get hurt, don't worry. We'll just take things as they come, it's no good lookin' for trouble.'

Tommy could sense the tension in Sadie's voice and led her thoughts away from what lay ahead. 'The market was dead busy today, wasn't it, Sadie? We were rushed off our feet from the time we opened.' His chuckle echoed in the dark deserted street and his breath hung in the air. 'There's a lot of poor buggers gettin' a second-hand hammer for Christmas.'

'Oh, that's not all they're gettin',' Spike said, his voice full of laughter. 'They're gettin' a box of tacks to go with them! The women were buying the hammers off you, then comin' to us for the tacks. I bet the wives have got jobs lined up for the poor sods over Christmas. I can hear them now, "Just put a tack in the lino on the stairs for us, love", or, "Ay, light of my life, will yer put a tack in that shelf in the kitchen for us? Go on, it'll only take yer a minute".'

'Aye, women are crafty articles, yer can't be up to them,' Tommy said. 'They've got their men cornered on Christmas Day because there's nowhere open. No pubs to have a pint, no bookies' runners on the street corner to have a bet, and no trams to take them off somewhere out of the way.'

'Ah, you poor things, me heart bleeds for yer.' Sadie clicked her tongue against the roof of her mouth. 'You men are all alike. Yer think yer badly done to but yer don't know yer born compared to the worry a woman has.'

Tommy gave her a dig in the ribs. 'Sixteen yer are, Sadie, and already I can hear a whine in yer voice. It's funny how all women have that whine – must be born with it 'cos I'm damn sure they wouldn't go out and buy it.'

'I'll have to think of an answer to that some other time,' Sadie said, coming to a halt at the corner of Pickwick Street. 'This is where I live.'

Tommy gazed down the street of two-up two-down terraced houses. It was much of a muchness to hundreds of other streets in Liverpool, including his own. 'Come on, let's get it over with, I'm starving. Me tummy thinks me throat's been cut.'

Walking between them with her head bowed, Sadie could feel the nerves of her own tummy tighten. It was easy to use brave words when you were miles away, saying you weren't frightened. But right now she'd give anything to turn tail and run. Her eyes slid sideways as they passed the Youngs' house, but the curtains were drawn over and she couldn't see inside. 'This is it. I think our Jimmy will open the door 'cos he knows I'm coming. If he does, will yer give him the parcel and then wait under the lamp for us?'

'If that's what yer want, Sadie,' Spike said. 'Whatever you say is all right with us.'

Sadie lifted the knocker and banged hard. 'I'll let yer know if I need yer, don't worry about that.'

Jimmy had been hovering by the front door for over an hour, wanting to be the first to see Sadie and warn her that their dad was in a foul mood and just waiting for someone to vent his anger on. So he had the door open even before the echo of the knock had died away. 'Don't come . . .' His voice trailed off when he saw the two big blokes standing either side of his sister.

'Jimmy, will yer take that parcel for us? This is Tommy and Spike, they've come with me in case me dad takes off.'

'He will take off, our Sadie. He's been in a terrible temper since he came in from work 'cos me mam didn't have enough money to get him some drink in for tomorrow. I've had a few belts off him, and so has our Ellen and Les. If he sees you he'll hit the roof.'

'Oh, to hell with that, I'm goin' in there.' Tommy raised his foot to mount the step. 'He sounds like a right bastard to me – he wants puttin' in his place.'

Sadie put a restraining hand on his arm. 'No, Tommy, please.' Suddenly she wasn't afraid any more. Knowing her father had hit the children turned her fear to anger. On Christmas Eve, when most children were excited about Father Christmas coming down the chimney to fill their stockings and leave their presents, all her brothers and sisters could expect was a clip around the ear. 'I'll be all right, I promise you.'

'Don't come in, our Sadie, he'll go for yer.'

'I'm going in whether he likes it or not. I've got a few things I want to say to the man who we are unfortunate enough to have for a father. So step into the street, Jimmy, and let me past. I'll go in first.'

Coming from Sarah's spotlessly clean, warm and comfortable home, the living room looked worse than Sadie remembered, and the smell was overpowering. Like the click of a camera, her mind photographed the whole scene. Her mother was sprawled on the couch next to Sally, who was banging on a battered pan lid with a spoon, while her father was slouched across the table facing Ellen and Les, eyeing them with venom in his eyes and a sneer on his lips. The two children looked petrified, as though they were too terrified to even blink for fear of feeling the back of his hand. Of her sister, Dot, there was no sign.

It was several seconds before Sadie's presence in the room registered in George Wilson's brain. Snarling like a wild animal, he sprang to his feet with such force he sent the chair crashing to the floor. 'Get out of my house, yer bleedin' bitch! Go on, out with yer, an' take those things with yer.' When Sadie didn't flinch, he became more enraged. 'If yer not out of this house in two seconds I'll pitch yer out into the street, and yer bleedin' parcels after yer.'

'I'll leave this house when I'm good and ready to leave, and not before.' Sadie was shouting herself now, more angry because she'd seen Ellen smile when she saw her, then quickly lower her head for fear of her father's wrath. 'You don't scare me one little bit.'

'Oh, no? Well, we'll see about that.' George made a move towards her. 'This is my house an' anyone I don't want in it, I'm entitled to throw out.'

'I would advise yer to stay right where yer are.' Sadie's tone was so full of confidence it had the effect of slowing George down. 'If you lay one finger on me I'll bring two of me friends in to sort you out. And I don't think yer'd like that 'cos they're big lads and you're only used to lashing out at children.'

'Don't you threaten me, yer lying little bitch.' Like a raging bull, he lunged towards her. 'I'm going to give yer what I should have given yer years ago, a bloody good hiding.'

Sadie bent her arm at the elbow and held it out to him. 'Go on, touch me.' She turned to Jimmy. 'Yer know what to do if he does, Jimmy. Yer go and bring Tommy and Spike in.'

Jimmy was so enjoying seeing someone stand up to his father, the excitement showed on his face. And it made him bold enough to say, 'They're great big men, Dad, they'd make mincemeat out of you.'

George's beady eyes narrowed. Although he was within an inch of his daughter he made no effort to touch her as his mind tried to work out what to do. Then he thought, to hell with it, he wasn't going to let a chit of a girl make a fool of him. 'I've told yer I'll say who comes in my house an' I don't want you or yer bleedin' friends in, so off yer go and take that load of shite with yer.' He nodded at the two parcels. 'And don't bother sendin' any more 'cos I'll throw it on the fire.'

Sadie put her open hand on his chest and pushed for all she was worth. 'Don't you stand near me, I hate and detest yer. Call yerself a father, do yer? What a laugh that is. Anyone less like a father I've yet to see. I will certainly never acknowledge you as being my father, I'd be too ashamed. What you are is a dirty man, dirty in mind and body. What you are is a cruel man who likes to beat the living daylights out of the children. What you are is a mean, selfish man who spends every night in the pub supping pints while his family sit in the cold because there's no money for coal. There's no money for food either, or for decent clothes for them, so they go hungry and walk around like tramps.' Sadie knew she was shouting but didn't care. She had to get it off her chest and at the same time let him know he wasn't going to have things his own way in future. 'Seeing as you won't buy the children clothes, I'll keep sending them as often as I can afford to. And don't try throwing them on the fire 'cos me friends outside wouldn't take kindly to that. Nor would they take kindly to yer ill-treating the children, so in future keep yer hands to yerself.'

Leaving her father looking as though he'd like to kill her but was afraid of the consequences, Sadie turned to Jimmy. 'Will yer go and tell Tommy and Spike that I'm all right and I'll be with them in a few minutes. I'll just give these presents out.' She picked up the doll wrapped in coloured paper. 'This is from Father Christmas, Sally, and yer mustn't open it until tomorrow when yer wake up.'

The child was round-eyed. She clutched the parcel and tilted her head. 'Sadie?'

'Yes, darling, I'm yer sister Sadie, and I love yer very much.' She kissed the upturned face with tears in her eyes before handing Ellen and Les their presents. 'Don't open them until tomorrow, d'yer hear? And there's clothes in there for all of yer.' After kissing the two children Sadie stood and looked down at her mother. Not one word had the woman uttered since she'd entered the house. I wonder why, she asked herself. Is it because she's ashamed, or guilt-ridden? If she was any kind of a mother at all she'd be both.

Sadie turned at the door. 'Have a nice Christmas, kids, and I hope yer like yer presents and clothes.' She glared at her father and forced her lips into a sneer her face had never experienced before. 'I have a few warnings for you. If you take any of the kids' things off them I'll find out and I'll make you sorry you signed. And if you threaten any of them with sending them to an institute I'll have you beaten to a pulp. I've never been vindictive in me life, but I am now where you're concerned. Keep your filthy hands off the children or suffer the consequences.'

Jimmy was standing talking to Tommy and Spike, his arms waving and his thin face animated as he told them how his sister had stood up to their dad. 'You didn't half tell him where to get off, our Sadie, I couldn't believe it!'

She hugged him and gave him a big kiss. 'There's a present on the table for yer but yer mustn't open it until tomorrow. And will yer help our Ellen to sort the parcel of clothes out? There's something there for

273

each of yer so yer'll all look posh on Christmas Day. Me dad won't bother yer no more, I think he's had his balloon burst tonight.'

Jimmy put his arms around her waist and lifted her up. 'Yer a smasher, our Sadie, I'm real glad yer me sister.'

'I've got another surprise for you and our Ellen for Boxing Day, but yer must give me yer solemn promise yer'll keep it to yerself. Yer both invited to tea in the house where I'm living.'

'Go 'way! D'yer really mean that, our Sadie? We're comin' to see where yer live?'

Sadie nodded. 'Leave the house at half-one and tell me mam yer going to the park or somewhere. Walk towards town, then ask someone how to get to Scotland Road. When yer get there, keep walking until yer come to the Rotunda. I'll meet yer there at two o'clock.' She gave him another quick kiss. 'Go in now, or the queer feller will be asking you all sorts of questions.'

'I won't tell him nothing, Sadie, I'll just act daft.' He grinned up at Tommy and Spike. 'But I will tell him yer had two giants with yer.'

'He's a corker, that one,' Tommy chuckled. 'Accordin' to him, yer Tom Mix, Robin Hood and King Kong all rolled into one. In another couple of years yer won't need me an' Spike, he'll sort yer old feller out single-handed.'

'Come on, let's go.' Sadie was eager to be away and began to walk briskly down the street leaving the two boys no option but to break into a trot to keep up with her. 'I'll be glad when I'm back in me grandma's house.'

'Hey, what's the big hurry?' Tommy asked. 'I thought yer'd be feeling pleased with yerself the way things went. Mind you, we were on our way down there a few times when we heard the shouting. Ready for action, weren't we, Spike?'

'You certainly told him what yer thought of him, Sadie – yer were brilliant.' In the darkness, Spike narrowed his eyes as he stared at Sadie's bowed head. There was something not quite right here. 'We didn't hear everything of course, we could only hear your voice and yer old man's.'

They were away from Pickwick Street by this time and Sadie slowed down. 'That's all yer would hear 'cos nobody else spoke. I've got a sister thirteen and a brother of nine, who didn't even look at me for fear of gettin' a clip around the ear. Me mam never opened her mouth or even looked at me – it was as if I wasn't there.' The lump in her throat was growing and tears stung the back of her eyes. 'I've got a baby sister who was only eighteen months when I left home, and she didn't recognise me. I had to tell her who I was.'

Tommy looked across Sadie's head and shrugged his shoulders at

Spike. They weren't used to seeing a girl cry and didn't know quite what to do. 'I think yer looking at this the wrong way, Sadie.' Tommy put an arm across her shoulder and Spike followed suit. Between them they began to walk her to the tram stop in Park Street. 'All the kids are better off for yer going, aren't they? I mean, they'd have had no presents or new clothes only for you.'

'And yer've got the old man off their backs,' Spike said. 'I can't see him touching them again in a hurry. If he does, yer know yer can always count on me and Tommy.'

Sadie sniffed up. 'It was seeing the place again that's upset me. I'd forgotten just how bad it is. And me heart breaks when I think of them having to live there.'

'Yer can only do so much, Sadie, an' yer've done more than most people would have done in the circumstances. Gettin' all that stuff together for them, out of the wage you get, well, I think yer bloody marvellous.'

'Yeah, me too!' Spike nodded. 'And yer've got something to look forward to on Boxing Day, with yer brother and sister coming to see yer. And it doesn't have to be a one off. They can come and see yer often – Sarah won't mind. That way, yer'll be able to keep tabs on the whole family, make sure they're being treated right.'

Spike's words lifted Sadie's spirits. He was right, she could see Ellen and Jimmy as often as she liked, as long as Grandma and Grandad didn't mind. She knew she could trust the children not to give her secrets away.

Sadie put her arms around their waists and pulled them closer. 'You two are good mates, yer know that, don't yer? Yer've done a lot for me tonight and I'll not forget.'

Chapter Twenty-Three

'Oh, yer've just missed it!' Florrie Young's eyes were flashing and her face flushed with excitement as Harry came through the door. He was late getting home tonight because he'd gone for a Christmas pint with the blokes from work. 'Ten minutes earlier and yer'd have heard a right performance from next door. Aren't I right, Jack? We've never heard nothin' like it before.'

'Yer mam's right, son – there was a real humdinger of a row.' Jack leaned forward and rested his elbows on his knees. 'We couldn't help but hear it. They were shoutin' so loud the whole street must have heard.'

Harry made his way to the hearth and held his hands out to feel the warmth from the glowing coals. 'Nothing unusual about him shouting his head off, he never does anything else.'

'Aye, well, he had someone to answer him back tonight.' Florrie's head nodded as her lips pursed. She wanted to be the one to tell Harry; she felt she owed it to him. 'The daughter turned up and by golly did we know it. You know the one I mean, you used to speak to her ... Sadie, isn't it?'

Harry straightened up, his cold hands forgotten. 'Sadie was next door?'

'And how! The first we heard was the queer feller bawling his head off, telling her to get out and calling her a bleedin' bitch. It was only as the row went on we were able to make out that she must have taken Christmas presents for the children and he said if she didn't get out he'd throw her out and the parcels after her.'

Harry took a long deep breath. 'Yer mean yer heard her being threatened and not one of yer got off yer backsides to see if she needed help?'

'Hold yer horses, son,' Jack said. 'Wait until yer've heard the full story.'

Florrie picked up the thread. 'The next thing, we hear her voice and, oh boy, was she giving it to him. She said she'd leave when she was good and ready and not before. And she said he didn't scare her one little bit. That set him off again, saying it was his house and anyone he didn't want in he was entitled to throw out. He must have gone for her,

277

'cos she warned him that if he laid a finger on her she'd bring her two friends in to sort him out.'

Jack took over now. 'We heard the table being pushed then, as though he'd made a grab for her, then her voice daring him to touch her. We heard her telling that young brother of hers to run and bring Tommy and Spike in if he laid a finger on her. Who the hell Tommy and Spike are, God only knows.'

Harry was shaking his head. 'Yer heard all that through the wall?'

'Yer haven't heard the half of it yet,' Florrie said. 'We were worried when he yelled that he was goin' to give her a good hiding, so yer dad told our Paul to go and stand by their door and knock on our window if things started to get nasty.' She looked across at Harry's younger brother. 'Tell Harry what yer saw, son.'

Feeling important, seventeen-year-old Paul gazed down at his laced hands hanging between his knees. 'I noticed these two strange blokes standing under the lamp, but I didn't give it a thought. But when I stood outside next door listening for sign of trouble, one of the blokes came down and asked what I wanted. I was goin' to ask him what it had to do with him, but he was such a big bloke, Harry, I decided I'm not cut out to be a hero. So I just said me mam had sent me to make sure the girl was all right, and he said him and his mate were there to make sure she was. He was nice about it, thanked me for me concern and I was to tell me mam that she needn't worry about Sadie.'

Harry could feel his insides turning over. While he was having a pint with his mates, Sadie had been so close, just next door. He hadn't really wanted the flaming pint, anyway – he'd only gone to be sociable. And now he'd missed the one person who was never far away from his thoughts. 'And that was that?'

'Was it hell!' Florrie smoothed the front of her floral pinny before folding her arms and hitching up her bosom. 'Your friend, Sadie, told him a few home truths and she did it so well I felt like clapping.' Florrie took on the part of Sadie. ' "Call yerself a father, well that's a laugh. I'll never acknowledge you as my father, I'd be too ashamed. What yer are is a dirty man, and a cruel man who likes to beat the daylights out of the children. Yer a mean and selfish man who stands in the pub every night supping pints while yer family sit in the cold because there's no money for coal. No money for food or clothes, either, so the kids go hungry and walk around like tramps".' She glanced at her husband to bear out that what she was saying was the truth.

'I know I haven't got it right word for word, but it's near enough, isn't it, Jack? Then she said, if he wouldn't buy the children clothes, she'd be sending them some as often as she could afford to. And she warned him that if he threw them on the back of the fire her friends wouldn't take kindly to it. Nor would they take kindly to him hitting the children, so in future he'd better keep his hands to himself.'

Jack coughed to draw his wife's attention, and when she looked at him, he raised his brows. 'Isn't there something you want to say to Harry, love?'

'Yes, there is. I was wrong about Sadie, son, and I'm sorry. Children can't help who they are born to and I should have had the intelligence to work that out for meself. She stuck up for those kids tonight and it made me feel so ashamed for treating them like dirt and the terrible names I've called them. I've had my eyes opened tonight, believe me. The girl I thought of as being as common as muck speaks better than I do! While her father was coming out with all the vile words yer could think of, never once did she resort to using swearwords. And to think she's spending all her money on clothes for the children! She must really be as good and as nice as you've always said, Harry.'

'Mam, from the day Sadie was old enough to talk, she has always been a little lady. I've never heard a bad word cross her lips.' Harry let out a deep sigh. 'I wish I'd been here, I'd like to see her. What time did all this happen?'

'Just before you came in,' Florrie told him. 'Our Paul went out to the door and she was walking down the street with her two friends. I don't know how yer missed them – yer must have passed them.'

Harry closed his eyes. Oh, dear God, he *had* passed them! He was turning into the street as three people went by, two blokes with a girl walking between them. He looked at his brother. 'Paul, was Sadie wearing a scarf?'

Paul was still nodding when Harry grabbed his coat and headed for the door. 'I'm goin' to see if I can catch them up. Keep me dinner warm, Mam.'

Florrie and Jack exchanged glances. 'Yer'll never catch them up now,' Florrie shouted. 'They'll be miles away.'

They heard him say, 'With a bit of luck they may be waiting for a tram.' Then the door banged behind him.

Paul pulled a face. 'What's got into him?'

'Never you mind,' Jack said, giving Florrie a significant look. 'And when he comes back I'd advise yer to keep yer trap shut unless yer fancy a black eye.'

Harry ran so fast he had pains in his chest. He tried the tram stops either side of the road going to and from the city, then ran down to Mill Street to see if he could catch sight of them by the stops going to Aigburth. He knew in his heart he was wasting his time. They could be

279

anywhere, gone in any direction, but he had to try.

It was an hour later when Harry fitted the key into the lock. Florrie heard it and made straight for the kitchen, throwing a warning glance at Paul as she passed. When she came through with a steaming plate in her hands, she said softly, 'Here yer are, son. It's a bit dried up now but that can't be helped.'

Harry threw his coat over the arm of the couch and pulled a chair from the table. 'Can I just have a cup of tea, Mam? I really don't feel hungry. It must be the pint I had, I feel bloated.'

Florrie opened her mouth to argue, for there was nothing she disliked more than having good food wasted. But seeing the look of despair on her son's face she held her tongue. 'I'll put it back in the oven; yer might feel like it later.'

Jack jumped to his feet. 'I'll put the kettle on – I could do with a cuppa meself.'

Harry wiped a hand across his forehead. 'While we're all here, can I ask yer to do me a favour? If any one of yer sees Sadie again, don't let her go without finding out where she lives. I was very fond of her and I'd like to know how she's getting on.'

'I'll do that, son,' Florrie said, picking up the plate. 'Even if I have to sit on her until yer come in, I'll not let her get away.'

'What about the older children?' Jack asked. 'They should know where she lives.'

Harry shook his head. 'I've asked the boy, Jimmy, but he said she won't tell them in case their father beats it out of them.'

'I'll keep me eyes open,' Paul told his brother. 'If I see her I'll throw her over me shoulder and bring her here.'

'We'll all keep our eyes open, son, yer can rest assured on that.' Florrie jerked a thumb at her husband. 'Now, Jack Young, where's that cuppa yer promised to make? Get a move on before we die of thirst.'

Sadie lay in the darkness staring up at the ceiling. Not that she could see it clearly, it was too dark in the room. How Peter could count the cracks in his bedroom ceiling she didn't know, unless he had the light on. Then Sadie pulled the sheet over her mouth to stifle a giggle. Fancy her believing anything that Peter came out with; he'd say all sorts to get a laugh. But wasn't it better to be like that, than going around with a face as long as a fiddle?

Turning her head on the pillow, Sadie stared at the alarm clock with the illuminated hands. She'd bought it from one of the market stalls the week she started to work for Mary Ann, to make sure she didn't over-sleep. Many's the morning she'd cursed its loud tinny screech for interrupting her sleep, but this morning, when she wanted the time to pass quickly, the hands seemed to be moving very slowly. It was still only six o'clock, far too early to get up. There'd be plenty of households up and about at this time, especially if there were young children in the house, eager to see what Father Christmas had brought them. But Sadie was no longer a child and it was too early to wake her grandma and grandad even if it was her first real Christmas.

Not that she had any intention of waking them until she'd got everything ready. She wanted to put their presents on the tree, rake the grate out and have a fire burning up the chimney for them, dust and tidy around, and set the table for breakfast. That should take her an hour, then fifteen minutes to get washed in the kitchen sink and put on her new clothes.

The sheet was brought up to her mouth again as a giggle threatened. New clothes! She couldn't remember ever having anything that wasn't someone's cast off. But it hadn't done her any harm, so why worry? There were lots of people worse off than her. Those simple words passing through her mind were enough to take her thoughts to her brothers and sisters. If only they could be here, her happiness would be complete. Christmas was a time for families to be together, and although she wasn't in a position to do anything about it now, she would work towards having the children around her in the not too distant future.

Sadie's eyes swivelled to the clock. It was still only half-six but she'd be better off working downstairs than lying here dreaming. She didn't want to be sad today – it would spoil things for her grandparents and for herself, for that matter. There was so much to look forward to, today and tomorrow; she'd be better off thinking of the good things in life rather than worrying about something she couldn't change.

Sadie swung her legs from under the bedclothes and shivered when her feet came into contact with the freezing cold lino. Her teeth chattering, she felt for the cardi she'd left on top of the bed so it would be easy to find in the dark. Then she groped with her hand until she found the chest of drawers where she'd left a candle standing in a saucer next to a box of matches. The light from the flickering flame cast shadows on the walls as she crept silently to the door and then out onto the landing. She could feel the warmth from the candle on her face but her feet were like blocks of ice. She'd buy herself a pair of bedroom slippers after the holiday – nice warm fleecy ones with a bobble on the front. The third stair from the top was one that creaked, so holding onto the bannister she lowered herself down to the next stair. Sarah was such a light sleeper the least sound woke her up.

Safely in the living room, Sadie closed the door behind her. It was warmer in here because the fire was still bright when they went to bed. She stood for a few seconds making a mental note of the jobs she had to do. First job was to get some light in the room so she could see what she was doing. Standing on one of the wooden dining chairs, she pulled on the chain at the side of the gas-light and held the candle to the gas mantel. After a gentle plop, the room was filled with light, making it at once feel warmer and more homely.

Kneeling down in front of the grate, Sadie took some old newspaper and a bundle of firewood from the coal scuttle, laid them on the hearth and began to rake the ashes through the bars and into the ash-can beneath. Her eyes kept straying to the Christmas tree and she could feel her excitement rising. It was going to be a lovely day, with turkey and mince pies and even a glass of sherry with their dinner. Oh, she was indeed a lucky girl!

The pieces of newspaper were twisted into tight balls and placed in the grate with the firewood on top. Then, using the tongs from the companion set, Sadie picked out a dozen pieces of coal from the scuttle and placed them carefully on top of the firewood. The first match she struck was sufficient to set the newspaper alight, and thinking that luck was certainly on her side today, she watched as the wood caught fire and the flames began to lick around the pieces of coal. Sitting back on her heels, she waited for five minutes to make sure there was no chance of it fizzling out before brushing the hearth and emptying the ash-can.

By a quarter to eight, Sadie was sitting in Joe's chair by the side of the fire, willing the hands on the clock to move faster. She'd made two trips upstairs, once to get the presents which now hung from the tree, and a second time to collect her best clothes. Now, as she waited patiently, feeling very pleased with herself, her eyes swept the room. Everything had been dusted, the table was set for breakfast, the fire was burning brightly and the big black iron kettle was on the hob ready to mash a pot of tea at the first sound of movement from above. Talk about being all dressed up and nowhere to go isn't in it, she was thinking when her eyes caught the movement of the door handle. She was smiling broadly when Sarah's head appeared. 'Surprise, surprise, Grandma!'

'Well I never! It certainly is a surprise, sweetheart, 'cos when there was no sound from yer room I thought yer were still sound asleep.' A smile covered the lined face. 'Here's me, coming down the stairs backwards on all fours so I wouldn't waken yer up. It's a good job no one could see me, they'd have thought I was doolally.'

Sadie hurried to take the frail body in her arms. 'A Merry Christmas, Grandma.'

'And to you, too, sweetheart, and may you have many more.'

'Oh, I intend to.' Sadie smothered the old lady's face with kisses. 'You and Grandad won't get rid of me that easy. I'm here to stay.'

'I'd better go and get Joe up.' Sarah turned towards the door. 'He is awake, but I told him to stay in bed where it was warm until I got the fire lit.'

Sadie reached for her arm. 'Yer not climbing those stairs again. I'll give him a knock.'

Sarah didn't argue. Sadie's presents were in the cupboard at the side of the fireplace and she could have them on the tree by the time the girl came down. 'I'll make a pot of tea, then. He likes a hot cuppa these cold mornings, does my Joe.'

Sadie had already cut three thick slices off the tin loaf, and while Sarah saw to the tea, the girl squatted on the floor to toast the bread in front of the fire with the aid of a long-handled fork. And this was the scene that met Joe's eyes when he entered the room. His mind flashed back to all the previous Christmases when there didn't seem to be anything to celebrate. Now they had Sadie, and she had enriched their lives more than they'd ever thought possible. And when she ran towards him with her arms outstretched he couldn't help the tears that ran slowly down his lined cheeks.

'Ay, come on, Grandad.' Sadie could taste the salty tears in her mouth. 'Yer can't cry on Christmas morning.'

'Don't mind me, queen, they're tears of happiness. And why wouldn't a man be happy with two lovely women to take care of him?'

'We'll have a bite to eat first,' Sarah said, spreading butter on the toast. Like her husband, she was feeling a happiness she hadn't known in years. 'Then we'll open our presents.'

'You open yours first, Grandad,' Sadie said when they'd finished eating and the dishes had been carried out to the draining board to be washed later. ' 'Cos you're the oldest.'

'Well, that's a back-handed compliment if ever I heard one.' But Joe was content to sit back and watch as Sadie lifted three brightly wrapped parcels from the tree. One was quite bulky, weighing the branch down, and the old man reached for it eagerly. 'I'll save that till the last.'

Sarah's eyes shone with love for her husband. 'It's like a child yer are, Joe O'Hanlon, saving the best till the last.'

'I feel like a child, Sarah, love. Younger than I've felt for many a long year.' Joe ripped the paper from the bedroom slippers and chuckled with delight. 'Just the job, they are. I'll be able to get rid of these old ones, they're falling to pieces.' He kicked his old slippers off, threw them on the fire and slipped his feet into the new ones. 'Thank you, queen, they're a welcome present.' Next came the tin of tobacco and he insisted on lighting his old briar before opening the last gift. 'I'll not be short of baccy for the next week, thanks to you, queen.'

Sarah watched him puffing contentedly and tutted. 'D'yer mind, Joe O'Hanlon? We'd like to open our presents, yer not the only one in the house.'

Sadie's inside was bursting with excitement. Buying this extra present for Joe, and one for Sarah, had left her penniless. But it was worth it. She didn't need money, anyway – she had everything she wanted to last her until next pay day. 'Shall I open it for yer, Grandad?'

'Not on yer life! Half the pleasure is in the opening.' The paper was torn to shreds in his eagerness and his gasp of delight was all the reward Sadie needed. The thick woollen cardigan was in a dark beige and had two deep pockets. 'By, that's grand, queen. With this to keep me body warm, me new slippers on me feet and me pipe in me mouth, I'll be in me element. But yer shouldn't have spent so much money on us. Yer must have left yerself skint.'

'I'm all right, Grandad, I've got everything I need. And the cardi didn't cost that much. I bought it from me superior-quality clothes stall.'

'Well, come and let me give yer a kiss, then Sarah can open her presents. She's givin' me cow's eyes for making her wait so long.'

Sadie picked the three presents from the tree and presented them to Sarah with a flourish. And when Joe saw his wife put the largest parcel on the side of her chair he took the pipe from his mouth and chuckled, 'It's like a child yer are, Sarah O'Hanlon, saving the best till the last.'

'Put the pipe back in yer mouth, man, and let me enjoy meself in peace.' Sarah opened the gloves first and exclaimed in delight, 'Oh, sweetheart, they're lovely. Me hands will be as warm as toast in these.' The slab of Cadbury's had her giving her husband a warning. 'This is mine, Joe, so keep yer eyes and fingers off it. You have yer baccy an' I'll have me choccy.'

Sadie was fidgety with excitement. 'Come on, Grandma, open the other one so I can see if yer like it.'

'I'm sure I will, sweetheart.' Sarah was careful with the wrapping paper. Having to be practical with money, she hated waste. And if the paper wasn't torn it could be put away for next year. But when she saw the deep maroon cardi, all thought of being economical fled and the paper was allowed to fall to the floor when she jumped to her feet. 'Oh, child, it is beautiful! Joe, will yer just look at this? It's me favourite colour, too!'

Joe coughed to clear his throat before gazing at Sadie's beaming face. 'Listen, queen, I'm an old man so yer'll have to forgive me if I shed a few tears. Me and Sarah, we haven't enjoyed Christmas for the last fifty years. We have tried a few times, buying each other a present and pretending to celebrate, but our hearts weren't in it and we weren't fooling anyone, least of all ourselves. But this year everything's changed. Last night we had the smell of the turkey wafting through from the kitchen, this morning we come down to a tree with presents on. And lovely presents they are, too. But the most precious gift me and my Sarah have been given is you.'

Sadie swallowed hard. 'I'm not going to cry, Grandad, even though I want to. If I let one tear escape then I'll be finished. I'll end up bawling me head off and spoil Christmas for everyone.'

'Yer'll do no such thing, child,' Sarah said, shaking her head and tutting at her husband. If she could keep her tears under control, why couldn't he? Mind you, Joe had always been an emotional man, and wasn't that one of the things she loved about him? 'You just sit back and puff on yer pipe, Joe O'Hanlon, and give Sadie a chance to see her presents.'

'Don't shout at him, Grandma,' Sadie said, ruffling the old man's hair. 'What he said was lovely, and when I think of it in bed tonight I'll have me cry then.'

'Well, here yer are, sweetheart.' Sarah handed over two parcels. 'They're not much compared to what yer've given us, but I think yer'll like them.'

Sadie gasped before squealing with delight as she lifted the blouse from its wrapping. It was in a fine, soft material, with a pink background patterned with splashes of pale blue. It had long wide sleeves gathered into a tightfitting cuff, and a wide frill set off the round neck. And it was brand new; it still had the label attached. 'Grandma, this is the prettiest blouse I've ever seen.' Sadie was overcome. 'I don't know what to say, except that yer shouldn't have spent so much on me, but I'm glad yer did 'cos I love it.'

'You can put it on when yer've opened yer other present. Me and Joe are dying to see what yer look like in it.'

'I'll wear it today, and tomorrow for when our Ellen and Jimmy come. Ooh, I could kiss yer both to death, and I will when I've opened this.' The slippers were just what Sadie had been promising to buy herself, and she was over the moon. 'As me Auntie Mary would say, there's no flies on me, not today there isn't. I'm so happy I could dance in the street.'

'Well, forget about dancing in the street, sweetheart, and go upstairs and put yer new blouse on. I'll rinse the few dishes through and then make us a nice cuppa before I start on the vegetables and potatoes.'

'I'll do all those,' Sadie said, on her way to the door. 'I'm going to wait on you today so yer can both take it easy.'

When Sadie came downstairs, Joe gazed at her for several seconds before calling, 'Sarah, come in here and see this.'

Sarah's hand went to her mouth. No matter what Sadie wore, she would always look beautiful. But they had never seen her looking as beautiful as she did in that blouse. It was a perfect fit, the style suited her and the colours brought out the vivid blue of her eyes. 'Child, yer look like an angel.'

'She looks like a film star.' Joe had never seen an angel but he had seen Jean Harlow and Constance Bennett. 'In fact, she looks better than a film star.'

A loud knock on the front door brought a look of surprise to Sadie's face. 'Who'll this be, on Christmas Day?'

Sarah kept her face straight as she shrugged her shoulders. 'It'll be one of the neighbours come to wish us the compliments of the season. I'll see to the door while you pour the tea out.'

As Sadie walked into the living room with two steaming hot cups of tea in her hands, Peter was coming in through the other door. 'Was that you knockin' on the door?'

'Well, it wasn't all of me, Sadie, just me hand. It's very impetuous, me hand, has a mind of it's own an' I can't do a thing with it. If it wants to knock on a door then it will do, no matter what I say.'

Still holding the cups, Sadie asked, 'What are yer doing here on Christmas Day?'

Peter turned to Sarah. 'This niece of yours is very rude, Auntie Sarah; she's got no manners at all.' He winked broadly at the old lady. 'But I've got to say she looks very delectable today – she even beats the fairy on top of the tree. D'yer think I should forget she's been rude to me and wish her a Merry Christmas?'

Joe had noticed Peter's hand behind his back and chuckled. 'Yes, son, wish her the compliments of the season like it should be done.'

Sadie was wary. She didn't trust Peter when he was in this mood. But before she even had time to put the cups down, he was standing between her and the table with a huge cheeky grin on his face and a piece of mistletoe in his hand. 'Don't you dare, Peter Townley, I'm warning yer.'

'Oh, I wouldn't miss this chance for the world.' Holding the mistletoe over her head Peter planted a kiss on her cheek. 'Have a happy day, Sadie Wilson. I know I've caught yer on the hop, with yer hands full, so to speak. But yer must admit that if I'd been a gentleman and asked yer permission to kiss yer, I'd have got me face slapped good and proper.

And as I'm not partial to having me face slapped I decided to strike while the iron was hot and sneak one in. Mind you, I'd have risked it for a proper kiss 'cos it must be said that yer do have very kissable lips. Not that yer don't have kissable cheeks, or a kissable neck, but a peck on the cheek is not worth getting a slap across the face for.'

Sadie's face was red with embarrassment. Fancy him doing that in front of her grandma and grandad! She looked at the cups in her hand and had the desire to throw the tea all over him. He deserved it for what he'd done. Then she heard Joe's hearty chortle and it was as if a light had been switched on in her head. Why was she being so miserable? Peter had come in all bright and cheerful, and here she was putting a damper on things. It was supposed to be a day of joy and happiness, for goodness sake! Where was her sense of humour? 'I'll get you for this, Peter Townley,' she said, setting the cups down. 'I'll pay yer back double, you see if I don't.'

After a sly wink at Joe, Peter handed her the mistletoe. 'Oh, yes please, Sadie. But instead of a double kiss on me cheek, can I swap it for just one kiss on me lips? I think that would be a very fair exchange, don't you, Auntie Sarah?'

'I'm saying nothing. You two young ones must fight it out between yerselves,' Sarah said, finding the whole incident hilarious. 'I'll see to a cup of tea for yer.'

'Yer not leaving this room until I have me Christmas kiss, Auntie Sarah.' When Peter took the old lady in his arms Sadie noted how gentle he was with her. It wasn't often he showed his serious side, but behind the jokes and the laughter, he was a kind and considerate boy.

Joe tugged at Sadie's skirt, and when she looked down at him and saw the mischievous glint in his eyes, her heart swelled with love for him. 'What d'yer want, Grandad?'

Joe nodded at Peter and pointed to the mistletoe before mouthing, 'I dare yer.'

Sadie's eyes flew open. Much as she'd like to give the old man a laugh, she couldn't bring herself to do as he asked. Or could she? It was only in fun, after all.

'Can I borrow yer mistletoe, Peter, so I can give me grandad a kiss?'

'Yer a lucky man, Mr O'Hanlon,' Peter said as he handed it over. 'From the looks of things I'm goin' to have to wait until I'm your age before she gives me a kiss.'

'Ah, me heart bleeds for yer. I couldn't be so cruel as to keep yer waiting all that time.' Sadie grinned and held the mistletoe over her head. 'Yer can have yer kiss, Peter Townley, but I'm not givin' it to yer, yer'll have to take it.'

Peter was flabbergasted. 'Oh aye, what's the catch? Yer teasing me, aren't yer?'

'Take it while it's on offer, son,' Joe laughed. 'If I was your age I wouldn't give her time to change her mind.'

The look of bewilderment on Peter's face was enough to chase away Sadie's doubts and embarrassment. At last she'd got the better of him and was giving him a taste of his own medicine. He wouldn't have the nerve to kiss her now.

'I'm going to count to ten, then the offer will be withdrawn.' She turned to Joe. 'He's scared, Grandad, 'cos I've called his bluff.'

While she was turned away from him, Peter seized the opportunity. 'I'll show yer whether I'm scared or not.' He pulled her to him, put one arm around her waist, a hand behind her head so she couldn't struggle, and before she knew what had hit her, his lips were covering hers.

Sarah came in carrying a cup of tea and gaped at the scene that met her eyes. 'Okay, that's enough, break it up now.'

When Peter raised his head he had the look on his face of someone who had just heard that a rich relative had died and left him a fortune. He didn't have a rich relative of course, but if he had, and they were generous enough to leave him a fortune in their will, then that's how his face would look. 'Auntie Sarah, yer a spoil-sport. I was just enjoying meself then. Couldn't yer go back out and come in again, in about half an hour?'

Sadie disentangled herself and gave him a kick on the shin. It wasn't a hard kick, just enough to make him wince. 'I'll get you one day, Peter Townley, you just see if I don't.'

'If yer could make it down a dark entry one night, Sadie, I'd like that. In fact, if I was to speak the truth, and you all know what a truthful bloke I am, then I'd have to say, without doubt, I'd positively enjoy letting yer get me one day.' He grinned into her face. 'I don't suppose yer could make it a week on Wednesday, by any chance? That would give me time to get meself in peak condition for the big moment.'

Sarah waved him to a chair. 'Will yer sit down and give yer tongue a rest, Peter.'

'Don't yer mean give our ears a rest, Grandma?' Sadie asked. 'Honest, once he starts he forgets to finish. I can never get a word in edgeways with him.'

Peter waited until Sadie sat down then pulled out the chair next to her. 'I promise I won't open me mouth until yer've told me what Father Christmas brought for you and Mr and Mrs O'Hanlon.'

That suited Sadie down to the ground. It was with great pleasure she showed him all the presents. Then she pointed to the Christmas cards standing on the mantelpiece and sideboard. 'See all the cards I got from me customers and friends at the market? I've never had so many cards in me life.'

'Oh, strewth!' Peter slapped an open palm on his forehead. 'I nearly forgot, I've got two cards for yer.' He pulled two crumpled envelopes out of his pocket and handed them to her. 'One's from me, and the other's from that feller yer once told me yer were courting strong. Only yer couldn't have been courting that strong, 'cos yer don't go out with him now.'

Sadie looked surprised. 'How did you get that?'

'He gave it to me at the dance last week, when you were up dancing with Tommy. He said he didn't like handing it to yer, and he couldn't send it because you would never tell him where yer lived.' Peter took advantage of Sadie's bowed head and winked at Sarah. 'He says on the card that he loves her, Auntie Sarah.'

Sadie gave out a loud cry. 'Do you mean to tell me that Geoff gave yer a card for me, and you opened it?'

'I didn't have to open it – he hadn't stuck it down.'

'You had no right, that's a sneaky thing to do.' Sadie's eyes were blazing. 'Grandma, will you tell him off for me? If I start on him I'll scratch his eyes out.'

'Let's get it straight first.' Sarah squeezed her husband's hand because she could hear him chuckling softly. 'Peter, what's the picture on the front of Geoff's card?'

Peter was caught off-guard for a second; he hadn't been expecting that. 'Er, I didn't look at the front of the card, only what was inside. I mean, I can't have an ex-strongly courted bloke sending Sadie cards, can I? He still fancies her, yer see, Auntie Sarah, and I don't want him blighting me life again. I'm getting nowhere fast with her as it is. If he comes back in the picture I'll be out of the running altogether.'

'You are not in the running, Peter Townley, I've told yer that often enough. You never have been and never will be. And neither is Geoff, even though he is more of a gentleman than you. At least he wouldn't be sly enough to read a card belonging to someone else.'

Sarah tutted. 'Peter, yer in deep water as it is, don't make it worse for yerself. Tell us exactly what Geoff has written on the card.'

'I don't know, Auntie Sarah, I'm on tenterhooks waiting for Sadie to open it. But I'm saying now, in front of witnesses, that if the word "love" appears on that card I'll set Tommy and Spike on to Geoff at the dance next week.'

While Sarah's shoulders shook and Joe rocked back and forth in his chair with laughter, Sadie gaped. 'Do you mean to tell me that we've gone all through this, Peter Townley, and you've only been pulling me leg?'

'I've been havin' yer on, Sadie, not pulling yer leg. If I ever got the chance to really pull one of your legs I'd have a look of pure bliss on me face 'cos I'd be in heaven. I hate to admit it in case yer get big-headed, but yer have got very shapely legs.'

'That's enough now.' Sarah wiped the back of her hands across her eyes. 'Yer startin' to get too personal and I'll not have it in my house.'

'I've got to try every trick in the book, Auntie Sarah. Don't forget I'm competing with Tommy and Spike, as well as this Geoff feller.'

Sarah couldn't resist. 'And Harry!'

'Harry!' Peter's voice was shrill. 'Who the hell is Harry when he's out?'

Sadie's heart had lurched when Sarah mentioned Harry's name, but the expression of bewilderment on Peter's face brought forth gales of laughter. He was flummoxed and she took great delight in the fact. 'Harry's an old friend of mine.'

Peter's eyes narrowed. 'How old? As old as Mr O'Hanlon?'

'Just about.' Sadie didn't want to talk about Harry so she changed the subject. 'Tell us what you got off Father Christmas.'

'The same as I get every year – socks, hankies and tie. Nothing to get excited about.'

'It's not easy to buy for boys, though,' Sadie said, making allowances for Mrs Townley. 'There's not the same selection as there is for girls.'

'Sadie, before we get to discussing the price of fish, are yer goin' to open yer cards?'

'As soon as yer out of the door I'll have them open and stood with the rest. While yer here they stay in the envelopes.'

This could go on all day, Sarah thought, and we've still got the veg and potatoes to see to. So she tried to hasten things along. 'We'd better get started on the dinner, Sadie, or we'll be having it at tea-time. And I've got some baking to do for tomorrow. Have yer told Peter that yer brother and sister are coming for tea?'

'No, she didn't tell me, Auntie Sarah.' Peter got in first. 'She's a bit of a dark horse on the quiet, is our Sadie.'

'I am *not* a dark horse! I just didn't think yer'd be interested.'

Joe was sucking on his pipe, listening with a wily look in his eyes. 'Why don't yer invite Peter, queen? The more the merrier, make a party of it.'

'No!' Sadie shook her head vigorously. 'Peter doesn't want to be bothered coming to tea with children – he'd be bored stiff.'

'On the contrary.' Peter pushed his chair back. He intended getting out quickly before the invitation was withdrawn. 'I'd be only too pleased. What time would you like me to be here, Sadie? Or should I be asking Auntie Sarah, seeing as it's her house?'

'Three o'clock, son, and now will yer get going. Sadie will see yer out.'

'No!' Peter could see by Sadie's face she wasn't too pleased, and if she got him on her own she'd tell him he needn't bother putting in an appearance. 'I'll see meself out.'

Chapter Twenty-Four

As the Rotunda building loomed nearer and nearer, Sadie's eyes were peeled for sight of her sister and brother. There were plenty of people out, all wrapped up against the cold wind as they made their way to visit family or friends for a Boxing Day celebration. But there was no sign of Ellen or Jimmy, and Sadie's heart sank. Perhaps they hadn't been able to get away, or maybe they'd got lost. She'd die of disappointment if they didn't come, she was so looking forward to seeing them. And it would be a let-down for Sarah, who had got everything ready for a tea party. When Sadie had left the house, the old lady had been putting the finishing touches to the jelly creams, sprinkling colourful hundreds and thousands over the top of them.

Sadie was passing a row of shops when a hand reached out from a doorway and pulled her to a halt. 'We're in here, Sadie.' Jimmy grinned, his cheeks whipped to a bright red by the wind. 'We were freezing standing on that corner, weren't we, Ellen?'

'I'm not surprised.' Sadie stared at them in dismay. Neither of them were wearing coats; their only protection from the cold were the woollen jumpers and gloves she had given them for Christmas. 'Don't either of yer possess a coat, or any sort of jacket?'

'Nah, but we're all right.' Jimmy pulled on the cuff of a glove and spoke with bravado through chattering teeth.' We're used to the cold, aren't we, Ellen?'

'We might be used to it, but that doesn't mean we don't feel it.' Ellen had her arms folded across her body with her hands tucked under her armpits for warmth. 'I'm like a block of ice, our Sadie. Even with these gloves on me fingers feel cold enough to drop off.'

'A quick five-minute walk and yer'll soon be sitting in front of a nice big fire.' Sadie undid the buttons on her coat and slipped it off. 'Come here, Ellen, and we'll put me coat across our shoulders. Cuddle up close and put yer arm around me waist.' She pulled a face at her brother. 'I'm sorry I can't help you, Jimmy, but we'll walk fast and that'll warm us up.'

Sarah had been watching through the window and the door was opened before Sadie had time to knock. 'In the name of heaven, they'll catch their death of cold comin' out in this weather without a coat on their backs.'

'They didn't have much choice, Grandma.' Sadie's glance told Sarah not to pursue the matter. 'Come on, kids, get in the warmth.'

Jimmy didn't need telling twice. He could smell the heat and made a beeline for the living room, but he pulled up sharp when he reached the door. He was expecting a fire, but not one that roared up the chimney, with dancing flames giving out both warmth and welcome. The few times they had a fire at home, it was just half a dozen pieces of coal lying so low in the grate there was no heat from it. And when he spotted the gaily decorated tree, his eyes became as round as saucers and his mouth gaped wide.

'Come in, son, and get a warm.' Joe beckoned the boy over. 'Sit on the floor and yer'll soon be as warm as toast.'

Jimmy saw the kindness shining from the old man's eyes and a smile lit up his face. 'That's a fire and a half, that is, mister!' He squatted on the floor and held his hands in front of the flickering flames. 'Ooh, that doesn't half feel good.'

Sadie had a job getting her sister to move, the girl was so shy. 'Come on, our Ellen,' she coaxed, 'let's get yer in the living room and I'll introduce yer proper.'

'I don't like.' The girl's voice was a mere whisper. At thirteen years of age she hadn't got a single friend and had never been in another house before. 'I won't know what to say.'

Sarah was closing the door behind them and couldn't help but overhear. 'We'll not eat yer, sweetheart, and it won't matter if yer don't say a single word. Just go in and get yerself warm while I make a nice cup of tea.'

Sadie breathed a sigh of relief when she saw Jimmy sitting on the floor looking as though he felt perfectly at home. Thank goodness he wasn't as shy as Ellen. 'That's our Jimmy on the floor, and this is our Ellen. Me brother will talk to yer until the cows come home, he's a bit like Peter from next door. But me kid sister here, she's the shy one. The cat seems to have got her tongue right now so we'll just leave her until she gets it back.'

Sarah bustled out to the kitchen, saying, 'Leave the girl to come around in her own time. It won't do no good to rush her.'

Jimmy patted the rug in front of the fire. 'Come and sit down here, Ellen, yer'll soon get warm.' He waited until she'd settled herself as close to him as it was possible to get, then grinned into her face. 'How about that for a fire, eh? Ain't it a smasher?'

Sadie tutted, 'Jimmy, there's no such word as ain't, and yer should know better.'

'Yes, there is.' Jimmy drew his knees up to his chin. 'It's a slang word.'

'Well, yer shouldn't use slang words, should he, Grandad?'

Jimmy's brows flew up to disappear under a lock of his unruly hair. 'Grandad!' His eyes settled on Joe. 'Why is our Sadie callin' yer Grandad?'

Sadie gasped. 'Ay, our Jimmy, don't be so blinkin' hard-faced!'

'I only want to know, an' if I don't ask I'll never know, will I?' Jimmy stared her out. 'How can he be your Grandad and not ours?'

Joe chuckled as he sucked on his pipe. 'There's a lad after me own heart. Anyone that goes through life without being inquisitive usually ends up as thick as two short planks.'

'In that case,' Sadie said, 'our Jimmy should end up a real brain box 'cos he never stops askin' questions.'

'I don't always get answers, though, do I?' The lad shuffled his bottom to move away from the heat of the fire. 'I usually get fobbed off or told to mind me own business. That's if I don't get a clip around the ear. Anyone would think I was a two-year-old instead of twelve, going on thirteen.'

'I won't fob yer off, son, so you ask away.' Joe smiled at him. 'As long as yer don't ask me for the loan of ten bob.'

Jimmy's laugh filled the room. 'Would I be in with a chance if I only asked yer for the loan of two bob?'

'Yer'd have as much chance as a snowball in the fires of hell, son, I'm afraid. I'm what some would call financially embarrassed, or, in other words, stony broke.'

Sarah came through carrying a tray. 'Here yer are, get a warm drink down yer. It'll keep yer going until tea-time.'

Sadie jumped to her feet. 'I think I'll give Peter a knock, Grandma, and ask him to leave it until half-three. It'll give the children a bit more time to get to know you and Grandad.'

The old lady cast a meaningful look at Ellen's bowed head. 'I think that's a good idea, sweetheart. Run along now but don't stay, I've poured yer a cup of tea out.'

Joe sat back in his chair watching as Ellen pulled on her brother's pullover. He saw her mouth the words, 'Go on, ask them.'

'All right, give us a chance, will yer?' Jimmy hissed, straightening the pullover that was his pride and joy before looking from Sarah to Joe. 'Why is our Sadie callin' you Grandma, an' him Grandad?'

'It was what we all wanted.' Sarah told him. 'Now she's living here it's more friendly than having to give us our full title all the time.'

Joe knocked his pipe against the side of the grate. 'I think they're old enough and intelligent enough to be told the truth.' He looked from one pair of deep brown eyes to another. 'Yer can keep a secret for Sadie's sake, can't yer?'

Jimmy looked indignant. 'I don't tell no one about our Sadie. She's good to us, always has been. Better than me mam and dad.'

Ellen raised her head. 'I can keep a secret, honest.'

'Right then.' Joe leaned forward and clasped his hands between his knees. 'Yer both know why Sadie left home, so we don't need to go into that. But because we didn't want the neighbours being nosy and asking questions, we told them she was our granddaughter. It was the best thing we could have done, because no one has ever asked where she lived before. Except for the boy next door, Peter, who has a crush on Sadie. He's always asking questions but she just tells him to mind his own business. He'll be in to see yer later and I think yer'll like him – he's a nice boy, full of fun.'

Jimmy was only half-listening. He'd made up his mind as soon as he set eyes on the old man that he liked him. He could tell he was gentle and kind, and he'd bet he never got bad-tempered and used dirty words, or let fly with his fists. 'What do me an' our Ellen call yer, mister?'

Joe tapped his chin as though deep in thought. 'Well now, what would yer like to call me and my dear wife?'

'I want to call yer what our Sadie calls yer.' Jimmy turned his head to glance over his shoulder. 'What about you, our Ellen?'

Embarrassed by her own shyness, Ellen lowered her eyes. 'If they'll let us.'

'Of course yer can, sweetheart,' Sarah said, damning in her mind the man and woman who didn't appreciate the gift they had been given in these wonderful children. What sort of parents were they to have allowed them out on a cold day like today without a coat on their backs?

'We'd be honoured.' Joe smiled that slow smile that endeared him to everyone he met. 'But I'd like to ask a favour of Ellen. Will yer lift yer head, queen, so we can get a good look at that pretty face of yours?'

When the girl raised her head she was blushing to the roots of her hair. No one had ever said she was pretty before. She'd made the most of her appearance today because she didn't want to let Sadie down. She had an abundance of black hair which she'd washed last night and put in rags, and now her pale face was framed by curls reaching down to her shoulders. She knew she was looking her best in the jumper and skirt she'd got off her sister – but pretty? No, she wasn't pretty, not by a long chalk.

Sarah sat on the arm of her husband's chair and tilted her head. 'You two are very alike, but yer as dark as Sadie's fair.'

'Our Sadie and the baby, Sally, take after me mam, she's got blonde hair. But the rest of us take after me dad.' Jimmy felt contented sitting in front of a warm fire, in a room that was comfortable and spotlessly clean, and facing two old people whose genuine warmth seemed to reach out to him. 'But I'm not goin' to be like me dad when I grow up. I'm goin' to live in a nice house like this, an' if I ever have children I won't be hittin' them all the time, I'll look after them proper.'

Sadie came through the door then, bringing a waft of cold air with her. 'Honest, yer stand more chance of stopping a train between stations as yer do trying to stop Peter from talking. He can't half gab.'

'I'll pour yer a fresh cup of tea, sweetheart, then we'll tell yer what we've been talking about while yer were out.'

'Oh aye, talking behind me back, were yer?' Sadie rubbed her arms briskly. It had been freezing standing on next door's step while Peter nattered on. 'I hope it was nothing bad that yer had to say?'

'I wouldn't never say nothin' bad about you, our Sadie,' Jimmy said. 'And I'd crack anyone that did.'

'I know yer would, sunshine, yer the best brother in the world. We wouldn't swap yer for a big clock, would we, Ellen?'

There was spirit in Ellen's voice when she answered. 'I wouldn't! He's good to me, is our Jimmy, he looks after me. He's had many a clout off me dad for stickin' up for me.'

Jimmy's chest swelled with pride. He'd always look out for his sisters because he loved them dearly. Even when they were older, he'd still keep an eye on them to make sure they didn't marry a man like their father. No man would ever lay a finger on them while he was around. He let his eyes roam the room, repeating in his mind that, yes, one day he would live in a house like this. 'You're lucky, our Sadie, living here.'

'Oh, I know how lucky I am, Jimmy, that's for sure. But as I've told yer, in a year or two you'll be able to do the same as I did. And I'll keep me promise and help yer.'

'Don't forget about me, will yer?' Ellen said. 'I'm fourteen in May, but I can't leave school until the summer holidays.'

Sarah handed Sadie a fresh cup of tea. 'In special circumstances they'll let yer leave school when yer fourteen without staying on until the break.'

Ellen's face lit up with hope. 'They won't, will they?'

Sarah nodded. 'If the family are poor and need the child's wages coming in, yes they will. There's a woman at the bottom of the street, she's a widow and the family were living hand to mouth. They let her girl leave school the week she was fourteen.'

Ellen's face dropped. 'They wouldn't let me leave 'cos me mam's not a widow and me dad's working.'

'Ay, I'd be all right if they did that.' Jimmy wagged his shoulders from side to side. 'It's my birthday in March. If I was fourteen instead

297

of coming up thirteen, I'd leave without tellin' anyone.'

'Don't be gettin' ideas in yer head, Jimmy,' Sadie told him. 'The School Board would be round to the house like a shot.'

'If I'd run away from home they wouldn't be able to find me, would they?'

Joe gave a hearty laugh. 'The boy's got something there. They're not going to send a search party out lookin' for him, just for the sake of sending him to school for a few weeks.'

'Grandad!' Sadie wagged a finger. 'Don't be putting ideas into his head, he's bad enough without you egging him on. Anyway, let's talk about it some other time. I want to show them me bedroom before Peter comes. He'll be here before we know it.'

Ellen and Jimmy took their seats at the table, their eyes round with wonder at the display of sandwiches, fairy cakes with coloured icing on, trifles, jelly creams and biscuits. And in the centre of the table was a large sandwich cake with a Father Christmas and a tree on the top.

Jimmy's grin stretched from ear to ear. 'Ay, Grandad, these look good enough to eat. It's a pity I'm not hungry, isn't it?'

Joe gave him a conspiratorial wink. A bond of genuine liking and respect had grown between the two and it was hard to believe they'd only met an hour or so ago. 'Do yer best, son, otherwise my dear wife will get upset. She's been all morning getting this ready and she won't take kindly to anyone not eating. Besides which, I'll be getting the leftovers for me breakfast, dinner and tea for the next few days.'

Peter was sitting next to Jimmy and he gave him a dig. 'Me Auntie Sarah's a witch, yer know. She's got a big broom she keeps in the coalshed.'

Jimmy returned the dig. 'Where do yer keep yours?'

The loudest laugh came from Peter. 'Nice one, Jimmy. I can see I'm goin' to have a bit of competition in the laughter stakes.'

'That will make a change,' Sarah said with a smile. 'It's not often anyone can get the better of you.'

Peter looked across the table at Ellen. Apart from a brief nod when he came in, he hadn't been able to get a word out of her. 'What did yer get off Father Christmas, Ellen?'

Her eyes on the plate in front of her, Ellen said in a low voice, 'A jumper and skirt and a pair of gloves.'

Sarah gave a cry as her hand went to her mouth. 'We've been that busy talkin' since yer came, I forgot that Santa had left yer a present each on our tree. It's only chocolates, but at least he didn't forget yer.'

Jimmy was very quick to take advantage of the opening. 'Can we leave them on the tree, Grandma, and pick them up next week when we come to see yer?'

Sadie had to smother a gasp. She tried to kick her brother under the table but he was crafty and kept his legs well out of reach. 'Yer'd better take them with yer today,' she said, 'otherwise me Grandad will eat them. He's a holy terror for chocolate.'

Joe raised his hands in mock surprise. 'Me! It's my Sarah that's got a sweet tooth, not me. You leave them here, son, no one will touch them before yer come.'

'The Father Christmas we had this year was no good,' Peter said. 'I'll swear he was new at the job 'cos when he came down the chimney he brought half the soot with him. Me mam was hairless when she saw the state of the hearth. If she could have got hold of him she'd have strangled him. He was a cheeky blighter, too!' He saw that Ellen was looking at him with a rapt expression on her face, and he leaned forward and spoke just to her. 'D'yer know what he did, Ellen?'

He wasn't half nice-looking, Ellen was thinking as she shook her head. She couldn't understand why Sadie was so off-hand with him.

'Well, me mam always leaves a tray set for him, with a glass of sherry on and two mince pies on a plate. And she does it up nice, with a doily on the plate and a paper napkin. But this was no ho-ho-ho, ha-ha-ha Father Christmas, not on yer nellie he wasn't. Can yer guess what he did, Ellen?' He waited for the girl to shake her head then his eyes went around the table. 'A tanner for anyone who can guess what he did.'

For a tanner, Jimmy was going to have a go. 'He dropped crumbs on the floor or broke yer mam's plate?'

'Sorry, Jimmy, yer not even warm.'

'He trod soot all the way through the house?' Sarah's guess was answered with a shake of his head.

'He made himself a cup of tea?' Sadie raised her brows at him.

'Sadie, I'd love to say yer were right, but unfortunately your imagination isn't as good as one would expect from someone with a face as pretty as yours.'

'I know,' Joe said, his shoulders shaking with laughter. 'He got the tin bath off the nail in the kitchen wall, stoked up the fire and gave himself a good soak to wash the soot off.'

'Yours is the best guess, Mr O'Hanlon, and very worthy of the prize. But I can't show favouritism – the rules of the game have to be strict and fair. Especially when it's my tanner that's at stake.'

Jimmy stared at him in amazement. 'Yer don't half use some big words, Peter. Yer sound just like my history teacher.'

'Your history teacher must be a very clever man, then, Jimmy.'

'My history teacher's a woman, Peter, but I've got to say she does look like a man. She wears her hair cut short like yours, but she's got a moustache an' you haven't.'

Amid gales of laughter, Joe banged his fist on the table. 'Can we get back to this Father Christmas of yours, before I die of curiosity.'

His face a picture of innocence, Peter asked, 'What Father Christmas is that, Mr O'Hanlon?'

Joe put his turkey sandwich down. 'The one yer were telling us about.'

'Was I tellin' yer about a Father Christmas?' Peter scratched his head. 'D'yer know, I can't remember.'

Sadie's eyes rolled to the ceiling. 'I told yer he was two sheets to the wind, didn't I, our Jimmy?'

All eyes focused on Ellen when she spoke. 'The one who brought the soot down the chimney with him and made yer mam hairless.'

'Oh, that one!' Peter snapped his fingers. 'Oh yeah, wait till I tell yer what he did, the cheeky blighter.' With that he stretched out to pick up a fairy cake and demolished half of it in one mouthful. 'I'll just have a bite to eat first.'

Sadie sucked in her breath. 'Peter, the kids have got to leave at five o'clock, will yer put a move on?'

'What have they got to leave at five o'clock for?'

'Because me mam and dad will be worried about them goin' home in the dark.'

Peter turned to Jimmy. 'Where do yer mam and dad live, Jimmy?'

Sadie said quickly, 'Tell him to mind his own business.'

Jimmy felt like pinching himself to make sure he wasn't dreaming. This was a different world to the one he was used to. He'd never known people to be so friendly and laugh so much. 'I've been told to tell yer to mind yer own business, Peter.'

'Okay, Jimmy, don't take it to heart, I'm used to it.' The other half of the cake was popped into Peter's mouth and he wiped the crumbs from his lips with the back of his hand. 'Now back to this feller who turns up once a year in a red suit and a white beard. When yer come to think of it, he must be a lazy beggar, only workin' one day a year.' He heard Sadie's tut of impatience and decided now wasn't the time to say he was going to apply for the job himself next year because it was a cushy number. 'When me mam had got over the shock of seeing soot all over her clean floor, she noticed a letter propped up against the glass on the tray. The cheeky devil had written to say the mince pies weren't to his liking, not enough mincemeat in and too much fresh air. He suggested that next year she buys them from the Co-op because they're his favourites.'

Encouraged by the loud laughter, Peter went on. 'Me mam said if she knew which way his reindeers had gone, she'd follow him and give him a piece of her mind. I told her I didn't think that was a good idea because if he thought the mince pies were full of fresh air, what would he make of her mind?'

Sarah wiped a tear away. 'Peter, if you're like this all the time I wonder how yer mam puts up with yer. I don't know where yer get all these ideas from.'

'I thought it was dead funny.' Jimmy started on his third jelly cream. 'D'yer know who he reminds me of, our Sadie? That bloke next door, Harry.'

'Harry!' Peter was quick off the mark. 'Is he the Harry who —'

Sadie cut him short. 'No, he's not.'

However, Peter wasn't satisfied and turned to Jimmy. 'How old is this Harry?'

'Don't you dare tell him, our Jimmy!'

'Yer've got to mind yer own business again.' Jimmy had never felt so happy in his life. With no one to tell him to shut his mouth or belt him one, he felt as free as a bird. With a cheeky grin he added, 'Yer must have a good business, Peter, 'cos yer spend best part of yer life minding it.'

Joe chuckled. 'He's met his match in you, son, yer make a good comedy pair. Almost as funny as Laurel and Hardy.'

Ellen had little to say for herself; she was content to sit and listen and laugh. Her eyes kept going to the clock on the mantelpiece, dreading the fingers reaching the hour of five. But all the wishing in the world didn't help, and all too soon Sadie said it was time they were on their way.

'Ah, ay, Sadie, just another ten minutes?' Jimmy pleaded. 'I'm not half enjoin' meself, an' so is our Ellen.'

'I'm sorry, Jimmy, but yer did promise yer'd go when it was time. I'll walk home with yer and we can have a good natter on the way.'

'I'll join yer,' Peter said. 'The walk will do me good.'

Sadie shook her head. 'It's good of yer to offer, Peter, but I want a bit of time with me brother and sister. I don't see them very often and we've a lot of talkin' to do.'

Peter held up his hands. 'I won't open me mouth, I promise. I'll be that quiet yer won't know I'm there.'

'Uh, uh.' Sadie was adamant. 'Go home now, Peter, so I can get them ready. They'll be in trouble with me mam and dad if they're out too long.'

Ellen looked at his crestfallen face and felt sorry for him. 'It's not that we don't want yer, Peter, but Sadie's thinkin' about us gettin' into trouble.'

He smiled across the table at her. 'I'm not upset, Ellen, I'm used to your sister. Yer wouldn't think she was head-over-heels in love with me, would yer? I know she's got a funny way of showing it, but she's crazy about me. In fact, she's begged me to take her to the pictures on Wednesday night, and being a gentleman I couldn't refuse. I won't be holding her hand, though, or puttin' me arm around her shoulders. And a kiss in the dark is most definitely out of the question.'

Sadie's tummy was shaking with laughter. 'Those are the only true words yer've spoken today. There'll be no hand-holding, no cuddles, and as yer said, most definitely no kissing in the dark.'

Peter winked at Jimmy. 'Next time yer come, remind me to tell yer about the cracks in me bedroom ceiling.'

Sarah felt sad that the afternoon of jollity was coming to an end; it was many a long year since this house had known the sound of so much laughter. But she was comforted by the thought that there'd be many such afternoons to come. 'Get yerself off now, son, and yer'll see the children again next time they come to visit.'

Jimmy piped up. 'Saturday, we'll see yer.'

'Not Saturday, Jimmy, I work all day.' Things were moving too fast for Sadie. If she didn't watch out, Peter and everyone else in the street would know her whole history. But looking at the eagerness on her brother's face, her heart went out to him. He had so little to look forward to; coming here again was important to him. And to Ellen, who wasn't as outgoing as her brother but whose eyes expressed her hope. 'Make it Sunday afternoon.'

When Sarah was showing Peter out, Sadie nodded to the littered table. 'You two take some of the dirty dishes out while I go upstairs for me working coat. Ellen can wear it on the way home, save her freezing to death.'

Sadie had her foot on the bottom stair when Joe called her back. 'I don't know whether it'll be any good, but I've got an old donkey jacket hanging under the stairs. I haven't worn it for years, but it might do for Jimmy to go home in.'

'Will yer show our Jimmy where it is, Grandad, while I sort Ellen out? I don't know what excuse they're going to make for being out so long. There's nowhere open, so me mam and dad are going to think it's fishy if they say they've been wandering the streets for about six hours.'

'Come on, son, I'll get the coat for yer.' Joe pushed himself up from the chair. 'It'll probably be moth-eaten by now, but it's better than nothing.'

'Better than a kick in the teeth, eh, Grandad?'

'Yes, son, better than a kick in the teeth.'

When the coat was brought out into the light it was easy to see it had had many years of wear, but fortunately the moths had left it alone. And it turned out to be a good fit for Jimmy. His face was agog as he fastened the buttons and stuck his hands in the pockets. If it had been a brand new expensive coat he couldn't have been more happy. 'How about that, then, Grandad?'

Sarah came into the room and stood with her arms folded watching Jimmy pull the collar of the jacket up to cover his ears before swaggering across the room. 'Yer look very grown up in that coat, Jimmy – it suits yer.'

'When I start work I'll save up and buy meself one.'

'You can have that one to be going on with, son,' Joe said. 'I don't wear it and it seems a shame to leave it hanging there doin' nowt.'

'He can't have it, Grandad,' Sadie said, coming into the room dressed in her best blue coat and carrying her working coat over her arm. 'Where can he say he got it from? I'd let our Ellen have this one with pleasure, but no one in their right minds is goin' to believe that a stranger walked up to them in the street and gave them a coat each.' She closed her eyes against the disappointment on Jimmy's face. Today she'd given them a glimpse of how happy life could be; now she was taking it all back and returning them to the misery that was their real life. 'What I could do, I could meet both of yer on the first day of next term as yer come out of school and I could bring the coats with me. That way yer won't have to tell no lies. Yer can say I gave them to yer.'

Jimmy's face brightened considerably. 'Thanks, our Sadie.' He turned to Ellen. 'We'll be proper posh then, as good as any of them.'

'Come on, Ellen,' Sadie coaxed. 'Get yerself muffled up and we'll be on our way. We'll put our thinking caps on and see what excuse we can come up with for where yer've been all afternoon.'

'There are some places open on Boxing Day, queen,' Joe said. 'I don't like to encourage the children to tell lies, but I think the old saying about necessity being the mother of invention is true, so in this instance I don't think a little white lie would go amiss.'

Sarah looked sceptical. 'What are you up to, Joe O'Hanlon? I don't want you teaching the children that it's all right to tell lies.'

'Grandma, if we had halfway decent parents I'd clout the kids for telling lies.' Sadie linked her arm through Ellen's and pulled her close. 'But we don't have decent parents and I'd lie through me teeth to save the kids from gettin' a hammering off them. So if Grandad has a suggestion, I'd like to hear it.'

'Yer might not like it, but it's all I can think of. They'll not get away with saying they've been walking the streets all this time without warm clothing on.' Joe leaned back in his chair and smiled at Ellen who was looking worried. 'The Salvation Army is open all over the Christmas holiday, so is the Seamen's Mission and a couple of churches. They open to feed the tramps, the down-and-outs and the poor. They're not really places where children would go, but they could say they were walking past one of them, decided to go in out of the cold and were invited to stay. It isn't likely, but it is possible.'

'I know where the Salvation Army place is, I've often gone past it and seen people goin' in,' Jimmy said, happy to let them see he wasn't completely thick and there were some things he did know. 'We could easy say we've been there.'

'Oh well, that takes care of that,' Sadie said with a sigh. 'I can't see me dad gettin' off his backside to go and see if yer telling the truth.'

Jimmy grinned. 'I can't see me dad ever gettin' off his backside to go anywhere except the pub on the corner. He could have bought that place twice over with the money he spends there.'

'Aye, well, if he's taught us nothing else, he's taught us how *not* to live our lives.' Sadie took her arm from Ellen's and pushed her forward. 'Say goodbye to Grandma and Grandad, thank them for the lovely party and give them a big kiss.'

Ellen hung back until she saw Sarah open her arms wide, then with her eyes glistening with tears, she walked into them. 'Thank you, Grandma.'

'Thank you for coming, sweetheart, and me and Joe will look forward to seeing you both next Sunday.'

Jimmy's face was crimson as he shook hands with Joe and gave Sarah a kiss and a hug. He wasn't used to these niceties but knew he would like the opportunity of getting used to them. 'Ta very much, an' we'll see yer on Sunday.'

Sadie sat next to Peter in the picture house on Wednesday night and bit on her bottom lip to stop herself from laughing. The film was a sad one with Janet Gaynor, but Peter's antics were pure comedy. He'd tried every trick in the book to get hold of her hand but she'd thwarted him at every turn. Now, having fidgeted through half the film, he was raising the armrest to see if he'd have more luck. In the end, Sadie held her hand out. 'If this will keep yer still, it's a small price to pay. But don't get too attached to it 'cos I want it back.'

A look of pure bliss came over Peter's face as he clasped her hand. 'Yer see, I knew yer were crazy about me, Sadie.'

Mindful of the people around her, Sadie kept her voice low. 'Peter, how old are you?'

'Going on seventeen.'

'That means yer sixteen, the same age as me. It's far too young to be going out serious with anyone.'

'Ah, but think of the time it gives us.'

'Time for what?'

'To practise for when we're old enough to get serious. If we practise hard enough we'll be dab hands at it when the time comes.'

'D'yer think yer could keep quiet now, Peter, so I can watch the film and find out why Janet Gaynor's crying?'

'She's crying 'cos she was sorry for me 'cos yer wouldn't let me hold yer hand. But she'll stop now, you just watch.'

Sadie rolled her eyes. They'd have been better off staying in with Sarah and Joe, then Peter could have kept them all amused. There wasn't much point in coming to see a sad film with someone who saw humour in every situation.

When they came out of the picture house Peter refused to let go of her hand. 'Uh, uh, if I let go I'll never get it back again.' He grinned down into her face. 'It wasn't half sad, Janet Gaynor dying, wasn't it?'

'Oh, yer did notice, did yer?'

'Well, I wouldn't have done only yer nails were diggin' into me hand 'cos yer were upset. That's something I'll never understand about women. Why they bawl their eyes out at a sad film. I mean, Janet Gaynor didn't really die, did she? If I'd thought for one moment that she was really gasping her last breath, I would have cried me flippin' eyes out.'

With her hand clasped tightly in his he began to swing their arms between them. He walked with a spring in his step as though he didn't have a care in the world. And glancing sideways at him, Sadie grinned. He was a nice lad, she was fond of him and grateful that she had him for a friend. When she was with him he took her mind off her concern for her brothers and sisters. She had left Ellen and Jimmy at the corner of their street on Boxing night and she was dying to know how they got on. But the schools were still closed for the holiday period so she'd have to wait until they came for tea on Sunday. If their dad had laid a finger on them she'd ask Tommy and Spike to go up there with her and put the frighteners on him.

'You're very quiet, Sadie,' Peter said. 'Yer not worried about what to wear for Janet Gaynor's funeral, are yer?'

'No, I've got a little black number in me wardrobe – I'll wear that.'

'I'll go half with yer for the wreath.' Peter's head went back and he laughed. 'Yer realise that yer getting as daft as me, don't yer?'

'Yeah, but I do have me serious moments – you don't.'

'That's where yer wrong, Sadie – I do have me serious moments. I never let anyone see them, like, but I do have them.'

'I find that hard to believe. What are you ever serious about?'

'Me future. I intend to make something of meself when I'm older. I'm an apprentice engineer now and there's so much progress in engineering I mean to keep up with it. I get the practical experience at work, but I go to night school once a week to learn as much as I can about new technology.'

'I didn't know that! You've never mentioned going to night school.'

'I didn't want to bore yer. But I am ambitious, Sadie, I intend gettin' on in life.' He let her hand drop and put an arm across her shoulders. 'What about you? Don't you want to get on, move a few rungs up the ladder?'

'Not particularly. I just want to be happy, with enough money to get by on, of course. And I want to see me brothers and sisters happy.'

'I liked your Ellen and Jimmy, they're nice kids. I don't think yer need worry about Jimmy, he's got enough nous to get on in the world. Ellen's very shy, though, isn't she?'

'She'll come out when she starts work and is mixing with people.'

'Would yer mam let her come to Blair Hall with the gang of us? We'd all look after her, and she'd soon get over her shyness in Tommy an' Spike's company.'

'We'll see,' Sadie said as they stopped outside her house. Ellen's future was too uncertain to make plans. 'Thanks for takin' me to the pictures, Peter, even if I haven't got a clue what the film was about.'

'What! No good-night kiss? Ah, ay, Sadie, don't tell me I sat through Janet Gaynor's death scene and I don't get a reward for it.'

Sadie grinned. What would you do with him? She held her head sideways. 'You can kiss my cheek. And before yer start moaning, yer lucky to get that far on a first date.'

'Don't take yer face away, I'll come for me kiss after I've worked something out.' Peter started ticking off on his fingers. 'First date, kiss on the cheek. Second on the forehead, third on the nose and after that the chin. Seeing as that takes care of all yer face, it figures that the fifth date is the big one where I finally get to kiss yer on the lips.' He leaned closer to peck her on the cheek. 'I can hang out that long.'

Chapter Twenty-Five

Half-past six. Sadie shivered and pulled the eiderdown up to her chin. Another fifteen minutes and she'd get up and light the fire so Sarah would have a warm room to come down to. The winter seemed to be neverending; they'd had a few heavy falls of snow and it was so cold standing in the market she sometimes thought her toes were going to drop off. Mind you, she couldn't complain. Mary Ann had made the one day a week off into two days while the bad weather was on. There wasn't much doing during the week and one could manage the stall on her own. But they were into March now and the weather should be improving soon, then it would be back to normal.

Sadie curled herself into a ball to keep warm, while her mind wandered. Nine months she'd been living here with Grandma and Grandad, and every day she counted her blessings. Since Christmas, Ellen and Jimmy had come every Sunday for tea and they loved it. Those few hours were the highlight of their lives, and the change in the children was nothing short of miraculous. They had blossomed in the warmth and the love they were given so generously. Especially Ellen. Gone was the shy girl who hung her head when spoken to. Now she was talkative, and when Peter came in for the Sunday tea, she gave him back as good as she got.

Their visits gave Sadie the opportunity of keeping up with the events at home. She knew the place was still a hovel, that food and heating were always in short supply and that their father still spent every night down at the pub. But, thankfully, Les and Sally were never at the wrong end of his temper because they were usually in bed when he came home from work. Her sister, Dot, hadn't changed from all accounts. She was off flying her kite each night with every Tom, Dick and Harry, her face caked in make-up, and coming home all hours. She wasn't popular with the children because she was too handy with her fists. Jimmy said you only had to look sideways at her and she'd land you a fourpenny one.

Sadie lifted her head from the pillow and cocked an ear. Yes, there it was again, the creaking of a stair. Surely Sarah wasn't getting up before she'd had time to light the fire? Pushing the clothes back, Sadie swung her legs over the side of the bed and moved her feet around until they came into contact with the warm slippers. Then she drew the curtains back so she could see her way around. It wasn't broad daylight out, but it was light enough to find the cardi which had slipped from the bed onto the floor. And as she struggled to get her arms in the sleeves, she made her way to the door. She was on the landing when the light in the living room went on and she hurried down the stairs.

'Grandma, what are yer doing up this time of the morning? Why didn't yer stay in bed until I had the fire going?'

'The old lady next door knocked on the wall, she mustn't be well.' Sarah was pulling her long black skirt on over her nightdress. 'She looked terrible when I saw her yesterday and I told her to give me a knock if she wanted anything.'

'Yer mean Mrs Benson? What's wrong with her?'

'She was as weak as a kitten and the sweat was pouring off her. I told her to make a bed up on the couch and keep the fire going, but yer might as well talk to the wall. She never has a decent fire in the grate and the whole house is damp, yer can smell it as soon as yer go in.' Sarah's blouse was topped by the thick black woollen shawl she was never without in the cold weather. 'I know she has a hard time making ends meet, but I'm fed up telling her that keeping herself warm is more important than anything. When yer get to our age a cold can quickly turn to pneumonia.'

'I'll go into her, Grandma – you stay and get me breakfast ready.'

'No, sweetheart, it's best if I go. Maggie might be embarrassed with a young girl like you. I can let meself in 'cos she's left the key hanging on a string inside the letterbox. I'll just see how she is and come right back.'

'Don't you go gettin' a cold, Grandma. Take yer own advice and keep yerself warm.'

Sarah kissed her cheek. 'I'll do that, sweetheart. You see to things here while I nip next door.'

When Sadie had the fire crackling merrily, she swilled herself down at the kitchen sink before getting dressed. Still there was no sign of Sarah and the girl was beginning to worry. Her grandma was too old to be rushing out in the cold this time of the morning. She was debating whether to go next door or put the toast on for breakfast, when she heard the key in the lock.

'About time, Grandma, I was beginning to get worried.'

'I'm that anxious about Maggie, love, I don't like the looks of her at all. That bedroom of hers is in a terrible state – the walls are wringing wet with damp.' Sarah shivered and moved to stand by the fire. 'I think she should be brought downstairs and a big fire lit, but she'd never make it on her own and I'm not strong enough to be of any help.'

'Can't she have a fire in the bedroom? That would save a lot of trouble.'

Sarah sighed. 'She's never had a fire in the grate up there since she moved into the house fifty years ago. Her son-in-law has nailed a piece of wood across it to stop the draught coming down the chimney.'

'I'll light a fire in her living room for her, then I'll help bring her downstairs. Mary Ann will understand if I'm late.'

Sarah shook her head. 'No, sweetheart, it's best if you go to work. But what yer can do to help is run next door and ask Mrs Townley to come here. She knows where Maggie's daughters live and I think they should be sent for in case a doctor's needed. So go and give her a knock, there's a good girl, while I put yer toast on.'

It was Peter who opened the door and his face broke into a smile. 'I'm sorry, Sadie, but I can't come out to play right now, I've got to go to work.'

'Get yer mam for us, Peter – quick, it's urgent.'

'What's up?'

'Old Mrs Benson's ill.'

Peter was down the hall like a flash to return with his mother. 'What is it, Sadie?'

'Me grandma said could yer go an' see her, Mrs Townley? The old lady next door is ill, yer see, and me grandma's worried.'

Betty Townley patted the dinky curlers in her hair. She'd put up with the agony of sleeping in them all night and now wished she hadn't bothered. She and Peter were very alike in colouring, features and humour. 'I'm not lookin' me best this time of the morning, girl. I do wish people wouldn't be so inconsiderate as to get sick before I've had time to take me curlers out and doll meself up.'

'I've offered to stay off and help, but me grandma won't hear of it. It's her I'm worried about. She's too old now to be seeing to someone sick.'

'I'll just get me coat, girl, then I'll be with yer. And don't worry about Sarah – I'll make sure she doesn't overdo it.'

'Thanks, Mrs Townley,' Sadie said as she hurried away, too upset to even say ta-ra to Peter. Her tea was poured out when she got home and a plate of toast was waiting. She'd just taken her first bite of the golden crispy bread when Peter's mother arrived and began to question Sarah.

'Right,' Betty said when she'd heard the story. 'I'll get in there and light a fire. As soon as the room's warm, I'll help her downstairs.'

'I'll come with you,' Sarah said, reaching for her shawl, 'and give yer a hand.'

'Will you heckerslike! It doesn't take two to make a blinkin' fire!

309

You get some hot tea and toast down yer, then get your feller out of bed. By that time I should have Maggie downstairs, please God, and you can sit with her while I fetch her daughter. Doreen only lives off Westminster Road, I'll be there and back in no time.'

Sadie threw her a look of gratitude. She felt better already, seeing the way Peter's mam had taken charge. 'Thanks, Mrs Townley.'

'Yer welcome, girl. And don't you worry about Sarah here, I'll see she doesn't go doin' cartwheels down the street showin' her fleecy-lined bloomers off to all the men.'

'You can go home if yer want, girl.' Mary Ann was wearing a man's heavy coat which nearly reached the ground and her black shawl was wrapped tightly around her head and shoulders. She said she was keeping her hair covered 'cos it was a different red to her nose and the two colours clashed. 'It's slack here for a Friday, so I'd manage on me own.'

'Me grandma would kill me if I went home,' Sadie told her. 'When I was coming out she said I got paid to do a day's work an' I should earn me money.'

'I don't think yer've any need to worry about Sarah. She knows her limits and won't try to do anything too strenuous.' The stall-holder gave her a gentle nudge. 'Ay, out, here comes Maggie and Florrie. Even if they don't have any money to spend we'll get a laugh. And my old mam, God rest her soul, used to say that a good belly laugh does yer more good than a full pan of scouse.'

Florrie, having heard the last part, said, 'I remember yer ma, Mary Ann, she was the salt of the earth. Always bright and cheerful, she was, and a kind word for everyone.' When her false teeth had settled back into place, she jerked her head at her friend. 'I'm not mentioning any names, mind, but she wasn't like some of the miserable sods that are around these days.'

Maggie's folded arms hitched up her mountainous bosom. 'Ay, Florrie, I hope that wasn't intended for me? I agree I might be a miserable sod for six days of the week, but on pay day yer won't find a happier or more sociable person if yer travelled the length and breadth of Liverpool.'

'Yer've done it now, Florrie,' Mary Ann laughed. 'She's cut to the quick, is Maggie.'

Florrie shrugged her shoulders. 'Yer know what they say, Mary Ann, if the cap fits then wear it.'

Maggie's bosom was now nearly up to her chin as she eyed the felt hat Florrie was wearing. When it was new, donkey's years ago, it had been a lovely navy blue. Now it was several shades of blue with a hint of green. 'If yer don't apologise, Mrs Florrie bloody-Know-it-all, I'll ram that bloody hat down yer mouth.'

'Ah, don't do that, Maggie.' Sadie held up her hands in mock horror. 'It's the only one the poor woman's got!'

'Listen to me, you two,' Mary Ann said, hands on hips, 'if yer going to have a fight then I'm goin' to be referee. And yer'll fight by the rules, all fair and square. If you dare lay a finger on her, Maggie, before she's had time to take those bleedin' false teeth out, that'll be counted as hittin' below the belt and a point against yer.' Oh, how the stall-holder was enjoying this. It had quite livened up an otherwise miserable day. 'And if yer play yer cards right, yer could both be winners 'cos I've got a proposition to put to yer. If yer put yer heart and soul into it, and have a good go at each other, yer could draw a big crowd to me stall. So for every article we sell while you two are bashing each other, I'll give yer a farthing each. Now I can't be fairer than that, can I?'

'Well, the bloody cheek of you! Did yer hear that, Florrie?'

'I most certainly did, Maggie. I never thought I'd live to see the day when Mary Ann would encourage two gentle, well-brought up ladies like ourselves to have a scrap just so she can make a few coppers. D'yer know what, Maggie, if her dear mother was alive she'd turn in her grave.'

The four of them doubled up with laughter and the happy sound had Sadie thinking it was a sign that spring was in the air.

Sadie ran all the way home and was gasping for breath when she burst into the room. 'How is Mrs Benson, Grandma?'

'She's bedded down on the couch, sweetheart, with a fire up the chimney and a hot water bottle on her tummy. Betty Townley was a godsend, I can tell yer. I'd never have managed on me own, I wouldn't have known where to turn. Betty went for the old lady's daughter, and as soon as Doreen saw the state of her mother she ran around for the doctor. He played merry hell over the house being so cold and damp, said he was surprised Maggie hadn't died of pneumonia before now. Anyway, he said he'll call again in the morning and if she's no better she'll have to go into hospital. He would have sent her today but she flatly refused. She said if she's goin' to die she'd rather die in her own home.'

Sadie had taken her coat off and draped it over her arm. 'She's not going to die, is she, Grandma?'

'No, I don't think so, sweetheart.' Sarah wasn't going to voice her misgivings and upset the girl. 'Hang yer coat up while I fetch yer dinner in.'

Sadie gave Joe a kiss before going out to the hallstand. 'She's not in the house on her own, is she?'

'No, she's not on her own, queen, so don't fret yerself,' Joe said. 'Her daughter's staying the night with her. Sarah's told her to knock if she needs us.'

When Sarah came through from the kitchen, Sadie closed her eyes. 'Don't tell me, let me guess.' She sniffed up. 'Steak and kidney pie.'

'Right first time, sweetheart. With mashed potatoes and carrot and turnip.'

'I'll make short work of that, I'm famished.' Sadie pulled her chair nearer the table and picked up her knife and fork. 'I bet Mrs Benson doesn't make herself a proper dinner every day like you do, Grandma.'

Sarah lowered herself onto the end of the couch. 'That's her whole trouble. She's got her priorities wrong, but will she listen to yer? Will she heck! Instead of buying nourishing food and coal, she saves her pennies to give to her grandchildren when they come. She's soft-hearted, is Maggie, and she gets a lot of pleasure out of giving them money for sweets. I can understand that, but not when she's killing herself in the process.'

Joe nodded his head in agreement. 'Yer told her daughter that, didn't yer, love?'

'I did, and she went mad. She said she'll put a stop to it and make sure her mother spends what little she gets on herself. In fact, the first thing Doreen did was to run around to the coalyard and asked them to drop two bags of coal off. There's a fire roaring up the chimney right now, and that's a sight I've never seen before in that house.'

'I'll give a knock when I've had me tea, shall I, and see if they want any messages from the corner shop?'

'That would be neighbourly, sweetheart, Doreen would appreciate that. And Betty said she'd send their Peter to fill a couple of buckets of coal for them. They'll have to keep the fire banked up day and night while Maggie's so ill, and it'll save Doreen havin' to go down the yard in the middle of the night.'

Sadie grinned. 'D'yer know what the soft nit said to me when I knocked this morning? Seven o'clock it was, I was half-asleep and he was as bright as a button. "I'm sorry, Sadie, but I can't come out to play now 'cos I've got to go to work".'

'He's a hero, that lad,' Joe chuckled. 'Whoever gets him will be getting a good one.'

There was a loud rat-tat on the window and all three gave a start. 'Speak of the devil and he's bound to appear.' Sarah was smiling as she eased herself up. 'This'll be him now – he's the only one who ever knocks on the window.'

Peter breezed in with his usual cheerful grin. He looked at the plate in front of Sadie and asked, 'Oh, are yer havin' yer dinner?'

'You need glasses, you do.' Sadie had learned that if you didn't look in his eyes when you were talking to him, it made it easier not to smile. 'Having me dinner, indeed! Can't yer see I'm knitting a pair of socks?'

Peter snapped his fingers. 'Silly me, of course yer are.' He looked across at Joe and winked. 'I hope they fit yer, Mr O'Hanlon. They look a bit on the small side to me, and I can see she's dropped quite a few stitches.'

Sadie chewed the last of the pie and laid down her knife and fork. 'Yer've always got an answer, Peter Townley, but one of these days I'll be the winner.'

'What d'yer mean, one of these days? You are always the winner!' He held his open hands out and appealed to Sarah and Joe. 'When you hear my tale of woe yer hearts will bleed for me, so have yer hankies at the ready. I've had three dates with Sadie since Christmas and I need another two before I get to the big prize. But will she go out with me? Will she heck.'

Sarah knew she was walking into his trap but she fell for it. 'What's the big prize?'

Peter plonked his bottom on the arm of the couch, his eyes deliberately avoiding the warning look on Sadie's face. 'It's a bit complicated, Auntie Sarah, and I've never played the game before so I don't really know the rules. But it goes something like this. On yer first date yer can kiss her cheek – well, I've had that one. On the second date yer get to kiss an area somewhere in the vicinity of her ear, and I've had that too. I've also kissed her nose, which she kindly allowed on our third date. So by my reckoning her chin comes next and after that the big prize.'

Sadie's face was crimson. 'I'll kill you, Peter Townley.'

Peter once again appealed to the old couple. 'See what I'm up against? All I'm after is a little kiss and she's talkin' about murder! Now I ask yer, what chance have I got?'

'Yer've got no chance at all now,' Sadie told him, 'yer've just blown it.'

'How about a little compromise?' Sarah suggested, promising herself a good laugh after they'd both gone out. 'It's yer birthday in two weeks, isn't it, Peter?'

'Yeah, sweet seventeen and never been kissed.' Then he wagged his head from side to side, a wide grin on his face. 'That's a bit of an exaggeration 'cos I've been kissed loads of times, but this is a special kiss I'm after, a collector's item.'

'Are you buyin' him a present for his birthday, Sadie?' Sarah asked.

'Huh! I'm not buying him anything for his birthday, and he needn't think I am. I've got better things to spend me money on.'

'I can think of a solution that will make yer both happy.' Sarah could hear the soft chuckle of her husband that always gladdened her heart. 'If yer make a date with Peter as his birthday present, that won't cost yer a penny. And I don't think yer so miserable yer wouldn't let him kiss yer chin, are yer? And as for Peter, well, he'd be over the moon 'cos it would be one down and only one more to go.'

Sadie couldn't hide her smile any longer. 'Grandma, yer a crafty old lady and you and Grandad are really enjoying yerselves at my expense. But I love every bone in yer bodies and every hair on yer heads.'

'That goes for me, too.' Peter stood up and stretched himself to his full height. 'I think your suggestion has met with the approval of Sadie and meself so that's me birthday sorted out. And now, Miss Sadie Wilson, are yer comin' next door with me to help me stock them up with coal? I'll hold the torch while you shovel it into the buckets.'

'Some hope you've got, soft lad.' Sadie pushed her chair back and picked up her empty plate. 'Don't you be givin' me orders, I'm no skivvy.'

'Leave the plate, sweetheart, I'll see to it. You poppy off with Peter and try not to come to blows in front of Maggie. Remember, she's a sick woman.'

Lily Wilson's eyes kept going to the clock as she paced the floor. It was two o'clock on a Saturday afternoon in May and her husband hadn't come home yet with his wages. She hadn't a penny to her name and not a piece of bread in the house. If she didn't get down to the corner shop soon and pay for what she'd had through the week, they wouldn't let her have any more tick and then she would be in queer street. 'Go and see if there's any sign of yer dad.'

'He'll be in the pub,' Jimmy said, 'and they won't let me go in there.'

'Ask someone to have a look for yer. Go on, do as yer told and don't be givin' me any of yer bleedin' lip or I'll belt yer one.'

As Jimmy stepped into the street he caught sight of his father coming out of the pub so he turned on his heels and went back into the house. 'He's on his way, I've just seen him comin' out of the pub.'

'I'll pub him if he's spent me wages.' Lily picked her coat off the couch and was slipping her arms in the sleeves when her husband staggered in. 'Where the bleedin' hell have you been until this time?

Yer knew I 'ad no money and would be waitin' on yer.'

George hiccupped and a silly grin spread over his face. 'I only went in for a pint. I'm entitled to a pint after workin' hard.'

'Hard? Yer don't know what hard work is! Now hand yer money over so I can get to the bleedin' shops before they close.'

Holding onto the door for support, George fumbled in his pocket and brought out a crumpled pound note. 'Here yer are, I'll give yer the rest later.'

Lily snatched the note. 'When our Dot decides to come home, you can lay the law down with her. She's to come straight home from work on a Saturday 'cos I need her money. You tell her that 'cos you're the one who's bleedin' spoiled the jumped-up little bitch.'

George flopped into a chair and his head lolled back. 'Take the baby out with yer. I don't want her cryin' and gettin' under me feet.'

Lily tutted but didn't argue. 'Jimmy, put the baby in the push chair an' I'll take her with me. Les, you can come as well to help me carry me bits an' pieces. And you make yerself useful, Ellen – get a pot of tea made for yer dad. There's no milk in the 'ouse so he'll have to make do without.'

'What's for me dinner?' George whined as he saw her making for the door. 'Me belly's rumbling.'

Lily turned. 'Yer can have the same as we've had – sweet bugger all!'

When Jimmy came back into the room, Ellen was handing her father a cup of tea. But George was making no move to take the cup from her, and the look on his face sent cold shivers down Jimmy's spine. He could see Ellen was terrified because her hand was shaking and the tea was slopping over the rim of the cup. There was complete silence as George leered at his daughter. Then he said in a slurred voice, 'I can't drink tea without milk, so why don't I send Jimmy to the dairy to get some, eh?' With his mouth wide open he belched loudly, causing Ellen to close her eyes and turn her head. But she was too afraid to move away and remained like a statue. In this mood her father was capable of anything.

George suddenly leaned forward and grabbed Ellen's free arm. 'You stay where yer are while I find a penny for the milk.'

There was a look of desperation on Jimmy's face. 'Me mam's bringin' milk in, she won't be gone long.'

George handed him a penny. 'Yer heard what I said, now get goin' and don't forget to take a jug with yer.' When the boy hesitated, he roared, 'Do as yer told, yer little bleeder, or I'll take me belt to yer.'

Jimmy didn't go to the kitchen for a jug, he picked up a dirty one from the table. He didn't know what it had been used for, but if wishes were granted it would be full of poison. Right then, seeing how distraught his sister was, he wished his father dead. 'I won't be a minute.' His words were directed at Ellen. 'I'll run all the way.' He left the room with his father's evil laughter ringing in his ears. But he was filled with apprehension for his sister and even with the threat of getting belted with his dad's buckle, he couldn't bring himself to desert her. So he didn't go any further than the front door.

'Dad, can I put the cup on the table?' Ellen's voice trembled with fear. 'I'll make yer a fresh one when Jimmy comes back with the milk.'

'No, you stay right where yer are until I say yer can move.' The wickedness in George's voice had the hairs on Jimmy's neck bristling as he listened outside. 'You be a good girl and do as yer dad says.'

'No, Dad! Leave me alone! That's dirty, that is! Stop it, Dad, please!'

Jimmy had heard enough. He pushed the door open and was filled with anger and disgust when he saw his father leaning forward, a look of pure lust on his face as his hand went further up Ellen's dress.

'You dirty, filthy bugger.' Jimmy grabbed Ellen and pulled her away, placing himself in front of his father. 'Yer nothin' but an animal, you are, yer dirty swine.'

George was momentarily taken aback. His brain was numbed by the three pints of beer he'd had and it took him a while to come to grips with what was happening. Then, his hands going to the buckle on his belt, he roared like a lion. 'I warned yer, didn't I? Well, now I'm goin' to flay yer within an inch of yer life.'

Jimmy was too angry to feel fear. He put his two hands on his father's chest and pushed him back in the chair. 'I hate you, d'yer hear? I wish yer was dead.' His eyes blurred with rage, the lad didn't see the clenched fist coming towards him until it was too late. He took the full force of the blow on the left side of his face and stumbled backwards.

Ellen looked on in horror until she saw Jimmy holding his face, then she flew at her father. The brother she loved had been trying to help her and this man, this evil man, had hurt him. She pummelled his body with her fists, her anger giving her the strength to rain blows that really hurt. 'I hate you, too, and I wish yer were dead.' Then, remembering the shame and humiliation he'd caused her over the years, she wanted to see him cower in agony. So she raked her nails down both of his cheeks and delighted in his cries of pain.

'Leave him now, he's not worth it.' Jimmy pulled her away. 'We can't stay in the house with him, he's insane. Get yer coat and let's get out of here.'

'Are we goin' to wait in the street until me mam comes back?'

'What good would that do? She'll only stick up for him, she always does. Anyway, yer not going back in there, ever.' Jimmy held on tight to

Ellen's hand. 'We'll go to our Sadie's, she'll know what's best.'

'She'll be at work.'

'We'll call in the market, she won't mind.'

They were walking down the street when Ellen said, 'Jimmy, yer eye's all red. Another hour an' it'll be black and blue.'

He shrugged his shoulders. 'I'll live.'

'Thanks for stickin' up for me, Jimmy, I'll always love yer for that.' Ellen stared down as their feet covered the ground. There was something on her mind but she was too shy to know how to say it. 'Jimmy, we won't have to tell anyone what me dad was doin', will we? I don't want anyone to know.'

'We'll have to tell our Sadie, so she'll know that yer can't ever go back home. But I won't say anythin' – you can tell her in private, like. She'll understand 'cos she knows what me dad's like.'

'But what about you? I'll worry about you going back 'cos me dad'll kill yer after this. If you go back, I'm comin' with yer.'

'Not if I've got anythin' to say about it, yer won't. But we can't do anythin' on our own 'cos we've no money and no one to turn to except our Sadie. But she will help us, I know she will, so let's wait an' see what she has to say.'

Sadie smiled and waved when she saw the children coming towards her, but as they got nearer and she saw the distress on their faces she left the stall and ran to meet them. The first thing she noticed was Jimmy's swollen black eye. 'What on earth happened to you?'

It was Ellen who told her, the words pouring from her mouth. 'Me dad did that to him just 'cos he was stickin' up for me. And I battered me dad and scratched his face. Look – I've got blood under me nails.'

Sadie's mouth gaped. 'Oh, my God! What brought all this on?'

Jimmy kicked the ground with the toe of his shoe. 'He asked for it, Sadie, he's been askin' for it for years. He was undoin' his belt to flay me and I pushed him in the chest. The next thing I knew he'd landed this punch on me.'

'But what started it off, and where was me mam?'

'Me dad was late gettin' in with his money, he'd been to the pub as usual, and me mam left to go to the shops as soon as he got in. She took Les and Sally with her, so there was only me an' Ellen in. He sent me to get some milk, but I didn't go 'cos I knew he was up to no good. So I stood outside the door and listened. When I heard Ellen cryin' I went in, and that's how it started.' Jimmy looked uncomfortable. 'Our Ellen's got somethin' to tell yer, private like. But I can't go and talk to Mary Ann, she'll wonder where I got me black eye from.'

317

'Tell her!' Sadie saw his startled expression but didn't care. She was so mad, so furious, she wanted the whole world to know what her father was like. She didn't need Ellen to tell her what he'd been up to, she knew him from old. And to think it took a young boy to put him in his place. 'Yer've no need to tell her everything, not about Ellen. Just say he was going to give her a hiding and yer tried to stop him. For that he gave yer a black eye and he did it deliberate.'

Jimmy hesitated, reluctant to go until he'd said what he knew his sister would be too shy to say. 'She can't go back home, Sadie. It wouldn't be right 'cos she's not safe where me dad is.'

'I know that, Jimmy, but it's all happened so quick I haven't had time to get me head together. It's not only Ellen I want out of that house, it's you as well. But I haven't the foggiest idea where yer could go. Ellen will be all right, I know Grandma will let her sleep with me, but there's not room enough for you.'

'I'll be all right, Sadie, as long as yer see to Ellen.'

Sadie felt like throwing her arms around him and weeping on his shoulder. At his age he should be enjoying his childhood, not having the responsibility of a grown man thrust on him. 'You go and talk to Mary Ann, we'll be with yer in a minute. But don't interrupt her if she's serving a customer.'

Sadie listened in silence as Ellen, her eyes on the ground, told her what had happened. 'And I've scratched all his face, Sadie, it was bleeding. I wouldn't have had the nerve to do it only I got mad when I saw what he did to our Jimmy.'

'Good for you! He'll have a job explaining the scratches away. But what you've got to remember is that none of this is your fault, so don't be feeling embarrassed or ashamed. No one will know the real story, not even me grandma and grandad. So hold yer head up, sunshine, and look everyone in the eye.'

Mary Ann was waiting, eyes blazing and nostrils flared. 'He's one bleedin' bastard, is that father of yours. I'd hang him up by the feet until he screamed for mercy.'

Sadie sighed. 'I know, Auntie Mary, but right now I've got a problem about what to do with our Jimmy. I'd give anything for him not to have to go back home, but even if I had somewhere he could go, which I haven't, there's his school to think of. If I tried to change his school there'd be all sorts of questions asked and they'd contact me mam and dad.'

'I'll go home, I'll be all right.' Jimmy put on a show of bravado but inside he was feeling anything but brave. He knew that as soon as he put his foot in the door his father would be waiting for him with his belt in his hand. 'If he touches me, I'll run away.'

Sadie made a quick decision. 'Yer'll go home, but it won't be alone.' She took hold of Ellen's arm. 'Go and stand by my stall, sunshine, put a smile on yer face and start selling. Yer've watched me the last few Saturdays, so yer know what to do. Everything on the stall is sixpence so that's all yer've got to remember. If yer get stuck, ask Auntie Mary, or even the customers – they'll help yer.'

Ellen looked uncertain. She'd watched her sister with the customers and envied the ease with which she spoke and laughed with them. But she wasn't like her sister, she was shy with strangers. 'Where are yer goin'? Can't I come with yer?'

'Ellen, I can't be in two places at once and don't forget I'm supposed to be working. So you get on that stall and do my job, while I go somewhere with our Jimmy.'

With her hand on her brother's elbow, Sadie pushed him through the crowd of people to Tommy's stall. He and his father were both serving but Tommy looked up briefly to give them a nod. Then when he'd exchanged a second-hand saw for threepence, he walked along the stall to where they were standing. 'Hello there, young . . .' His words petered out when he saw the ugly bruising on the boy's face. 'What's happened to you, lad? Walked into someone's fist, did yer?'

Sadie looked to where his father was chatting to a customer. 'Mr Seymour, d'yer mind if I have a word with Tommy?'

'Have three if yer like, queen, we're not exactly rushed off our feet.'

Tommy came from behind the trestle table. 'What's up, Sadie?'

'Yer can see what's up, Tommy.' She pointed to her brother's face. 'My brave father did that to him.'

'Bloody hell! He knows who to pick on, doesn't he? Were yer giving him cheek, lad?'

Jimmy shook his head. 'He was givin' our Ellen a hidin' and I tried to stop him. I did give him cheek then, I said I hated him and wished he was dead. That's when he fisted me.'

'There's a bit more to it than that, Tommy,' Sadie told him. 'When Ellen saw what he did to Jimmy, just for sticking up for her, she had a go at me dad and scratched his face. She said it was bleedin' so it must be bad.'

'Serves him right. If I'd been in Ellen's place I'd have taken the poker to him.' Tommy gazed with sympathy at the angry bruises which covered the boy's eye and came halfway down his cheek. 'Yer did right to try and protect yer sister, young Jimmy, and I'm proud of yer. A little hero, that's what yer are.'

'I'm not lettin' Ellen go home again, she's in danger in that house 'cos me dad can't keep his hands off her,' Sadie put in. 'He was like that with me, but I'm not as gentle as our Ellen. Anyway, I'm asking me grandma if she can live with us, and I'm positive she'll say yes. And because she's just turned fourteen, I'm going to find out if she can leave school early. But our Jimmy's a different kettle of fish; he's got another year at school so he'll have to go back and face the music. And I'm afraid for him. After what's happened, me dad will tear him limb from limb. He'll get Ellen's punishment as well as his own.'

'Not if me and Spike take him home.'

Sadie sighed with relief. 'Tommy, yer an angel, I was praying yer'd say that. I know we're all supposed to be goin' to Blair Hall tonight, but we could still go even if it means being a bit late.'

'Hang on, I'll get Spike over.' Tommy put two fingers in his mouth and blew out a loud whistle. When he caught his friend's attention, he waved him over. 'I know Spike will agree with me, but it's policy to ask.'

Spike took one look at Jimmy's face, asked how it happened, then shook his head sadly. 'Yer not letting the lad go home on his own, are yer?'

Tommy grinned. 'No, you an' me are goin' with him. Yer such a kind-hearted bloke I knew yer wouldn't mind me offering yer services.'

'Yer should have let us go in last time, Sadie – I did warn yer.' Spike's normally smiling face was serious. 'I knew yer father was a bad 'un from what yer told us. When children are so afraid of their father that they daren't open their mouths, then there's something radically wrong. A smack on the backside when they're naughty is one thing, but takin' a belt to them is something else. Anyway,' he cocked his head at Tommy, 'are we goin' straight from here or goin' home first?'

'If we go straight from here we'll catch me dad before he has time to go to the pub.' Sadie nodded, 'Yeah, I'm coming with yer.'

'There's no need. Me and Spike can sort it out. You'd only get yerself all upset.'

'I'm takin' our Jimmy home, Tommy, and no amount of talkin' will change me mind. I want to see the look on me dad's face when he sees you two. I want to see the same sort of fear on his face that he puts on the children's. I know it makes me sound as hard as nails, and perhaps I am, but if I am then that's how he made me.'

'Aw, you're not hard, Sadie,' Tommy said. 'Yer as soft as a brush.'

'Yer nicer lookin' than the brush me mam's got, though.' Spike grinned into her face. 'If me mam's brush was as nice-lookin' as you, I wouldn't let her brush the floor with it. Oh no, I'd make her sit it on a chair and we could all spend our time admiring it and saying, "Isn't she like Sadie Wilson?".'

Jimmy forgot his painful eye and Sadie smiled. 'You two are as mad as hatters, but I'm glad I've got yer for me mates.'

'Yeah, me too.' Jimmy was wishing the next few years of his life away to the time when he was as big and manly as these two. 'When I leave school, would I easy get a job on the market?'

'What, a hero like you? Of course yer would, especially if I recommended yer.' Tommy threw his chest out. 'I'm very highly thought of, I am.'

'Ay, come on, I'll have to get back to me stall 'cos Ellen will be having a nervous breakdown. She can go to me grandma's now and tell her what's happened and that I'll be late. And she'll have to tell Peter, as well. He can go on to the dance and we'll meet him there.'

'Yeah, okay. Me and Spike will pick yez up when we've cleared away for the night.' Tommy ruffled Jimmy's hair. 'Don't you be worryin', lad, 'cos it'll be all right, I promise. Your dad has hit you for the last time.'

Chapter Twenty-Six

Ellen was filled with mixed emotions as she made her way to Sarah's. She ran like the wind, and her mind raced at the same speed. It was hard to take in that she'd never have to go back to the home she had come to hate. And to live with Grandma and Grandad was a dream she never expected to turn into reality. Mind you, they hadn't yet said she could live with them, but Sadie seemed so sure and her sister was usually right. The only blot on her horizon was the plight of her brother, Jimmy. If only he didn't have to go home then her happiness would be complete. She couldn't imagine life without him because since Sadie had left he'd always been there to look out for her. He wouldn't be in this trouble now only for trying to protect her.

With her head so full of conflicting thoughts, Ellen ran on, her eyes not seeing the people she passed. She pelted round the corner of Penrhyn Street at breakneck speed and straight into the arms of Peter Townley.

'Hey, steady on, Ellen.' Peter held her at arm's length. 'What's the big hurry?'

She took several deep breaths to calm her nerves. 'I've got a message for Grandma from our Sadie, and I've got one for you, as well.' She screwed her eyes up to try and halt the flow of tears, but it was no good, they began to roll down her cheeks. 'Oh Peter, it's been a terrible day. Me dad punched our Jimmy an' he's got a terrible black eye. And I got so mad at what he did to me brother I scratched me dad's face.'

'I'm sure things aren't as bad as yer think, Ellen, so dry yer eyes. It'll all blow over, you mark my words.'

'It won't, yer know.' Ellen sniffed up, wishing she had something to wipe her nose on. 'I'm not goin' home no more. I'm hoping Grandma will let me stay with them.'

'Yer can't just run away from home without yer parents' permission. They'll be worried sick about yer.'

'They don't worry about us at all. If they did they'd look after us better and not be clouting us all the time. We're not allowed to open our mouths, an' if we even look sideways we get a belt.'

Peter dropped his hands and his eyes were thoughtful. 'Is that why Sadie left home?'

Without thinking, Ellen said, 'Yeah, she'd had enough. She looked after us when she was home, our Sadie did, that's why we all love her so much. But when she left there was only our Jimmy and he's no match for me dad.'

'Look, let's get to Auntie Sarah's. There's no point in yer having to go over the whole story twice.'

Sarah's smile was one of welcome when she opened the door to see Peter standing there with his arm across Ellen's shoulders. But when the old lady saw the girl's tearful face her expression turned to one of concern. 'In the name of God, sweetheart, have yer had an accident?'

Peter got in first. 'Ellen's got a message for yer from Sadie, and one for me. But I think a cup of tea would work wonders right now.'

Sarah walked straight through to the kitchen without saying a word, leaving Joe to see to their visitors. 'Hello, queen, this is a pleasant surprise.'

'Hello, Grandad.' Ellen sat on the very edge of the couch, her head lowered as she picked nervously at her nails.

When no further information was forthcoming, Joe raised his brows at Peter who shrugged his shoulders. 'Ellen's a bit upset now, but she'll tell us about it after she's had a cup of me Auntie Sarah's miraculous brew.'

'Here yer are, sweetheart, I've put plenty of milk in it so it's not too hot.' Sarah kept hold of the cup and held it to Ellen's mouth. 'Drink it all up, there's a good girl, an' yer'll soon feel better.'

Ellen gulped the tea down, eager to say what she had to and get it over with. No sooner was the cup away from her mouth than she blurted out, 'Grandma, can I stay here?'

Sarah looked puzzled. 'Yer mean for tonight?'

Oh dear, how could she answer that? If she said she wanted to live there for good, they'd think she had a cheek. But she was spared from answering when Peter came to her aid.

'Ellen was telling me that her and Jimmy had some trouble at home with their dad. Perhaps that's got something to do with why she's here.'

It took some gentle coaxing from Sarah for the sorry tale to come tumbling out. It was when Ellen was saying that her dad had hold of her arm that she hung her head and sobs shook her body. In her mind she was reliving those moments of shame and fear. She could feel her father's hand going up her bare leg and his fingers pushing under the elastic in the leg of her knickers. She could hear herself begging him to stop, and the relief she felt when Jimmy dashed in.

Peter came to her aid once again. 'Yer father was goin' to give yer a belt, wasn't he?' He waited for her nod. 'And Jimmy came in and tried to stop him, is that right?'

Ellen raised her tear-stained face. 'I didn't do nothing wrong, Grandma, honest I didn't! And our poor Jimmy didn't either. He pulled me away from me dad, and I remember him saying he hated him, then the next thing, I heard this crack and me brother's holding his face. I love our Jimmy, and he didn't deserve that, so I went for me dad. I was punching him as hard as I could, then I scratched his face. I don't know how I had the nerve 'cos I've never even answered him back before. But I'm not sorry I did it, and I'd do it again if I saw him hitting our Jimmy.'

Sarah let out a deep sigh. 'What happened then, sweetheart?'

'We ran out of the house. Me dad had been drinkin' yer see, and when he's drunk he gets in a terrible temper. He'd have killed us if we'd stayed.'

Joe took a neatly folded pure white hankie out of his pocket and handed it to her. 'It is clean, queen, so give yer nose a good blow.'

'Where was yer mother, sweetheart? Couldn't she have stopped this?'

'She'd gone to the shops with the young ones, but she wouldn't have stopped it anyway. She always sticks up for me dad no matter what he does. He's always hittin' one of us and she never stops him. So our Jimmy said we'd go to the market and tell our Sadie.'

'And is that why yer want to sleep here tonight?'

'Sadie said I'm never to go back home because I'm not safe where me dad is. So she said I was to ask yer if I could stay here until she sorts something out for me.'

'Of course yer can, sweetheart. Me and Joe would love to have yer.'

Joe, with the wisdom of his years, sensed there was more to what happened than the girl was telling them. If what he was thinking was true, then the father needed horse-whipping. 'Yer can stay as long as yer like, queen,' he agreed. 'I'll be waited on hand and foot with three women to fuss over me.'

Relief flooding her body, Ellen went on to give the rest of the message. 'Sadie said not to have a dinner ready for her, Grandma, 'cos she's taking our Jimmy home. Tommy and Spike are goin' with them to give me dad a good telling-off and a warning about what'll happen to him if he doesn't keep his hands off the children.'

Peter was none too pleased. 'I'd have gone with Sadie – why didn't she ask me?'

'Well, she didn't see yer to ask yer, did she? They're goin' straight from the market so they'll be back in time to get ready for the dance. Sadie said to tell yer to go on an' they'll meet yer inside.'

'Will I thump! I'll be here when she gets home to find out how they got on,' Peter huffed. 'I should be with them, never mind gettin' told to go on to the dance. Just wait until I see Sadie, I won't half give her a piece of me mind.'

'Don't you go shoutin' at our Sadie,' Ellen said with spirit. 'She's got enough on her plate, worryin' about me an' our Jimmy.'

Joe chuckled. He could see Peter having a lively time with the two sisters to contend with. Ellen was as timid as a dormouse most of the time, but now and again she showed that there was steel under the surface, and when push came to shove she could hold her own. 'I think yer in for a rough ride, Peter. It'll be battle stations, with two against one.'

'Nah, I can handle two of them, easy-peasy.'

Sarah pursed her lips. 'Don't put yer money on it, son, don't put yer money on it.'

Sadie bought Jimmy a tuppenny bag of chips and scallops from a chippy in Mill Street, knowing there was little chance of him getting anything to eat at home. And the speed with which he was devouring the delicacy showed not only how hungry the boy was, but also what a rare treat it was to walk along the street eating chips from a piece of newspaper in the company of people who treated him like a human being.

Spike had his arm loosely across Jimmy's shoulder as they strolled along, quizzing him without seeming to. 'Who's yer favourite cowboy, Jimmy? Is it Tom Mix?'

'I dunno, I've never seen him.'

'Never seen Tom Mix! Don't yer ever go to the Saturday matinée?'

Jimmy shook his head. 'No, I've never been.'

'What d'yer spend yer pocket money on, then? Don't tell me yer've got a girlfriend and yer spend all yer money on sweets for her?'

Jimmy pushed two fingers into the hole made in the newspaper wrapping and pulled out a long chip which he blew on before popping it into his mouth. 'Don't get no pocket money an' don't have no girlfriend.'

'Yer must get some pocket money – every kid gets pocket money.'

Jimmy shook his head. 'Not in our 'ouse, they don't.'

'Go 'way,' Tommy said. 'The poorest kids in our street get money to go to the matinée to see Tom Mix. They mightn't have no arse in their kecks but they'll find the money from somewhere to go and see the cowboys and Indians, even if they 'ave to take empty jam jars back to get it.'

'Our Jimmy's tellin' yer the truth,' Sadie said quietly. 'None of us have ever had pocket money. When I left home I was sixteen years of age, had been working for two years, and I received the grand amount of a shilling a week. Out of that I had to buy me own dinners, me own clothes, and even soap to keep meself clean.'

'Bloody hell!' Tommy snorted. 'The more I hear, the more I wonder what's wrong with yer old man.'

They reached the corner of Pickwick Street and by silent consent they stood and waited until Jimmy had finished eating. Although he wouldn't for the world show it, now the time had come to face the music he was quaking inside with fear.

'Come on, let's go and get it over with,' Sadie said. 'I'm not looking forward to it but it's got to be done.'

Spike put a hand on each of Jimmy's shoulders and looked down into his face. 'Remember this, lad. Never let the enemy see that yer frightened, 'cos if yer do, yer'll lose the battle.'

'Come on, Spike, let's move.' Sadie slipped her arm through her brother's. 'We'll stick to the plan, me and Jimmy go in first. Oh, and Jimmy, I'll see yer at Grandma's tomorrow, same time as usual.'

Young Les opened the front door and his jaw dropped in horror. 'Ooh, our Sadie, I wouldn't come in if I were you.'

'Shush.' Sadie put a finger to her lips. 'Is the baby in bed?' When Les nodded, she said softly, 'You go upstairs and sit on the bed out of the way.'

'Me dad's in,' the young lad warned. 'He's not goin' to the pub 'cos of his face.'

From the living room came an angry roar, 'Shut that bleedin' door or I'll knock yer bleedin' teeth down yer throat.'

Sadie bent to kiss Les. 'Don't forget I love you.' She patted his bottom. 'Up the stairs yer go and don't come down again, there's a good boy.' Then Sadie took Jimmy's hand and squeezed it tight. 'Ready, sunshine?'

George Wilson was slumped in the chair, picking his teeth with the end of a dead match. Sadie was taken aback when she saw the red scratches down both of his cheeks, but there was no pity in her heart because she knew why they were there. Lily was sprawled on the couch and was the first to see the two children. She opened her mouth but no sound came out. It was the expression on her face that caused her husband to turn his head. 'Why, you pair of bastards.' He jumped from his chair but before he reached them, Sadie said, 'There's someone outside waitin' to see yer so I would keep me hands to meself if I were you.'

George's eyes narrowed. 'Who wants to see me?'

'I dunno.' Sadie shrugged her shoulders. If she didn't lie, he'd never go out to see who it was. 'It must be one of yer mates from the pub.'

George ambled towards the door, hoping no one would be able to see his face. How could he explain the scratches away? As he passed Jimmy, he hissed, 'Just wait till I start on you, yer little bleeder, yer won't know what day it is.'

Sadie held the living-room door open to see what happened. Her father was standing on the top step and she heard Tommy's voice. 'Are you Mr Wilson?'

'What the hell's it got to do with you? Now bugger off, I don't know yez from Adam.'

Then Spike's voice. 'We'd like a word with yer.'

The next thing Sadie saw was her father's feet leaving the floor, then he disappeared from sight altogether. She shut the door and led Jimmy to stand in front of their mother. 'Yer haven't seen yer son's face, have yer? Well, take a good look at what yer brave husband did to a young boy.'

'He asked for it.' Lily's eyes were like slits. 'What about yer dad's face, eh?'

'Now if anyone asked for it, he did. Jimmy tried to get him away from our Ellen, and I don't need to tell yer what he was doin' 'cos your mind's in the muck midden with me dad's.'

Lily lowered her eyes without answering. She hadn't believed her husband's story about Ellen going for him just because he'd asked her to make a cup of tea. But she'd had to pretend to believe him because he was her husband, after all.

'Can I ask yer a question, Mam?' Sadie addressed the top of Lily's head. 'Why did yer have six children when yer didn't want them? When yer didn't love them and weren't prepared to give them a decent life?'

Lily's head jerked up. 'I don't have to answer any of your questions! Who the bleedin' hell d'yer think you are? Snotty-nosed little upstart.'

'I am, unfortunately, one of the children you didn't want and don't love. And no, Mam, yer don't have to answer me question. Yer don't have to do anythin', do yer? Don't have to keep the house clean, don't have to feed or clothe yer family properly, don't have to wash or iron, don't have to speak without using filthy language and don't even have to keep yerself looking respectable. You're a disgrace, Mam, and I'm ashamed that I was ever born to you an' me dad. I wouldn't care if I never set eyes on either of you again, and that's a terrible thing for a daughter to have to say.'

Sadie waited to see if her mother would respond. When she didn't, the girl went on: 'I don't suppose it'll worry yer, but yer've lost another daughter now. After what happened this afternoon our Ellen's not coming home again. And I'm warning yer in advance that as soon as Jimmy's fourteen, I'll take him away from this hell-hole.'

Lily raised her head and for the first time showed some emotion. 'You get our Ellen back here or I'll go to the police. It's you what's puttin' ideas into their heads, they wouldn't be talking of leavin' only for you enticing them.'

'Bring Ellen back so she can be a skivvy for yer, like I was? Not on your life! You go to the police by all means, if that's what yer want. I'm more than prepared to talk to the police, and so are Ellen and Jimmy.'

'Sadie's not puttin' ideas into our heads.' Jimmy's voice was deep with anger. 'Our Ellen doesn't want to come back 'cos she doesn't like it here. I don't like it, either, an' I'll be glad to get away.'

'If yer like, Mam, I'll call into the police station and tell them meself. I can take Jimmy with me so they can see his face.' When there was no answer, Sadie went on, 'Two of me friends are outside with me dad, giving him a last warning. I'll tell you what it is so yer'll know to be careful in future. If either of yer lay one finger on Jimmy, or the other two children, then just watch out. I'll not stand by and see them used as punch bags, and neither will me friends.'

Sadie turned her head so her mother wouldn't see her wink at Jimmy. 'I'm goin' now, sunshine, but I'll meet yer outside school one day to find out how you and Les and Sally are. Don't worry, I'll be keeping me eye on yer.' She put her arms around him and hugged him tight. 'I love you, Jimmy.'

'And I love you, Sadie.' There were tears in his eyes but he refused to let them fall. Grown boys didn't cry, only cissies did that.

Sadie was stepping into the street when her father pushed past her, holding a hand to his face and making whimpering sounds. 'Oh dear, what happened to him?'

'He's a very unreasonable man, your father.' Tommy's hand was clenched and he was rubbing his knuckles. 'We couldn't get him to see sense, could we, Spike?'

'Wouldn't have none of it, Sadie. We tried to be reasonable with him but it was no use. They were his children and it had nowt to do with us.' Spike knew it was no time for joking, but he couldn't help it. 'I'll tell yer what he's brilliant at, though, and that's swearing. Workin' on the market I thought I'd heard everything, but some of the choice words your father came out with had me baffled. Never heard nothing like them. If the circumstances had been different, if we'd had more time, like, I'd have asked him to explain what some of them meant.'

The scarf Sadie was wearing over her head as a disguise began to slip back and she was re-tying the knot under her chin when Tommy said, 'He wasn't so bad after we'd taught him the error of his ways though, was he, Spike? More understanding altogether, he was.'

'What did yer say to change him?'

'Well, we'd done our level best to get him around to our way of thinkin', but we weren't gettin' anywhere, and we decided, me and Spike, that talkin' wasn't the answer. So we gave him a demonstration, and it worked a treat.'

Sadie stood between them, linked their arms and started to walk down the street. 'How d'yer mean, yer gave him a demonstration?'

'You know what a demonstration is, Sadie,' Spike said. 'It's when yer show somebody with actions instead of words.'

'I know that, soft lad! What I meant was, what did yer demonstrate?'

'How to give someone a black eye.'

Sadie came to a halt. 'Yer gave me dad a black eye?'

Tommy's face was serious but there was laughter in his voice. 'I can't promise he's got a black eye right now, probably more of a pink. But give it an hour or so an' he'll have a better shiner than Jimmy's. In fact, if me knuckles are anythin' to go by, he'll put yer brother in the shade.'

'Oh dear,' Sadie said. 'I don't know whether to laugh or cry.'

'Well, while yer makin' up yer mind on that, I've got a bone to pick with the feller on yer other arm.'

'Oh aye, Tommy, what's that then?'

'Considerin' yer supposed to be so clever, how come yer told young Jimmy never to let the enemy see that yer frightened? Even I know it should have been that yer never let the enemy see the whites of yer eyes.'

'I'm afraid yer in for a let-down if yer think yer've caught me out on that,' Spike told him. 'I was afraid that if I told him not to let the enemy see the whites of his eyes, he might walk around with his eyes shut, bump into a lamp-post and end up with another black eye.'

Sadie pulled on their arms. 'I'll make up me mind whether to laugh or cry when yer tell me our Jimmy's not goin' to get a hiding.'

'Then yer can laugh yer head off, Sadie, 'cos yer dad has given us his solemn promise not to touch him again.' Spike looked over her head. 'Isn't that right, Tommy?'

'That's right, Spike. And don't forget to tell her he was on his knees when he made the promise, with his hands together as though he was praying.'

'Yeah, but he wasn't praying for forgiveness from the Good Lord, he was beggin' you not to hit him again.'

'Oh, you two.' Sadie clicked her tongue on the roof of her mouth. 'Can't yer ever be serious?'

'We were dead serious tonight, Sadie,' Tommy told her truthfully. 'After seein' the state of young Jimmy's face, and listening to him sayin' he didn't know who Tom Mix was – well, it really got to me. But we accomplished what we set out to do, made sure the kids were safe, so I think we're entitled to be pleased with ourselves.' He squeezed her arm. 'If yer have a mind to return the favour, Sadie, we'll call it quits if yer save me the first tango.'

Sadie cried in mock horror, 'Oh, no! Not the tango!' Although Tommy's dancing had improved considerably, they never let him forget the mayhem he caused during his first dance with Sadie. 'Have pity on me, please, I beg you. Any dance but the tango.'

'Oh, go on, then. Seein' as yer nice-lookin', I'll make it the rumba.'

'Ay, lad, don't do her no favours, will yer?' Spike said. 'I would have thought Sadie had had enough problems for one day without having to cope with your idea of how the rumba should be danced.'

'Oh, aye, hark at Fred Astaire! Yer supposed to enjoy dancing, not be as stiff as a board like you, with a dead earnest expression on yer gob as though one wrong step an' yer'd be sent to the gallows.'

Sadie grinned. If these two weren't with her she'd be a nervous wreck after what she'd just been through. But they didn't give her time to think, which was just as well. She wasn't proud or happy about what she'd done, but it was the only way she knew to help her brothers and sisters. And she'd do it again if one of them was in danger.

Peter had taken a seat next to Ellen at Sarah's table. He was wearing his best suit and his patent leather dance shoes had been laid on the floor next to the sideboard. 'I thought Sadie would have been home by now, it's nearly half-seven.'

'Don't look at me, son,' Sarah said. 'Yer as wise as I am.'

'She'll not come to any harm with Tommy and Spike with her.' Joe was not to know that as far as Peter was concerned, he was pouring oil onto troubled waters. 'With two big lads like them, she'll be as safe as houses.'

'She'd have been just as safe with me,' Peter said, his face without a smile for once. 'I can handle meself, yer know.'

'I've no doubt about that, son, I'm quite sure yer can more than hold yer own.' Joe tried to repair the damage to the lad's ego. 'It's just that the other two were on the scene, so to speak. If Sadie had been at home then I'm sure it would have been your door she knocked at.'

The old man's words went some way to restoring Peter's humour, and Ellen went even further when she touched his arm. 'Yer look very smart, Peter. I bet all the girls at the dance will be after yer.'

'Thank you, Ellen.' A smile was back on Peter's face. 'It's nice of yer to say so. That sister of yours has never once said that I look smart.'

Ellen bridled. 'Don't you call our Sadie that sister of mine, like that. If she doesn't want to say yer look smart, then she doesn't have to, does she?'

Sarah and Joe exchanged amused glances as they sat back and listened.

'Well, I'm always telling her she looks nice,' Peter said. 'It wouldn't hurt her to return the compliment now and again.'

'Our Sadie always looks nice, she doesn't need you to tell her.' Ellen's deep brown eyes flashed. 'She's beautiful, she is. I bet none of the other girls yer go out with are as beautiful as my sister.'

'I don't go out with other girls.' Peter was wondering how he'd got himself into this when they heard a key turn in the lock and silence descended.

'I'm sorry I'm late, Grandma, but what a day it's been.' Sadie lifted her brows in surprise when she saw Peter. 'What are you doin' here? I thought yer'd have gone on to the dance.'

'Well I didn't, did I? And don't you start on me 'cos this sister of yours has been giving me a really hard time.'

Sadie smiled at Ellen. 'Are yer all right, sunshine?'

'Oh Sadie, I'm so happy I can't believe it.' Ellen wrapped her arms around her body and hugged herself. 'I keep pinchin' meself to make sure I'm not dreaming.'

'Next time yer feel like pinchin' yerself, let me know an' I'll do it for yer.' Peter grinned into her face before asking Sadie, 'How did yer get on? Come on, we're all dying to know.'

'Hang on to yer last breath until I'm ready. It's first things first.' Sadie went to Sarah and hugged her. 'Yer didn't mind me sending Ellen, did yer, Grandma? I was at me wit's end, I didn't know what to do.'

'Yer did the right thing, sweetheart. She's more than welcome.'

Joe lifted his face for his kiss. 'Like me dear wife said, we're more than happy to have Ellen. This house has never known such activity since the day it was built.' He winked at her. 'Mind you, if Peter and your sister ever come to blows, it might not be standing much longer.'

'Shall I get yer dinner out of the oven, sweetheart?'

'Not yet, Grandma. I'll tell yer what happened first, and get it over with. It won't take that long, then I can have me dinner, a quick swill and change me clothes.' Sadie pulled a chair from under the table and positioned it so she could see all four of them. Then she began to relate the day's events, quickly and without interruption. And as she talked, it was Joe's face she watched. His lined face was full of character, clearly showing his changing emotions as they moved from anger to silent laughter.

'So there yer have it.' Sadie sat back and clasped her hands in her lap. 'That's the lot, practically word for word.'

Ellen's mouth was open, her eyes as round as saucers. 'Yer mean me dad's got a black eye as well as the scratches on his face?'

'I haven't seen the black eye, but according to Tommy it'll be a belter by now. But I did see the scratches and they are very noticeable. I can't see him turning into work for a few days, or makin' any trips to the pub.'

'And yer really said all those things to me mam?'

Sadie nodded. 'Every word, sunshine.'

'Ooh, yer not half brave, our Sadie.'

'That's what you think,' Sadie laughed. 'Me knees were knocking so loud it's a wonder the whole street couldn't hear them.'

'Did yer not see anyone yer knew in the street?' Sarah was thinking of Harry. Sadie hadn't mentioned his name since the day they took the Christmas tree down and she'd held the little teddy bear in her hands. 'I'm goin' to keep this for ever, to remind me of the best friend I ever had, or am ever likely to have.' Those had been Sadie's words, and it set the old lady wondering if this was the boy who'd stolen her heart. She certainly didn't let any of the boys she went out with get too close. Any one of them, Peter, Tommy or Spike, would give their eye teeth to be her sweetheart, but the girl kept them at a distance.

'No, Grandma, I didn't see anybody. I just kept me head down and walked as fast as me legs would carry me.'

Sarah pressed her hands on the couch and eased herself up. 'We'll have plenty of time tomorrow to go over it all again in detail, but if yer don't make a move, sweetheart, yer'll be getting to Blair Hall in time for the last waltz. The kettle on the hob is full of hot water, so bring it through and have a quick swill while I see to yer dinner.'

There was a small square of thick cloth kept near the grate for carrying the hot kettle, and after making sure her hands were well protected, Sadie carried the water through to the kitchen. 'Grandma, I'm awful selfish, I haven't even asked yer how Mrs Benson is?'

'She's just the same, sweetheart – no better but no worse. The doctor said if she stays nice and warm, gets plenty of drinks and soups down her, there's a chance she'll make it.'

'Oh, that's good. I'll say a prayer for her tonight.' Sadie poured some of the hot water into the sink and set the kettle on the gas stove. Then she put her arms around Sarah. 'Thank you for letting Ellen stay here,

Grandma, you really are good to me. She'll be no trouble to yer, I promise. She's a good girl, not cheeky or forward. And she'll do her share in the house; she's not frightened of work. And I know she'll love you and Grandad as much as I love yer.'

Sarah stroked the long blonde hair that shone like silk. 'Get yerself ready, sweetheart, and enjoy yerself tonight. Forget all yer troubles for a few hours and we'll talk about Ellen's future in the morning. Everything's going to be fine, you'll see.'

On Sunday morning they sat having breakfast, a fire crackling in the grate and bacon and egg on their plates. Ellen felt as though she was living in a dream. She'd never known such peace, such a feeling of well-being. And a proper breakfast was something she'd never had. At home they were lucky to get a round of bread and dripping and it would be stuck in their hand to eat off a dirty, cluttered table. And the air would be filled with shrill voices screaming obscenities at children too afraid to bat an eyelid. Here, there were no raised voices, no bad language; the table was set with a nice white cloth and the room was clean, warm and comfortable. She'd slept like a log in a clean bed with plenty of bedclothes to keep her warm and her sister to snuggle up to.

'Yer very quiet, Ellen,' Sarah said. 'But I suppose it's all strange to yer and it'll take yer a while to settle down.'

'Oh, it's not strange to me, Grandma, it's lovely. I'm quiet because I was thinking what a lucky girl I am.'

Sadie laughed. 'I bet yer didn't think yer were lucky when I made yer get up early this morning.' She winked at Sarah. 'I thought we should start as we mean to go on, so while I lit the fire, Ellen dusted and tidied the room. She knows where everything is now, so she's no excuse for gettin' out of doing any work.'

'Yer awful, you are, our Sadie. I wouldn't try and get out of doing any work.'

'I know yer wouldn't, sunshine, I was only pulling yer leg. I've already told Grandma what a smashing little worker yer are.'

Joe was eyeing the *News of the World* which was folded on his chair. He loved Sunday mornings when he could spend the whole time reading about what was going on in the rest of the world. 'Would you ladies excuse me while I retire to me chair?'

Sarah's smile for him was full of love and tenderness. 'It's not the chair that's attractin' yer, Joe O'Hanlon, it's the newspaper and that old pipe of yours.'

'Partly true, love, partly true. But I did think it would be better for you ladies if there wasn't a man sittin' listening to every word yer say. I know yer've got a lot to talk about.'

Ellen waited until Joe was settled in his chair, then asked the question that had been burning in her mind. 'Will I be able to get a job now?'

'Grandma says yer will, but I don't know. I hope yer will because we could do with yer contributin' to the housekeeping.'

'Don't be worrying the child about money, sweetheart – we'll not starve.' Sarah smiled at Ellen who was looking a little less happy. 'The school leaving age is fourteen, and if yer've a good reason for leaving then, I can't see them stopping yer. I'll take yer to the Labour Exchange in the morning, explain that yer've come to live with me and there's not much point in me putting you in a school around here for the sake of a few weeks.'

Ellen sighed with relief. 'Ooh, thanks, Grandma.'

'What sort of a job would yer like, sweetheart – in a shop or a factory?'

'I don't mind.' Ellen was feeling really grown-up with someone asking her opinion. 'Any job would do.'

'There was a notice in Irwin's window the other day asking for a junior shop assistant, but the job may have gone by now.'

Sadie leaned forward, her interest sparked. 'When did yer see the notice, Grandma?'

'A couple of days ago, sweetheart, I can't remember the exact day.'

'We could take a walk along there if yer like, Ellen.' Sadie thought a job in a shop was more suitable for her sister than working in a factory. 'The sign might still be in the window.'

'Ooh, er.' Ellen pulled a face. 'Would I be any good in a shop?'

'Of course yer would. Everyone has to learn when they get a job – look at me at the market. I never thought I'd have the nerve to do it, but I soon learned. And I've tried to drum it into yer that you are as good as anybody else, Ellen, don't ever forget that. No matter who they are or what they do, you're as good as them.'

Joe lowered his paper. 'Yer sister's right there, queen, yer up there with the best.'

'I'll wash yer hair for yer tonight, after our Jimmy's gone, and I'll rout some of me clothes out for yer to wear until we get yer some of yer own.' Sadie eyed her sister's blossoming figure. She definitely needed a couple of dresses that would fit her properly, and she needed to wear a brassière. 'We'll have a good sort-out tonight, and in the morning, before I go to work, I'll doll yer up to the nines.'

Ellen was all eager. 'Can we walk to Irwin's now, see if the notice is still in the window?'

'Hey, hold yer flippin' horses, sunshine!' Sadie raised her brows. 'Are yer just goin' to walk out and leave the table for someone else to clear?'

Ellen blushed with embarrassment. Her first day and she was making herself out to be selfish. 'I'm sorry, Sadie, sorry, Grandma. It's just that I'm so excited, me heart's racing like mad. I don't know whether I'm comin' or going.'

'I'll clear away,' Sarah said. 'You two poppy off out.'

'We will not.' Sadie was very definite. 'That would be a fine start, wouldn't it? Two young girls buzzing off and leaving you with all the work? Not on your life, Mrs Woman. Ellen can clear the table and I'll do the washing up. After that we'll do the spuds and the veg.'

Ellen began to stack the plates. 'I wonder how our Jimmy got on? I can't wait to see if he's all right.' She began to giggle. 'And I want to know what me dad said about how he got a black eye.'

'Yer'll find out soon enough, now get crackin'. The quicker yer move the quicker we get to Irwin's.'

Sadie's words had Ellen moving like a flash of greased lightning. If she got a job she wouldn't be a child any more; she might even be able to go dancing with Sadie . . . and Peter.

Chapter Twenty-Seven

Ellen skipped backwards in front of Sadie, her face alive with excitement. They were coming back from Irwin's, where the card advertising a job for a junior shop assistant was still on display in the window. 'D'yer think I've got a chance of gettin' the job, Sadie? It would be marvellous if I could, it's so near home.'

'It depends how yer get on at the Labour Exchange. If they agree it's not worth yer goin' to school for a few weeks, then yer stand as good a chance as anyone of getting in at Irwin's. I'll make sure yer look presentable, so if yer do get an interview all you've got to do is be pleasant and civil. Yer good at sums, aren't yer? I mean, yer can add up?'

'Yeah, I'm good at adding up.' Ellen turned to walk beside her sister. 'I'll say me prayers tonight, and you'll say a prayer for me, won't yer?'

Sadie grinned. 'I will, sunshine, and we'll get Grandma and Grandad to say one for yer too. With all those prayers winging their way up to heaven, God is bound to listen to them.'

'I hope so, 'cos I want to be able to pay Grandma for me keep.' Ellen slipped her arm through Sadie's. 'I haven't thanked yer properly for what yer've done for me, but I want yer to know I really am grateful an' I'll love yer all me life and never let yer down.'

'I know yer won't let me down, sunshine,' Sadie said as they turned the corner into their street. 'And I know yer'll be happy with Grandma and Grandad.'

'Happy? I'm like a dog with two tails. I still can't get it into me head that I won't ever have to go back to our house.' Ellen pulled her sister to a halt just before they reached the front door. 'We could have been a happy family except for me mam and dad, couldn't we, Sadie?'

'We'll be a happy family one day, sunshine, in spite of me mam and dad. There's two of us now, and our Jimmy's fourteen in less than ten months. With a bit of luck there'll be the three of us this time next year.'

'Ooh, I can't wait for that, our Jimmy's me very best mate.' Ellen had second thoughts and added, 'And you, yer both me best mates.'

'Buttering yer bread on both sides, are yer, sunshine?' Sadie laughed. 'Anyway, let's get in and if there's any hot water in the kettle I'll wash yer hair. We might even have time to sort a decent dress out for yer before Jimmy comes.'

'Is Peter comin' in, too?'

'Oh yeah, yer might know that nose fever won't miss anything. When I left him at the door last night he said he'd be in.'

'He'd like to be yer proper boyfriend, wouldn't he? I don't know why yer won't let him, 'cos I think he's nice.'

'Of course he's nice, he's a really decent lad. And he's very funny, there's never a dull moment where Peter is.' Sadie turned the key in the lock and pushed the door open. But before she stepped inside, she said. 'I'm not ready to settle down yet, sunshine, so me and Peter are just good mates. The same goes for Tommy and Spike. All good blokes but at the moment, not for me.'

After passing on the news to Sarah and Joe about the advert still being in the shop window, Sadie washed Ellen's hair in the kitchen sink, wrapped a towel around her head and took her up to their bedroom. 'Give it a good rub and get the wet out, we don't want yer catching yer death of cold. I'll see what I've got for yer to wear.'

When Sadie handed a brassière to her sister, the girl blushed to the roots of her hair. 'I've never worn one of them, Sadie.'

'Yer need to, sunshine, and yer clothes will look better on yer. When yer've had it on for ten minutes yer'll forget it's there. I only possess three, so I'll have to ask Mary Ann to keep her eyes peeled.' She found a dress she thought would suit Ellen and passed it over. 'Try them on and see if they fit.'

Ellen hung her head. 'I don't like getting undressed with you standing there watchin' me, I'd die of shame.'

'I'll make meself scarce then, and give Grandma a hand with the dinner. Shout down the stairs when yer ready and I'll come and brush yer hair.'

Ellen went up the stairs a young girl, and came down a young lady. The transformation left Sarah and Joe open-mouthed. 'I wouldn't have believed it if I hadn't seen it with me own eyes,' Sarah said as she gazed on the neat figure and the luxuriant long black hair which had been brushed until it shone. 'Yer look lovely, sweetheart.'

Joe gazed from sister to sister, one so fair, one so dark. Sadie would always stand out in a crowd because her flawless complexion, vivid blue eyes, jet black brows and lashes and her light blonde hair, combined together made for a perfect beauty. But her sister had the makings of a very attractive girl who would catch the boys' eyes and hold her own in any crowd. 'You and me are goin' to be very busy, love.' Joe winked at his wife. 'Every boy in the neighbourhood is goin' to be beating a path to our door.'

Sadie doubled up with laughter when there was a loud knock on the door. 'Blimey, Grandad, news doesn't half travel fast, doesn't it?' She was chuckling happily until she opened the door to see Jimmy standing on the step. Right away she thought there'd been trouble at home. 'What's happened? Are yer all right?'

'Yeah, I'm fine. I came out early to get away from me dad's moaning.' The boy's grin stretched from ear to ear. 'Yer should see his face, Sadie, it's in a right mess.'

'Have yer seen yer own face?' Sadie held the door wide to let him pass. 'It looks worse than it did yesterday.'

'Oh, my God!' Sarah put a hand to her mouth when Jimmy entered the room. 'I never thought it was that bad. You poor thing, yer must be in agony.'

'Nah, I'm all right.' The lad's eyes lighted suddenly on his sister and he gaped before puckering his lips and letting out a shrill whistle. 'Ay, our Ellen, what's happened to you? Yer look all grown-up and posh.'

'Don't be daft.' Ellen ran and put her arms around him. 'Yer face looks awful sore, Jimmy, is it very painful?'

'Yer could do with holding a wet cloth to yer eye, son,' Joe said. 'It would take some of the swelling down and ease the pain.'

'Did any of the neighbours see yer like that?' Sadie asked.

'Only Harry, the bloke from next door. He asked me what had happened an' I told him I'd been in a fight.'

'Oh.' Sadie turned to straighten the runner on the sideboard. 'How is he?'

'I dunno, I didn't ask. He asked me if I'd seen you and if I knew where yer were living. But I didn't tell him nothing, Sadie, honest. I said I didn't know where yer lived. Yer didn't want me to tell him, did yer?'

'No, sunshine, yer did right.'

Sarah sighed inwardly. Sadie had told her she wasn't good enough for Harry, and his family certainly wouldn't touch her with a barge-pole. But the least she could do was see the boy and let him decide for himself what he wanted.

Sadie pulled a chair from the table. 'I'll make yer a cup of tea in a minute, Jimmy, but sit down first and tell us how yer got on with me dad after we'd left.'

'He didn't say a dickie-bird to me, too busy moanin' about his pains. So I made meself scarce and went to bed. I heard him and me mam shouting downstairs but I stayed out of it. Me mam told him he could say he'd picked up a stray cat and it went for him, clawing his face. But me dad got real sarcastic with 'er over that, asking if he should say the cat had given him the black eye as well. There was ructions then, with me mam tellin' him he'd got himself into the mess so he could get himself out.'

'What was he like with yer this morning? Did he have anythin' to say?'

'Not a word. He sent our Les out to get a paper an' he just sat reading. He's touchin' his face all the time and making funny gruntin' noises. But he wasn't shoutin' like he usually is, and he kept his hands an' his feet to himself.'

'Well, now, that's a blessing,' Sarah said. 'Let's hope he's been taught a lesson.'

'Tommy's knuckles were terrible sore last night,' Sadie told them. 'So he must have given me dad a real good thump.'

Jimmy's tummy was rumbling. 'Can I have a cup of tea, Sadie, please? I haven't had nothin' since those chips yer bought me last night.'

'Oh, yer poor thing!' Sarah was already on her way to the kitchen. 'I'll make yer a buttie to keep yer going until the dinner's ready.'

'I'll give yer a hand.' Sadie followed her out. 'I'm sorry about this, Grandma, but Jimmy can have half of my dinner.'

'We'll manage, sweetheart, so don't fret yerself. It'll mean one less roast potato each, but we won't starve.'

Joe got more pleasure from watching Jimmy eating than he got from his own dinner. The bruises on the young lad's face looked raw and angry, but they didn't seem to be bothering him as he tucked in with gusto. He was the first to clear his plate, rub his tummy and lick his lips. 'I didn't half enjoy that, Grandma, it was lovely.' He sat back in his chair, happy and replete. 'I'd lick me plate but I know our Sadie would give me a go-along.'

'I would too! We'll have some manners at the table if yer don't mind.' Sadie laid down her knife and fork. She too was feeling happy and replete, but it wasn't from the food – it was because she had two of her family near her. 'Yer can help Ellen clear the table while I wash up. And make it snappy because Peter will be here soon.'

Sadie was standing on the kitchen step shaking crumbs from the tablecloth into the yard when she heard the front knocker. 'One of yer open the door, please.'

'I'll go!' Ellen was down the hall like a shot and giggled when Peter stared at her in amazement.

'I'm sorry, but I must have come to the wrong house,' he said. 'I've never seen this pretty maiden before.'

'Don't be daft – it's only me.' Ellen closed the door after him. 'Our Sadie did me hair for me an' lent me one of her dresses. Do I look nice, Peter?'

'I'll say! A sight for sore eyes, that's what yer are.'

Ellen ran ahead of him, too young to realise that not only had her looks been changed in the last few hours, but also her feelings towards boys. 'Peter said I look nice, Sadie, an' I'm a sight for sore eyes.'

'Holy sufferin' ducks!' Peter looked stunned by the injury inflicted on Jimmy. 'I hope Tommy gave your dad a real belter, 'cos that's what he deserves.'

'Oh, he did! If yer think I look a sight, yer should see him – he looks ten times worse.'

For the rest of the afternoon Peter went out of his way to include Jimmy in all the conversations. He felt sorry for him and wanted to show that he was welcome and they were all his friends. 'D'yer know how to play cards, Jimmy?'

'Dunno, I've never tried.'

'Shall we have a game of rummy, Sadie?' Peter cocked an eyebrow. 'It's an easy game to learn.'

'Yeah, that's a good idea.' Sadie was sitting next to her brother, facing Peter and Ellen. 'I'll teach Jimmy, you see to Ellen.' She went to the sideboard drawer and brought out a pack of playing cards. 'You shuffle and cut them, Peter, then I'll deal.'

She dealt out seven cards each then turned over the one at the top of the remaing cards. 'Before yer pick them up, I'll tell yer briefly how to play. Yer've got to get either three cards alike, say three fours, and they don't have to be the same suit. Or yer can get a run, that means numbers that follow on, say two, three and four. But they've got to be the same suit. As soon as yer get any three, lay them down in front of yer.'

'Ooh, er,' Ellen said, pulling a face. 'I'll never learn all that.'

'Of course yer will, Peter will help yer.' Sadie leaned forward and said in a loud whisper, 'But watch him, he's the biggest cheat going.'

'I am not!' Peter looked suitably shocked. 'Fancy saying that about the man yer going to the pictures with on his birthday. Which, incidentally, is in ten days' time.'

'Ooh, is it yer birthday, Peter?' Ellen turned wide eyes on him. 'Can I come with yez to the pictures?'

This time the look of shock on Peter's face was genuine. 'Yer most certainly can not!'

'Ah, go on,' Ellen pleaded, 'don't be mean.'

'I am mean! I'm the meanest man on earth, didn't yer know? I don't want anyone looking on when I get me birthday present off yer sister.'

Jimmy had picked up his hand of cards and was sorting them in order when he asked, 'What are yer buyin' him, Sadie?'

'I'm not buying him anything, Jimmy, so take no notice of him.'

'Yeah, she's right there.' Peter nodded his head in agreement. 'What she's givin' me won't cost her a penny.'

'Oh, aye?' Jimmy laid his cards face down on the table. If you could get something for nothing he wanted to know what it was. 'What's she givin' yer, then?'

'She's lettin' me kiss her chin.'

'Yer what?' Jimmy looked disgusted. 'Is that all? A kiss on her flippin' chin?'

'Never mind "is that all". I'll have you know it's taken me six months to work me way up to that. Yer see, yer sister has a points system—'

Four young heads turned at the loud burst of laughter. Sarah and Joe were doubled up, tears of merriment streaming down their cheeks. 'Oh dear, oh dear, oh dear.' Sarah ran the back of her hand across her eyes. 'I couldn't keep it in any longer.'

'Bloody hysterical, it was.' Joe held a hankie to his face. 'Peter's expression at the thought of being deprived of his kiss was a picture no artist could paint.'

'Oh, aye,' Peter's serious face belied the laughter going on in his head. 'I suppose you didn't mind having an audience when yer kissed me Auntie Sarah?'

'Yer Auntie Sarah didn't have a points system, son, so I was lucky, I got to go straight to the bull's-eye. I agree that Sadie's way of working could be a handicap to a young man.'

All this talk of systems and handicaps was way over Ellen's head. All she understood was that Peter was taking Sadie to the pictures just so he could kiss her chin. She looked around at the happy smiling faces and, in all innocence, said, 'If yer take me to the pictures, Peter, I'll let yer kiss my chin as well.'

This was met with hoots of laughter and it continued throughout the afternoon. They did eventually get down to playing a few hands of rummy, and Jimmy, quick on the up-take, won most of them. Mind you, he had help from Peter. There were quite a few cards exchanged under the screen of the chenille cloth. Sadie saw what was going on but was so grateful to Peter for putting a satisfied smile on her brother's face, she kept quiet. Ellen didn't see what was going on and thought her brother must be the cleverest boy in Liverpool to have learned the game so quickly.

On the Monday morning Mary Ann was waiting for Sadie. 'I've been worrying meself sick all over the weekend, girl. I couldn't get the young lad's face out of me mind. Hurry up and tell me how he got on.'

Sadie lifted a bundle of clothes onto the table, and as she sorted through them she told her friend everything that had gone on. 'Our Jimmy seemed all right yesterday, except for his face of course, and that doesn't seem to be bothering him much. As long as me dad keeps his hands to himself, Jimmy can put up with the rest.' She folded the sheet and laid it on the table before reaching for another bundle. 'I don't know what I'd have done without Tommy and Spike, though, Auntie Mary. I wouldn't have known where to turn. They were marvellous and I'll never be able to repay them.'

'I bet they were glad to help yer out, girl – they think the world of yer. And it was a bit of excitement for them.'

'Excitement!' Sadie let out a long, deep sigh. 'It's the kind of excitement I can do without, Auntie Mary. I wouldn't like another day like Saturday, I can tell yer. Me nerves wouldn't stand the strain.'

'And what about Ellen? Is she settling in all right?'

'Settling in? She doesn't know she's born! She's wallowing in all the affection she's getting, and the decent food and the clean house. She's never got a smile off her face, even when she's asleep.' Sadie put her arms around the stall-holder and hugged her tight. 'To think it's all through you that so much happiness has come into my life.'

Mary Ann smiled. 'I often think of the first day I saw yer. Yer were that shy, yer face the colour of beetroot when yer asked me if I had a brassière. I took to yer right away, girl, an' I'll always look back on that day as bein' one of the luckiest in me life.'

After a quick hug, the women began to fill the stalls out. 'I don't suppose we'll do much, it being a Monday and hard-up day. Still, we've got to make the effort, girl, and show we're willing. Yer never know, someone's husband may have come up on the gee-gees.'

'Our Ellen's hoping to go after a job at Irwin's. I hope she does, and I hope she gets it. If looks were anything to go by, she'd walk it. I got her ready this morning and she really looked nice. So keep yer fingers crossed for her, Auntie Mary, and say a little prayer. She's coming in to let us know how she got on.'

It was eleven o'clock and Sadie was serving one of her regular customers when Mary Ann called, 'Here they come, girl, Sarah and Ellen.'

Ellen's face was beaming. 'I got the job, Sadie! Ooh, me head's spinning and me tummy's turnin' over and over. I can't believe it, I can't!'

'Calm down, sunshine, calm down.' Sadie cupped her sister's face and planted a kiss on her lips. 'I'm proud of yer.' She turned to Sarah. 'Thanks, Grandma, I know you had a hand in her good fortune.'

'Nonsense! Ellen did very well for herself without my help, both at the Labour Exchange and Irwin's. She was a bit nervous, that's only natural, and I think it worked in her favour. They could see she wasn't the pushy type. She was very polite and answered their questions with her head held high and a smile on her face.'

'Now, Grandma, yer telling fibs.' Ellen wagged her finger under the old lady's nose. 'Yer didn't tell us yer knew the manager at Irwin's, did yer?'

'I'm bound to know him with doin' me shopping there for so long. There's been about five managers in that shop in my time. But I couldn't have got the job for yer if he hadn't thought yer were right for it.' Sarah smiled at Sadie. 'He gave her some sums to do, to make sure she could add up, and she had them finished in a flash. Mr Keene, that's the manager's name, said all the girls who'd applied before couldn't add two and two together.'

'Grandma, yer not half a big fibber,' Ellen said. 'I heard him saying that if you recommended me then I must be all right.'

Mary Ann rejoined them after finishing serving the customer Sadie had been attending to. 'Nice goin' that, girl, getting the first job yer go after. There'll be no stoppin' yer next week when yer start work and are earning a few bob. I hope yer buy yer clothes from yer sister's superior-quality clothes stall an' keep the money in the family.'

'Not next week, Auntie Mary,' Ellen said, a gleam of excitement in her eyes. 'I start work in the morning.'

Sadie gasped. 'Tomorrow!'

'Mr Keene asked me to 'cos they're a junior short, an' I said I would.' Ellen wiggled her hips and shouted, 'Yippee! Oh boy, oh boy, oh boy! I feel like jumpin' up in the air and singing, I'm that happy.'

'And I'm happy for yer, sunshine,' Sadie said. 'Yer see, the prayers worked. God was listening.'

'Come on, sweetheart.' Sarah took the girl's arm. 'Let's go and tell Joe the good news. He'll be on tenterhooks waitin' to see how yer got on.'

Sadie and Mary Ann looked on as Ellen put her arms around the frail shoulders and kissed the old lady. 'Grandma, our Sadie said I would love yer, and she was right. I love you and Grandad to bits.'

'Oh, here we go.' Mary Ann rolled her eyes. 'I thought Sadie was the only one who could reduce me to tears, but now her sister's gettin' in on the act. Take her home, Sarah, before she has me bawlin' me eyes out. It's a bleedin' good job she's not comin' to work in the market, I've only got three hankies to me name and they'd be soppin' wet in half an hour with these two. Soft as butter, the pair of them are,' she winked at Sarah, 'thank God.'

As Ellen took hold of Sarah's elbow and they began to walk away, the two watching women heard her say, 'Wait until I tell Peter I've got a job, I bet he'll be pleased.'

Sadie chuckled. 'She's got her eyes on Peter, all right. She thinks he's marvellous.'

Mary Ann tilted her head and asked, 'Wouldn't she be steppin' on your toes?'

'No, of course not. Me and Peter are just mates, that's all.'

'Like Tommy's just yer mate, and Spike's just yer mate? I've never known a girl have so many boys as mates. I'm surprised they've stuck around so long when yer don't give them any encouragement.'

'I'm very fond of each one of them, Auntie Mary, but that's all. I can't pretend to feelings I don't have, it wouldn't be fair on anybody. And they don't have to stay around if they don't want to. I'd be made up for them if they found themselves nice girls.'

'I've got some spare wool at home,' Mary Ann said, jerking her head back. 'I'll knit yer one if yer tell me what sort of feller yer after. Or don't yer know yerself what yer want?'

'Oh, I know what I want, all right. But we can't always have what we want, Auntie Mary, can we?' Sadie looked away. 'So you go ahead and knit me one, but could he have dimples in his cheeks, please?'

'Put that curtain back, sweetheart, there's a good girl. Sadie would go mad if she thought yer were spying on 'er.'

'I only want to know if she enjoyed the picture.' But Ellen did as she was told and let the curtain fall back into place. 'And I want to ask Peter if he's had a nice birthday.'

'Now we're getting to the truth.' Sarah raised her brows at Joe before saying, 'It's Peter yer interested in seeing, not yer sister.'

'No, it's not!' Ellen blushed. 'I only want to know what the picture was like.' She'd had to work a week in hand at Irwin's, so this Saturday would see her with her first wage-packet. She had settled in happily at the shop and loved the work. 'I might want to go an' see it meself when I get some money.'

'Own up, queen,' Joe said, smiling at her. 'Yer've got yer eye on Peter, haven't yer?'

'He's all right.' She tossed her head, sending her long hair swinging about her shoulders. 'Anyway, our Sadie's not really his girlfriend, she told me so.'

'He's older than you, sweetheart.'

'Only three years, and lots of girls have boyfriends older than themselves. Mavis, one of the girls in work, her boyfriend's three years older than she is.'

'Doesn't Peter have any say in the matter?' Sarah didn't let her smile show. The girl was young and naive, she didn't understand the ways of boys. 'Will yer take a bit of advice from an old woman, sweetheart? Never throw yerself at a boy. If yer do, yer'll scare him off and he'll run a mile. Just be natural with Peter, don't gush over him. If he's goin' to fall for yer, let him do it in his own time.'

'But he doesn't even see me when our Sadie's around.'

'Bide yer time, queen, bide yer time.' Joe was of the opinion that Sadie's cool attitude towards Peter would gradually wear him down and he'd be looking for pastures new. But Ellen was very young, perhaps too young for the boy to take seriously. 'Take yer grandma's advice and let things take their course.'

While he was being discussed inside the house, Peter stood outside with Sadie. 'I don't feel any different now I'm seventeen than I did yesterday, at sixteen. Wouldn't yer think nature would be kind and make yer feel more grown-up?'

'Don't be wishing yer life away, Peter. Enjoy yer youth while yer've still got it.'

'Right, I'll do that, Sadie. And can I begin to enjoy meself by taking what yer promised me, a kiss on yer chin?'

Sadie tipped her head back. 'Be my guest, Peter.'

The lad took the liberty of kissing her on the chin then moving his lips down to kiss her neck. 'I was lying in bed last night and it suddenly came to me that yer neck might be on this points system of yours, so I decided to get it over and done with. Now on our next date I should get a proper kiss. And yer can't say I haven't been patient, Sadie, 'cos I think I've been a flippin' saint.' He held her hand in his, suddenly feeling shy. 'When's your birthday? Perhaps we could go out together then?'

'Not for another six or seven weeks.' Sadie tried to erase the pictures that filled her mind of the outing she'd had with Harry on her last birthday. It was over ten months now since she'd seen him and there wasn't a day passed that she didn't think of him.

'Blimey! Have I got to wait that long to get a proper kiss?'

'No, you can have it now.' Sadie made up her mind so suddenly she surprised herself. But since her conversation with Mary Ann, she'd asked herself many times why she couldn't feel more towards the boys who, given the slightest chance, would be her sweetheart. Was it the way she was made? Was there something missing in her make-up?

'Are yer pulling me leg, Sadie?'

'Of course I'm not pulling yer leg.' Peter was as nice a boy as she'd find and she was fond of him. If she allowed herself to, could she become more than fond of him? Would a kiss awaken feelings she didn't know she had? 'But it doesn't matter if yer don't want to.'

Peter ran the back of a hand across his lips before pulling her into his arms. 'I'm not givin' yer time to change yer mind.' His lips covered hers, soft and smooth. The kiss lasted several seconds and when Peter lifted his head he was grinning with pleasure. 'It was well worth waitin' for, Sadie. Better than a cream bun any day.'

But for Sadie there had been no stirring of the senses, no shiver running down her spine. It seemed she was incapable of romantic, loving feelings, and she was incapable of pretence. She wouldn't allow the thought to linger in her head that she'd been spoilt for any man by one with deep brown eyes, dimples in his cheeks, a crooked grin and a caring, loving disposition. 'I'd better get in, Peter, 'cos our Ellen won't go to bed without me. I'll see yer tomorrow.'

He lifted her hand to his mouth and kissed it. 'Sleep well, fair maiden.' Then he chuckled. 'I'll sleep like a top tonight with a grin on me face. I'm glad I filled in the cracks in me ceiling. I couldn't be bothered countin' them tonight, I've got more pleasant things on me mind.'

Chapter Twenty-Eight

Business at the market was booming as lightweight blouses and dresses were sought for the glorious summer weather. The busy time put a stop to the mid-week day off for Sadie and Mary Ann, but neither of them minded as they thrived on the hustle and bustle, the laughter and the smiles on faces of satisfied customers.

Sadie's superior-quality clothes stall did very good business, particularly on a Saturday when she usually sold out. One of her best customers was her sister. Ellen had been working for two months now, and every Wednesday, on her half-day off, she would make straight for the market to see what Sadie had set aside for her to add to the wardrobe she was building up for herself. The girl had good dress sense and was always well turned out. She turned a few heads, too, as she blossomed into a very pretty girl.

But Sunday was Sadie's favourite day. Jimmy came for dinner regularly now and stayed until after tea. They were like a big happy family then, with a grandma and grandad the children respected and adored. Peter still came in for a game of cards and a laugh, but Sadie hadn't dated him since the night of his birthday. No amount of coaxing or wheedling could change her mind and Peter had by now given up hope. They still went to Blair Hall every Wednesday with Tommy and Spike, but the two market lads usually got off with a couple of girls and would walk them home. Sadie was glad for them, and she certainly didn't want for dancing partners or offers to walk her home. But she always turned the offers down and said she was already spoken for. Peter had so far kept to the old routine of walking home with her, but one day he too would find someone who took his fancy.

On this particular Sunday, after they'd finished their dinner, Sadie asked Jimmy to give her a hand in the kitchen. 'I want to have a talk with me brother, it's ages since we had a really good natter. So you three can relax, put yer feet up and read the paper.'

'I'll give yer a hand,' Ellen said. 'He's my brother, too, yer know, an' I'd like to have a natter with him.'

'You can talk to him as much as yer like when we've finished the dishes,' Sadie told her. 'But right now do as yer told and make yerself scarce. Go upstairs and titivate yerself up for Peter coming.'

This had the desired effect, and as Ellen made for the stairs, Jimmy grinned. 'She fancies him, doesn't she?'

'I think yer could say that.' Sadie grinned back. 'The only one who doesn't seem to know is the lad himself. He either can't see or doesn't want to see.' She slipped a stack of plates into the warm water in the sink. 'Now, how's things at home, sunshine?'

'Just the same. The house stinks, there's never enough food, me mam and dad are always shoutin', an' the air's blue with their language.'

'But me dad doesn't hit yer any more, does he? Or the other kids?'

Jimmy shook his head. 'He hasn't laid a finger on any of us since the lads give him that black eye. But I hate them, Sadie, an' I still want to leave when I'm fourteen. Yer will keep yer promise, won't yer? I mean, yer will help me?'

'I'll do me best, Jimmy, I promise.' Sadie could see by her brother's face that her answer wasn't definite enough. 'If I tell yer what I'm hoping for, yer won't tell anyone, will yer? Yer see, I haven't even told Grandma, and it mightn't come off, anyway.'

'I can keep a secret, yer know that, our Sadie. I know when to keep me mouth shut.'

Sadie spoke in a low voice. 'Yer know the old lady next door, Mrs Benson? Remember she was very ill a few months ago? Well, her daughter wants her to go and live with her family and they're trying to talk the old lady into it. So far she won't hear of it, and in a way I'm glad because me and our Ellen couldn't afford to rent that house on our own. But if she hangs out until you leave school we could afford it with three wages comin' in. It would be a struggle, but I wouldn't mind that if we were together.'

Jimmy nearly dropped a plate in his excitement. 'Ooh, ay, our Sadie, wouldn't that be the gear! Just fancy, you, me and our Ellen livin' in our own house.' Then he thought of something that took the sparkle from his eyes. 'But what about Grandma and Grandad? They wouldn't like yer to leave, would they?'

'No, they wouldn't, sunshine, and I wouldn't want to leave them. But I can't be all things to all men, can I? You need help and I made you a promise. And we'd only be next door. We'd be seeing each other every day and we'd be on hand if they wanted anything or one of them got sick and needed help. They're part of my life, Jimmy, and they always will be.'

Jimmy had another dark thought. 'Would the rent man let us have the house? I can't see him renting it to three kids, 'cos that's all we are.'

'We'll cross that bridge when we come to it. And until then, not a word to a soul.' Sadie passed him a plate to dry, and as she did so, she met his eyes. 'Jimmy, how come yer never mention our Dot? Yer talk about Les and Sally, but yer never mention yer big sister. Why is that?'

' 'Cos I've got nothin' to say about her. She just comes an' goes as she pleases, never hardly speaks to anyone. She gets in from work, has whatever there is to eat, then she's off out an' I'm in bed by the time she comes 'ome.'

'Who does she go out with, a girlfriend or boyfriend?'

'I honestly don't know, Sadie, she never talks to anyone. Even me mam doesn't know where she gets to 'cos I've heard her tellin' me dad.' Jimmy bent to put the plates away in the kitchen cabinet. 'She doesn't hit us no more, that's one good thing. And she doesn't put so much muck on her face. Honest, she used to look like a clown when she went out, with two big round patches of that red stuff on her cheeks. If she hadn't been me sister I'd have been laughing an' pokin' fun at her.'

'Don't ever do that, Jimmy, 'cos after all, as yer said, she is yer sister.' Sadie's voice was so low as she bent over the sink, Jimmy had to cock an ear to hear what she was saying. 'Whatever our Dot is, me mam and dad made her that way. I know she's hardfaced and not very nice, but don't forget she had a lousy childhood, same as us.' She swished her hand around in the water to make sure she hadn't missed any small items of cutlery, then pulled out the plug and leaned against the sink to watch the water drain away. 'Let's forget about Dot, now. Have yer no other news?'

'Only that I earned an extra penny at the market yesterday. Yer know Tommy and Spike usually give me a penny each for runnin' messages for them? Well, they gave me a thruppenny joey between them yesterday 'cos they said I'd worked hard.'

'Good for you! Yer could get a nice summer shirt with that from the market. Yer'll need one with the weather picking up.'

'Nah, I'm goin' to save it to buy yer a present on yer birthday. I've never bought yer a present before 'cos I've never had the money.'

Sadie dried her hands on the towel hanging from a nail on the kitchen door. 'You spend yer money on yerself, sunshine – yer worked for it. Don't be worrying about me, I've got everything I want or need.'

Jimmy gave her a mischievous grin. 'Just wait and see, yer won't half get a surprise.'

Sarah came to the kitchen door. 'It's takin' a long time for yer to wash the dishes. I hope yer haven't washed the pattern off the plates.'

'We've finished now, Grandma, the dishes and our little talk.'

'Well come along in, Peter's here.'

Ellen waited for her sister to sit down before asking, 'Can I come to the dance with yer one night, Sadie?'

Sadie glanced across at Sarah. 'What d'yer think, Grandma? Is she too young?'

'That's up to you to say, sweetheart.'

'Go on, let her come,' Peter said. 'She can't come to no harm while she's with us.'

'Don't be mean, our Sadie,' Ellen pleaded. 'Let me come with yer on Wednesday, go on, please?'

'Oh, all right. If I say no I'll never hear the last of it.'

'Well, instead of playing rummy, why don't we teach her a few dance steps?' Peter said with a smile on his face. 'Just in case some poor fool asks her for a dance.'

Ellen was bobbing up and down on the chair. 'Ooh, yeah, that would be brilliant.'

Joe and Sarah were all for it. 'Push the table right back, queen, and make more room,' Joe said. 'Me and my dear wife might have a go as well. They say yer never too old to learn.'

Sarah chuckled. 'Yes, we might come with yer to Blair Hall, as well.'

The table and chairs were pushed right back, and amid laughter and cheers, Ellen had her first dancing lesson.

Jack Young watched his reflection in the mirror over the fireplace as he straightened his tie. 'I won't be out long, love, just a pint to whet me whistle.'

'I don't mind yer goin' out, yer know that,' Florrie told him, then laughed. 'As long as it's only every Preston Guild.'

'I wouldn't bother, meself, but when I met Bill Curtis on the tram coming home from work and he asked me to go for a pint with him, I didn't like refusing. Like meself, he's not a drinker, so we certainly won't be there until the towels go on.' Jack turned to his son who was sitting at the table reading. 'D'yer feel like comin' out for an hour, Harry? Just down to the pub on the corner?'

'No, Dad, I don't feel like it,' Harry said, 'but thanks for asking.'

'Oh, go on,' Florrie tutted, 'don't be so flamin' miserable. It's a lovely night, the fresh air will do yer good.'

Harry grinned. 'It's about thirty steps away, Mam, about six breaths of fresh air and we'd be there. I'm not being miserable, I just don't feel like it. Yer know I'm not a drinker, I wouldn't care if I never saw the stuff.'

'Okay, son, it was only a thought.' Jack kissed his wife on the cheek. 'I'll be gone an hour or so, love.'

Florrie went to the door with him. 'Yer've no need to hurry back.

God knows it's not often yer go out. But a warning, Jack Young, don't you come rolling home.'

Jack laughed as he walked away. 'Fat chance of that, love.'

Bill Curtis was sitting in a corner of the pub, his coat over a chair to reserve the seat for his friend. 'Sit yerself down, Jack, and I'll get the drinks. Pint of bitter, is it?'

'I'll get them in.'

'No, this is my round.' Bill moved his coat from the chair. 'Park yer backside an' take the weight off yer feet.'

The two men had been neighbours for years and had a mutual respect for each other. As they sipped their pints, conversation came easy. They discussed the weather, their jobs and their families. 'Talkin' about families,' Bill said, leaning closer, 'there's a miserable specimen of manhood standing at the bar who could do with a few lessons on how to raise a family.'

Jack turned his head to see George Wilson leaning on the counter. 'You're telling me. He's a bloody disgrace, and that's putting it mildly. And a bloody mystery! One of his daughters went missing nearly a year ago, and now it seems another one has left home – just disappeared into thin air. No one knows where they are, an' he goes around as though he hasn't a care in the world.'

'Can yer blame them for wanting to get away from that house? I certainly don't. And the blonde one seems to be doing all right for herself. She looks better since she got away from his clutches. She's a fine-lookin' girl, and a worker.'

Jack looked surprised and puzzled. 'Yer mean yer've seen her?'

'Yeah – I've seen her a few times. She works in Paddy's market.'

'Go 'way!' Jack's heartbeat was racing but he didn't want to sound too interested. 'What does she do there?'

'She works on a second-hand clothes stall for a woman called Mary Ann. Everybody knows Mary Ann, she's a well-known character around Scottie Road. Very popular she is, with a sharp wit and a smile for everyone. Good businesswoman, too. Her stall does a roaring trade.'

'And Sadie works for her?'

Bill looked puzzled. 'Who the hell is Sadie when she's out?'

Jack nodded to the figure holding up the bar. 'The queer feller's daughter, the blonde one.'

'Oh, I get yer now. Yeah, she works there, I've seen her with me own eyes.'

'Have yer spoken to her? Has she seen yer?'

' "No" to both questions, Jack. I never spoke to her while she was livin' in the street, so she'd think it was queer if I went out of me way to

353

speak to her now. And she's never seen me, 'cos the market's so crowded yer can't see anyone. It would be like lookin' for a needle in a haystack.'

'What do you go to Paddy's market for? I would have thought St John's market would be nearer for you from here.'

'It probably is, but I enjoy the atmosphere at Paddy's market. I go there for lots of things, like second-hand tools, bits of wood if I'm makin' something, any old odds and sods. There's nothing yer can't get there, and for only a few coppers.'

'I see.' Jack wanted to rush home to tell Harry, but he had to get his round in first. 'I'll have to try it some time.' He picked up the empty glasses. 'Same again?'

Over the second pint, Jack thought things through and decided not to say anything to his son until he was sure of his facts. It would devastate Harry to have his hopes raised and then dashed again. He'd go to the market and see for himself first.

So in bed that night, Jack told Florrie of what he'd learned. 'I'll go on Saturday afternoon, just to make sure and see how the land lies.'

'I'll come with yer.' Florrie couldn't rid herself of the guilt she felt. If she hadn't been so down on the family next door, Harry would have brought his feelings for Sadie out into the open. She was responsible for the change in her son and she deeply regretted it. 'We'll go together.'

'No, love, don't be rushing at it like a bull at a gate. If we don't get things right, we'll do more harm than good. One might go unnoticed at the market, but not two. Let me do it my way, love, and trust me.'

The crowds were three deep at each of the three tables and hands were coming over the tops of heads or between bodies. Just the sight of a certain colour could have someone straining to reach it. They might not want it when they got to it, but they wanted to be certain they didn't want it before someone else got there before them. And the old hands had a few tricks up their sleeves. If they spotted something they liked the look of, but couldn't get near the table, they weren't beyond giving the person in front of them a kick on the shin, and while the hapless victim was bending down, the perpetrator would push her way to the front while murmuring sounds of sympathy.

Mary Ann clicked her tongue as she anchored a lock of stray hair behind her ear. This had to be the busiest day they'd ever had. It had been non-stop since nine o'clock and there was no sign of a let-up. It was a good job her feller had brought a few extra bundles just to be on the safe side. She turned her head sharply at the sound of a scuffle and rushed to where two women were fighting over a blue and white striped blouse. They were playing tug-of-war with it, first it would go one way, then the other. 'In the name of God, will yer just look at yerselves? Women are supposed to be the fairer, weaker sex, but you two look like prize-fighters! Eyes screwed up, nostrils flared and teeth ground together, anyone would think yer were going to kill each other. Well, let me tell yer there'll be no murder committed at my stall, unless I can sell tickets for it. If yer've ripped that blouse, then yer'll pay for it, d'yer hear? Now give it here to me.' The women looked shamefaced as the blouse was handed over. 'I saw it first, Mary Ann, and this one grabbed it out of me hand.'

'You bleedin' barefaced liar! I saw it first!'

'Will you two behave yerselves and act yer age, before I come round there and bang yer bleedin' heads together?' Mary Ann shook the blouse before holding it up. 'Nellie, and you, Vera, seein' as both of yer have got breasts as big as footballs, how did yer intend gettin' into this? It wouldn't cover one of them, never mind two.'

The women eyed the blouse then looked down at themselves. 'I never got a chance to see it proper, Mary Ann,' Nellie said. 'I'd only just picked it up when this one snatched it out of me hands. Quick as bleedin' lighting she was.'

Vera's look was scornful. 'I hope when yer go to Confession that yer tell the priest how many lies yer tell. Every time yer open yer gob the lies just pour out.'

'Oh, aye? The bell's gone for the second round, has it?' Mary Ann thought of a way to put a halt to it. 'Well, yer can stop it now 'cos I'll sell yer the blouse. The first one to hand thruppence over can have it.'

'I don't want it,' Nellie said. 'It's no good to me.'

'What's the use of buyin' somethin' that doesn't fit?' Vera asked. 'Yer must think we're short on top, Mary Ann, or we've got money to burn.' She turned to Nellie. 'She's not soft, is she, girl? It's no wonder she's loaded.'

'We'll look for something else, eh, Vera? I fancy somethin' in blue.'

Vera frowned. 'Ay out, Mary Ann, some kid's just nicked one of yer jumpers.'

'Oh dear, oh dear,' Mary Ann sighed. 'D'yer know, when I get home tonight I'm goin' to be too tired to count me money.' She saw the figure of a young boy pushing his way through the crowd, a grey jumper swinging from his hand. 'It's all right, he's Aggie Armstrong's son, she'll pay me next time she comes. If she doesn't, I'll give him a thick lip.' The stall-holder's brow creased. There was a man standing just at the back of the stalls, and she'd noticed him a few times. At first she thought he was waiting for someone, but he'd been there ages and each time she'd looked he seemed to have his eyes on Sadie. That's all he was doing now, standing with his hands clasped behind his back, his eyes on her young assistant. He was up to no good, that was a dead cert, but she'd soon send him packing.

'Sadie, I know yer up to yer neck, girl, but I've got to go to the lavvy or I'll burst. Will yer hold the fort for a few minutes?'

'Of course I will, Auntie Mary.' Sadie smiled. 'I'll keep me eye out.'

Without further ado, Mary Ann squeezed through the gap in the tables, walked to the back of the stall and confronted the man. 'Well?'

Jack Young took a step back in surprise. 'I beg yer pardon?'

'Don't come the bleedin' innocent with me, my man. I've been watchin' yer for the last fifteen minutes and all yer've done is stand there gawping at me young lady assistant. Now I want to know why.'

'You mean I've been watching Sadie?'

Mary Ann was taken aback. 'Yer know her?'

'She used to live next door to us. My name's Jack Young.'

'Harry's father! Oh, my God! And here's me thinkin' all kinds of evil things about yer. But what are yer doin' here?'

'She's mentioned Harry to yer, then?'

'Er, let me see. He's got dark curly hair, deep brown eyes, white teeth and dimples in his cheeks. He's kind and caring, the best friend she ever had. Yes, as yer can see, she has mentioned him to me.'

'Is she courting?'

Mary Ann shook her head. 'Plenty of offers but I think your son put her off other men for life. She'll go dancing or to the pictures with them, but if they start to get serious then that's it.'

'Harry's never been the same since she went away without telling him. He's tried to find her but the other Wilson children say they don't know where she is. Me and me wife blame ourselves – if it wasn't for us he wouldn't have been frightened to say how he felt about her, but if yer knew her family yer'd understand.'

'Oh, I understand all right, and so does Sadie. She said she wasn't good enough for Harry or his family. But I'll tell yer this much, Mr Young, there isn't a man on earth that Sadie Wilson isn't good enough for. She's the nicest girl I've ever met and I love the bones of her.'

'Does she live with you?'

'No, she lives with an elderly couple who think the world of her. The other sister, Ellen, she lives there as well. Young Sadie spends most of her hard-earned money on her brothers and sisters, otherwise they wouldn't have a stitch to their backs. She really is one in a million, Mr Young, believe me.'

'The name's Jack, and I know you're Mary Ann.' He quickly told her how he'd come to hear where Sadie worked. 'What do I do now, Mary Ann? Do I just go home and tell Harry?'

'No! Where's the romance in yer, Jack? It has to be something really special and I've got a brilliant idea. But I haven't got time to work it out with yer now, so I'll give yer the address where she lives and yer can go and see the old couple. Sarah and Joe O'Hanlon, they are. They know Sadie's best memory is going out with your son on her last birthday. Well, her birthday's come around again and it's only a few days off. I'm sure Sarah can think of a good way to surprise her and give her the best present she could ask for.' Mary Ann chuckled, 'Yer know, Jack, I've never said so much without bleedin' swearing. It just goes to show I can be a lady when I want. Young Sadie must be a good influence on me, 'cos if ever there was a lady, it's my junior assistant on the superior-quality clothes stall.'

'I can see she's got a good friend in you.' Jack smiled. 'Anyway, I'll nip home and pick up the wife. She can come with me to see the O'Hanlons. If I left her out of this she'd kill me.'

'Sadie and Ellen get home about half-six, so yer'd have to be away by then. I'll find out what yer decide 'cos Sarah comes to the market a few times a week. Anyway, thanks for comin', Jack, yer've really made my day. I'm bound to see yer again, and yer wife, I hope, 'cos Sadie's like a daughter to me.' Mary Ann sighed with happiness. 'Aren't I glad I noticed yer, even if I did think yer were a dirty old man.'

As Florrie Young sat down her eyes took in the spotlessly clean room and she nodded in appreciation. 'Yer keep yer home nice, Mrs O'Hanlon.'

'Call me Sarah.' The old lady smiled and won the hearts of Florrie and Jack. 'I'll not take all the credit, I get a lot of help. Sadie and Ellen do their own little jobs before they go to work. Me and my Joe don't know we're born since Sadie came into our lives, do we, sweetheart?'

Joe brushed aside the packet of cigarettes Jack was offering him and reached for his pipe. 'You go ahead and light up, Jack, I'll get me old pipe going to keep yer company, be sociable, like.' He opened the tobacco tin and proceeded to fill his briar. 'What me dear wife said about Sadie is quite true. Twelve months ago she came to us like a breath of fresh air, and the air's been sweet ever since. She has so much love to give, and she gives it with all her heart. Ellen is a nice kid, too, but Sadie will always be special to me and my Sarah. She's kind and thoughtful and hasn't got a selfish bone in her body. And considering she's got the looks of a film star, she's modest and completely natural.'

'Has she ever talked to yer about our Harry?' Florrie asked.

'Oh, I know all about your son.' Sarah smoothed down the front of the pinny she was wearing when she'd answered their knock. She hadn't been expecting visitors so they'd have to take her as they found her. 'And if your comin' here today means what I hope it means, then yer very welcome in our home.'

Florrie told them about the change in Harry over the last year. 'He used to be so full of fun, always crackin' jokes and never without a smile on his face. And he used to be out dancin' nearly every night – now he seldom goes anywhere.' Florrie dropped her head and there was a quiver to her voice when she said, 'And it's all my fault.'

Jack patted her hand. 'Now, don't be gettin' yerself all upset, love. It wasn't anyone's fault. If Sadie hadn't left the way she did, things might have worked out different.'

Sarah's heart filled with pity for the woman who was trying so hard not to break down. 'Florrie, there isn't a woman breathing who wouldn't worry about the family her son married into. Yer only human, sweetheart, doing what yer thought best for yer son.'

'That's all in the past,' Jack said. 'Now we've got the chance to make up for it, to bring the two young ones together.' He cocked an eyebrow at Sarah. 'Mary Ann said it would be nice to do something on Sadie's birthday. She said you were the one with ideas, that you would find a way of surprising the girl and making it into the best birthday she's ever had.'

Sarah smiled. 'When I answered a knock on me door and saw two strangers there, I was curious. When they told me who they were I felt like jumpin' for joy. Yer see, Sadie has become so precious to me and my Joe, if I had it in my power I would give her the sun, the moon and the stars. But what brought you here today will mean far more to her than anything else on earth. And if yer'll forgive an old lady for being sentimental, and presumptuous, I'd already started to plan how best to surprise Sadie before yer were sat down.'

Joe looked so happy anyone would think he'd won the pools. He was chuckling as he said, 'That's my dear wife, always ahead of the field.'

Sarah gave him that special look that was reserved solely for him. A look that said she loved him as much now as when they first married. Then she turned to Harry's mother and father. 'I hope yer'll not be offended if I take the liberty of having a hand in making this the happiest day of me granddaughter's life?'

Jack and Florrie exchanged glances. It was funny but neither of them felt like strangers in this house. Like the old couple, it seemed to welcome them as old friends. 'We're in your hands, Sarah,' Jack said. 'And happy to be so.'

Sarah pursed her lips and folded her arms. 'Well, it's like this. It's

Sadie's birthday a week on Monday and I had planned a little party for her on the Sunday afternoon. She doesn't know yet, it's going to be a surprise for her. So here's what we'll do.'

Sadie was tired but happy as she walked home. She'd been on the go all day and her feet were aching, but it had been worth it. Mary Ann had been delighted with the takings and had insisted Sadie take an extra two shillings in her wages. When she'd refused, the stall-holder had said she'd add it to the money she had saved up. It was over six pounds now, that was a lot of money and not to be sneezed at.

'Sadie!'

Startled out of her wanderings, Sadie turned her head to see her sister, Dot, leaning against the side wall of an end shop. Fear made her speak sharply. 'What are you doin' here?'

Dot moved away from the wall and stood in front of her. 'I came to talk to yer.'

'How did yer find out where I lived?'

'I followed our Jimmy. I knew he must be meetin' yer, going out the same time every Saturday and Sunday.'

'Are yer trying to tell me yer followed him all that way an' he never saw yer? Pull the other one, it's got bells on.'

'It took me three weeks. I followed him so far one day, then the next week I left home before him and waited at the spot I'd left him at the week before. The third week I saw him turn down a street along here, but I couldn't tell which house he went in.'

'Well, yer've gone to a lot of trouble for nothing, Dot, 'cos you and I have nothing to say to each other.'

'Won't yer let me talk to yer, just for five minutes?'

Sadie was about to refuse when she remembered how she had reminded Jimmy that this was their sister. And she was surprised by the change in the girl facing her. Her pale face was devoid of make-up, the hard look had gone from her eyes and she looked sad and unhappy. 'Five minutes, that's all. I've been run off me feet all day an' I'm tired.'

'I just want to say I'm sorry.' Dot's eyes went to the ground. 'To you, and the other kids.'

Sadie huffed. 'It's a bit late in the day for that, isn't it? I wrote you off a long time ago as bein' a lazy, crafty, heartless, hard-faced bitch. An' if yer think the kids are goin' to forget all the belts yer've given them over the years, then yer've got another think coming.'

'I know what I've been, Sadie, an' I'm not proud of meself. I want to change, but how can I when I've no friends? You know yer can't have friends when yer home's a pigsty. I started dressing like a tart just so the boys would notice me, but the only ones I got were out for no good.'

'You didn't do much to clean up the pigsty, did yer? When you lifted yer hand it was to hit the kids, not to do anythin' to improve their lives.'

Dot closed her eyes. 'I don't hit them no more. I know I've been no good, me dad taught me how to be that. I'm so ashamed of meself, so unhappy, I feel like throwing meself under a train.'

'That's no way to talk! Yer only fifteen, Dot. If yer make up yer mind to change and make somethin' of yer life, then yer can do it. I did.'

'I want to be friends with yer, Sadie, and with the other kids. I want them to love me like they love you.'

'Yer can't ask for that, Dot, yer have to earn it. Make up yer mind from right now that yer going to be a different person. Prove to the kids that yer love them, and prove to me that the words coming from your mouth are not just hot air. If yer can do that then I'll have a sister I can be proud of and we can be good mates.'

Tears rolled unchecked down Dot's cheeks and the sight of them melted Sadie's heart. This girl, this sister of hers, had done a lot of bad things, but like herself she was a victim of their father. She opened her arms. 'Come here, yer daft ha'porth.'

This was how they were when Ellen came upon them. Her mouth gaped when she saw Dot, and she asked, 'What's she doin' here?'

Sadie dropped her arms. 'Wipe yer eyes, Dot, and yer can start being the changed you right this minute. I think yer've got somethin' to say to Ellen.'

Ellen was too startled to move away when Dot put her arms around her. 'I'm sorry I've been a bitch with yer, Ellen, but I'm goin' to make it up to you, I promise. And to the other kids.'

Ellen's eyes were wide as they looked over her shoulder at Sadie. There was a question in them that Sadie answered. 'Yer sister has had the guts to say she's sorry, I hope you have the good will to accept. And remember, I helped you when yer needed it, and I'm going to help Jimmy. Dot is also a member of our family.'

Ellen wasn't prepared to forgive and forget graciously. She'd suffered too many hidings off this sister of theirs. 'Only if yer never, ever, hit our Jimmy again.'

'I'll never raise me hand to anyone, ever again.'

'Oh, that's all right, then.'

'We'll have to go, Dot, otherwise they'll have the police out looking for us.' Sadie couldn't help feeling pity for the forlorn figure. 'I work at Paddy's market. Come and see me there one Saturday afternoon and we'll see how things are going. Ta-ra for now.'

'Ta-ra, Sadie, ta-ra, Ellen.'

Sadie's dig in the ribs brought a response. 'Ta-ra, Dot.'

Sarah was standing on the step waiting for them. 'What on earth kept yer? I've been in an' out like a yo-yo.'

'There was a surprise waiting for me at the top of the street.' Sadie pulled out a chair and sat down. Then she quickly related every word that had been said. She ended by saying, 'I know I've called her every name under the sun, but I can't help feeling sorry for her.'

Ellen wasn't so generous. 'I don't feel sorry for her. Why can't she just leave us alone?'

'Would you like to be back in that house with me mam and dad?'

Ellen blushed and hung her head. 'No.'

'Then let's give her the benefit of the doubt, shall we? I've got a feeling she meant every word she said, and if she did then I'm going to try and help her.'

'And so yer should, both of yer. She is yer sister, after all.' Sarah was nodding her head in time with Joe's. 'Blood is thicker than water and families should stick together.'

'But she can't leave home an' come here – there's no room for her.' Ellen wouldn't have admitted to it, but she was jealous. 'And yer've promised to help our Jimmy. Where's he goin' to live?'

'There's always Mrs Benson's next door,' Sarah said softly. 'When she leaves yer could rent that between yer.'

Sadie almost gasped aloud. Why the crafty, lovely, adorable old lady! She must have heard her talking to Jimmy about it. 'We're too young, the landlord wouldn't let us.'

'I have mentioned it to him,' Sarah said. 'I knew yer'd be looking for somewhere for Jimmy to live, and being selfish I wanted to keep yer near. And Maggie's told me she won't be able to take the big furniture with her because her daughter's house is full already. That means the house, when she finally decides to move, will be furnished.'

Sadie couldn't believe her ears. 'What did the landlord say?'

'That as long as he got the rent every week he didn't care how old yer were.' Sarah crossed her fingers and prayed forgiveness for the lie. The rent man had said they were too young, but what had happened today changed things. Harry was twenty, old enough to rent. Something could be sorted out before Maggie made up her mind to move out.

Joe covered his mouth to stop the chuckle. There was his dear wife, ahead of the field again.

Chapter Twenty-Nine

'Me and Joe are slipping next door to see Maggie,' Sarah said on the Sunday afternoon. 'We won't get a chance when Mary Ann and Tom come, and yer know I like to go in every day just to make sure she's all right.'

'Can I come with yer, Grandma?' Ellen asked, on cue. 'I haven't seen Mrs Benson for nearly a week.'

'You're all goin' out and leaving me on me own?' Sadie looked apprehensive. She'd never had a birthday party before and was sick with nerves and excitement. 'What if the visitors start to arrive and there's only me here?'

'They won't be here for another hour or so, sweetheart, and we'll be back well before then. Anyway, there's only Peter and his mam and dad, and Mary Ann and her feller. It's not as though there's any strangers coming.'

'Okay, I'll let yer off,' Sadie grinned. 'If I get stuck I'll knock on the wall for yer.'

Left on her own, Sadie walked through to the kitchen and eyed the cakes and sandwiches Sarah had prepared. There seemed to be an awful lot for the few people that were coming, but as her grandma said, what didn't get eaten today would keep for tomorrow. And it wasn't only a few people because there was Jimmy, and she'd sent word with him to their Dot to say she was welcome if she felt like coming. That had been Sarah's idea. Give the girl a chance and a helping hand, she'd said. And when Sadie had seen Jimmy at the market yesterday he told her that Dot had apologised for being a lousy sister. 'She speaks to me and the kids now, and she even brought some sweets in for us to share. She doesn't have much to say to me mam and dad though, an' I don't blame her 'cos they're horrible with her, always making snide remarks about her and sniggerin' like a pair of idiots.'

So an apology and a change of attitude would satisfy Jimmy; he wouldn't be holding any grudges against his sister.

There came a loud rat-rat at the knocker and Sadie's hand flew to her mouth. Oh Lord, who could this be? She wouldn't mind if it was Mary Ann, but if it was next door she'd panic. She was all right with Peter, but she'd be tongue-tied with his parents. It was probably only Jimmy,

363

though, too impatient to wait until four o'clock. He hadn't been happy when Sarah said she'd be too busy to make a roast dinner today, so he was not to come early or he'd be under their feet. She looked in the mirror over the fireplace as she passed, stroked the long blonde hair that was already perfect and went to open the door.

'Hello, Sadie.'

Sadie's breath caught in her throat, her mind ceased to function, and her heart stopped beating. It was as if time and the whole world stood still. For a few seconds, shock took over. Then she drank in the smiling face with the deep dimples, the tender smile and that special look that made her tingle all over. As a cry left her lips she jumped from the top step, sailed through the air and landed in Harry's waiting arms. Saying his name over and over, she clung to him, afraid that if she let go he would disappear.

'Would you invite me in, Sadie? I can see all the curtains twitching, the whole street are probably watching and I'd much rather do this in private.'

She took his hand and walked ahead of him into the house. After closing the door, she asked shyly, 'Can I have a kiss, please, Harry? Just so I'll know I'm not dreaming.'

Harry held her tight. 'Just a kiss, or one of me smackeroos?'

'I don't mind, as long as you're here, that's the main thing.'

'Just a brotherly kiss for now, eh? Then I'd like to sit down and have a good talk to yer before anyone comes.'

Sadie tilted her head back to ask, 'How did yer know I lived here?'

'It's a bit complicated, Sadie, so can we sit down?'

Sadie led him to the couch, holding his hand in a tight grip. 'Now, how did yer find out where I lived?'

'I've got so many questions bottled up inside me, Sadie, let me set me mind at rest before anything else. First of all, have yer missed me?'

'Every day, Harry. I've thought about yer and missed yer so much it hurt.' Sadie suddenly jumped up. 'Hang on a minute, I've got something to show yer.'

Harry heard her taking the stairs two at a time, then within seconds she was on her way down again, jumping the last three stairs. She sat down beside him and held out the little teddy bear. 'Remember this, Harry? Never a night goes by that I don't kiss him good night. And this,' she opened her other hand to reveal a silver sixpence nestling in the palm, 'this is the last sixpence yer gave me. Even when I was skint I wouldn't spend it 'cos you'd given it to me.'

Harry gazed into her eyes before slipping a hand into his trouser pocket. He pulled out a paper sweet bag and handed it to her. 'Those are yours.'

Sadie stared down at the bag full of sixpences. 'What are these, Harry?'

'There's fifty sixpences there – one for every week yer've been away. The first night yer didn't turn up I didn't worry 'cos I thought yer couldn't get away. The next time I still thought the only reason yer didn't come was because yer weren't well or something. So I put the sixpences away, never dreaming you were no longer living next door. I wouldn't let meself believe I'd never see yer again, even when the months passed and there was no further word from yer and no sight of yer. The only thing that's kept me going was the thought that one day I'd catch up with yer. I didn't know how, it was just a feeling I had.'

Sadie dropped the bag onto her lap and cupped his face. 'I'm sorry for what I did to yer, Harry, it was mean of me. But I had to get away from that house, I couldn't take any more. And the only way I could do that was by not telling anyone, in case me mam and dad found out where I was.' She kissed his cheek before asking, 'How did yer find me, Harry?'

'Me nerves are ragged, Sadie, I've got to ask yer something first. Then I'll tell yer the very long and complicated story.' He held her hands in his. 'Will you be my girl, Sadie? Not just me girlfriend, but me sweetheart?'

'Yer don't need to ask, Harry, but I'll tell yer all the same. I'll be anything yer want me to be, I'll even fly to the moon with yer, like yer once asked.'

'I love you, Sadie, so much that it's frightening.'

'And I love you, Harry. I think I have done since yer came down the entry that day and found me crying. But I wouldn't let meself admit it because I knew it wouldn't do no good. Your mam would never accept me as yer girlfriend.'

'That's all part of the story I've got to tell yer, but one more question first. Will yer get engaged to me on yer birthday?'

Sadie closed her eyes. She felt as though she was floating on air. 'There's nothing in the world I'd like more, but what about your family? I don't want to cause trouble between you and yer parents.'

'We'll come to that in a minute, Sadie, just answer me question. Will yer get engaged to me on yer birthday?'

'That's tomorrow, Harry, and I work on a Monday.'

'So do I, but I've asked for the afternoon off. And you've been given the afternoon off, as well, so yer've no excuse.'

'I don't understand! How do you know I can have the afternoon off?'

' 'Cos Mary Ann told Mrs O'Hanlon yer could.' His questions answered, his heartbeat back to normal and his nerves calm, Harry laughed aloud at the startled look on Sadie's face. 'Why do yer think yer grandma and grandad have taken themselves next door? And taken Ellen with them?'

'They knew you were coming, didn't they?' Sadie didn't know whether she was on her head or her heels. But she did know she was happier than she'd ever been. 'Harry Young, if you don't hurry up and tell me what's going on, I'll take me kiss back.'

'Sadie Wilson, the only way yer can take a kiss back is by putting yer lips on the mouth yer've kissed. I'm quite happy to oblige if that's what yer want.'

'You can have as many kisses as yer like, once yer've told me what's going on.'

'Before I do, I've got to tell you that you are lovelier than ever, that I love you with all my heart, and that there's fifty sixpences in that bag which entitles me to fifty kisses – all of them me speciality smackeroos.' He held up his hand, 'Okay, here we go.'

Harry started at the night she went home with Tommy and Spike and his family heard the row. It was that night his family found out how deep his feelings for Sadie were. Then he told how his dad was in the pub with Bill Curtis when his friend just happened to mention he knew where Sadie worked.

When he'd finished, he sat back and sighed. 'So now you have it, lock, stock and barrel.'

Sadie was struck dumb for a while as her mind tried to take it all in. Then, her voice a mere whisper, she asked, 'Yer mean your mam and dad have been here, to this house?'

Harry nodded. 'I take me hat off to me dad, it was a good bit of detective work he did. And I'll be grateful to him for the rest of me life.'

Sadie bit on her lip. 'I can't believe it, it just won't sink in. I'm so happy I feel like crying me eyes out.'

'Oh, no, you don't! The gang will be here in about ten minutes and we've got to get fifty kisses in by then. And don't try and cheat by givin' me little pecks, 'cos although me mind isn't workin' right at the moment, I can still count.' He pulled her close. 'Mind you, whenever I was with you me mind never worked right, it was always somewhere in the clouds.'

When the door-knocker sounded, Sadie grabbed Harry's hand and pulled him along the hall. 'I don't know who it is, but you're comin' with me. I'm not lettin' yer out of me sight.'

She thought nothing would surprise her any more, not after Harry turning up on the doorstep. But she was wrong. This time she opened the door to all the friends she'd made in the last year. Fronted by a beaming Sarah and Joe, they were all there. Mary Ann and Tom, Peter and his parents, Betty and Frank, and towering above them all, Tommy and Spike. And standing close together at the edge of the group were her sisters, Dot and Ellen, and her brother, Jimmy.

Sadie shook her head. 'I don't believe it! Where did you all spring from?'

It was Mary Ann who told her. 'It was this grandma of yours. She had us all use the entry to get to Mrs Benson's, just so yer wouldn't see us passing the window.'

'Well, I thought it would be more of a surprise if everyone turned up at the same time, instead of coming in dribs and drabs, so we arranged to meet next door.' Sarah was feeling very proud that everything had gone according to plan. There was one more surprise in store for Sadie, and that would be the one to complete her day of happiness. 'Now are yer going to stand aside and let us in, so we can meet this young man of yours?'

'I don't want to meet him, I want to break his neck,' Tommy said. 'A complete stranger, someone by the name of Harry, comes along and steals our girl! It's just not blinkin' well on, is it, Spike?'

'Yer right there, pal,' Spike growled. 'He should be taught a lesson. I'll tell yer what, Tommy, I'll hold 'im down while you beat the daylights out of him.'

Harry came out of the shadow of the hall and stood on the step next to Sadie. With his arm across her shoulders, he asked, 'Who's the one goin' to beat the daylights out of me?'

Spike pretended to size Harry up. 'It wasn't me, pal.' Speaking out of the side of his mouth like he'd seen Edward G. Robinson do in a gangster film, he said to his friend, 'Yer on yer own, pal, this one's no pushover.'

'What are yer looking at me for? I haven't done nothing.' Tommy looked suitably hurt. 'Why do I always get the blame?'

'Oh, stop messing you two and let's get in.' Sarah took Joe's hand as she mounted the step. 'We're the oldest so we get priority.'

'I'm goin' to be posh, Grandma, and introduce each one to Harry on the way in. And who better to start with than the two people I love so dearly.'

His mother and father had spoken so well of the old couple, Harry had been curious about what was so special about them. But it only took one look, one smile, and he was in Sarah's arms. And he felt at home there. He whispered in her ear, 'Thank you for looking after Sadie for me.'

'It's been our pleasure, sweetheart, and we'll keep on looking after her until someone comes along to take over.'

'I start learning from tomorrow,' he told her, 'when we're getting engaged.'

Everyone was so cheerful and friendly as they trooped in and were introduced that Harry didn't feel in the least awkward. He couldn't remember all their names, but he'd get to know them better as the day wore on. They were certainly a happy bunch, no doubt about that. And there was no doubt about their genuine affection for Sadie.

The three children were the only ones left now, and while Ellen and Jimmy did what they'd seen the grown-ups do and shook hands with Harry, Dot hung back. She was shaking inside at the thought of looking Harry in the face, remembering how she'd cheapened herself in front of him. But Sadie had paved the way and he greeted her as a friend. 'Come on, Dot, there's no need to be shy with me, we've known each other long enough.'

Jimmy made a bee-line for the kitchen to see what the food situation was, while Ellen made straight for Peter. 'Yer haven't said yer like me new dress, Peter.'

'I like yer new dress, Ellen, yer look very nice.'

'Yes, I do, don't I? Are yer goin' to dance with me after, Peter?'

'Ellen, are yer asking me, or telling me?'

'I'm asking yer to ask me first, Peter, 'cos that's proper. But if yer say no, then I'll have to ask you. It is all right for girls to ask boys, I've seen them doin' it at Blair Hall.'

'Ellen, this isn't Blair Hall.'

Still looking the little innocent, Ellen said, 'No, it's a bit smaller, isn't it? But we'll manage.'

Everyone had been listening to the exchange, now the room erupted with laughter. Peter's mother, Betty, thought it was hilarious and doubled up. 'I'll say one thing for yer, girl, yer not backward in coming forward.'

'That's right, Ellen,' Tommy roared. 'Don't you stand no messin' from him. Let him know who's the boss.'

Spike had to add his twopennyworth. 'Start as yer mean to go on, girl.'

Peter took it all with good humour. After all, Ellen was looking good enough to eat in her new dress, with her lovely hair bouncing on her shoulders and her pretty face smiling. 'Before I commit meself, I want to make sure she doesn't have a points system, like her sister.'

There were only four people in the room who knew what he was talking about. Sarah and Joe were shaking with laughter and Sadie gasped. 'Peter Townley, I'll kill you!'

'Well, I think we men must stick together,' Peter said, his face serious. 'And I think Harry should be warned that he probably won't get to give Sadie a proper kiss until they've been out on a date six times. And even then he'll have to have a letter from Our Lord.'

'Is that how it works?' Harry was leaning against the sideboard with his arm around Sadie's waist. 'This is goin' to take some figuring out. Let me see, I haven't seen Sadie for nearly a year, so at a rate of two dates a week, that's a hundred kisses.' He stroked his chin thoughtfully. 'I've only had fifty off her this afternoon, that's all the time we had before you lot came. So she still owes me fifty kisses and I owe her a letter from Our Lord.'

Ellen was the other person to know of the points system. 'I don't have no system, Peter. I wouldn't make yer kiss me chin or me forehead.'

Peter chuckled. 'In that case I'll ask me mam if I can dance with yer.'

'There's work to do before yer think of dancing, Peter, sweetheart,' Sarah said. 'I want yer to go next door with Tommy and Spike and fetch the crate of beer and the two bottles of port wine.'

'Grandma, you haven't been splashing out on drink, have yer!' Sadie shook her head, worrying that her grandma and grandad would leave themselves short. 'We don't need drink to enjoy ourselves.'

'You speak for yerself, Sadie.' Tommy was already on his way to the door, followed by Spike and Peter. 'Yer can't have a proper knees-up without a drink. And this party is definitely goin' to be a jars out, knees-up party.'

When they'd gone, Sarah told Sadie, 'I haven't paid a penny out, sweetheart. Mary Ann and Tom, Betty and Frank, and Tommy and Spike, it was their idea and they clubbed together for the drink. They wanted this to be a birthday party yer'll never forget.'

Sadie was close to tears. 'I'll never forget this day as long as I live, Grandma. I keep thinking I'll wake up and find it's all a dream.'

'Listen, girl,' said Mary Ann, 'don't you start me off crying like yer usually do. This is a bleedin' party, not a wake, and I intend to enjoy meself.'

Sadie sniffed up. 'All right, I won't start getting sloppy. But just tell me, Auntie Mary, where would I have been today if it weren't for you and Grandma and Grandad?'

'And me!' Ellen knew how lucky she was and wanted everyone to know that she appreciated the new life she had. She might act childish in front of people, but that was only to make them laugh. In her mind she was grown-up enough to know her happiness and good fortune had been brought about by the people in this room. 'Where would I have been?'

'Oh God, we've got two of them now!' Mary Ann rolled her eyes. 'One I can take, girl, but two, never on your life. Now go and gee those boys up with the drinks, me throat's parched for want of a bottle of stout.'

'I'll go,' Tom, her husband said, before looking across at Peter's dad. 'Are ye comin' with me, Frank?'

'Aye, I might as well.'

'Don't you be havin' a drink on the sly,' Mary Ann called after them. 'Otherwise I'll get the poker to yer.'

'And I'll get the rolling pin,' Betty Townley shouted. 'Tell our Peter.'

Dot cut a lonely figure standing by herself just inside the door. She was very like Ellen, same build and colouring. And she looked just as pretty in a pale pink blouse and navy-blue skirt. But she didn't look at ease. She didn't know anyone, only her sisters, and didn't feel part of this happy group of friends. She would love to go over and talk to Sarah and Joe, but she couldn't pluck up the courage. Perhaps later, when she got over her shyness.

One hour later the room was filled with talk and laughter.

'It's amazing what a few drinks can do, isn't it?' Mary Ann said between sips of her milk stout. 'It certainly loosens the tongue.'

'It seems to have more effect on your tongue than most, chick,' Tom said. 'I'm just waitin' for it to reach yer legs and we get to see yer party piece.'

'Oh, aye, Tom?' Frank leaned forward. 'What's her party piece?'

'It's hard to describe, Frank. I can only say it's a cross between the Irish jig, the Scottish reel and *Knees Up Mother Brown.*'

Betty winked at Mary Ann. 'I'll be yer partner, girl, when yer ready. I do a mean jig, even if I do say it meself.'

Sadie was standing close to Harry, his arm tight around her waist. 'They all seem to be enjoying themselves, don't they? The old ones are having a good natter, Peter is keeping Ellen and Jimmy amused, and look at the difference in our Dot now that Tommy and Spike are talking to her. I was worried before because she looked so lonely.'

Just then Tommy's voice could be heard, saying, 'Aren't I right, Spike? Wasn't the feller I had a fight with at the market about six foot six?'

'If you say so, pal.'

'Never mind if I say so, you saw him, and he was at least six foot six, wasn't he?'

Dot was looking from one to the other, her pale face animated, her eyes sparkling with laughter.

'I don't think I saw that fight, pal,' Spike said. 'I must have been away at the time.'

Tommy snorted in disgust. 'Yer were standin' there, watching!'

'I must need glasses, then, pal, 'cos the feller I saw yer fightin' was about four foot ten.'

Harry chuckled. 'They're a pair of comics, those two.' Then he whispered, 'Let's go in the kitchen so I can hold yer properly and kiss yer.'

Sadie blushed. 'We can't do that, everyone will know.'

'I want everyone to know, everyone in the world.'

'We'll have plenty of time to ourselves tomorrow, about ten whole hours.' Sadie smiled at the heavenly prospect. 'What are we going to do?'

'First we're going to choose an engagement ring, that's top priority so I'll know for definite that yer belong to me. Then, if yer agree, we'll go to New Brighton like we did last year.'

'Ooh, yes, please! I'd love that, Harry.'

'Sadie, are yer deaf, sweetheart?' Sarah called. 'There's a knock at the door.'

'Are yer expecting anyone, Grandma?'

'No, it'll only be one of the neighbours lookin' for change for the gas. You go, there's a good girl.'

Harry took her hand. 'I'll come with yer.'

He was teasing her as they walked along the hall, trying to steal a kiss, and Sadie was laughing as she opened the door. But when she saw his mother and father standing outside she became shy and dropped her head. She'd lived next door to them all her life but couldn't remember having exchanged a single word with them.

Harry broke the silence. 'Sadie, this is me mam and dad.'

'Hello, Sadie,' Florrie said. 'Yer don't mind us gate-crashing yer party, do yer?'

'No, not at all.' Sadie stood aside. 'Come on in, yer very welcome.'

Florrie stepped into the hall and grasped Sadie's outstretched hand. 'I've got a lot of making up to do, love, if yer'll let me.'

'No, you haven't, Mrs Young. I'd have been the same in your shoes. So shall we forget the past and start afresh?'

Harry put his arms around them. 'I love both of you, and yer've no idea how happy it makes me to see you together.'

'Excuse me,' Jack said. 'Don't I get a look-in?'

Sadie grinned and put her arms around him. 'Thank you for finding me and bringing me and Harry together again.'

'Me wife hasn't told yer, but I will. We're both over the moon because we're getting the daughter we always wanted.'

They hadn't noticed the living room had gone very quiet. Sarah was standing at the door giving a running commentary on the proceedings. 'Get the glasses ready, they're coming in now.'

Sadie and Harry looked on in surprise as Florrie and Jack had a glass stuck in their hand. 'Hey, don't we get a drink?' Harry asked.

'Greedy, aren't yer, pal?' Spike grinned. 'Yer've got the girl an' now yer want a drink as well!'

'Hey, hang on a minute.' Sadie's eyes narrowed. 'Who gave our Dot and Ellen a drink? Ooh, and our Jimmy! They're too young to drink!'

'Don't flap, Sadie,' Tommy said, 'it's nearly all lemonade.'

Joe came to stand in front of Sadie. 'I'm proud to do this, queen, 'cos yer've brought so much love into this house. So I want everyone to raise their glasses to wish the nicest girl in the world a happy birthday.'

Glasses were raised and cheers echoed to the rafters. The only one who couldn't toast the birthday girl was Harry. 'Why haven't I got a drink? She is my girlfriend, after all.'

Sarah moved to stand beside Florrie and Jack. 'Are yer goin' to make an announcement now yer mam and dad are here, Harry? We're all waiting.'

Harry took a deep breath, pulled Sadie close and kissed the top of her head. 'After seeing the three handsome men who have been looking after Sadie for me, I thought I'd better step in quick and claim her. So tomorrow we're getting engaged.'

Once again the rafters rang to 'For they are jolly good fellows, and so say all of us'. There were many kisses exchanged, hands shaken and backs slapped. Sadie was caught up in the excitement, never did she think she'd know such happiness. The only time she got a lump in her throat was when Harry pulled her over to where her two sisters and brother were standing, wide-eyed with wonder. Never had they known such warmth and friendliness. As she hugged and kissed them, she told them she loved them and getting engaged wouldn't make any difference, she'd always be there for them. And when Harry hugged and kissed them they knew they hadn't lost a sister, they'd found another brother.

The only difficult moment was facing Harry's parents, even though he was gripping her hand tight to let her know that no one on earth had the power to separate them now. 'I hope yer don't mind me pinching yer son, do yer?'

'Mind? I'm delighted. Only you could put that smile back on his face. He's been as miserable as sin for the last year.'

Pleasantries over, the party started in earnest. Mary Ann and Betty did their jig, showing a great expanse of knickers in the process and bringing whistles and cheers from the men. Sarah and Joe sang a duet, *Just A Song At Twilight*, then Tommy, who had a fine, strong clear voice, sang a couple of smoochy songs, *Girl Of My Dreams* and *Who's Taking You Home Tonight*. Sadie and Harry danced close together, wishing they were alone and could say the things they wanted to. Ellen partnered Peter, but they didn't dance so close because his mam was watching. And Dot danced with Spike, much to the disgust of Tommy. When he'd finished singing he growled, 'Hey, mate, why don't you learn to sing? Yer not soft, yer not, leavin' me flogging me guts out while you get the girl.'

'Oh, I can sing, pal,' Spike said, leading Dot to the side of the room. 'But as yer've just said, I'm not soft.'

Soon it was time for the party to break up. It was an early rise the next morning, the start of a new week. Sadie was worried about Jimmy and Dot getting into trouble for being out late, but Tommy and Spike solved that problem by saying they were taking them home. When they were kissing good night, Sadie whispered in Dot's ear, 'Come to the market with Jimmy next Saturday – he'll show yer where I am.'

But her voice hadn't been low enough because Spike said, 'Yer'll be seeing her before then. She's comin' to Blair Hall with us on Wednesday.'

Soon after they'd gone, the Townleys left. And without Peter the party had lost its sparkle for Ellen and she took herself off to bed. 'We'd better be on our way, too,' Mary Ann said. 'But we've really enjoyed ourselves.'

'Yeah, we have as well.' Florrie stood up and held out a hand to her husband. 'Come on, love or I'll never get yer up in the morning.'

'Yer did say we could call and see yer, Sarah, didn't yer?' Jack said. 'Otherwise we'll never get to see our future daughter-in-law.'

'You are welcome any time – aren't they, sweetheart?'

'We'll be glad of yer company,' Joe told them. 'Any time yer like.'

Sadie stepped in and surprised even herself. 'I can't keep away from Harry's family all me life, so yer will see me. Me parents ruined me childhood, I'll not let them ruin the rest of me life.'

'Good for you, queen.' Joe's face told of the pride he felt in her. 'You walk down that street with yer head held high.'

As soon as all the guests had departed, Sarah gave her husband a knowing look as she stretched her arms and yawned. 'I'm dead beat, sweetheart, I'm off to me bed.'

'And I'll be joining yer.' Joe pushed himself up. His joints seemed to be getting stiffer every day, or perhaps it was because he wasn't used to parties any more. He held out his hand to Harry, 'Welcome to the family, son.'

The young couple listened as the old couple slowly climbed the stairs. 'No wonder yer love them so much,' Harry said. 'I've fallen for them meself.'

Sadie drank in the face she had thought was lost to her for ever. Harry was smiling and his dimples showed, a lock of his dark hair had fallen over one eye and he was looking at her with an expression that sent ripples down her spine. They were going to be like Grandma and Grandad, she could tell. Their love wouldn't go stale or lose its romance like some couples; they'd still be sweethearts in fifty years' time.

'I love you, Harry Young.'

'And I love you, Sadie Wilson. I know it was your birthday celebration today, and I don't want to steal your thunder, but this is a day I'll remember all me life. You are so beautiful, in every way. I can't believe me luck.'

'Well, take me to our own special moon, Harry, and give me the fifty kisses yer owe me.'

'I haven't got the letter from Our Lord – does it matter?'

'When you're kissing me, nothing in the world matters.'

When his lips touched hers, she sighed with contentment. This was where she belonged, where she'd always belonged, with the boy next door.